The Wabana Deception

Wabana Press
36219 Shoreview Drive
Grand Rapids, MN 55744

greg@gregpast.com

Prologue

Darkness and a dank smell—a misleading sense of tranquility permeated the air, creating a claustrophobic atmosphere in the cave, even though it was large and there was barely enough light to see the walls. She had been aware of this cave all her life; still, it fascinated her. Adventures in the cave were an integral part of her childhood memories. Tribal history slumbered here, a sleeping giant, waiting to be rediscovered by the world. After communing with the spirits in the cave, she left with a feeling of predestination, anxious to discover what the future held. Yet there was more, a riddle crying out to be solved. The key to that riddle was hidden somewhere deep within the cave. Once unlocked, the solution would give new meaning to her life.

The flashlight turned in her hand, illuminating the wall, shifting focus to the drawings. Images appeared, beginning with food sources. Rabbit, deer, elk, pine martens, and other animals not readily recognizable were prominently displayed. Observing the artwork from right to left, the artists' skill and power of observation improved. Upon closer examination, what looked like a deer in the first drawing was actually an elk. The elk disappeared from this area when the great white pine forests were harvested for lumber in the last century. Following the artwork as it made its journey along the wall, the paintings began depicting human activity, hunting and planting. Subsequent sets of paintings represented what appeared to be religious ceremonies. She felt a deep connection with these images.

She turned her attention to the center of the cave. The narrow flashlight beam provided tunnel vision of the objects it illuminated. She gasped in fear as the flashlight revealed a hideous face. It appeared as the bottom figure of the totem pole. Even though she had seen it many times before, her reaction was always the same. The face radiated evil. This was Chief Wabana. Wabana, the namesake of the township and lake. The totem pole stood behind a fire ring and had a profound effect upon the casual observer. The ring was composed of fieldstones arranged in a circle four feet in diameter; a stalagmite protruded from

5

the ground at its center. The stalagmite was four feet tall and, upon closer examination, it was hand polished to a razor-sharp tip. There were bits and pieces of charred animal bones surrounding it, a legacy of ceremony and sacrifice.

Sacrificial ceremonies were a part of primitive cultures, but the totem pole told a story that sent a chill up her spine—a saga that started with Chief Wabana at the bottom, followed by an image of a woman dancing, perhaps a tribal priestess. The next image portrayed a ceremony which appeared to be a fertility rite. Above that was a depiction of a traditional burial mound, and the last carving was an eagle—a bald eagle—the consummate predator. The eagle's wings were spread and its talons extended, as if poised to gather prey. The eagle's mouth was open wide. It was screaming.

She pondered. Was the purpose of the totem pole to ward off evil spirits or intimidate? All of the other totem poles she had seen were taller, with more images. This one appeared truncated.

Next she turned her attention to the hole in the ceiling of the cave. The cave was approximately twenty-three feet high. The hole was directly above the fire pit and was designed to let the smoke out. How many generations of people had used this cave? It was large enough to hold several families. It must have provided shelter from the winters for the tribe. The artwork on the wall was their story. It was time to make her contribution to the story. She had her art materials with her.

A noise! Was she alone? Stepping back in trepidation, she was startled by a cold sensation in her feet. She relaxed and laughed at herself. She had stepped into the stream that flowed from the back of the cave out the front entrance. She was easily spooked in this cave. Her imagination ran wild.

She arranged her art materials, positioned the light on the wall, and began to paint. Painting was always easy for her. Perhaps it was a sense of intuition; she felt she was predestined to paint on the wall. There was more to add to the story. It would not have been allowed before; now was the time. She finished her artwork, then stepped back, assessing it.

Another noise; this time, she was sure she heard it. She darted alongside the stream to the back of the cave. There was a tall, narrow opening in the back of the cave where the stream emerged. How many times had she wondered how powerful the stream must have been at one time to carve out this cave? Could there be other caves behind this one? It looked like a person could turn sideways and fit into the opening. She gathered her courage and did just that, seeking shelter in the opening.

A shot rang out! The bullet ricocheted off the stone next to her head. She moved quickly into the opening. Another shot. She felt herself melting away into the darkness.

Chapter 1

I wonder what they were like?

Lomasi was lost. Not lost in the woods—she took the same walk through the woods every morning on the same path behind her house. She never knew her parents. All she had were photographs. It was like wandering through the world alone without anyplace to call home. When Sandy and Dan disappeared, she lost her reference point in life. All she could do was carry a picture of them wherever she went.

Lomasi lived with Sara, her grandmother. Sara assumed the role of mother. Lomasi never found out what happened to her parents. Were they murdered? Could they have just left her behind?

Did they love me?

This was the foremost question in Lomasi's life, yet the love she sought remained a stranger to her.

They must have loved me. My grandmother loves me. My fellow students love me. Everyone loves me.

Love was not a need for Lomasi, it was an obsession.

On the wall in her room was a self-portrait of her mother, a charcoal drawing. Lomasi often thought the drawing captured the essence of her mother. She liked to think that her mother created this image for her. Even though the portrait was black and white, her eyes seemed exotic—almost glimmering. There was beauty in her perfectly formed face. Her coquettish smile was enigmatic. Lomasi always thought that smile suggested a secret happiness her mother would share with her. More than anything else, the drawing was a comfort to her. Lomasi felt that her mother was watching over her, especially while she slept.

Lomasi would ponder the drawing for hours. *What are you trying to tell me?*

Her mother just smiled back in silence. Lomasi felt compelled to decipher Sandy's message, the meaning behind the smile.

It was spring in northern Minnesota. Flowers were blossoming and the trees were turning a vibrant shade of green only springtime can produce. The morning air felt cool and crisp on Lomasi's skin as she walked along. Majestic, towering red pines shaded the forest studded with an occasional white pine. The sun shone brightly though the breaks in the forest canopy. The rays of light warmed her as she ambled along the path with her thoughts spinning around her.

At seventeen, it was also the springtime of Lomasi's life—she was blossoming into an attractive young woman. Her long black hair reached to her lower back, shimmering in the sunlight. Her dark complexion and sultry brown eyes, combined with her slender, five-foot-five figure, were starting to attract the attention of both boys and men. She could sense heads turning as she walked down the hall at school. She would graduate from Grand Rapids High School at the end of the school year.

It was a time of life for choices. Like the path through the forest, Lomasi felt she was meandering through life. Like any orphan, she felt insecure. This was especially true for Lomasi, she was not certain she was an orphan. When she was eighteen months old, her parents just disappeared. She was too young to remember what happened. She had to accept Sara's explanation of the event.

Raising Lomasi was a challenge for Sara. She did the best she could, but the difference in generational lifestyles was tremendous. Sara grew up in a time when TV was changing the world; Lomasi grew up in a time when electronic devices were changing every aspect of our lives.

Lomasi felt Sara did not understand her. Sara would never talk in depth about the disappearance. It was frustrating because it appeared no one really knew what happened. What made it even worse, Lomasi felt someone did know what happened to her parents, and that person was content to remain silent.

Lomasi loved to write—she excelled in English class and wrote for the high school newspaper. Studying was easy for her. Her grades put her at the top of her class. In her spare time, she wrote poetry; some of her poems were published in the local newspaper, the *Grand Rapids Herald Review*. Yet it seemed to surprise everyone when Lomasi was accepted to the University of Minnesota for the fall term. Lomasi had already decided she was going to major in English Literature. She believed the highest calling in life was to be a writer. She wanted to write a novel.

Driven by a strong maternal instinct to protect Lomasi, it was only natural for Sara to desire a stable life for her grandchild. She wanted Lomasi to avoid the pitfalls she experienced growing up a Native American in a white-man's world. Sara was a single mom and now a single grandmother. She wanted Lomasi to follow in her footsteps in the medical field as a nurse practitioner. She did not want Lomasi to make the same mistakes she had made when she was young.

Sara worked in Grand Rapids at the Longfell Clinic. Being a pragmatic person, she recognized hard work as her ally. She began her career in medicine as a nurse's aide at the hospital in Grand Rapids. Through her own initiative and perseverance, she climbed the career ladder in the healthcare industry. She went to school at night, earning a bachelor's degree in nursing, then pursued her master's degree in nursing, becoming a certified nurse practitioner.

As a highly trained healthcare professional, Sara was in demand and well paid. She wanted the same thing for her granddaughter and could not understand Lomasi's desire to be a writer. Sara felt Lomasi was following a youthful romantic dream rather than being realistic. She wanted to help Lomasi avoid making lifestyle and career choices that would hinder her success in the future. Sara felt Lomasi should embark on a profession that provided security, good pay, and advancement. Even though it may have sounded exciting, what were the chances Lomasi would write a successful novel?

Lomasi, on the other hand, was certain about her future. As she reflected on her childhood, the pleasant memories of campfires with her family and friends, she realized there was more to her goal than being a writer; she had to master the art of storytelling. The first story she wanted to tell was her story—the disappearance of Sandy and Dan. She needed closure; her writing would serve as therapy. It would make her life whole.

"I have to write about my life, my parents' disappearance," Lomasi argued with her grandmother, begging for more information about the event. "If I write about it and investigate, I know I can solve the mystery."

"You will be wasting your time," Sara replied. "I doubt you will discover anything new."

"You said yourself that many young Native American women have disappeared. My mother is one of them."

"Most of those girls had drug and alcohol problems. They were members of dysfunctional families with the same problems. I think a lot of them escaped their surroundings to go to the big city, where they could find more opportunity."

"What about your dream of opening a shelter for Native American women?"

"I still have that dream," Sara said thoughtfully. "There are too many young girls getting into trouble these days. They start drinking alcohol and the next thing you know, they are into sex and drugs, and ultimately prostitution. Then they disappear. Having a shelter where they could stay and sort out their problems would help immensely. Many families could benefit."

"I could use the profits from my first book to help you start a shelter."

"You're a dreamer," Sara said. "Your heart is in the right place, I'll grant you that. At least you care."

"Grandma, why do I feel you are not telling me everything you know about my past?"

Sara remained silent. Withholding information from Lomasi made her feel guilty. What was the point in revealing the truth? What was done was done. It would only cause more pain for both of them.

Sara's next-door neighbor was her stepbrother, Duane. They grew up together in Wabana Township. A single father, his adopted son Ahote lived with him. Duane bought Lomasi's parents' trailer when it was apparent they would not return. The proceeds of the sale would be used for Lomasi's education. The same age as Lomasi, Ahote had been her best friend through childhood. They shared many similar experiences. Unlike Lomasi, Ahote was not a stellar student. Through his desire to be a musician, he developed the undeserved reputation of a wastrel.

Duane was drafted into the army after high school and served in Vietnam in the infantry. He was a natural athlete. After basic training, he received paratrooper training, then joined the 101st Airborne Division in Vietnam. Injured in combat while rescuing a fellow soldier, shot in the leg just above the knee, his femur was shattered. He was evacuated to the United States, but his wound never healed properly. He walked with a slight limp. Duane spent the rest of his army career helping train new inductees into the army's regimen. The recipient of a medal, the bronze star, for bravery in combat, he was a wounded hero who did not receive a hero's welcome home.

Duane got a job with a local logging company after his discharge from the army. He was surprised to find that no one at work really appreciated what he did in Vietnam. While working at the logging company, he was treated as a second-class citizen by many of his coworkers because he was Native American. The work was difficult physically because his nagging leg wound hindered him. He became bitter and missed work, using his wound as an excuse.

Duane was finally awarded a small disability pension from the army. When rain approached, he noticed a throb and swelling in his knee. He spent his time learning to carve birds, especially loons, and researching the history of his ancestors.

One of Sara and Duane's favorite summer activities was to sit around the firepit in Sara's backyard at the end of the day with Lomasi and Ahote. Sara and Duane belonged to a generation of Native Americans that transitioned from the tribal community to the "Americanized" version of family life.

Native American culture was very important to Sara and Duane. It was their mission to convey to Lomasi and Ahote knowledge of tribal values and lore. They accomplished this by telling them stories while they sat by the campfire at night. Their ancestral history had been passed down from generation to generation, through storytelling. Sara and Duane shared a genuine concern that their descendents, Lomasi and Ahote, would become so immersed in the present-day culture of the United States that the stories of their ancestors would disappear along with their Native American culture.

Duane was a direct descendent of Chief Wabana, the last tribal chief in the area. They were pleased that both Lomasi and Ahote were interested in learning lore. Lomasi liked storytelling. She was their poet. Ahote loved the chants and music surrounding their culture. He was learning the dances that accompanied their rituals. He was proficient with the guitar. He was their musician.

Wabana Township was a sleepy place nestled in the Chippewa National Forest. Nothing much happened to change the tempo of life. Aside from a small human population, the environment was composed mostly of wildlife: bear, deer, wolves, ducks, and an occasional fox. Some days the call of a loon was the only thing that broke the silence of this peaceful area in northern Minnesota. Residents of the township liked it that way. It was an ideal location for people to retire.

The Wabana chain of lakes dominated Wabana Township along with a bevy of smaller lakes that provided lakeshore ideally suited for cabins and lake homes. On weekends the population swelled with families enjoying their vacation homes and sportsmen enjoying a day in the outdoors.

Wabana Township was located twelve miles north of Grand Rapids, Minnesota, which had a population of 10,000. The principal industries in the area were logging and mining. Both of those businesses had slowed down in recent years. Grand Rapids was located on the east end of the Mesabi Iron Range. The mining industry now was just a shadow of what it was in its heyday. Huge piles of overburden—discarded low-grade ore—could be seen as you drove through the Iron Range. The piles of overburden had been part of the landscape for so long that grown trees had made their homes on them.

Full-time residents of Wabana Township were greatly outnumbered by the part-timers that used the area as a recreational destination on weekends and vacations. The full-time residents were composed of a few couples who were raising a family and retired couples, many of whom lived here in the summer and became snowbirds in the winter, migrating to warmer climes.

In the winter, snow and cold dominated the landscape. Snowmobiling was a popular pastime. A snowmobile made it easy to explore the remote areas of the forests and lakes. There were trails designed specifically for the sport, which allowed enthusiasts to travel hundreds of miles in northern Minnesota to restaurants and different towns. A snowmobile could also be a practical mode of transportation when a winter storm dumped a foot or more of snow on the area.

Ice fishing was popular. At night one could look out on the lake and see the lights from the fish houses used to keep warm while people fished through holes drilled in the ice.

Residents lived and breathed hockey, encouraging their children to learn the sport by building ice rinks. The area produced top hockey players for high school and college sports programs. Cross-country skiing was also popular, with trails crisscrossing the area.

Protecting the environment was an issue that all residents agreed was important. The pristine waters and forest land must be guarded for future generations. Invasive species were a constant threat to the delicate balance of nature.

Most of the important players on environmental issues such as mining and water quality were groups that were not based in the area.

Mining concerns, environmental groups, and lobbying groups dominated the political landscape at the state legislature. Local residents sometimes found it frustrating that they must live by rules created by outsiders.

Something Sara and Duane found ironic was that Native Americans were the original environmentalists. They lived off the land, never taking more than was necessary to survive, assuring an abundant source of wildlife and natural resources for future generations. Now, after taking most of the lakeshore for private residences and cabins, polluting the water with their substandard septic systems and waste, the local residents wanted tight standards that would maintain a pristine environment. They failed to recognize Native Americans were the original good stewards of the environment.

Wabana Township was not a diverse community. White Caucasians dominated the human population. Sara and Duane found it ironic that in an area that was once dominated by their ancestors, they were now minorities. Even though they were the original residents of the area, they were now considered the least desirable resident—Native American trailer trash—a highly educated nurse and a Vietnam veteran! Perhaps that is why the disappearance of Sandy and Dan was not a cause for concern. The community just sighed in relief—good riddance.

It was a cold case now. It happened so many years ago that everyone just accepted the disappearance of Sandy and Dan as fact. The neighbors quit gossiping about it. There was occasional speculation that Lomasi's parents ran off to the West Coast. Some said they had gang ties and were abducted, then murdered, over a drug deal. It became a local legend that they were in their van at the bottom of Bluewater Lake. The fact remained that sixteen years ago, Lomasi's mother and father left their trailer on Bluewater Road and were never seen again.

Lomasi knew her parents were not drug dealers. She knew they would never desert her. How could the local residents make up such lies? It was cruel.

Lomasi's grandmother had lived in the trailer next door. She had the day off work and was babysitting Lomasi. She arrived at her daughters' trailer to pick her granddaughter up prior to Sandy and Dan leaving for work. They said goodbye—nothing seemed out of the ordinary. When they did not return home at the usual time, Sara was not alarmed. They probably just stopped at the grocery store and were running a little late. When it got to be 10:00 PM and they still were not home, Sara became increasingly concerned. Sandy and Dan were young; perhaps they stopped for a beer. At midnight she called the sheriff, inquiring if there had been any accidents reported.

Once law enforcement became involved, the investigation began in earnest. After it was established that Lomasi's parents had never arrived at work that day, the search began. They searched for the blue Ford van. Initially they focused their search in Wabana Township, canvassing neighbors, inquiring if anyone had heard or seen anything. They searched the back roads in the township for the van or anything unusual. Soon the search spread to Itasca County and eventually a missing person's bulletin was broadcast across the state. No results.

Lomasi moved to the house next door to live with her grandmother. Sara was Lomasi's closest living relative. She would take care of her until her parents returned.

Chapter 2

This is outrageous!

While driving Bluewater Road toward his home, Mike King encountered something that made his blood boil. As he approached Duane and Ahote's home, he saw his red Jaguar parked on the street along with a collection of other cars. Several young people gathered outside the garage. Music with a primitive beat was blaring from inside the garage. It really irked him that Emily, his significant other, was not in the Jaguar, but in the front of the crowd of people. Jealousy reared its vile head.

Emily was a young Native American woman. She was voluptuous, an exotic beauty with a figure that made her the center of attention wherever she went. Mike rescued her from a poor family situation on the reservation. Emily had been ready to run away and Mike was there to help her. Mike provided her with a lifestyle that she could only dream about previous to meeting him. She lived in a beautiful home, wore designer clothes, and had Mike's Jaguar available with a full tank of gas. Everything she wanted, including liquor and drugs, was available.

Emily had a naughty side. She liked being the center of attention. Now she was trying to attract Ahote's attention. Emily was dancing in place to the music, shaking her body seductively and waving her hands. She was not alone in her enjoyment; everybody seemed to be enjoying the music. Mike couldn't control himself. He got out of the car, walked over, and grabbed Emily by the arm.

"You're coming with me!" he hissed.

"Ouch—you're hurting me," Emily retorted as she obediently followed Mike. She knew she was in trouble but she couldn't help herself. Even though she had it really nice, life was a little boring living with a man more than twice her age. She had just stopped to enjoy herself. It was no big deal.

"Now, get in the car. I'll follow you home."

What could she do? Emily followed instructions. She got in her Jaguar and slowly drove Bluewater Road to the home she shared with Mike. She pulled into the driveway and walked into the house without saying a word. Mike followed her, looking like a crazed maniac. He grabbed her arm and turned her toward him. She stared at him defiantly.

"Don't you ever embarrass me like that again!" Mike said.

"I could say the same thing to you!" Emily replied. As soon as the words came out, she knew it was mistake. She became keenly aware of his rage and anticipated his actions. Pulling away from him, she ducked as he let a left hook fly. The punch went over her head, but she was off balance.

"Mike, I'm sorry!" she screamed as he picked her up over his shoulder and manhandled her into the bedroom like a Cro-Magnon man. He sat on the bed and put her over his knee.

"Mike, don't, I said I'm sorry!" Emily pleaded.

Mike pulled her skirt up above her buttocks and started to spank her. He continued until her screaming became unbearable, even to him. He was becoming aroused and he started to massage her buttocks and run his hand up and down her legs. She was so relieved that his rage was subsiding, that she started to respond. Mike sank back on the bed with Emily on top of him.

No one saw Emily again after that morning. Sadly, there was no one to miss her.

Lomasi's and Ahote's fondest memories together were of evenings with Duane and Sara gathered around the campfire in the back yard. They never tired of the stories Sara spun in great detail about their ancestors. They sang with joy the tribal songs that Duane taught them.

Ahote and Lomasi were the same age. While Lomasi was a studious person, serious about school and life, Ahote was the opposite. He was a gregarious child. About him glowed an invisible aura that was warm and alluring; he had a contagious laugh that spread joy throughout a crowded room.

Ahote was a musician. He had decided on his profession early in life and was pursuing it as much as a seventeen-year-old could. He had a band that played in the garage and occasionally at dances and community events. He fancied himself a singer and songwriter.

Ahote was six feet tall. He had a muscular build and long black hair that hung over his shoulders. He had a dark complexion and dark-brown, almost black, engaging eyes that twinkled with impishness when he smiled.

One night while they sat looking at the flames, Ahote said, "Hey, Duane, listen to this."

Ahote started playing a song he wrote with Lomasi. *"Wabana, Wabana, you call to me. Wabana, Wabana, you set me free…"* he crooned.

"Ahote, we don't need a totem pole to ward off evil spirits. Your singing is enough!" Duane chuckled as he continued, "As a matter of fact, we won't have any spirits around here, good or evil, with you singing."

"I can understand you being jealous of me, Duane, but Lomasi wrote the words. I composed the music," Ahote replied. "Lomasi, you should give up your ideas of being a novelist. We could be a songwriting team. We'll be famous."

"Forget it, Ahote," Lomasi said. "While you're standing in the unemployment line waiting for your big break, I'll be collecting a Pulitzer prize for my novel."

"We'll see who laughs when I am touring the world," Ahote replied. "You'll be stuck behind a desk in some basement apartment eating pizza and slaving over your manuscript."

A part of Lomasi was jealous of Ahote. He had such an easy style with people. He had grown into a very attractive young man. But he was just that, a young man. She could tell that he liked her and in a way she felt the same way about him. But, she had her whole life ahead of her and she was not going to waste it on someone from northern Minnesota who probably would not amount to anything. Still, they always had fun together—they connected on a deep level.

Ahote's band practiced in his and Duane's garage on Bluewater Road. The band had five members. Lloyd played drums. Tom played lead guitar and sang. Bill played bass guitar and Mary was their lead singer.

Ahote was the leader of the band. He played acoustic guitar. He wrote the music and songs they played. He was the go-getter who would look for jobs for the group; a spark plug for the enterprise. Ahote would be successful at any type of sales job. He was outgoing and driven in any endeavor. Being a skillful leader, he performed his job flawlessly while making each member of the band understand their contribution was important.

Initially the band was a minor nuisance to their neighbor, Sara. They played with the garage door open. Their music was loud, but there were no other neighbors in earshot to complain. They made quite a few musical mistakes and the drummer was just learning to keep musical time. The band members were dedicated. They practiced twice a week. Gradually they became a tight-knit group that had a set of twenty songs they could play for parties and dances.

Their practicing and hard work did not come without a price. Mike King, who lived on Bluewater Road, would drive by while the band was practicing and seethe. He did not like the primitive beat of the music. He especially did not like the volume of the music. He did not like anyone else being the center of attention and became deeply jealous when he drove by the band practicing with his latest acquisition, Emily, watching. She liked the music and thought the band members were cute. He had become uncontrollably jealous when he saw Emily was dancing, trying to catch Ahote's attention while the band played.

Mike never really worked hard for anything. He reaped the rewards of other people's work. He owned a resort on Bluewater Lake, just up the road from where Lomasi and Ahote lived. He had someone managing the resort for him. He owned a beautiful hand-scribed log home on Bluewater Lake with eight acres near the resort. He was a carouser and a womanizer. He would wake up late in the morning, spend a couple hours reviewing the day's business, then head to the bar. His motto was, "Up at the crack of noon, in the bar by 4:00." Mike always had a beautiful young woman on his arm.

Mike was used to controlling the environment surrounding him. He did not like the idea of a bunch of young upstart teenagers disturbing the peace of the neighborhood. He was also a Wabana Township supervisor. He had moved to northern Minnesota when his father died and left him a fortune. He lived the life of leisure and did not want to have his quiet lifestyle disturbed by some garage band. He knew what he had to do.

"Itasca County Sheriff's Department, Deputy Mason speaking; how can I help you?"

"Good day, deputy, this is Mike King. I live on Bluewater Road in Wabana Township. We have a noise problem out here. There is a group of young people that formed a band. They practice in their parent's garage and make so much noise it causes a public disturbance."

"They are disturbing the peace?" the deputy asked.

"They're causing a general disturbance in the neighborhood. I realize they are just young people having fun, but isn't there a more appropriate place for them to practice? I am a township supervisor in Wabana Township. This is a place where people spend substantial sums of money on their lake homes so they can enjoy the peace and quiet. People retire here. We don't need trailer trash making noise and disrupting our lifestyles."

"We'll send someone out there to look into it," the deputy replied.

The next day, a sheriff's deputy was dispatched to Ahote's house. Duane was not there, but Ahote was home. It was Saturday; he and Lomasi were sitting around talking about their future now that they were finally graduating from high school. Ahote was playing his guitar—it was a nervous habit—while they spoke. There was a knock on the door. Ahote peeked out the front window. He was surprised to see a sheriff's squad car parked outside his house and a deputy standing outside the door. He opened the door.

"Is there something wrong, sir?" Ahote asked politely.

"Are your parents home?" the deputy asked.

"No, Duane went to town; he should be back later today," Ahote answered.

"Are you Ahote?" the deputy asked.

"Yes."

"Duane is your stepdad?"

"Yes." Ahote was surprised. He wondered how the deputy knew so much about him.

"We received a complaint about your band making too much noise. Have you been practicing in the garage?" the deputy asked.

"Yes, we have," Ahote replied. "We like to think that we are playing music, not making noise." It was hard for Ahote to hide his sarcasm.

"Stop the wisecracks, young man," The deputy demanded. "We have a complaint from one of your neighbors that your behavior is disrupting the neighborhood. I am here to investigate."

"Who filed the complaint?" Ahote asked.

"Never mind who filed the complaint; I'm asking the questions here," the deputy replied.

"Our next-door neighbors are Sara and Lomasi. They don't care if my band practices in the garage. The next closest neighbors are over a mile away. Our amplifiers aren't powerful enough for them to hear us at that distance. I do not understand the problem, deputy." Ahote was starting to get mad.

"Well, if you must know, it was Mike King that called. He is a supervisor for Wabana Township," the deputy replied. "He is an influential person around here and we do not want any trouble from him or anyone else. Just try to keep your volume down when you practice. We don't want any more complaints!"

"Will do, deputy," Ahote said contemptuously.

"Can you believe that?" Ahote said to Lomasi. He had a skeptical look on his face as the deputy drove away. "There is no one that lives close enough to hear us practice except you and Sara. How could someone complain about noise?"

"They are just jealous," Lomasi replied. "Let's forget it. We have our graduation party to plan. Just because our neighbors are unhappy does not mean that we have to be."

"You're right," Ahote said. "I envy you going to the university this fall. I bet you don't get complaints about loud music around there. They would probably enjoy listening to us play."

"Why don't you move there, too?" Lomasi asked. "It would be a good place to launch your music career and I would have at least one friend there when I moved."

"Maybe I will," Ahote said thoughtfully.

Ahote looked out the window to ensure the deputy had left. He noticed someone parked on an all-terrain vehicle, an ATV, on the side of the road about one hundred yards away.

"Who is that?" Ahote asked Lomasi.

"I don't know," Lomasi replied. "I've never seen him before."

They sat and watched the stranger for a few minutes. He was parked off the road. He appeared to be watching Sara's and Duane's homes. Ahote and Lomasi knew almost everyone in the neighborhood, but this time of year, there were a lot of people in the area who had seasonal properties they used for recreation, so it was not unusual that they would not recognize this person. The stranger was wearing a crash helmet with tinted glass, so they could not see what he looked like. They watched him for a while. Finally Ahote said, "Maybe he is having problems with his ATV or he is lost. Let's go over there and see if he needs help."

Ahote and Lomasi walked down Bluewater Road toward the stranger. When they got close, Ahote smiled and asked, "Hi, can we help you?"

The stranger started his ATV and drove off into the woods.

"Strange," Lomasi said to Ahote as the man on the ATV drove from sight.

Chapter 3

A collective sigh of relief echoed throughout the auditorium as the last senior received a diploma, completing the graduation ceremony for Grand Rapids High School. The former students experienced long-awaited closure. Time to start a new chapter in life; it was time to celebrate!

"Let's organize a graduation party" Ahote suggested.

"It has to be something special," Lomasi added.

"I've been thinking—let's party in the cave," Ahote blurted without thinking.

"Do you think we should?" Lomasi looked at Ahote as if she had been betrayed. "We've always kept the cave a secret. It has been our clandestine meeting place since we were children."

"That sounds a little melodramatic—there is really nothing clandestine about us." He obviously did not understand how Lomasi felt. "Besides, this is a special occasion—the cave will be perfect."

They decided to invite their friends.

Lloyd's father owned a liquor store in Grand Rapids. He was able to finagle six bottles of champagne for the occasion. They all met in the parking lot at the beginning of the hiking trail on Bluewater Road and started their trek. The path that led to the waterfall was a quarter mile up the trail. Most of the group had been to the waterfall before; they were all surprised and delighted to hear there was a cave behind the waterfall. The group was filled with a sense of adventure as they made their way through the woods.

Warmth from the rising sun and blue sky greeted them as they approached the waterfall.

"It's a nice day to die!" Ahote stated with a smile. He was trying to set the tone for their adventure.

Everyone gave Ahote a strange look except Lomasi. She giggled.

"It's an old Native American saying," Lomasi explained to the group. "It's a custom, a way of saying it is a beautiful day." When there was no reaction from anyone, Lomasi added, "I guess you have to be Native American to appreciate it."

"Follow me," Ahote said as he led the way to the entrance of the cave. Ahote, Lomasi, and the rest of the group approached the waterfall and the entrance to the cave cautiously.

Mary said, "Why are we going in there? There's a nice pond and the waterfall out here. Let's party in the sun." She looked at the narrow entrance to the cave and wondered why anyone would try to squeeze through that small space. In reality, the entrance was not that narrow and it grew wider as you went through it, but Mary did not want to ruin her clothes; she had second thoughts about entering the cave.

"It gets bigger as you go inside," Lomasi reassured Mary.

The rest of the group was anxious, anticipating the adventure of exploring a cave that had been right under their noses all this time. They all slipped inside. As Ahote lit the torches one by one, the interior of the cave gradually revealed its secrets. Stalactites captured everyone's attention initially, hanging from the ceiling, water dripping from them to the floor. Light from the flickering torches danced across the walls and brought the paintings to life, like ghosts with a story to tell. Finally everyone focused on the totem pole.

"Where did that come from?" Tom asked as he stepped closer to the totem pole to examine it with his flashlight.

"It's a totem pole," Ahote replied.

"How profound," Mary commented sarcastically. She was secretly jealous of Ahote's relationship with Lomasi.

Ahote realized he had just stated the obvious and added sheepishly, "It is designed to ward off evil spirits."

"It looks like it is an evil spirit," Tom retorted.

"Everything in this cave seems primitive; some of it seems ancient. It is like walking into another world," Mary said thoughtfully. "Yet the totem pole has to be a recent addition. Otherwise it would have rotted by now."

"Ahote and I found the cave when we were kids," Lomasi said as she lit the fire—she and Ahote had gathered wood and prepared the firepit ahead of time. "The totem pole has been here ever since we can remember."

"Well, it's creepy!" Mary exclaimed. "What is that sticking out of the firepit?"

"It's a stalagmite," Ahote replied. "It's just like the stalactites hanging down from the ceiling only this one has a sharpened point. We think the firepit was used for sacrifices at one time. They probably impaled the animal being sacrificed, then burned it in the fire."

"What if it wasn't animals?" Tom asked.

Everyone looked at each other, but no one dared to answer.

"Who are *they?*" Lloyd asked.

"The people who originally inhabited this land, our ancestors," Ahote said, pointing to Lomasi and himself. "This cave is full of history. Look at the paintings on the wall—they tell a story."

"A creepy story," Mary said. "The last few paintings look like orgy scenes. And look at that totem pole—the artist must have been preoccupied with murder and rape."

"I never noticed that before," Lomasi observed.

"It takes a mind like Mary's to imagine something like that," Bill said.

"It's hard to tell when these were painted," Lomasi said as she walked over to examine the most recent. "Obviously, whoever painted these was more talented than the previous artists," she said knowingly. "The colors are more distinct and the details intricate."

"Does anyone use this cave besides you?" Lloyd asked.

"I don't know," Ahote replied. "We always thought it was just a forgotten cave, but it is possible others know about it and keep it to themselves."

"Maybe it's a secret society," Mary said.

"Come on, Mary," Lomasi said. "Remember, this is Wabana Township. The most exciting thing that happens around here is the ice melts off the lakes in the spring."

"You should tell someone at the University of Minnesota about this cave," Bill said. "I bet they would love to study this. You would be making a contribution to history. People would learn more Native American culture. Native Americans would be thought of as a race of people with history and art, rather than a bunch of drunks that can't make it without a casino monopoly."

"What are you talking about? Most Native Americans do not receive any benefit from the casinos. We're not all drunks!" Ahote retorted. He resented racism. He couldn't count the number of times he had heard the argument that gaming was the only way Native Americans could achieve success.

"Quit arguing! Can't you two get along, even for a little while? This is a graduation party," Mary said. Then she turned and said thoughtfully to Lomasi, "It wouldn't be a bad idea to have the university look at the cave."

"We thought about it," Lomasi said as she looked at Ahote. "We decided to keep it for ourselves. We even debated whether we should have the party here. If we told outsiders about this, our lives would change. The burial mounds beyond here have already been raided and desecrated. There would be people from the academic world studying the area. There would be looters. Bluewater Road would carry a lot more traffic. They might excavate. You can imagine how things would change. It could become a tourist trap."

"Yeah, they might scare off the evil spirits," Tom said as he chuckled to himself.

"Those are just old superstitions. Chief Wabana is dead. His spirit doesn't haunt the area," Lomasi replied.

"Speaking of spirits," Lloyd interrupted, "I brought champagne along to help us celebrate our graduation. Let's not forget we came here to party, not for a historical field trip." He reached in his backpack and pulled out a bottle of champagne and some plastic glasses.

"Yeah, let's sit by the fire and enjoy ourselves," Tom said.

"We graduated!" Mary yelled. "Yes! Let's party."

They all shuddered as Mary's voice reverberated in the cave. It was spooky. Everyone settled down around the fire pit. Lloyd started pouring the champagne. He made sure they all had a full glass.

"A toast," Ahote said, "to us. We made it. We finally graduated."

Everyone raised their glasses.

"To our future," Lomasi said. There was more drinking.

"Lomasi," Lloyd said. "You're always so serious. Here, fill up everyone's glasses. Let's not worry about the future, let's have fun now. We deserve some enjoyment."

"Yeah," Mary said. "Drink, everyone. Let's see who can down theirs first."

Everyone emptied their plastic glass of champagne. Lloyd opened another bottle and filled their glasses again. "We're starting to get low on bubbly already," he said. "I only brought six bottles."

"Don't worry," Tom said. "I brought along some of the noble weed." He pulled out a couple marijuana cigarettes.

"Tom was always the thoughtful one; he wants us to get stoned in the cave," Bill said. He was drunk enough to think he was being clever.

26

Everyone was pleased except Lomasi. She did not want to say anything against smoking marijuana. Everyone was always telling her she was too somber, that she should lighten up. After all, this was a graduation party—she did not want to put a damper on the celebration.

Tom lit a joint, took a large drag off it and passed it on to Bill. Lloyd in the meantime was making sure everyone had a full glass of champagne. The light from the fire cast shadows in the cave. Tom lit another joint and started passing it. Everyone was getting high.

"I should have brought my guitar," Ahote said. "I bet the acoustics in this place would be great for live music."

Lomasi took her turn at the joint but did not inhale the smoke. She could already feel the effects of the champagne. Her head was starting to spin.

Mary was sitting next to Ahote. She started giggling and could not stop. "Ahote, all you ever think about is your music. Don't you ever think about girls?" she said as she leaned her head against his shoulder.

Ahote laughed. "I think about you all the time, Mary," se said with a coy smile.

Bill was jealous. He could feel the effects of the marijuana and the champagne. He had a crush on Mary. He stood up and pushed Ahote and said. "Leave her alone, can't you see she's drunk? She's not your squaw!"

Ahote fell back against the floor of the cave. He was mad; another racial slur. He and Bill were rivals; the drugs and alcohol exacerbated the rivalry. He got up and pushed Bill back. "You're just jealous, white boy. If you quit acting like such a fool, maybe women would like you, too!" Ahote yelled at Bill.

Bill was enraged. He charged across the fire ring at Ahote, disturbing everyone who was sitting in the ring. He grabbed Ahote in a bear hug. His momentum knocked them both to the floor. Bill was on top of Ahote, flailing away with his fists. Lloyd and Tom grabbed Bill. They were pulling him off Ahote when Tom shook loose and kicked Ahote in the groin. Ahote fell over in pain on the floor of the cave. Lomasi sat next to Ahote, holding him and trying to ease his pain.

In her drunken state, Mary got jealous. "You stay away from him," Mary said as she pushed Lomasi away.

Lomasi fell backward and hit her head on one of the stones of the fire ring. Lloyd grabbed and dragged her away from the fire so she would not get burned. He set her down. Everyone in the cave was pushing and shoving. It was general melee. Lloyd stepped into the fray also. Mary felt guilty—she could see her friend Lomasi lying unconscious on the floor of the cave while all the men were pushing and shoving. Fists started flying and everyone was yelling.

"Ahhhhhhhhhhhhhhhh!" A blood curdling scream echoed thoughout the cave. Suddenly, tom-tom drums were playing a primitive beat and ancient chants fill the air.

Everyone stopped fighting and looked at each other. Paranoia gripped them. The combination of alcohol and marijuana clouded their thoughts.

"What is that?" Lloyd asked.

"I don't know, but I'm not sticking around to find out."

Everyone panicked and made a beeline for the only exit from the cave. They slipped outside, made their way from under the waterfall, and beat a hasty retreat down the path that lead to the hiking trail. When they reached the trail, Ahote stopped and asked, "Where's Lomasi?"

"The last time I saw her, she was lying on the floor of the cave, unconscious," Mary said.

They all looked at each other. Ahote said, "We have to go back. What if something happened to her?"

They started back down the path to the waterfall entrance to the cave. Everyone was acting brave, but it was just that—an act. When they reached the entrance to the cave, everyone looked at each other. No one wanted to go in the cave. Silence!

Finally Ahote said, "I'm going in," he disappeared into the entrance of the cave.

He could hear Mary say, "Be careful!" as he looked around the cave. He made a thorough search and came back out.

"She's not in there," he said with a sad expression.

"Not in there?" Tom asked with a pained look. "How can she not be in there?"

"We would have seen her if she left," Lloyd said. "She didn't go past us. She has to be around here someplace. Let's search the area."

"Are you sure she isn't in the cave?" Mary asked. "Did you look everywhere?"

"Go look for yourself," Ahote retorted.

"I'm never going into that cave again," Mary replied.

"We're wasting time," Lloyd exclaimed. "Lomasi hit her head—she was hurt. We need to find her fast before something bad happens, if it hasn't already. Now let's spread out and search the area."

The group acted as a team instinctively. They fanned out from the cave entrance to look for Lomasi. They searched for over an hour. One by one they showed up where the path to the waterfall intersected the walking trail. Bill was the last one to show up.

"No luck?" Ahote asked.

"No sign of her whatsoever," Bill said.

"Oh, what could have happened to her?" Mary said as she started crying. "She was my best friend."

"Your best friend?" Bill asked. "You just assaulted her because you were jealous of her and Ahote."

"That's different," Mary said. "I was jealous, but I didn't intend for her to get hurt. What if something really serious has happened to her now? What if she is dead?"

"There is nothing further we can do here," Ahote said. "We need to call the police."

"Call the police!" Tom repeated. He was clearly distressed. "Oh, sure, we'll just explain to them we were sitting around in the cave smoking joints. We were also illegally drinking champagne—all of us are underage. Maybe they will be kind enough to give us adjoining cells, so we can keep each other company."

"He's right," Lloyd said. It would be foolish to call the police until we have an explanation for her disappearance. We need a story that we can all stick to."

"We should call Sara," Mary said. "She will be worried if she does not hear from Lomasi."

"We won't be calling anyone from here," Ahote said. "You forget we have no cell phone reception here. There is barely any reception at my house."

"We have to tell Sara," Mary said. "She's Lamosi's grandmother. She can decide what to do."

"Oh, sure, Mary," Bill said. "We just tell Sara we were all in this hidden cave with a totem pole and ancient drawings. We were drinking champagne and smoking joints when you attacked Lomasi. Then there was a loud scream, drums, and chanting. We ran out of the cave scared out of our wits and left Lomasi there. Now, Lomasi has disappeared."

"It sounds too fantastic to believe," Tom said. "If I wasn't there, I would not believe it myself."

"We have to go tell Sara." Ahote asserted his leadership skills. "We have a responsibility to Lomasi and to ourselves. We just graduated from high school. We are adults and we have to do the right thing, regardless of the consequences. It has been a couple hours since we have seen Lomasi. If we want to see her again, we have to act fast. Let's go tell Sara."

"It makes sense," Mary said.

They all started down the hiking trail to the parking area. They drove to Lomasi's house and parked.

"Who tells her?" Lloyd asked.

"I will," Ahote said. "I know her best."

"Tell her we're sorry," Mary said. She was thankful Ahote took charge of the situation and they were doing the right thing.

Ahote got out of the car and knocked on the door.

"Hi, Ahote." Sara said as she opened the door. "What's up?"

"We don't know where Lomasi is…"Ahote started to say. He was stumbling over his words.

"Lomasi is in her room sleeping right now," Sara interrupted. "I don't think she is feeling too well. She came home about an hour ago; her clothes were wet. I asked her what she had been doing, but she just wanted to go to bed. She won't be able to join you guys if that is why you're here."

It took Ahote a couple seconds to grasp what Sara said. "Yeah, we were going have a picnic to celebrate graduation. It doesn't sound like Lomasi will be able to join us."

"I'll tell her you stopped by," Sara said.

"Thanks," Ahote said as he walked back to the car. He opened the door and sat down inside.

"What did she say?" Mary asked.

"She said Lomasi came home about an hour ago and is sleeping," Ahote said in disbelief.

"How did she get back here before us?" Mary asked. "For that matter, how did she get out of the cave?"

Silence hung in the air as they drove away.

Chapter 4

A bass drum was pounding a steady rhythm that reverberated through her head. A queasy feeling radiated throughout her body. Was it the champagne, the marijuana, the blow to the head, or a combination of them all? *I guess I'm just not a partying person. All my friends think I am too serious. I am serious. I have things to accomplish.* Nevertheless, Lomasi woke in the morning with the same niggling feeling, the recurring question that never went away: *Who am I?*

She focused on positive affirmations: *I am Lomasi and I am proud of it! I am successful! I accomplish my goals!* Self-doubt remained. She knew her grandmother loved her. Sara had spent a good part of her life raising Lomasi. She was going to pay Lomasi's tuition. Still, Lomasi could not help but wonder, did Sara ever resent the fact that Sandy had disappeared and left her to raise her granddaughter?

These misgivings made life arduous for Lomasi. Coping with the same problems any adolescent teen faced coupled with the additional problems only an orphan encountered was a daunting task. She longed for the day she would understand her purpose in life. She longed for the day she would know what had happened to her parents.

Maybe that is why I have been so successful academically, Lomasi thought. *Maybe I had a greater need to please my teachers because I had no parents to please.*

That is why Lomasi spent so much time exploring the cave. She knew that the paintings on the wall and everything in the cave had something to do with her story. She felt a strong connection with the cave.

"Lomasi, it's time to get up," Sara yelled from the kitchen. "Breakfast is ready and this is your first day of work. We don't want to be late."

Lomasi forced herself to get out of her bed, put on her robe, and go have breakfast. It was oatmeal and muffins. It was always the same breakfast. Well, today would be a break from her routine. She would work for the summer at the Longfell Clinic. Sure, it would be mostly gofer work, but what did she expect? She was new to the workforce and if she wanted to fulfill Sara's expectations and work in the medical field, the clinic would be a valuable starting point. Besides, it would be nice to have money she had earned for herself.

"Are you ready to start work?" Sara asked.

"Sure, I'm as ready as I'll ever be," Lomasi replied.

"Don't sound so excited," Sara said.

"Oh, Grandma, I am excited to start something new," Lomasi justified her lack of enthusiasm. "It's just that I was getting used to sleeping late. I guess the long summer vacations are over for me."

"Welcome for the workforce," Sara said. "Now, remember, I will be your boss along with Dr. Longfell and you will help our receptionist, Ashley, also."

"I know, Grandma—I am at the bottom of the totem pole," Lomasi said, resigned to her fate. "You have to start somewhere."

"Good, I'm glad you understand," Sara said. "Now go get ready for work."

Sara had recently purchased a two-year-old BMW. She felt she deserved a treat for herself, plus it demonstrated to Lomasi what hard work can do. Sara had finished the nurse practitioner program at the College of Saint Scholastica in Duluth. It had seemed like she was making that ninety-minute drive from Grand Rapids to Duluth forever. Sara was proud of her accomplishment. Now she could help Lomasi find a rewarding career in healthcare.

Lomasi got in the BMW. "I'm ready," she said as Sara pulled out of the driveway. It was a sixteen-mile drive to the clinic from their home. They drove down Bluewater Road. As they approached County Road 60, they noticed an older gray pickup parked on the side of the road facing them. The driver waved at them vigorously as they approached.

"Do you need help?" Sara asked as she slowed to speak with the stranger.

The man just shook his head and looked forward.

Sara looked at Lomasi and rolled her eyes. They continued their drive. "Just what we need, a weirdo on Bluewater Road," she said. "I wonder why he was just parked on the side of the road? There are no houses around here. He seems to be sitting around watching everything and waiting."

"Weird is putting it mildly," Lomasi said. "That huge beard and the long gray hair are creepy. With that unusual hat, he seems like a comic character. He waved at us like he knows us."

"Everyone waves on Bluewater Road," Sara said. "People get mad if you don't wave at them."

Lomasi laughed. "Yeah, I know," she said. "Ahote and I saw the same guy parked on the side of the road a couple days ago."

"What was he doing?" Sara asked.

"He was sitting on his four-wheeler. It looked like he was staring at our house," Lomasi explained. "Ahote went over to ask him what he was doing, but he just drove away."

"Are you sure it was the same guy?" Sara asked.

"He was wearing a crash helmet with a tinted visor, so I did not get a good look at his face," Lomasi said. "But I think it was him."

"Well, we have to get to work now," Sara said. "I don't think he is harming anyone. Maybe we'll check with the sheriff later to see if there is any suspicious activity around here, but there isn't a law against parking on the side of the road."

"Still, it never hurts to be careful," Lomasi said.

"It's even better to be on time for work your first day," Sara said. "We better get going." Sara stepped on the gas as the sped towards town.

Cyrus Longfell sat in his clinic wondering if he had made a mistake hiring Lomasi for the summer. He had taken a chance hiring Sara as a nurse practitioner. At the time, nurse practioners were a new commodity. Some of his patients had been with him since he started his clinic years ago. The patients that visited frequently were elderly, saddled with the infirmities of age. Would something new, like a nurse practitioner, make them feel they were not getting their money's worth? After all, they came to see him, a medical doctor.

Then there was the fact that Sara was Native American—an American Indian. Grand Rapids was not exactly a bastion of diversity. There were few minorities in the area. Cyrus found that, outside the clinic, he was not necessarily accepted. Even though he had practiced in Grand Rapids for several years, many of the local residents still viewed him as an outsider.

The gamble had paid off in Sara's case. She was a competent medical practitioner. She presented herself to the patients as knowledgeable yet caring. The fact that she grew up here and was a local success story helped. Sara also had a flair for dealing with people. She had a sense of humor. She was very charming and made the patients feel welcome and appreciated.

On the other hand, Lomasi was a different story. She was a young woman—albeit an attractive young woman—an unknown quantity. Sure, she had graduated at the top of her class—she was obviously smart. It would be better for her if she gave up her association with that troublemaker Ahote. He had a reputation around town as someone who bucked the system. Sure, he was well liked among the young people in the area. He was even thought of as their leader because of his way with the guitar and singing. If he would just cut that long hair and behave as everyone else. Every time Cyrus thought of Ahote, he became angry—realistically, he was jealous.

Cyrus thought back to his humble beginnings. He recognized that not everyone had the opportunity to attend a private school and get the best educational opportunities. Cyrus grew up in Florida. His mother was a single mom. She had to struggle to make ends meet. She worked as a maintenance worker at Saint Mark's Preparatory School in Florida. Even though she was dealt difficult cards to play in the game of life, she had a good attitude and worked hard. She took advantage of every educational opportunity presented to her. She won the respect of the headmaster of the school and the instructors.

Cyrus' mother recognized early on her son's intellectual abilities. When Cyrus turned five years old, she proposed to the headmaster of the school that Cyrus be admitted. She pointed out that Cyrus scored high on the intelligence tests for a child his age. She proposed that she work an extra fifteen hours a week to pay for her son's education.

The headmaster and the admissions board liked the idea. Over the years the school had gotten a reputation for educating the elite. By educating Cyrus, not only would the school be helping a person of lesser means gain an education and improve himself, the school would be helping a single mom with the upbringing of her child. The decision was made and Cyrus's mother was informed that tuition would be free as long a she worked at the school.

Cyrus looked back on this now as the springboard to his career as a medical doctor. Who knows what would have happened if he had gone to a public school in Miami instead. Certainly he would never been accepted into the University of Miami. He probably would never have attended Harvard Medical School.

Cyrus had also made lifelong friends at Saint Mark's Preparatory School. Mike King went to school with Cyrus. He was a few years ahead of Cyrus. At first, Mike looked down on Cyrus. Of course, all the upperclassmen looked down on the youngerclassmen. That was the culture of Saint Mark's. Many there saw Cyrus as a charity case, knowing that his mother worked at the school and that Cyrus' father had left him in the lurch.

Mike acted out in school. He was mischievous. He seemed to know exactly how far he could stretch the limits. The Catholic Fathers at the school were tolerant, but their patience could be worn thin. When they could catch him at one of his nefarious acts, they punished Mike. But Mike seemed to enjoy it—he had a callous air about him. There was always a tension that bordered on violence between Mike and the people in authority at the school, even some of his fellow students.

In time, Mike and Cyrus became good friends. They hung around with classmates Jake and Tony. The four of them played pranks on their fellow students. They snuck off the campus to meet girls, go to movies, buy a bottle of gin, and generally let loose. They became a gang of four. Cyrus, as the youngest, enjoyed tagging along with his older peers.

As Cyrus looked back on this now, he chuckled. Mike had become a respected citizen in the community. He lived in an expensive home on Bluewater Lake. His true business activities were hidden behind shell corporations and offshore tax shelters.

Because of his background, Cyrus felt an obligation to help Lomasi. She was a diamond in the rough. Lomasi was going through a period in her life where she was experiencing growing pains. Once she finished her education and began working, she would mature into a thoughtful, competent medical professional. She would contribute to the profession and the well-being of humanity because of his help. Perhaps he was being a little too grandiose. After all, Lomasi was just working at the clinic for the summer.

"Good morning, Cyrus," Sara said.

Cyrus looked up from his desk. "You startled me," he said. "I didn't hear you come in. I was just preparing for today's patient load."

"You remember Lomasi," Sara said as she walked into Cyrus's office with her granddaughter.

"Yes, I have been looking forward to seeing you again," Cyrus replied. "You've grown up since the last time I've seen you." Cyrus was surprised. He was expecting to see someone younger. What he saw was a blossoming beauty with long straight black hair, black eyes, and a figure that could stop traffic.

"Thank you for the opportunity to work at the clinic this summer," Lomasi said humbly.

"Thank you for helping," Cyrus said politely. "Our patient load grows in the summer. We get our regular patients plus the seasonal folks that live here during the warmer months. We will keep you busy."

"I am hoping to gain some practical experience in the medical field that will help me in the future," Lomasi said.

"Well, you came to the right place," Cyrus replied. "Sara will fill you in on your duties. If there is anything I can do to be helpful, just let me know. Now it is time for us to get ready for our first patients."

Sara and Lomasi left Cyrus. Sara started showing Lomasi around the clinic, explaining to Lomasi what needed to be done daily.

Cyrus closed the door to his office. He thought to himself, *That's Lomasi? Maybe this will not be a bad summer after all.*

Friday morning, Lomasi was ready for the week to be over. She had learned most of her job duties, so she could do her job with little direction. It was established that she would get paid every Friday so she would become accustomed to immediate reward for hard work.

"Well, how do you like it so far?" Sara asked Lomasi as the day was coming to an end.

"I've enjoyed it so far. I'm glad the week is almost over. It will be nice to relax this weekend."

"You deserve it. You've worked hard this week and you've done a good job," Sara complimented Lomasi.

They were done with patients for they day. It was just a matter of cleaning up and preparing the clinic for Monday. Sara was glad to have Lomasi there, because Ashley was not much help when it came to anything other than being a receptionist.

"Let's go out for pizza after work. You deserve a treat," Sara suggested.

"That sounds like fun."

"Let's go see if Cyrus would like to join us," Sandy said. They went to his office; the door was open, but he was not there.

"That's what happens around here on Friday. Everyone is ready to get out of here and start the weekend. Why don't you start restocking the treatment rooms with supplies so we can get out of here on time?"

Lomasi went to the supply closet. She could not open the door. She could hear giggling coming from inside. She tried the door again, more forcibly this time. *It must be locked,* she thought. She went to find Sara to get the key.

"I don't know of a key for that closet," Sara said. "I have never seen it locked."

Lomasi was sitting in Sara's office. She heard a door open and looked toward the supply closet. She saw Cyrus walk out of there. She thought that was odd. The she saw Ashley follow him out. *The closet must be for more than supplies,* she thought to herself.

That night there was a solitary figure on Bluewater Road. It moved with a catlike grace. Its figure, barely outlined by a new moon, appeared to slither through the night. Dressed in dark clothes like he was going on a commando raid, the intruder blended with his surroundings. First he inspected Lomasi's house for any sign of life. Everyone appeared to be asleep. Then he did the same with Ahote's house. Finally he snuck up to Ahote's car and carefully opened the door. He took a plastic bag from his pocket and slid it under the driver's seat. He placed another object under the seat. It made a metallic sound as he accidentally scraped it against the seat mechanisms. His heart skipped a beat as he waited for someone to wake. Satisfied no one had heard the sound, he closed the door to the car as quietly as possible, then surveyed the area visually. Pleased that he had remained undetected, he disappeared into the darkness.

Chapter 5

Fall 1985

I am lucky! Cyrus said to himself. This was not an affirmation—to Cyrus, this was predestination. Dwelling inside of him was a strong belief that he was meant to do something great, a Horatio Alger rags-to-riches success story. A pauper from birth, finishing his education at Saint Mark's Preparatory School, Cyrus was a serious child. Work hard and taking advantage of every educational and cultural opportunity a private school could offer, he'd graduated with honors, establishing character traits that would form the foundation of his future.

Cyrus was delighted by his admission to the University of Miami. At orientation, he received a surprise that evoked both joy and consternation. There was Mike King, a classmate from Saint Mark's, sitting in the same auditorium.

"Hey, Mike, what are you doing here?" Cyrus asked Mike as he approached him. "I thought you were in the Army."

"Cyrus, it's nice to see you." Mike was surprised to see Cyrus. He explained, "I served my time and received an honorable discharge. I am using my GI-bill benefits to attend college."

"Well, let's sit together in the orientation," Cyrus suggested cautiously.

"Sounds great," Mike replied. "It will be nice to have a friend; everyone here is a stranger to me."

"Me, too," Cyrus replied, relieved they were friends. "Have you decided what your major will be?"

"I was an MP in the army. I didn't like it," Mike said. "I am going major in business administration."

"MP, as is military police?" Cyrus was surprised. After getting to know Mike in prep school, he would never have imagined him a police officer.

"Yup, I spent four years in the Army," Mike explained. "I really enjoyed it, but I didn't like being an enlisted man. Having attended a private school like Saint Mark's, my educational background was much more advanced than my peers'. I applied to the Army's Officer

38

Candidate School but was turned down because I did not have a college degree."

"It's a little late for that, isn't it?" Cyrus asked, wondering why Mike was attending college now.

"I just spent four long years serving my country. I want to play, have some fun. What better place than the University of Miami? The fact I can get a degree is a bonus."

"Why don't you just go to work for your father?" Cyrus asked.

Mike was the son of an entrepreneur. His father was a real estate developer. He owned several nursing homes, assisted-living facilities, retirement condominiums, and townhomes. Business was good. As a matter of fact, business was so good, there were rumors that these businesses were investments for racketeering profits. In any case, Mike could go to work for his father and live a life of leisure.

"Working in the nursing-home industry the rest of my life is not for me," Mike replied. "I want my life to be exciting."

Cyrus thought back to his days at Saint Mark's with Mike. Mike was always a character, a spark plug with an engaging personality that attracted others to him. Mike liked the feeling of feeling of being in control—the center of attention—and he was good at it. Natural athleticism allowed him to participate in every sport available at Saint Mark's. He particularly liked contact sports and excelled in boxing. Mike could be intimidating. At Saint Mark's, that did not seem unusual since it was a school for boys that was almost a military school. Cyrus was wondering how Mike would fit in at the university. Cyrus was also concerned how he would fit in at the university. Having Mike as a friend seemed a good fit.

After the orientation, Mike said to Cyrus, "Why don't we go to my place? We can sit by the pool and have a beer."

"You own a house?" Cyrus was surprised.

"No, it is my dad's house. He doesn't live there anymore. I take care of it for him."

"I should study," Cyrus protested.

"What do you mean, study? We haven't even started classes yet."

"It never hurts to be prepared."

"Come on, Boy Scout—let's relax for a little bit. You can study tomorrow after you actually attend a class."

Mike led Cyrus to his car and drove him to his house.

"Wow, this is quite the house," Cyrus said.

"It is just one of the houses my father owns."

"Is that a river in your backyard?"

"No, it's Lake Belmar. It's actually a protected harbor. If we get in my boat and head east, we end up in the Atlantic Ocean," Mike explained as he reached in the refrigerator for a couple beers. "Come on, let's sit by the pool and relax."

"Good idea, thanks."

"You'll have to come out here when Jake is here sometime."

"You're referring to Jake from Saint Mark's?"

"Yeah, referring; you always sound so formal. Tony is managing my nightclub. Jake works for him."

"Nightclub?" Cyrus asked.

"Yup, when I got out of the service, I explained to my father that I did not want to go into the nursing-home business. I told him I wanted to own a string of nightclubs. He agreed to help me buy a nightclub if I would go to school and major in business administration."

"So Tony manages the nightclub?"

"He went to college straight from Saint Mark's. He worked as a bartender while attending school and eventually became manager of the Barracuda Club. I bought the place on his recommendation."

"It would be nice to see him again." Cyrus was impressed by his friend's business acumen. Mike seemed very nonchalant about it.

"You never told me," Mike said. "What is your major?"

"I'm majoring in plant biology," Cyrus replied.

"What are you planning to do, research?" Mike said.

"No, I am planning to attend medical school," Cyrus replied.

"So you are going to be a professional student?" Mike said.

"Yeah, pretty much," replied Cyrus. "I like school and I like the idea of helping people."

"We'll see what you say after the first year is over," Mike said. "For me college is like a break from being in the military service. I get GI-bill education benefits. I am going to enjoy the next four years."

"I thought about taking a break and working for a year before starting school, but I have so much school ahead of me, I wanted to get going right away," Cyrus said. "I might even go to summer school."

"Summer school?" Mike asked. "You should go with me up to my father's resort on Bluewater Lake in Minnesota for the summer. It's on a four-lake chain surrounded by forest. We could play for the summer. All we have to do is the maintenance work for my father's resort. He'll pay us to do it. We can also do odd jobs for the cabin owners around there. We'll have a blast."

"I'll have to think about it," Cyrus said. "It sounds like a lot of fun. One of the things I always wanted to do when I got out of school is get away from Florida. Miami was a great town to grow up in, but I like the idea of northern Minnesota. It fits in with my love for plants and animals and it isn't always hot there."

"Well, think about it," Mike said. "You don't have to make a decision until next summer. By then you might be tired of taking all those science classes and will need a break."

Cyrus started to think about what Mike said. Spending the summer in northern Minnesota did not sound all that bad. He was also surprised at his friendship with Mike. All during his time at Saint Mark's, Mike was ahead of him. He was bigger and stronger than everyone else and had a superior attitude toward his classmates. Now that they were in college together, they were equals—best friends. *We are certainly not equals financially,* Cyrus thought.

Cyrus watched how Mike progressed over the school year. He went out for every sport. He was good at contact sports; he especially liked football. Cyrus was surprised at how well Mike did in his studies since his primary occupation seemed to be partying and women. Cyrus was just the opposite. He was reserved. He excelled in his studies, but the last thing he wanted to do was go out for sports. He was shy around women and though people liked him, he was not really popular. Yet the friendship between Cyrus and Mike grew and as the summer break approached, Cyrus became more interested in taking Mike up on his offer to spend the summer in northern Minnesota.

After spring-quarter finals, Cyrus and Mike spent a day partying on the beach with their classmates. They finished their freshman year in college and were full of themselves. The sun was shining, the ocean was calm, and everyone was in a good mood. They enjoyed volleyball and beer, snacks and beer, and swimming and beer. Now as the sun was setting, there was a red tint on the horizon and everyone was sad the day had to end.

"Hey, everyone, let's gather some driftwood and start a fire," Cyrus said. He had enough beer and sun inside him that he had lost his shyness.

"There's no firewood on the beach. Even the driftwood gets snapped up," someone said.

"I brought some firewood," Mike said. "It's in my truck."

After much deliberation on how it should be done, Mike took matters into his own hands—he crunched some newspaper in a pile on the sand, put kindling on top of it, and lit the flame. The flames reached for the sky just as the moon added its silvery presence to the end of a perfect day.

Everyone was talking about what they were going to do for the summer. Some had plans to work, some had plans to play all summer, and the more ambitious were planning to attend summer session.

"What are you going to do?" someone asked Cyrus. Everyone assumed he would be attending summer classes.

Cyrus surprised everyone by saying, "Mike and I are going to northern Minnesota to work at the Bluewater Resort."

"I heard the mosquitoes are so big, they can fly away with you up there in the summer," someone said and everyone laughed.

"They're not quite that bad," Mike said. "My father owns the resort. We'll do the grunt work of running the resort and odd jobs for the seasonal cabin owners up there. It's a great way to earn extra money in the summer. In our spare time, there's fishing, swimming, and girls. What could be better?"

"I'll tell you what could be better," someone said. "Mike, why don't you share some of that weed you've been selling around school?"

"I just happen to have some along," Mike replied as he took a couple joints of marijuana out of his shirt pocket. He lit one and passed it on. When that one was done, he passed a couple more. Everyone was getting stoned except Cyrus. He was taken aback by the fact that Mike was dealing drugs. He wondered where Mike got the time to do that along with everything else that he was involved in.

The next morning, Mike and Cyrus packed their belongings into his pickup truck and started out.

"How far is it from Miami to the resort?" Cyrus asked.

"I don't know," Mike replied. "I always just drive it from wherever I start. From around here, it takes about thirty-two hours if we drive straight through."

"Are we going to drive straight through?" Cyrus asked.

"It's our summer break," Mike said. "Why spend almost a day and a half in a car? I'm for taking three days, maybe even four days to drive there. The way I see it, what's the hurry?"

Nothing further was said about the drug episode the night before. Mike had sensed that Cyrus would not approve of drug dealing. On the other hand, Cyrus did not want to upset his relationship with Mike.

It took most of the day to get to Chattanooga, Tennessee. They stopped for something to eat.

"We could drive for the rest of the night," Mike said. "That way, we would only have a day's drive to get to the resort. What do you think?"

"I'm for driving straight through," Cyrus replied. "I am excited about seeing the resort."

"Let's see how we feel about it when we get to Champaign, Illinois," Mike said.

"I won't be tired," Cyrus said. "I am excited about northern Minnesota and making new friends."

"I should warn you," Mike said. "A lot of the people we will meet at the resort will be guests. We have to be careful; it is not our purpose to make friends—although that can be a side benefit. We want to make sure the guests enjoy themselves and want to come back again."

"I understand," Cyrus said.

"Another thing," Mike said. "Before I was in the service, I went up there for five years straight. It was a great time, but the locals are not necessarily all that friendly. At the end of five years, some of them still did not want anything to do with me, even though my father owns the resort."

"So what makes northern Minnesota different than Miami?" Cyrus asked.

Mike thought for a minute. "Yeah, I guess you're right."

Cyrus and Mike arrived at the Bluewater Resort two days later. It was a sunny day with no wind. Cyrus was impressed with Bluewater Lake. The surface of the water was like glass and it reflected the azure hue of the sky. The beach was white-sugar sand that invited the visitor to tan in the warmth of the sun. There were towering white pines mixed in with the red pines competing to reach the sky. It was a paradise. Cyrus and Mike had three months to live there.

Mike took Cyrus to the main lodge, where they would stay for the summer. It was a large house, the first structure you see when you drive into the resort. They unpacked their things in their rooms. Then Mike took Cyrus on a tour of the cabins.

"There are seven cabins," Mike explained. "We rent them from Saturday to Saturday. Our job is to keep the grounds clean, to ensure the guests have everything they need, and to prepare the cabins for the next guests after the current guests check out."

"How much work can that be?" Cyrus asked.

"It might not sound like much, but wait till you've been here a while," Mike said. "The guests will be here Saturday—then it starts. This is our largest cabin. It has four bedrooms."

Cyrus drew a breath as he entered the cabin. It was made of hand-scribed red-pine logs that had to be twelve inches in diameter. They had been stained to a rich brown, which lent a glow of warmth to the cabin. There were oak hardwood floors. The great room had walls covered with tanned animal skins and deer heads. A bearskin rug rested in front of the fieldstone fireplace that occupied the greater part of an outside wall and towered to the apex of the vaulted ceiling. The cabin exuded a rustic northwoods charm that said welcome to Cyrus.

"Are all the cabins like this?" Cyrus asked.

"They are all similar but smaller in size," Mike replied. "Come on, I'll show you the rest of them, then we start work."

"Who does your dad have run the resort?" Cyrus asked.

"For the last four summers, he has had locals manage the resort," Mike explained. "This year, we are managing the resort."

"Do you have the necessary experience?" Cyrus was a little uncomfortable with the responsibility.

"Sure, I've worked here since I was a little kid," Mike retorted. "Besides, the resort pretty much runs itself."

"You've seen my housekeeping skills," Cyrus objected. "I'm no good at that."

"There is a couple that lives on Bluewater Road, Dan and Sandy, who kept the resort going. Dan worked at the paper mill and helped with odd jobs on his time off. Sandy did the housekeeping. We will hire Sandy to do the housekeeping if she is still around."

"All right, tell me what we have to do, boss," Cyrus acquiesced.

"Let's get the place ready," Mike said with confidence.

"Why not?" Cyrus asked. "It sounds like fun and who can do a better job than us?"

There was a lot to get ready before the first guests arrived. The resort had a gentle downhill slope from the road to the lake. There were twenty-five acres in total with over a quarter mile of sandy shoreline. The cabins and the actual grounds of the resort took up a small portion of the land. There rest of the land was forest with hiking trails for the guests. The beach area of the resort was a thousand feet of prime, sandy shoreline. Three docks rested on the sand, waiting to be put in the water. At the center of the beach, a large communal fire ring dominated the landscape with smaller fire rings next to each cabin for private use. Guests frequently made use of the fire rings for roasting marshmallows and hot dogs. Volleyball was popular with the guests—there was a court set up for that purpose in the sand along the lake. The parcel of land the resort occupied was the nicest property on Bluewater Lake.

Cyrus was intrigued by the property. The possibilities for the summer seemed endless. "Why don't you just live up here, Mike? It seems perfect."

"Have you ever lived through a Minnesota winter?" Mike asked.

"No, I've always lived in Florida," Cyrus replied. "I've never seen snow."

"Well, you have to give it a try before you commit to living here full-time," Mike said. "The winter can be very cold and there is no heat in the cabins except for the fireplaces. The water pipes can freeze and snow removal is a daunting task."

Within a few days of their arrival, Cyrus and Mike fell into their daily routine. Guests arrived at the resort on Saturday. True to his word, Mike had no trouble getting the resort up and running.

"Most of the guests have been here before, but some of them are new to the resort. They will ask you how to get to the Joyce estate," Mike explained. "Bluewater Lake is part of the Wabana chain of lakes. In order to get to the Joyce estate by water, you take the channel from Bluewater Lake to Wabana Lake; from there is a channel to Little Trout Lake, which connects by channel to Trout Lake.

"In 1917, David Gage Joyce launched the construction of a forty-seven-building camp he called Nopeming. David was the heir to a logging empire that harvested the white-pine forests in northern Minnesota. He purchased 2600 acres along the Eastern shore of Trout Lake that included a point where he would set the foundations for his compound. The estate was ultimately transferred to the US Forest

Service in 1974 after the death of the remaining heir to the Joyce estate. The estate went into a state of decay after that, but the buildings and their surroundings make it an interesting place to visit.

"Guests can access the Joyce estate by water or by hiking trails. The closest hiking trail is accessible from Bluewater Road. I'll have to take you to the Joyce estate when we get some free time," Mike said.

"I'll look forward to it," Cyrus replied. He did not want to be rude, but he was tired of lectures and was glad this one was over.

"Don't mention this to anyone, but there are rumors of spirits haunting the area by the hiking trail."

"Spirits?" Cyrus asked skeptically. He was used to Mike's antics.

"Yes, it is rumored that the spirit Chief Wabana, a Chippewa Indian, haunts the area."

"Are you putting me on, Mike?" Cyrus asked.

"I don't believe in evil spirits, but the guests may ask about it. Refer them to me. It doesn't hurt business!"

Chapter 6

It was the end of another glorious spring day in northern Minnesota. The sun, a golden sovereign, settled slowly on the horizon, painting the sky with a pink hue. Cool, crisp air was filled by a choir of birds chirping their mating songs to greet the triumphant return of spring. Lomasi, Ahote, Sara, and Duane gathered at the firepit behind Sara's house for their evening meal.

"We wrote a song," Ahote announced.

"We?" Duane asked.

"I wrote it with Lomasi. It's called 'Ode to Wabana,'" Ahote explained.

"You two are songwriters?" Duane asked as he winked at Sara.

"We're a team," Lomasi chimed in. "I write the words, Ahote provides the musical accompaniment. It works."

"Can I hear it?" Duane was unable to hide his amusement.

"Of course," Lomasi said.

Ahote grabbed his guitar and played the introduction, then he and Lomasi sang in unison:

> *Wabana, Wabana, you call to me.*
> *Wabana, Wabana, you set me free.*
> *It's here I feel my spirits soar.*
> *This wild beauty that I adore.*
>
> *Wabana, Wabana, I call to you.*
> *Wabana, Wabana, when day is through.*
> *It's here I long to feel your touch.*
> *All that is you, I love so much.*
>
> *Clear waters, blue skies*
> *Delight my eyes.*
> *Pine forests and deer*
> *Draw me here.*

The stars that shine above
Bring out my love, for,

Wabana, Wabana, you call to me.
Wabana, Wabana, you set me free.
It's here I want to end my days.
I love you in so many ways.

"That was terrible!" Duane complained. He was secretly proud that the time he had spent teaching Lomasi and Ahote about their Native American heritage was paying dividends. By memorializing Chief Wabana, they had recorded tribal history in writing and music for future generations. Duane felt he was achieving one of his goals— transmitting Native American culture for posterity. Duane softened his criticism with a smile and said, "Your song tells a story of our people. What did you think of it, Sara?"

"It was nice," Sara said begrudgingly. Sara was not as pleased as Duane. She did not want to encourage Lomasi to write songs with Ahote. Sara believed that Lomasi was wasting her time and talents writing songs.

"It reminds me of the old days," Duane reminisced. "I wish we could bring those days back. Once, the winds of fate blew more favorably. We were a great nation. Our people inhabited the whole region. We existed in peace and harmony with the environment and our neighbors. There was community. We hunted together, played together, our families grew up together, and we grew old together. We were like the workings of a fine watch—each of us performed our part and the second hand of time ticked evenly and unremittingly. We lived with dignity. Now look at us.

"True," Sara agreed. She looked knowingly at Duane and said, "Now there are alcohol and drug problems. All of our land is parceled off to private ownership and we are relegated to reservations and living in trailers while the rest of the country prospers. It is very sad."

"We were the original environmentalists. We respected the land and the animals that inhabited it. We harvested only what we needed. Buffalo roamed the land in abundance. Our streams and rivers were full of fish. The great white-pine forests stretched across the land. Lomasi and I incorporated those themes into our song," Ahote added with zeal. He promoted his music relentlessly.

"Lifestyles are evolving. It is not all bad," Lomasi said. "Now we have cars, computers, and the Internet. What would we do without modern conveniences?"

"Still, there is something romantic about sitting around the fire at night telling stories," Sara said. "It's these simple things I appreciate the most."

"That is why I want to be an author. When you write a book, you're just telling a story. I want to be a storyteller," Lomasi lobbied. "Think of the audience you can reach with a book."

"Change is not necessarily good for everyone," Duane observed. "Some people adapt to change better than others. What is good for some is bad for others."

"Oh, Duane, you are such a philosopher," Sara said sarcastically. A part of her thought of Duane as a hypocrite. *If only these kids knew the true Duane,* she thought.

Lately, Lomasi noticed things about Duane she hadn't seen when she was younger. She had always thought of him as her great uncle, someone kind enough to adopt Ahote and take care of him. As she matured, she noticed that Duane was shrewd. He was intelligent; perhaps sly was a better word to describe him. He dissembled when discussing social issues that were important to her.

Lomasi wondered about Duane's background as a Vietnam War veteran. Over the years, she heard Duane arguing with Sara when they thought she was sleeping. He would complain about how Vietnam veterans were treated when they returned from their tour of duty in the war. He would grumble about how African Americans and women were treated as a special class of citizens while Vietnam veterans were largely forgotten. People were promoted based on sex and race and enjoyed special privileges in our society. He especially resented the fact that only men were drafted to serve in Vietnam. Over sixty thousand men died. Could there be any discrimination worse than death?

Then there were the late-night parties. Lomasi wondered what went on at his house. Sara just seemed to ignore it. Lomasi had trouble sleeping when she heard the primitive beat of the tom-tom drums. It was wanton, sexual. The privacy fence lent a veil of secrecy to the goings on in the backyard. When she casually mentioned it to Ahote, he remained close-lipped.

She was wakened from her thoughts when Ahote pointed to the woods. "Is someone out there?"

"You're too jumpy, Ahote," Sara said. "It's probably just a raccoon or some animal."

"I heard it, too!" Duane added.

"Ever since we started seeing that strange guy sitting on the side of the road watching everybody, I feel jumpy," Lomasi said.

"You're both imagining things," Sara said. "There is probably some explanation for the guy in the pickup we saw the other morning. Maybe he was waiting to meet someone."

"I don't care," Lomasi said. "It still gives me the creeps."

"I think you're all wrong," Duane said. "I think that noise was the spirit of Chief Wabana. He liked your song."

They all laughed.

"Let's put the fire out and go to sleep. Lomasi and I have to go to work in the morning," Sara said.

Lomasi's sleep was troubled that night. She sensed the presence of someone or something lurking out there, waiting, watching for their opportunity. She gradually drifted into a deep sleep as the fire slowly burned itself out.

Up at the crack of dawn, Sara and Lomasi prepared for their drive to town as the rising sun ushered in another day. Sara enjoyed having her granddaughter at work, where she could observe her progress. Sara could provide a positive role model for Lomasi, while her granddaughter could observe the important role she played in healthcare as a nurse practitioner. It also served to keep Lomasi away from Ahote; he was a bad influence. Ahote was always playing and never serious about anything but music. To him everything was fun, life was a party. Sara did not want this for Lomasi.

"It's time to leave," Sara yelled to Lomasi. "We don't want to be late for work. We have to open the clinic this morning."

"I'll be right there," Lomasi replied. She stretched her arms and yawned as she got out of bed. It was a new day, but she awoke in the same way, with a niggling feeling that she didn't belong.

"Too many campfires, not enough sleep," Sara said. She could sense Lomasi's unrest.

"No, I'm not tired," Lomasi replied. "I just always wake up with this feeling that I do not know who I am."

"Come on," Sara said. "I thought you were over that by now."

"I'll never be over it until I find out what happened," Lomasi said.

"I understand your frustration," Sara asserted. "Don't forget, Sandy was my daughter. There will always be a part of me missing, too."

"Do you think we will ever find out what happened?" Lomasi asked.

"I hope so," Sara replied. "But I sometimes wonder. The sheriff's investigation stalled—no new information—so it was put on the back burner. Now that the case is so old, it is forgotten. The only way something will happen is if we find their bodies or someone comes forward with new information."

"You make it sound hopeless," Lomasi said.

"It is hopeless," Sara said. "Nevertheless, I will call the sherrif's office this morning when we get to the clinic. It never hurts to keep bothering them about it. Maybe something will turn up."

"It's hard to believe they would just get up and leave us wondering," Lomasi said. "Someone must know what happened."

"They never found a trace of them," Sara said. "Their pickup truck was never found. They left one morning and disappeared off the face of the earth."

"When I look at that drawing of Mother on my bedroom wall, I feel like she is calling to me. I'm drawn to her because she is saying something. I want to write about how I feel. I want to analyze the information. I need closure."

"You should forget writing and focus on your career," Sara said. "Healthcare is a meaningful way to make a contribution to our society. We are needed. Plus the money is good. You have to think about your future. Duane and I will not be here forever and the mystery of your parents will probably remain unsolved."

"I am going to major in English in college next year," Lomasi said. "Writing songs, stories, and poetry is what interests me."

"Right now, what interests me is opening the clinic on time," Sara said. "It won't do to have patients waiting for us to unlock the door."

"I hope we don't see that creep in the pickup truck on Bluewater Road again this morning." Lomasi was thinking out loud. "Something tells me he is responsible for all this mystery."

They drove to work without incident. Lomasi learned quickly and did her job well. She exceeded all expectations. She looked up to Dr. Longfell and her job performance reflected her admiration. She was eager to please. It was no surprise she was very popular with the patients and got along well with everyone in the clinic.

It was Friday afternoon. The day supplies were delivered. One of Lomasi's duties was to restock the supply closet. She had learned to enjoy the job because the closet was in the rear of the clinic and isolated from everyone. She could be alone with her thoughts, take her time, and help prepare the clinic for the next week.

While she was putting the supplies on the shelf, Cyrus walked in.

"Hi, Lomasi," he said. "I didn't know you were here."

"Oh, it's you, Doctor Longfell. You startled me." Lomasi's mind flashed back to the day she saw him and Ashley emerge from the closet.

"Don't mind me, Lomasi. I just came back here for some aspirin samples. I've got a headache."

"They're right here," Lomasi said as she reached up to the top shelf. She felt Cyrus grind up against her rear end. They were probably reaching for the same thing. She let him reach over her and get the aspirin.

"You've been doing an excellent job, Lomasi."

"Thank you," she replied. She was too embarrassed to turn around. She just hoped Cyrus would leave. Then she felt his hands cup her breasts. She turned and said, "Doctor Longfell, this is inappropriate."

"Now, now," Cyrus said. "You just do what the doctor orders." He put his hands on his shoulders and pushed her down on her knees. Lomasi was shocked to see his erection pointing straight at her. She was about to object, when to her surprise, he put his member in her mouth.

"That's a good girl," Cyrus said as he began to undulate in her mouth. Lomasi didn't know what to do. She was confused, so she just acquiesced. Cyrus finished with an explosion in her mouth.

"Swallow," he ordered. She obeyed.

"We'll just keep this between ourselves," Cyrus said as he zipped his trousers and left the supply closet.

Lomasi just sat there on the floor. What had just happened? She couldn't believe it. She felt violated. What should she do? Should she call the police? Would the police believe her? She didn't put up much of a fight; as a matter of fact, she went along with it. Who would the police believe, her or a doctor? *I should have bitten him,* she thought.

Then she thought of her grandmother. She worked at the clinic. What would happen to her if Lomasi reported rape? They would both lose their jobs. Lomasi just sat there feeling guilty. She could not help but feel it was her fault. She had let it happen. Finally she just got up and finished stocking the closet.

On the ride home, Sara said to Lomasi, "You're awfully quiet. Are you thinking about what you will do this weekend?"

"Huh?" Lomasi said.

"You haven't been listening to me the whole ride home," she said as they pulled into her driveway.

"I'm sorry, Grandma."

Kids these days, Sara thought. They're off in a world of their own.

Chapter 7

Mike King's adrenaline flowed as he prepared for his trip downtown. Like a wolf stalking its prey, he sensed a moment of weakness in his quarry and was moving in for the kill. His weapon of choice was persuasion and innuendo. He would verbally maneuver his opponent into a corner, incite a feeding frenzy, and let others move in for the kill.
.   Every week he met with a circle of friends at a local café and had lunch. It was an informal get-together that Mike had cultivated over the years. There was someone from every walk of life—at least every walk of life Mike felt was important. It was an all-male crowd. They discussed sports, politics, and religion; whatever topic was of interest at the current time. Each member considered himself a wizened sage and knew what was best for the community.

This morning there were seven present. Their favorite waitress, Tracy, put two tables together for them.

Mike had rehearsed what he was going to say the previous evening. His words had to evoke the desired response and everyone needed to believe his solution was their own idea. He strove to introduce the topic with finesse. He let someone else begin and waited his opportunity.

"Someone spotted a cougar up by Wabana Lake this week," Paul the banker said. "I heard it on John Latimer's phenology report on KAXE."

"I read an article in the paper that the young male cougars are on the move," Roger said. "There was one that attacked a horse down by Aitkin."

"All right, boys, what'll you have?" Tracy interrupted. She was a tall, slender, sultry blond. She was accustomed to stopping the conversation. Everyone at the table appreciated any attention she gave them. She took their orders and retreated into the kitchen area.

"I read in the paper that crime is on the rise in Itasca County," Paul said. "I don't know if that is a result of high unemployment or if kids are influenced by television shows."

"You're right," Sam Whitman said. Sam was a deputy sheriff. "It's not making our job any easier."

"It's drugs," Mike King added. *What a delightful segue,* he thought.

"Sam, I can't understand law enforcement these days," Roger said. "They let known criminals roam the streets. They seem more interested in issuing traffic tickets."

"We do our job," Sam replied. "Public safety is part of it, so, yes, we issue speeding tickets. But there is more to it than that. The courts tie our hands. We arrest a criminal, they throw the charges out. The court system deserves the criticism, not law enforcement."

"I know the criticism seems unfair, Sam, but realistically, there are too many drugs and illegal guns on the street," Mike said.

"Guns and drugs aren't the problem. It's the people who use them," Sam said. "I think it is wrong to blame the young people of this community just because of a few rotten apples."

Like a cat poised and patient, Mike saw his opportunity and pounced. "What if I told you we have a drug-dealing ring operating right under our noses?" Mike asked.

"Mike, you have been watching too much television," Sam said. "If we had a drug dealer in town, we would know about it."

"I'm not talking about in town here. I'm talking about Bluewater Road, where I live," Mike explained. "I may be retired but I am not senile. I've seen this with my own eyes. That Indian kid Ahote pretends to have a band, but he is using it as a cover to sell drugs."

"I know Ahote," Sam replied. "Sure, he may be a little wild, but it is just a phase he is going through. Wait and see—he'll find a girl, get married, and be a responsible citizen some day."

"You're the expert, Sam," Mike conceded. "Still, if it looks like a duck, quacks like a duck, it must be a duck. It's only common sense."

Soon the conversation turned to fishing and the group broke up. Mike had errands in town. He hoped he had done enough to plant a seed of thought in Sam Whitman's head that would blossom in the fertile soil of prejudice and racism. It didn't take a lot to start an avalanche that was waiting to happen.

Sam Whitman was working the night shift. He drove his county sheriff's patrol car through Grand Rapids. It was a sleepy night. The streets were deserted. The city rolled in the carpet and closed its doors early. He liked it that way. Only the gas stations were open and most of those were only self-service pumps. He was thinking about what his friend Mike had said. He was a little embarrassed by the conversation at lunch. He did not like to look incompetent to his friends. If someone was committing a crime, he did something about it. *I am a man of action*, he thought.

Sam parked in the Eagles Club parking lot, where he had a good view of the main drag. He was setting up a speed trap, hoping for a speeder or a drunk driver to provide his graveyard shift with some excitement . Providence smiled on Sam as Ahote drove past him. He stopped in the next block, picked up a young woman walking on the street, and kept driving down Pokegama Avenue. It looked suspicious to the deputy. Sam pulled out of the Eagles Club parking lot and followed Ahote at a distance.

Ahote stopped and dropped the young woman off, then continued on his way. Could that have been a drug deal? Sam noticed that Ahote's car had a taillight that was not working. The brake light wasn't working either. He decided to stop him.

Ahote was surprised when he noticed flashing red lights in his rearview mirror. He pulled over to the side of the road and rolled down his window.

"Can I see your driver's license, please?" Sam said as he shined his flashlight on Ahote.

"Why are you stopping me, deputy?" Ahote said. "I wasn't doing anything wrong."

"Your brake lights aren't working," Sam replied. "Now I need to see your driver's license and proof of insurance."

"Here is my driver's license," Ahote replied. "Hang on; I will get proof of insurance from my glove compartment."

While Ahote searched for his insurance information, Sam was thinking about what Mike King said earlier about drugs. Sam couldn't smell alcohol on Ahote's breath, but he needed a reason to search the car.

"Ahote, have you been drinking?" Sam asked. "You were weaving back and forth in your lane before I stopped you."

"No, sir, I was having an interesting conversation with Carol, the woman I just dropped off," Ahote said politely. "I didn't think I was weaving. If I was, it was because I was distracted."

"Would you get out of the car, please?" Sam asked.

"Sure," Ahote said as he got out of the car and faced Sam.

The deputy walked a few steps from Ahote and turned to face him. "Walk a straight line toward me."

Ahote walked to face Sam in a perfect straight line.

"Okay, raise your right foot and then touch your nose with your index finger."

Ahote complied with Sam's request. He displayed no evidence of being impaired. Sam was frustrated and disappointed but he would not give up, not with a known criminal.

"Now, look at your taillights—you can see that one of them is out," Sam said.

"I'm going to step on the brake. You tell me if a brake light is out." Sam got in the car and stepped on the brake.

"Okay, so the left brake light is out," Ahote said. "I'll fix it first thing in the morning."

"Do you mind if I have a look in your car?" Sam asked and then started poking around before Ahote could reply.

"Hey, what are you doing?" Ahote asked.

"I just want to make sure there are no alcoholic beverages in your car," Sam answered.

"I have nothing to hide," Ahote said. "I'm just a little surprised. Don't you have to have a warrant to search my car?"

"You just gave me permission." Sam shined his flashlight throughout the car. All he could see was a bunch of books and a guitar case. He was going to ask Ahote to open the guitar case, but he happened to glance at the floor. Protruding from under the driver's seat, he found the corner of a plastic bag. He pulled the bag out from under the seat.

"What's this?" Sam asked as he looked into the bag.

"I've never seen that before," Ahote replied.

Sam pulled out at 9mm Beretta and a bag of white pills.

"I suppose you don't know what these are, then?" Sam asked.

"What do you think you are doing?" Ahote cried. "Those are not mine. I don't own a gun."

"Well, then, what were these doing under your seat?" Sam asked. "I suppose someone put them there without your knowledge."

"Honestly, I do not know how that got there!" Ahote protested.

"You don't know what these are?" Sam asked as he held up the plastic bag of pills.

"Someone planted those in my car," Ahote replied.

"It looks like Vicodin. You are in possession of a narcotic. Do you have a prescription for these pills?" Sam asked.

"No, I never saw them before in my life," Ahote replied.

"Put your hands on the roof of the car," Sam ordered as he patted Ahote down for weapons. "You're under arrest. We can sort this out at the county jail. Please get in the car."

Sam opened the back door to his squad car and pushed Ahote inside roughly.

Ahote was alone in the cell. The walls were cement block painted white. The floor was a slab with a drain in the middle. The ceiling was white with a light in the middle protected by a metal cage. He inspected the cell for hidden cameras. *I wonder if anyone is watching. If there is a camera, it is probably hidden,* he thought. The door was metallic gray with a small window three quarters of the way up the door. It looked heavy. The bed was a mattress on a cement platform built up one foot above the floor. There was a thin blanket and a pillow. It was going to be home for a while. Ahote's attitude was as bleak as the cell.

The worst part of the whole thing was wondering what had happened. Where did the gun and the pills come from? What was going to happen to him for having them in his car? Which was worse, the gun or the pills? He didn't even know what kind of pills were in the plastic bag. He could not afford a lawyer, but maybe Duane would hire one for him. Could he get a public defender?

Ahote was seventeen years old. He didn't think he should be in the Itasca County Jail. The deputy didn't seem to care about any of that. He knew one of the taillights was out on his car and he was planning to repair it when he had the money. So the deputy had a legitimate reason to pull him over. Did that give the deputy a right to search his car? Ahote knew from watching TV that he would have to be charged within twenty-four hours or released. What would the charges be? He would not have to wait long to find out.

He heard the metallic sound of a key turning in the door and a deputy walked in carrying breakfast.

"Good morning. Here's something for you to eat," The deputy said as he handed Ahote the tray.

It was scrambled eggs, coffee, and toast.

"Thanks," Ahote said as he took the tray.

"I'll be back in a while for the tray. Someone will come for you later on to get the facts about what happened last night," the deputy said as he left.

Ahote heard the key turn in the lock after the deputy closed the door. He wondered how good the food was. Were they powdered eggs? At least it wasn't bread and water. He was hungry, so it did not make any difference. He would eat it.

Ahote knew he was in trouble. He would have to have a strategy. They were probably going to question him about what they found in his car. It would probably be the good-cop/bad-cop routine he had seen on TV. He should insist on having a lawyer present. If Duane did not visit him soon, he knew he would be on his own.

After the deputy returned for the tray, Ahote felt tired. He was alone. The cell gave him a cold feeling. Drowsiness overcame him; he lay down and drifted off into a restless sleep.

Chapter 8

Spring 1986

It was early morning. Already the sun was radiating heat, portending a sweltering, summer-like day. Even though it was early spring, the warm weather was a welcome change from the stretch of bone-chilling rainy days that had just ended.

Sandy lay in bed and wondered what to do. Waking up to a day off was a luxury. She didn't want to waste it. She knew Dan would want to work on his car, do errands in town. *How mundane,* she thought.

Dan and Sandy met at Grand Rapids High School. They had been together for so many years now, most people thought they were married. They purchased twenty acres from Sandy's mother and moved a trailer onto the property, where they set up housekeeping on Bluewater Road. Life had become a routine. She became bored. Sometimes she thought she had settled on Dan too easily. He caught her in a time of weakness, was her knight in shining armor. But was he what she really wanted in a man? She didn't have time to think about it right now.

Sandy knew she had to take control of the day in the morning if she didn't want to spend another dreary day working around the trailer and running errands. She shared with Dan a common interest in hiking. That morning she insisted they pack a lunch and drive north on Bluewater Road to the hiking trail that lead to the grounds of the Joyce estate. They had to hike three miles through the woods to reach their destination, but it was worth the effort.

They spread their blanket on the sandy beach of a beautiful point that extended into Trout Lake. The area was pristine, an unexpected jewel hidden in the northwoods. The sky was a deep azure. The slight breeze created ripples on the water that twinkled like diamonds in the sun. They ate their lunch and talked about their future. Sandy was lying on the blanket, the sunshine warming her as she prepared to nap.

"Let's go skinny dipping," Dan said. The azure color of the water in Trout Lake was beckoning them to swim. The noonday sun beating down on him compounded the desire.

"We can't skinny dip in public," Sandy said. "What if someone sees us?"

"We're miles from anywhere," Dan said. "Who will see us?"

"What about the boaters?"

"It's a weekday," Dan replied. "There is no one on the lake. We'll see anyone approaching from miles away."

Sandy acquiesced. The couple slipped into the aqua-colored water. The drop-off was perfect, and within a few feet, Sandy and Dan were in water up to their necks. They splashed and played, enjoying the outdoors.

Dan could not get over it. Sandy looked as lovely today as the day he met her. The intimacy in the water spurred Dan's primal instincts. He moved close to Sandy, taking her in his arms. He pressed her body close to his and said, "Someday we will bring our children here. We'll have family picnics."

Sandy was not as enthusiastic as Dan about having a family. She replied, "I'll have to think about that."

"Well, you don't have to think about this," Dan replied. He took Sandy's hand and led her from the water to the blanket on the beach.

"We can't do this here," Sandy protested. She knew it was hopeless to argue as Dan kissed her and their bodies melted together into the sand.

"Let's take a jog. It's a perfect afternoon and we could use a break," Mike told Cyrus. "I would like to show you something that is unique."

"Unique? This whole place is unique," Cyrus replied.

"Come on," Mike said. "I am talking about the Joyce estate. It's on Trout Lake."

"What about the guests?" Cyrus asked.

"It's midweek," Mike said. "They will be all right for the morning. We'll be back before the afternoon is over."

Mike and Cyrus started jogging at a slow pace the short distance down Bluewater Road to the hiking trail that lead to the Joyce estate.

As they approached Kremer Lake, Mike started to tell Cyrus some of the local lore. "At one time, this was all white-pine forest. The land was occupied by Chippewa Indians. The last Indian Chief was named Wabana. The lake and township became his namesake."

"What happened to Chief Wabana?" Cyrus asked.

"No one knows," Mike replied. "Legend has it that the chief was buried on Balgillow Island on Wabana Lake. The northern half of the island is owned by the US Forest Service. The grave has never been found."

"Can we go to this island sometime?" Cyrus asked.

"Sure," Mike replied as they jogged further down the trail. "There has always been a rumor that Chief Wabana's spirit still haunts the area. That his soul never rests because the 'white man' stole his land from him and stripped it of all the trees and wildlife. Chief Wabana's spirit has been charged with murder, the disappearance of animals, infertility, and cursing the area in general. Whenever something happens that cannot be easily explained, it is blamed on the chief."

"How could they blame a dead Native American chief? It sounds like superstition to me," Cyrus speculated.

"Even though this is the twenty-first century, people are still superstitious," Mike explained. "This path to the Joyce estate is one of the places people say is haunted. There have been sightings of the chief, apparitions."

"It seems like a beautiful nature area to me," Cyrus said. "The kind of place I would like to practice after I finish my medical training."

"Wait till you see the Joyce estate," Mike said as they continued to jog down the path. The first thing they saw as they approached the compound was the nine-hole golf course extending to the shores of Trout Lake. Since the Estate was abandoned, there had been no maintenance of the golf course; even so, it was an impressive site. Soon they approached the main compound; the water tank was intact. Cyrus was amazed to see the grounds.

"All of this was once manicured lawn. Imagine what it was like. It was the roaring twenties. It was the time of Prohibition and women's suffrage. This property was developed by a twenty-five-year-old multimillionaire as a summer home. Forty-five hundred acres, forty buildings made up the Adirondack-style camp. They led a swank lifestyle," Mike explained. "There was a staff that kept everything like a park until a few years ago. Now it has been left to disrepair."

"Who's that?" Cyrus asked. They could see two figures by the main lodge building. They kept walking towards them.

"Hi, Dan, Sandy," Mike said as they approached the couple. "What are you guys doing here?"

"We have the day off," Dan replied. "It's a perfect day for a picnic."

"We didn't mean to disturb you." Mike smirked. "I was just showing Cyrus the grounds. Cyrus, this is Dan and Sandy. They live on Bluewater Road. They used to help us out at the resort."

"Nice to meet you," Dan said. Mike was the last person he was happy to see. He knew he would not like Cyrus, if only because he was Mike's friend.

"Cyrus is a college friend of mine. We came up to run the resort for the summer," Mike explained. "We miss your help, Sandy," Mike said as he leered at her.

"Well, we are on the way home. It was nice to meet you, Cyrus," Dan said as they headed down the trail back to the Bluewater Road.

"Wow, she's really something to look at," Cyrus said.

"Yeah, when she helped at the resort, she was a teenager," Mike said. "She was really something then. All of the young guys that stayed at the resort would have jumped at a chance to date her, but she was stuck on that guy Dan. Then she married him or moved in with him. No one knows for sure. They probably came to the estate to look for something valuable that was left behind."

"Do you think there is anything to be found here?" Cyrus asked.

"The Joyce estate is what remains of a logging empire," Mike replied. "The family ended with Beatrice—BJ, she was called. The place has been looted of everything already. If there is anything of value here, it is hidden so well that no one has been able to find it."

"This place must have been something when it was fully operational. It would be fun to come back here with a metal detector," Cyrus said.

"It is valuable real estate," Mike said. "Look at the shoreline. It is perfect sand. The water is beautiful aqua and it has a perfect drop-off. There's probably ten, fifteen houses on the whole lake. It was a shame that the US Forest Service got it."

Mike continued to show Cyrus the estate. They looked at what remained of the main lodge and cabins and walked around the rest of the grounds. Then they started their jog back to the resort.

At the end of the day, Mike poured himself another glass of Jack Daniels and sat on the sofa. Seeing Sandy again had a long-lasting effect on him. His mind kept replaying the day he met her at the resort. He was sixteen years old. She had just graduated from Grand Rapids High School and was working at the resort for the summer while she decided what she wanted to do with her life. Sandy had never left the Grand Rapids area in her life, so working at the resort and meeting guests from all over the country appealed to her.

Initially, Sandy found Mike attractive, even though he was two years younger than she was. He was the son of a wealthy businessman from Florida. He was tall and animated.

Sandy had waist-length long black hair and shiny black eyes. She was slender with a great figure. Her movements were graceful. As she moved through the resort, her long legs accentuated the sway of her beautiful hair. She proudly noticed the male guests could not keep their eyes off the swell of her breasts.

She would take her breaks with Mike. They would go for walks on the many hiking trails. Mike took her out in his sailboat on Bluewater Lake. Even though she encouraged Mike at first, his immaturity showed and she soon grew tired of him. It was a difficult situation for her, since Mike was the son of her employer and eventually she quit the resort to look for employment in town.

She looks even better now, Mike thought as he dialed the phone.

"Sandy?" Mike asked.

"Yes," she replied.

"Hi, Sandy, this is Mike King from the resort."

"Hi, Mike, did you call to speak with Dan?" Sandy asked. After seeing Mike, she knew he was going to call. She still found him attractive but was not looking forward to speaking with him.

"No, I called to talk with you," Mike replied. "We're short handed at the resort this summer. We could use some part-time help. Would you be interested?"

"No, I'm not interested, but thank you for asking, Mike," Sandy said. "Dan and I are working full-time in town," she lied. "We just had the day off and decided to picnic at the Joyce estate. We are not looking for work."

"Sandy, I really just called to talk with you. It was nice to see you again. I didn't realize how much I missed you," Mike said.

"Mike, I'm complimented you called," Sandy lied diplomatically. "I'm happy with my relationship with Dan."

"I'd like to see you again, alone," Mike said.

"Mike, please do not call me about this again," Sandy said as she hung up the phone.

Mike just stood there frustrated for a minute. In a fit of rage, he hurled his glass at the wall. In his anger, everything seemed to happen in slow motion. He watched the glass travel to the log wall, then shatter, spreading shards of glass throughout the room. Seeing Sandy had rekindled the flame Mike held in his heart for her.

There was a knock on the door. "Are you all right?" Cyrus said as he opened the door.

"I'm okay," Mike replied. "I just dropped my glass."

"It sounded like something smashed on the wall. Remember, I'm in the room next door," Cyrus said. "What's the matter, Mike?"

"I'm just frustrated."

"Frustrated?"

"It's women!" Mike said. "I didn't tell you earlier, but I had a crush on Sandy when I was younger. I think she used to like me, too, until she met that guy Dan. I didn't realize how much I cared about her until I saw her today."

"She's married, Mike," Cyrus said.

"She told me she was happy with Dan," Mike said. "But haven't you ever wanted something and not been able to get it? It makes you want it all the more."

"But there are some things you just cannot have," Cyrus said.

"It's so frustrating," Mike replied. "I can offer her all of the advantages she never had, but she prefers this Indian loser. Who knows what they were doing at the Joyce estate this morning?"

"Mike, I never mentioned this to you before because we are friends," Cyrus admitted. "I have always been jealous of you ever since I met you back at Saint Mark's. You were always the popular one. You were the great athlete. Now that we are in college, you're still the popular one. You get all the girls, while I sit in my dorm room and study. So you meet one girl that doesn't want you—so what?"

"I never guessed you felt that way," Mike said. "I always thought you were just interested in plant biology or engineering— whatever it is you are studying."

"No, I'd like to go out on more dates in school next year," Cyrus admitted. "I already have a great grade point average. I would like some companionship. I get lonely."

"Why don't we go to town a little more often this summer?" Mike suggested. "I can give you a few pointers with the girls we meet."

Cyrus agreed with Mike that going to Grand Rapids weekend nights would liven up their summers. Who knows what might happen? Cyrus also remembered how vengeful Mike could be from Saint Mark's. He was probably a lot like his father—you didn't cross Mike King and get away with it. They had a resort to run; it was their responsibility for the summer, so Cyrus focused on work.

Chapter 9

Ahote was released from jail. He was perplexed. He felt like a wounded animal fleeing from an unknown predator—a predator with an unfair advantage.

He was charged with possession of a concealed firearm without a permit and possession of narcotics—codeine. He was scheduled to appear in court in thirty days.

Why would someone plant a gun and drugs in his car? Who hated him that much? He was a victim, not a criminal. Could he convince the judge or a jury he was innocent?

"Why were you driving around with a gun and drugs in your car?" Lomasi asked accusingly.

"I didn't know I was in possession of a gun and drugs," Ahote replied, thinking, *How can I convince a judge and jury? Even Lomasi thinks I'm guilty.* "You're just as bad as the rest—I'm innocent. It was almost as if the deputy knew to look under the seat of my car."

"I'm sorry. I guess it is easy to believe the worst." Lomasi shrugged in a conciliatory manner. "What happens now?" Lomasi asked.

"I'm scheduled to go to a hearing next month," Ahote replied.

"What happens to our band?" Lloyd asked.

"Nothing right now," Ahote said. "I spoke with the court clerk. He said that the hearing next month will be to determine if there will be a trial or not. If there is going to be a trial, the date will be set at the hearing."

"Are you scared?" Lomasi asked.

"Of course I'm scared," Ahote said. "Wouldn't you be? I could spend one to fifteen years in jail if I am convicted. That's a long time. Especially for something I didn't do."

"The story we heard," Lloyd said, "was that you were dropping a woman off at Country Kitchen after exchanging sex for drugs when the deputy pulled you over."

"That's just the type of rumor you hear in Grand Rapids because it is a small town," Ahote explained. "It was Mary Dunham I dropped off at Country Kitchen. We all knew her from school. She was walking down Pokegama Avenue; it was late. I stopped, picked her up, and gave her a ride to work. That was all that happened. I think the deputy watches too much television. He fantasizes that the situations portrayed on TV are really happening in our community. He sees himself as the hero, the star of the show."

"So you were just giving Mary a ride because you were concerned about her safety?" Lomasi was obviously jealous.

"Sounds suspicious to me." Lloyd chuckled. "I'd like to give Mary a ride, too!"

"You guys!" Ahote said. "Quit making jokes—this is serious. I could be sent to jail. I gave Mary a ride. I really do not know her all that well. We just went to school together. Sure, she is cute. But there were no drugs involved. Now everyone thinks I am a drug dealer and they are wondering if Mary prostitutes herself for her drug habit—a drug habit that doesn't exist."

"If you ask me, Mike King is behind all of this," Lomasi said. "He's a racist."

"Yeah, I thought about that," Ahote said. "Remember the day he came by here and started yelling at us over the fence?"

"He's like a shark that smells blood. He's had it in for you ever since he found that woman Emily outside your garage listening to us play," Lloyd said. "But do you think he would really plant a gun and drugs in your car?"

"He's ruthless," Ahote thought out loud. *The unknown predator.*

"Around here, he's pretty important. He's a township supervisor," Lomasi said. "He still owns the resort, plus he has numerous business interests."

"He thinks he runs everything around here," Lloyd chimed in.

"Grandma warned me a long time ago to watch out for him. He's a womanizer. He seduces young Native American women," Lomasi explained. "They go for his money and his looks."

"Yeah, he thinks he's really smooth," Ahote said. "He thinks Wabana Township is his country club and that only the rich should be able to join the club."

"He's really a sleazy character," Lloyd added. "There is nothing he would not do for his personal gain."

"Duane said Mike proposed a township regulation to make everyone remove the trailers from their properties and replace them with stick-built homes," Ahote said.

"Yeah," Lomasi replied. "The county wouldn't let him do it or we would not be living here now."

"Hi, Mike, it's Sam Whitman."

"I recognize the voice, Sam, thanks for calling," Mike King said into his cell phone.

"I just wanted you to know that our 'little problem' has been dealt with."

"Little problem?" Mike asked, pretending not to understand what that meant.

"Yeah, Ahote has been arrested and charged with possession of a concealed weapon and possession of drugs."

"Good work, Sam—you're a credit to the community," Mike replied. "The sooner that Indian kid is in jail, the better."

"There's a rumor going around that before I arrested him, he propositioned a young woman with drugs for sex."

"You're a crafty one, Sam," Mike said admiringly.

"Yeah, I've been doing this a while. I set up the court date so he would appear before Judge Martha Hamler."

"That's cruel, Sam. I wouldn't wish that on my worst enemy."

"Yeah, she'll toss him in a cell and throw away the key. I just called to let you know."

"Thanks, Sam. We all appreciate your good work. The community is a better place because of men like you," Mike said has he hung up.

"When do you appear in court?" Lomasi asked.

"In a month. The exact date is the 23rd," Ahote replied. "I checked the court calendar; my judge is going to be Martha Hamler, the man hater."

"The man hater?" Lomasi asked.

"Sure, haven't you heard?" Ahote said. "She gets the trials for crimes against women. She's a feminist that passes out harsh sentences against men, especially Native American men."

"Doesn't a judge have to use sentencing guidelines?" Lloyd asked. "In high school, they taught us that the legislature creates the laws, and a judge ensures the sentence matches the crime."

"That is true, but there is such a thing as judicial activism," Lomisi said. "Lawyers argue how the law should be applied in the case being tried. A judge can interpret, perhaps clarify, the intentions of lawmakers."

"Oh, thanks," Ahote replied. "That's just what I needed to know. I get a judge that hates men and can make her own rules."

"It's not that simple," Lomasi explained. "I did a paper about this for my advanced social studies class."

"Oh, great—Lomasi the scholar strikes again," Lloyd joked.

"You laugh," Lomasi said, "but education is the key to understanding how our society works. Women have experienced legal discrimination over the years because judges were all men. So in a rape case, for example, the defense lawyer simply said, 'She was asking for it,' and the defendant went unpunished."

"That doesn't seem like justice," Ahote observed.

"In this situation, a judge can interpret the law to cover a certain situation. For example, you may not know it, but Mary, the woman you gave a ride, has accused you of propositioning her."

"Well, the thought did cross my mind, I admit," Ahote said honestly. "But I didn't do anything illegal, I just asked her if she would like to come over sometime and listen to my music. What is wrong with that?"

"Mary says you are a sexist," Lomasi said emphatically.

"Women play the sexism card freely," Lloyd chimed in. "Whenever they don't get their way, they claim sexism. We men are getting a little tired of it."

"Sexism still exists in our society," Lomas retorted. "You have never experienced it."

"I am not trying to be insensitive to a problem in our society," Lloyd defended himself. "It's just that women seem to believe that everyone should have certain values, live in a certain way. In this case, Ahote asking Mary Dunham if she would like to come over to his place and listen to music sometime does not mean he is sexually propositioning her. It is not sexism. Would Mary be accused of sexually propositioning Ahote if she invited him over to her place to listen to music? Would it be interpreted as sexism? It is harmless behavior. It is another example of someone playing the sexism card inappropriately."

"It sounds harmless enough and perhaps you are right about the sexism card," Lomasi replied grudgingly. "But you have to understand, there are a lot of men and women in this community that are…well, racists, especially when it comes to Native Americans. They think they are high-minded moral individuals. But really what it comes down to is they don't like seeing an Indian guy hitting on a white girl."

"I don't think finding Mary attractive is a crime," Ahote stated.

"In their eyes, yes, it is a crime. But it is a bigger issue than that," Lomasi said. "It's so hard to explain."

Lomasi thought about what she would tell Ahote. She was jealous that he would ask Mary to come over to his place and listen to music in the first place. Why should she help him at all? On the other hand, what was happening to him was not fair. He was not a drug dealer and Lomasi was sure that he did not own a gun. But those accusations, drug dealing and gun possession, were symptoms of a larger issue. It was a question of equality for all races and the elimination of racism from our society.

"It's not fair; I should be able to talk to any woman I like without fear of retribution," Ahote said emphatically.

"Actually," Lomasi said, "that is the least of your problems. You have been charged with possession of drugs and a gun. For that, you could go to prison. We have to think of a way to prove you are innocent."

One month later, Ahote went to the Itasca County courthouse for his trial. Lomasi came with him for moral support. The building created a somber mood for them as they walked into its cavernous entrance. Whoever designed the building displayed their lack of imagination with straight lines and bland colors. The building stifled any creativeness and optimism a person possessed walking into it.

They climbed the stairs and went to the east end of the building to the courtrooms. There was a crowd of people gathered there when they arrived. Ahote and Lomasi took a seat on one of the benches and waited. Lomasi brought a book. They were a half hour early.

Eventually the bailiff appeared and asked everyone to report to the court clerk to check in. Ahote waited in line in front of the clerk. When Ahote's turn came, the clerk asked him if he would like a public defender.

"What do I have to do to get a public defender?" Ahote asked.

"You have to qualify financially for one. Fill out this form and turn it in to the bailiff when he asks for it," the clerk droned.

Ahote finished registering with the clerk, took the public defender form, and sat down to fill it out and wait. He waited for another half hour, until a bunch of prisoners in orange jumpsuits were brought into the courtroom. Ahote's mood turned somber as he imagined himself in prisoner's garb. Then the bailiff turned to the gallery, where everyone waited.

"Is there anyone applying for a public defender?" the bailiff asked.

Ahote raised his hand along with eight other people.

"Please hold up your right hands," the bailiff said. "Do you swear to me that all of the information you provided on this public-defender form is true?"

Everyone with his or her hand raised said, "I do."

"Please sign the completed forms and turn them in to me," the bailiff requested. "Then wait until your name is called to meet with the public defender."

Ahote handed his information to the bailiff and sat down with Lomasi. The judge had already entered and taken her seat. The bailiff called court to order. They started with the prisoners in orange jumpsuits. The first one was there for sentencing—armed robbery. Judge Martha Hamler sentenced him to seven years in Stillwater Prison. Suddenly, the gravity of what was happening dawned on Ahote. The possibility of spending time in jail was real! Then he heard his name called from the rear of the courtroom. He went to meet the public defender.

"Hi, my name is Clare Thompson," the public defender said as Ahote walked into the small office just off the main hallway. "I am the public defender and I am here to help you. I have the information the deputy turned in to the court. Tell me your version of what happened."

"It was late at night..." Ahote related what had happened to him.

"So, you did not know about the gun and codeine under the driver's seat of your car?" Clare asked.

"Honestly, I do not even know why I am here," Ahote said. "I thought teenagers were supposed to go to juvenile court."

"How old are you?" Clare asked.

"I am seventeen," Ahote replied. "I will be eighteen next month. I just graduated from high school."

"Ahote, your case was obviously mishandled," Clare said. "When I get done with interviewing all of my clients, I will talk to the prosecuter. I will get these charges dismissed."

"Thank you, Clare," Ahote said.

He felt like the weight of the world had been lifted from his shoulders. He went back to the courtroom and told Lomasi what had happened.

"You got lucky this time, Ahote," Lomasi said. "But someone out there is after you. That gun and those drugs did not just appear in your car. That deputy must have had a preconceived notion about you in order to stop you that night."

"Yeah, I think you are right," Ahote said.

Ahote knew then, his fate was sealed! It was time to move on.

Chapter 10

Lomasi was anxious and woke early. A chill permeated the autumn air—the sky was liquid copper as the sun peeked over the horizon. The summer, like a swan swimming in a pond, was moving gracefully toward its end. Lomasi felt a twinge of sadness as she watched the leaves create a multicolored carpet as they fell to the ground. A feeling of change hung in the air. She decided to walk in the woods. She was leaving today for Minneapolis for college. She was leaving her friends and home behind. The mystery of her parents still haunted her like a ghost. She was leaving that behind also, trying to forget it.

"Hey, why the sad face?" Sara asked her granddaughter.

"I was just thinking about leaving my home and going to the university," Lomasi said. "It dawned on me that I'm going to miss you."

"I'm going to miss you, too!" Sara replied. "But we will only be four hours away from each other. I can come and visit with you on weekends."

"I am going to go for one last walk in the woods before I leave. Care to join me?" Lomasi asked.

"I'd love to," Sara replied as they walked through the backyard to the trail in the woods.

"I want to see Breaking Dawn"—Lomasi had a pet deer she fed corn every day—"one more time before I left," Lomasi explained. "I am worried about her. Hunting season starts soon. Will Breaking Dawn survive another season?"

"That deer has survived several hunting seasons and has not been hit by a vehicle," Sara said optimistically. "I see no reason why she cannot do it for another year."

"I know. I'm just worried," Lomasi said. "I feel so alone this morning. I'm leaving you, Grandma. I've lost my parents, without ever knowing about them. I'm going someplace new to go to school."

"You'll be fine," Sara said. "You're going to be around people that are your own age that are sharing similar experiences. You will make friends with people that have backgrounds much different than yours."

"The big difference is they know where their parents are," Lomasi said. "They can call them every night."

"We've gone over that, Lomasi, again and again," Sara said. "I know it's hard for you, but eventually you just have to get over it."

"I can't help it," Lomasi cried. "It's like there is a big hole in my life. I've always felt that there is something you're not telling me about my mother."

"You know everything you need to know," Sara replied. She was hurt. "How do you think I feel? It was my daughter that disappeared. I am just glad that I have you. Together we will get through this. Maybe someday we will find out what happened to them." Sara felt a wave of guilt wash through her body as she spoke. Would the truth about Sandy really help her granddaughter?

"Maybe," Lomasi replied. "My life is always maybe."

Sara put her arm around Lomasi as they walked down the trail one last time before Lomasi left for college. She wanted to comfort her granddaughter, but she knew this was something Lomasi had to work out for herself. The only truth Lomasi needed to know was that her mother was gone and would not be coming back.

"You are working for something," Sara said. "You have done a great job at school and in the clinic this summer. When you finish college, you will be a healthcare professional. You will be able to support yourself and make a good living."

"I want to be a writer, Grandma," Lomasi said. "Novelists make a lot of money."

"Some novelists make a lot of money, but most do not," Sara replied. "You can do that, too, but first find a way to support yourself in case your writing career does not work out. Your grandmother is not always going to be around to help you."

They continued their walk discussing their plans to go to Minneapolis in the afternoon. They looked for Breaking Dawn in vain. The deer was nowhere to be found, so they headed back to their home to prepare for their trip.

Lomasi was amazed by Minneapolis. It was so much bigger and busier than her hometown of Grand Rapids. At first, she felt claustrophobic—everything was so close together. She unpacked her suitcases in her dorm room. Some of her classmates dropped by and introduced themselves as she was getting settled. She was glad Sara was there to help her.

"Now that you are unpacked, let's go for a walk. We'll scout the area," Sara suggested. "I could go for a little exercise after that long drive."

"I'm hungry," Lomasi said. "Could we get something to eat?"

"Let's walk first, then we'll check out one of the local restaurants," Sara said.

The Mississippi River separated the University of Minnesota into two campuses, one known as the West Bank and one known as the East Bank, then meandered slowly to the Gulf of Mexico. Lomasi's dormitory was on the East Bank, not far from the river. Sara and Lomasi decided to walk along the river.

"It's so different here," Lomasi said. "The river is much wider than at home."

"It gets bigger the further south you travel," Sara said. "It's beautiful. It never occurs to you when you are in Grand Rapids that you could float on the river all the way to the Gulf of Mexico."

"Minneapolis will take some getting used to," Lomasi said. "I think I am going to like it. It's a new adventure."

"You will make a lot of new friends," Sara said.

"Yes, at first I thought I would be alone in a strange new environment. After meeting some of the people in the dorm, it looks like everyone is in the same boat."

"I went to nursing school in Duluth when I was young," Sara said. "At first, I felt the same way, but eventually I found my life to be routine."

"I'll miss the woods and open spaces."

"You will adjust," Sara said. "We've gone far enough. Let's go find a restaurant."

Lomasi's first day of school was orientation. The president of the university spoke. He was followed by various speakers. Lomasi was bored already. At noon, the orientation broke for lunch. Lomasi opted to eat at the student-union coffee shop. She ordered at the lunch bar and sat down with a cup of tea. She noticed another student sitting at an adjacent table reading a book and looking over at her occasionally. She smiled at Lomasi. Lomasi returned her smile and said, "Hi."

The other student stood and moved to join Lomasi. "I'm Rachel."

"Nice to meet you, Rachel. I am Lomasi."

"You must be here for orientation."

"Is it that apparent?"

"You have the look of someone that just arrived," Rachel said. "I remember when I felt the same way. The university is a big school. It can be overwhelming at first."

"I have to admit, it appears that way. How long have you been going to school here?"

"It seems like forever, but it has only been two years. I am starting my junior year. I know my way around here, so if there is any way I can be helpful, let me know."

"Thank you, Rachel."

"Lomasi is an exotic name. What nationality are you?" Rachel asked.

"It's a Native American name. I am of Chippewa ancestry. I lived north of Grand Rapids, Minnesota, in Wabana township."

"How interesting," Rachel replied. "I am familiar with Grand Rapids. I have a home on Pokegama Lake. I go up there in the summer a lot."

"Where are you from, Rachel?" Lomasi asked. She was surprised someone that young would own property in her hometown.

"I am from Edina," Rachel replied. "It is an older suburb of Minneapolis, west of here. I bought a house on the West Bank on the Mississippi River. I live with four other girls. It is so much easier than driving back and forth every day. I did that for my first two years."

"So you know the town well?" Lomasi asked.

"Some parts of it," Rachel said. "It's such a beautiful day. I hate to waste it inside. Let's take our sandwiches and drinks and eat them by the river. After that, we can walk and talk."

Lomasi was bored with orientation already and there was something about Rachel she liked. Rachel was tall and slender with long blond hair. She had deep blue eyes and a lovely figure. Lomasi felt comfortable with her. She surprised herself when she replied, "I'm tired of the orientation already. A walk would do me good."

Lomasi and Rachel took their sandwiches and drinks to a park bench overlooking the Mississippi. After lunch, they walked on the sidewalk along the river. River Road was a scenic drive along the Mississippi. The city kept the area like a park. A steep bank led to the river one hundred feet or more below in some places. The flow of water created river flats—large areas of level ground that extend to the water's edge. The flats were largely left to grow wild with underbrush and trees—whatever the sandy soil would support.

"I never grow tired of this view," Rachel said. "Sometimes I play my guitar here. It feels great. The sun warms you. I think of all that must have happened along this river. There is a lot of history here."

"You play guitar?" Lomasi asked.

"Yes, I am a music major. My instrument is the piano, but it is kind of hard to carry one around, so I play the guitar also."

"My neighbor from Grand Rapids plays the guitar. We wrote a song together."

"You're a songwriter?" Rachel asked.

"We did it just for fun. I am a writer, or at least I am studying to be one. I am an English major."

"Can you sing?" Rachel asked.

"We used to sit around the campfire and sing in the summer. I don't know how good we were, but it was a lot of fun."

"I will have you over to my place sometime. We can sing and play. You can meet my roommates."

"That sounds like fun," Lomasi replied. She found Rachel interesting. They walked along the river and shared information about each other. After a couple hours of getting to know each other, they arrived back at Lomasi's dormitory.

"I had a great time, Lomasi. Let's exchange information. Here is my cell phone number," Rachel said. "I'd like to get together with you again. Maybe we can write some songs together."

"I'd like that," Lomasi said.

"I'll call you in the next few days," Rachel said as she strolled off to the parking lot to retrieve her car.

Chapter 11

Cyrus would have preferred to stay home and work in his clinic, where he felt comfortable. In reality, it was a humdrum existence. His day was predictably dull; there was rarely anything new. Some days, he wished excitement would escape its incarceration and invade his life.

In Grand Rapids, he was a big fish in a little pond. In Saint Paul, he wasn't even a fish, just a minnow amongst thousands of other minnows trying to get through the day without being gobbled by a shark. So he put the three-and-a-half-hour trip off as long as possible.

Cyrus went to his clinic early that morning to work for an hour before beginning the long trek to the state capital. On his way to work, he noticed Ahote hitchhiking on Pokegama Avenue with his guitar slung on his back and a pack on the ground. *Who would want to pick him up?* he wondered. Ahote would have a lot easier time finding a ride if he would cut that long hair and wear some decent clothes. Why couldn't he be like everyone else? Mike King had already gloated to Cyrus about how he finally got rid of Ahote, but he told Cyrus that Ahote was going to jail, not leaving town. Maybe he was on the run?

When he reached the office, Sara was already there preparing for her patients.

"Good morning, Sara," Cyrus said. "I am leaving for the Twin Cities in an hour or so. I will be back sometime tomorrow. Is there anything you need from me before I go?"

"Good morning, Cyrus," Sara replied. "No, I'm fine. I have a normal day of appointments today. Tomorrow is a little lighter patient load, so if anything comes up for you, I can cover it."

"Great," Cyrus said. "I just have some paperwork to complete this morning and I will be on my way."

An hour later, Cyrus put his briefcase in the trunk of his Jaguar and started driving towards the Twin Cities. He loved that car. He loved his life. As a doctor, he enjoyed many privileges that ordinary people just dreamed about. The most important privilege was income. He made more money in a couple years than most people made in their lifetimes. What amazed him was that it was not dependent on results. He hoped he would not wake up one day to find out it was all a dream.

Perhaps the biggest prerequisite of being a doctor for Cyrus was women—they were like doctor groupies. When he was young and in school, women would not give him the time of day. He was shy then and not very good looking. Today he was still shy and not very good looking, but he had a title. Women loved to brag to their friends that they were going out with a doctor. They loved the status that went with being Mrs. Doctor. And of course the greatest aphrodisiac of all—they loved the money. Yes, now women fell all over him. He felt like a puppeteer, pulling the stings of their lives. He could toy with one woman until the next one came along.

As he drove down Pokegama Avenue leaving town, Cyrus noticed Ahote was still in the same place he had seen him earlier, hitchhiking. He was leaving town—why not help him? He stopped to pick him up. After all, how far could he be going? In truth, Ahote was going nowhere—in life, he smirked to himself.

"Hi, Ahote," Cyrus said as rolled down the passenger window. "I'll pop the trunk. Put your stuff in there and hop in."

"Dr. Longfell," Ahote said. "Thanks for stopping."

"No problem. Always like to help friends when I get a chance. Where are you going?"

"I'm headed towards Minneapolis." Ahote pondered his elevated status as one of Dr. Longell's friends.

"Wonderful." Cyrus was nonplussed. He didn't really like Ahote all that much that he wanted to spend the next few hours with him. He had just stopped to be polite. In fact, he had a strange feeling come over him—jealousy. Why would he be jealous of this crude, uneducated, unsophisticated Indian kid? He was surprised to find that he viewed Ahote as a rival. All summer, Lomasi had worked at the clinic. Cyrus could not help but notice how she had blossomed into an attractive young lady. Even though there was a large age difference, Cyrus could not help being attracted to her. So when he found Lomasi alone in the supply closet, he had his way with her. Too bad she had to leave for school. Otherwise he could look forward to many secret rendezvous. Oh, well—there was always Ashley. But she was too easy—he needed a new challenge.

Sara had mentioned how Ahote and Lomasi were friends— perhaps more than friends. Sara was glad Lomasi had left for the university so she would not spend so much time with Ahote. Cyrus agreed.

"That is a coincidence; I am going to Saint Paul. It'll be nice to have some company."

They drove in silence for a few miles.

"What are you going to do in Minneapolis?" Cyrus asked.

"I'm moving there," Ahote explained. "I want to pursue a career as a musician and the Minneapolis/Saint Paul area offers more opportunity than Grand Rapids."

"There are a lot of good things about Grand Rapids, Ahote. You shouldn't berate the place you grew up."

"I'm not complaining about living in Grand Rapids. I like it there. But everyone here knows everyone else. The town shuts down early and there is no diversity. It is hard for a budding artist to grow. There is more opportunity in the Twin Cities."

"I understand what you are saying," Cyrus replied. It took me a while to adjust to Grand Rapids after finishing my internship in Chicago. Even after several years in my clinic, I sometimes feel like an outsider."

"Try being of Native American heritage," Ahote continued to state his case. It was funny. Ahote felt he could confide in Doctor Longfell. After all—if you couldn't trust a doctor, who could you trust? So he started to open up to Cyrus. "You already have one strike against you. No one believes you can write songs or sing except in a powwow."

"Grand Rapids is a progressive town and discrimination is a thing of the past," Cyrus said. "Too many people blame an abstract entity for their own shortcomings."

"That's easy for you to say, Cyrus," Ahote said. "You're a doctor. You have a great income and your profession has a corner on the marketplace. People have no choice but to be your customers."

"I earned the right to be in business. I went to school for many years and worked crummy hours as an intern for no money. You have to do the same."

"I understand what you are saying," Ahote said thoughtfully. "I didn't mean to be insulting. It is just different for a Native American. I want to write about it, not be penalized by the fact that I am one."

"I don't mean to be insensitive," Cyrus said, not wanting to sound like a racist. "My point is that it is the person, not the place, that determines how successful you will be. So in that respect, Grand Rapids is as good a place as any."

"I agree that everything is up to me in life. I have to take the initiative," Ahote said. "For example, the only open stage in a thirty-mile radius is at the local coffee shop. It's nice of them to have an open stage, but the opportunities at the open stages in Minneapolis are greater. You have the opportunity to play in front of a larger audience and the opportunity to see a greater diversity of musicians and to hear a greater variety of music."

"I guess I see what you mean," Cyrus admitted reluctantly. He couldn't help but think that some of Ahote's problems in the area were self-made. He had gotten a reputation as a rebel. He wanted to party all night long and seduce women instead of getting a steady job and working hard. Everyone in the area had heard about his run-in with the law. *You can't run away from yourself,* he thought.

"I want to grow as a person and a musician. I'd like to write poetry. I want to capture the spirit of America…the world. I want to do that through music and writing," Ahote said to Cyrus. "I know I need to improve my skills, but part of that is education that you can only gain though travel and practice—hard work. Grand Rapids will always be home, but that is why I am leaving."

"I wish you luck in your endeavors, Ahote. Where will you stay?"

"I don't know yet. I will probably stay in a motel at first, but after that, who knows? I'd like to rent a place, but I don't know where I would like to live yet."

Cyrus was staying at a motel on University Avenue between Saint Paul and Minneapolis, the Midway. He liked the central location. There was easy access to the freeway and there were plenty of restaurants and entertainment.

Cyrus dropped Ahote at the intersection of Oak Street and Washington Avenue, right in the heart of the University of Minnesota's East Bank community.

"I'm headed to downtown Saint Paul from here," Cyrus said. "This is probably as good a spot to start as any."

"Thanks for the ride, Cyrus," Ahote said as he got out of the car and looked around.

"Don't forget us," Cyrus said, then drove away.

Good riddance, Cyrus thought as he pulled away from Ahote. Mike was right about him. He was just a troublemaker. He picked up his cell phone.

"Hey, Mike, you'll never guess who I just gave a ride to Minneapolis."

"Who?" Mike asked, although he already had a hunch.

"Our local juvenile delinquent, Ahote," Cyrus replied.

"Yeah, I heard he beat the charges on a technicality." Mike sounded disappointed. "He claimed the gun and drugs were planted in his car. It would have been a pretty weak defense. It was Sam Whitman's fault. He should have taken him to the juvenile center instead of the county jail. Sam is a good man, but sometimes he doesn't think things through before he acts."

"Well he's out of our hair now," Cyrus said.

"Thanks for letting me know, Cyrus," Mike said as he hung up. He thought, *I still have a score to settle with Ahote. Who do I know in Minneapolis that can help me?*

Cyrus thought about his upcoming hearing in Saint Paul. He knew it was just a formality. Complaints against doctors were heard as a routine, but nothing was ever done about it. At most there was a slap on the hand or a suspended fine. Since he was being judged by his peers, he had nothing to fear.

Chapter 12

Fall 1981

Mike turned the page on another chapter of summers spent in northern Minnesota running the resort and prepared for the tedious drive to Miami. He and Cyrus fastened the shutters and turned off the lights at Bluewater Resort. It would remain dormant for the winter, silently waiting for another spring. Like migratory birds, the shorter days and the coolness in the air signaled it was time for the voyage south.

Mike and Cyrus were going through a metamorphosis, shucking their cocoons and emerging as butterflies. Time had transformed them into sophomores. They were experienced college students now and they were looking forward to their increased stature on campus. They were anxious to get back to school and share the adventures of the summer with their friends. The sun shone brightly, deepening the rich blue color of the ocean. Their surroundings seemed to be welcoming their return to Florida. As they pulled into Miami, they felt that primal urge to celebrate. The first thing they did was drive to the beach for a swim.

As they were drying off, Mike said to Cyrus, "I'm glad you decided to move in with me. You will like living off-campus much more than the dormitory."

"It's a great idea. It was good to take a break and work for the summer at the resort instead of attending summer classes. I feel refreshed and ready for another year of study," Cyrus said.

"We had a great summer at the resort. We can split the profits. All my Dad cares about is the place paying for itself. He looks at it as a real-estate investment. As long as he breaks even on the profit/loss statement, he is happy. He depreciates the property on his taxes when, in reality, lakeshore property in Minnesota is rapidly appreciating in value."

"Well let's follow your father's example and use our money judiciously," Cyrus suggested. "We need to make it last till next summer."

"Yeah, maybe by next summer, Sandy will get rid of that loser Dan and she will be available for a real man."

"I'm not interested in her," Cyrus quipped.

"I wasn't talking about you, fool!"

"I wanted to be independent of my father," Mike told Cyrus, "but what the hell? The house on Lake Belmar is perfect. It's about a half hour drive to school. Think of the parties we can have."

"Let's go take a look," Cyrus replied as they drove down Biscayne Boulevard toward their destination. They turned onto NE 91st Street; as they approached the house, Cyrus could not believe his eyes. "We're going to live here?"

"Yeah, it's pretty nice, huh?"

"We're on the water."

"It's more like a protected harbor. There is the dock; that's our boat. We can access the ocean from here."

"It looks good to me," Cyrus said. "I'm ready to move in."

The house was an older home on Lake Belmar. Miami was continually expanding, and that expansion brought bigger and better houses. To Cyrus, the house was a mansion. It was a single-level home with brick walls. There were three large bedrooms, a kitchen, and a dining-room area. The living room overlooked the swimming pool and the protected harbor. There was a twenty-foot dock on the harbor. A small boat—small for the ocean—rested on a canopied lift at the end of the dock. Cyrus sighed—this was paradise.

Living off-campus in a house afforded Mike and Cyrus prestige among their peers. They were men about town. They could furnish their fellow students with a place to party and get away from the college atmosphere. There were none of the normal restrictions.

Mike and Cyrus were complete opposites. Mike was extroverted; he was a partier. After spending time in the military, he was ready to have some fun. He was also interested in school and was seriously pursuing a bachelor's degree. While it looked like Mike just wanted to have fun, he was a good time manager and found time for his academic interests as well as recreation. Cyrus, on the other hand, was the serious student. His grade point average was always above 3.4 on a 4.0 scale, and he felt it should be above 3.75. He spent most of his time studying. In his spare time, he would exercise. He loved to jog and would take advantage of the miles to exercise with a view of the ocean.

"I told you this would be a sweet setup," Mike said to Cyrus as they drove to their first day of school.

"I'm glad you convinced me to move in with you. I was skeptical at first. I thought living in a dorm was for me. Once I saw the house, I couldn't resist."

"We'll be eligible bachelors at school," Mike replied. "The women won't be able to resist us."

"I can't believe I am living in this expensive house rent-free," Cyrus observed.

"It's not rent-free. You worked all summer at my father's resort. You earned a place to live while we attend school."

"It's great. We have more room than we need and a view of the water."

"Let's focus on school," Mike said. "Next summer we'll be back at the resort. Business is always good there and my father is grateful for someone to run it. We can earn pretty good dough every summer to pay our living expenses here."

Cyrus was always amazed at Mike's schmoozing skills. Once back at school, Mike started in right away meeting girls. He was organizing a party for Saturday night while Cyrus was busy planning for the quarter's tests, papers, and final exams. Cyrus wrote test dates and when papers he had to write were due on a calendar. He was amazed at the lackadaisical attitude Mike had toward planning the quarter. Cyrus scheduled his time around school, while Mike scheduled his time around dating and partying.

"We need to get ready for the party Saturday," Mike told Cyrus. "We'll need at least a keg of beer and music."

"How do you find time to study with all this partying?" Cyrus asked.

"I don't," Mike replied. "I give the instructor my full attention in class and I take good notes. Most of my classes have tests with essay questions and term papers."

"Still, don't you have to spend time in the library?"

"Yeah, but I like to organize discussion groups with other students," Mike explained. "We talk about our understanding of the subject. Then, when I take a test or write a paper, I can use other perspectives than just my own. It improves my understanding of the subject and it is fun. I get to know my fellow students."

One day when Cyrus came home from school, he was surprised to see one of his old classmates from Saint Mark's.

"Tony, what are you doing here?" Cyrus asked.

"Cyrus, great to see you," Tony replied as he stood up to shake Cyrus' hand. "It's been a long time."

"Too long," Cyrus replied. "Mike tells me you manage his nightclub."

"Now I manage two nightclubs," Tony said. "Mike just bought the Belmont Club."

"Amazing," Cyrus said thoughtfully. "He never seems to be working at anything except meeting girls. Now he owns a second club?"

"Yeah, you'd never guess it talking to him," Tony said. "He's pretty unassuming. I don't think he wants it to be known that he owns the clubs."

"Hi, Cyrus," Mike said as he entered the room. "You probably haven't seen Tony for a while."

"No, but he hasn't gotten any better looking," Cyrus quipped.

"I see him all the time, so I don't notice," Mike replied. "We're going to my new club—why don't you come with?"

"I'd like to," Cyrus said. "I'm tired of classes and studying."

"You two go ahead," Mike replied. "I have a few more things to do here. I will join you later."

"Come on, Cyrus, let's get out of here," Tony said.

Tony drove Cyrus to the Belmont Club downtown. They went inside. The lights were low, so it took a minute for their eyes to adjust. Cyrus was impressed with the swank interior. The stage was well lit. A dancer appeared and strutted her way down the runway. She was graceful, yet tall and lanky. Her moves were practiced. She captured every man's attention in the bar as she pranced up and down the runway. She mesmerized the audience, then in one fluid motion, she took off her top, teasing the audience while she did it. It took a moment for Cyrus to catch his breath so he could speak.

"So Mike bought another strip club," Cyrus observed.

"No one can get anything by you, Cyrus," Tony joked.

"Cut it out, Tony." All through school, Tony had made fun of Cyrus. Why should anything be different now?

"Seriously, it made sense to buy this club. The seller got into financial trouble. His overhead was too high. We can combine purchasing and management of both clubs and reap a healthy profit. Plus, as you can see, there are side benefits."

"I like the side benefits. Can I meet her?"

"Of course, just let her finish on stage, then I'll introduce both of us."

It was still early and there were not many people in the club. Tony was able to wave the dancer over without any problem.

"Hi," Tony said. "You looked great up there. I'm Tony Mankin, the new manager, and this is my friend Cyrus."

"I saw you here before, Tony. Hi, Cyrus, it's nice to meet you two. My name is Serena."

"I'll leave you to talk. I have some work to do," Tony said as he walked toward the business office.

"Serena, that's a lovely name."

"Thanks, it's my stage name."

"If I said you had a lovely body, would you 'hold it against me'?"

"That's an old line." Serena laughed. She caught the play on words right away. "No, I won't hug you, but I'll give you a lap dance for ten dollars."

"No, thanks. I'm a student—I can't afford it."

"Are you from Miami?"

"Yes, I was born and raised here. Are you from Miami?"

"No, I'm from northern Minnesota," Serena explained.

"Really? I just got back from there a few weeks ago."

"Where were you?" Serena asked.

"About sixteen miles north of Grand Rapids at the Bluewater Resort."

"I'm from Cass Lake. I used to live on the reservation. I moved to Miami a few years ago. How do you know Tony?"

"I used to go to school with Tony. I am Mike King's roommate. Tony works for Mike."

"You live with Mike? I'll probably see you Saturday night, then. He invited me to his party. Maybe I'll 'hold it against you' then," she said suggestively. She winked and walked away.

Cyrus could think of nothing else but Serena. When Saturday night finally arrived, Cyrus was still thinking of Serena. He was looking forward to the party. Cyrus was struck by the contrast between himself and Mike. One minute, it seemed like he and Mike were best friends, fellow students. Then there was the other side to Mike that Cyrus never got to know. He had bought another nightclub. He had employees. Tony worked for Mike. Did Mike sell drugs? It was all very disconcerting to Cyrus.

Guests started to stream in the door. At first it was mostly students. Mike had a buffet-style feast spread on a table by the pool. There was a keg of cold beer, wine, and liquor. When word got out around school that there was a party with free drink and food, students found a way to get there. Cyrus mingled with the students he knew.

"This is where you and Mike live?" Beth asked Cyrus.

"Yeah, not a bad place." Cyrus tried to act nonchalant. It was becoming easier as he drank more beer.

"Not a bad place?" Beth asked. "It's more like a mini mansion. I wouldn't mind having a swimming pool."

"Mike's father owns it. He lets us stay here free during the school year. Then we manage his resort in northern Minnesota in the summer."

It was getting late and as the beer flowed, the crowd was getting a little raucous. Suddenly the mood in the room changed. Cyrus looked up and saw Serena walk in the door along with four of her friends. Almost in concert, every male in the area was focusing on the newcomers. Rock 'n' roll filled the room, but it seemed time had stopped.

"Serena, thanks for coming," Cyrus said as he walked toward her. She rewarded him with a big hug.

"So this is where you and Mike live," Serena said. "Not bad. We came to liven up your party. Let's dance."

Serena's friends spread out in the party while Serena grabbed Cyrus's hand, led him to the center of the room, and started dancing. Cyrus was shy and had never danced much. It must have been a combination of the beer and Serena's heavenly scent; all of a sudden, he was an expert dancer. They danced to a couple songs.

"I have to go find Mike," Serena explained to Cyrus. "I'll see you later," she said. She hugged him and gave him a peck on the cheek.

Cyrus was floating on air. Since he danced with Serena, he noticed all the girls from school were much more interested in him. He went from being a geek to being debonair in a matter of a few minutes. It was a stroke of genius inviting Serena to the party. Mike always surprised him.

Later that evening, Cyrus awoke to a sharp noise. As his mind slowly emerged from a beer-tainted haze, he could hear screaming and shouting. He left his room to see what was going on and he saw Serena, half-dressed and carrying the rest of her clothes, fleeing the bedroom. He saw Mike storming out of his bedroom after her. Cyrus melted into the corner of the room into the darkness where he would not be noticed.

Serena bolted toward the front door. Mike dashed after her; he barely caught the ends of her long black hair and pulled backwards. Serena fell to the floor on her back. Mike climbed on top of her, pinning her shoulders with his knees. It was like a cat with a mouse— Mike had caught Serena, and now he was going to toy with her. Cyrus could only hope Serena would not suffer the fate of a mouse. Mike slapped Serena, then Cyrus noticed Mike held a stiletto in his right hand. Mike held the knife to Serena's throat.

"Don't you ever treat me that way, bitch," Mike said.

"Mike, I'm sorry. Please, put the knife away."

"You deserve the blade. If you weren't one of my dancers, I would give you a scar to remember me by."

"Mike, I love you! I would never do anything to displease you."

"I made you, Serena—you were just some starving Indian bitch before I took you off the reservation. I gave you nice clothes, gave you a lifestyle you only dreamed about before you met me."

"I know, Mike, I'm grateful," Serena lied. She knew she was being exploited for her body. She knew the ropes. Mike would pick up young, naïve, Native American girls and shower them with gifts and charm. Then he would put them to work as strippers in his club. What followed was drug addiction, then prostitution.

"Don't you ever turn me down again!"

"Mike, I don't do anal," Serena pleaded. "It hurts me. Please, don't hurt me."

Mike's eyes were almost bugging out of his head, his face was red with rage, and spittle escaped from his mouth as he spoke. "I said, don't ever turn me down again!"

"Okay, okay, but be gentle—it hurts me," Serena said. She was resigned to her fate.

Then just as quickly as Mike had flown into a rage, he was calm. He smiled at Serena and said, "Serena, I love you. I don't want to hurt you." Mike got up, took Serena by the hand, and stood her up. "Put on the rest of your clothes and go home. Get a good night's sleep and things will look better in the morning."

"Thank you, Mike," Serena said gratefully. She could not believe the change in Mike. She put the rest of her clothes on. She gave Mike a peck on the cheek and walked out the door.

Mike just stood there and watched her drive away. Then he sighed, turned, and went back to his bedroom as if nothing had happened.

What was that all about? Cyrus thought. Every time he thought he knew Mike, something else happened to give him a new perspective. It was like there was an on-off switch with Mike. He displayed super aggressive behavior, then passive behavior. Maybe Mike wasn't as good with women as Cyrus thought. Maybe Mike was too clever for his own good! Cyrus thought perhaps he was being too nice of a guy with women. One thing he knew for sure was that he better be very careful how he treated Mike.

Chapter 13

Rachel contemplated Lomasi as she strummed her guitar. She felt a connection with her new friend. It was like a warm glow they shared between them when they were together. It seemed so real, she missed it when they parted. Was she attracted to Lomasi? She had been with other women before. It was never something planned—it just happened. Now she felt like she was in pursuit of a relationship. It was intentional. *Am I the moth and is Lomasi the proverbial flame?* There was only one way to find out. Rachel picked up her phone.

"Hi, Lomasi," Rachel said. "I'm calling to see if you would like to go for a walk along the river."

"I'd love to," Lomasi replied. "I'm tired of studying."

"Great! I'll be there in a few minutes."

So far, so good, Rachel thought as she picked up Lomasi at the dorm. They drove to a parking spot on the West Bank of the river.

"I can never get over what a beautiful view there is here," Rachel said. "You can almost feel the history. Sometimes I imagine the spirit of the river and the people who populated this place before us."

"It is a special place," Lomasi observed. "Let's go down these stairs so we can walk the river flats."

Lomasi and Rachel navigated the stairs down the steep bank to the walking trails. Lomasi was in awe of the power of the ancient river. It carved its path through the land. The Mississippi was much wider here than it was in Grand Rapids.

"It's almost like we're out of the city and in the forest," Lomasi observed.

"I come here when I want inspiration. It awakens my creative abilities to walk here," Rachel said.

"I know exactly what you mean. Look—there's an old fashioned paddleboat."

"There are a few of them. You get on in Saint Paul. They will take you on a cruise up the river. You can almost imagine Mark Twain at the wheel."

"I really like this," Lomasi said. It was her first time walking the flats. "The river is timeless. It invigorates a person."

They continued to walk for a half hour. "Come on," Rachel said. "I'll show you where I live."

"Why do you live on the West Bank when you go to class on the East Bank?" Lomasi asked.

"The West Bank has its own atmosphere, flavor," Rachel explained. "The West Bank of the university is more artistic. It's more fun. All the sororities and fraternities are on the East Bank. It seems almost commercial. You'll see what I mean after you live here a while."

"Here we are," Rachel said as she parked in her driveway. "How do you like it?"

"Wow, it's beautiful." Lomasi saw an older home that seemed to smile and welcome her. It was built at the dawn of the twentieth century and radiated Victorian charm. The house was on River Road and overlooked the Mississippi River. It reflected the opulence and elegance of the time period in which it was built—it was a time when fortunes were made in the flour and logging industries.

The house had been restored to its unsullied, original state. It was surrounded by a white picket fence. The porch wrapped itself around the house from the front door to the side of the house, with a gazebo crowning the corner. The top portion of every window had stained-glass designs that sparkled in the sunlight almost as if they were putting on a show for you. The turret on the other front corner of the house extended to the third floor like a tower in a castle. A widow's walk kept watch on the lazy river. The lightening rods on the roof reached toward the heavens.

"How did you manage to find this house?" Lomasi asked.

"I was renting the lower floor of a duplex in a depressed neighborhood. Good housing is scarce around the university. This house was for sale. It was run-down and needed tender loving care. I adopted it and restored it to its original glory," Rachel explained.

"You did a wonderful job," Lomasi complimented. She couldn't help wondering where Rachel got the money do all the work. "It must have cost a fortune. It is so charming."

"Thank you. It's an investment," Rachel said. "I rent it to five other women that are attending the university. My father owns a construction business, so I had some help from the family in the remodeling process.

"You have a nice father," Lomasi said.

"Yes," Rachel replied. "It was a compromise. My father wants me to follow in his footsteps. He wants me to take over the family business. The reason he agreed to help remodeling a house on this side of the river is because the Curt Carlson School of Business is located on this campus. I agreed to take some accounting classes. We have an ongoing argument: I want to major in music; he wants me to major in business."

"I was lucky to hook up with you," Lomasi said. "I can see we are going to be great friends."

"What does your father do?" Rachel asked.

"I don't know," Lomasi said dejectedly.

"Don't know?" Rachel asked thoughtfully.

"My parents disappeared when I was a young child," Lomasi explained. "No one could find a trace of them. They got up one morning, left for work, and were never seen again. I was raised by my grandmother."

"The one that wants you to be a nurse practitioner?" Rachel asked.

"Yeah, I want to be a writer, but she wants me to do something she thinks is more sensible. She works as a nurse practitioner for Cyrus Longfell, a dirty old man that has a medical clinic in Grand Rapids."

"Dirty old man?" Rachel asked. "That sounds interesting."

"Maybe to you," Lomasi explained, "but I had to work for him all last summer. Every time I saw him, he seemed to be leering at me."

"What's wrong with that?" Rachel asked.

"It was more than that," Lomasi said. "Can you keep a secret? I really need to talk about this," Lomasi explained to Rachel what had happened to her in the supply closet. "That's why I say Cyrus gives me the creeps."

"Did he ever try it again?"

"No, it was the Friday before my last week working there. I made myself scarce the last week."

"It was rape. You should have reported it." Rachel was empathetic.

"I don't know. I didn't stop him. I should have, but I felt like I was in his control. I just went along with it—that's what bothers me. I thought about reporting it, but I was worried no one would believe me. After all—he's a doctor; I'm just a young girl. Also, he's my grandmother's boss. Would he fire her? It's sad, but I didn't do anything."

"Well, I think you just have to think of it as a lesson learned now. It happened; just don't let anything like that happen to you again unless you want it to happen. That is the best advice."

"I know—it just irks me that a doctor would take advantage of his position like that."

"He's just a man. You have to expect that type of behavior."

"I suppose." Lomasi shrugged.

"Come on; I'll show you around." Rachel changed the subject.

Lomasi was charmed by the interior of the house and the attention to detail when the house was restored to its original state. The oak floors shined, and the woodwork accentuated the tastefully decorated walls. There was a sitting room directly off the entry, then the entries to the living and dining areas were on opposite sides of the hall. The sun shining through the stained-glass portion of the windows cast a collage of colors on the walls.

"I love it," Lomasi said. "Can I move in with you?"

Rachel almost gasped. She wondered if Lomasi could read her mind. Did Lomasi feel the same way about her? She decided to play it safe in light of Lomasi's previous revelation. "We have no vacancies right now, but things are always changing, and later in the school year, there may be a spot for you," Rachel replied.

They continued their tour of the house.

"Lomasi, I would like you to meet Diane," Rachel said as they walked into the kitchen. Diane was just finishing her lunch.

"Hello, Lomasi. It's nice to meet you," Diane said. "Are you going to school at the university?"

"Yes, I am a freshman English major," Lomasi replied.

"That sounds interesting," Diane replied. "I am majoring in accounting. Lomasi is a unique name. Are you from around here?"

"No, I am from Grand Rapids, Minnesota." Lomasi was getting tired of people asking her about her name. She could guess the next question.

"You look like you are from the Middle East; you're an exotic beauty. You're probably Irish and I'm way off-base," Diane said as she laughed.

"No, I'm Native American."

"That's where you get that glamour look. You could be a model," Diane said. "You will be a big hit with the guys at school."

"Thanks for the good words," Lomasi replied. She felt like reading Diane the riot act. First, she did not come to the university to be popular with guys. She came here to become a writer. Second, she was tired of having to explain to everyone why her name was "unique." She was constantly explaining that she was Native American and that her mother had given her a Native American name. It brought out the anxieties she always experienced when the subject of her parents' disappearance was brought up. She would have to change her name.

Instead of being mad with Diane, Lomasi bit her tongue and said, "I am looking forward to getting to know you better, Diane. I am sure we are going to be great friends."

"Yes, we will have to meet for coffee and get to know each other better sometime soon," Diane replied.

"Can I use your bathroom, Rachel?" Lomasi asked.

"It's right down the hall." Rachel pointed the way to her.

"Where did you find the squaw?" Diane asked snidely after Lomasi closed the bathroom door.

"You're so crude," Rachel replied. "She's a nice young girl."

"Naïve, you mean."

"I like them that way." Rachel fumed. Silence filled the air and time seemed to stand still. She was about to say more when she heard Lomasi open the bathroom door.

"Lomasi, I almost forgot to tell you," Rachel said. "We're having a party here Saturday night! It's to kick off the new school year. We're going to start it right. You have to come. You can meet the rest of my roommates."

"That sounds like fun. I'll look forward to it," Lomasi replied. "I'd like to see the rest of the house."

Rachel continued the tour. "This is the master suite. These old houses by the river had amenities that you don't find in modern housing."

"It's perfect," Lomasi said as she took it all in. There was a sitting room with a picture window that yielded a panoramic view of the river. There was a bedroom with a master bath attached to it. It occupied the entire third floor of the house, and there was an entrance to the widow's walk from the sitting room.

"Yes, I have a lot of privacy up here, even though I have to climb three flights of stairs to take advantage of it."

"It's worth the climb," Lomasi said. After living in a trailer home all of her life, she was just starting to adjust to the more affluent lifestyles she was introduced to in her new city.

"Here is my guitar. I love this instrument even though I play the piano for my major," Rachel said as she picked up the guitar and strummed.

"Why do you play the piano if you prefer the guitar?" Lomasi asked. Rachel was so enthusiastic that Lomasi found herself looking at her as more than a friend. Rachel was adorable—she put it out of her mind.

"There is so much music written for the piano. It was the first instrument I learned to play. The guitar, on the other hand, is an instrument that is used in more popular music. Many guitar players cannot read music, nor do they have the need to read music. They understand the theory behind the music. I enjoy playing both instruments." Rachel sat on the sofa next to Lomasi and started to play.

"I have a neighbor back home that plays the guitar. We have a firepit in the backyard. In the evening, we used to sit around the fire and he would play and we would sing together," Lomasi said nervously. Rachel was a strong presence next to her.

"You sound like you have a great singing voice. What kind of songs did you guys play?" Rachel smiled invitingly.

"We wrote some of our own songs. I supplied the words and Ahote, my neighbor, supplied the music."

"I'd love to hear the songs," Rachel said. "Why don't you sing one? I'll play along."

Lomasi sang and Rachel automatically picked up the tune and played with Lomasi. She even improvised a solo. Lomasi was enjoying the strong connection she felt with Rachel.

"That was fun," Rachel said when they finished the song. "I like the song. Your neighbor must play the guitar well."

"His name is Ahote. He is moving to the Twin Cities soon."

"Is he going to pursue a musical career?"

"Yes, he had his mind set on being a musician in high school, and then after graduation, he was arrested. It was a setup."

"Did he have to spend time in jail?" Rachel asked. Ahote sounded interesting.

"No," Lomasi explained. "He was busted for drugs and possession of a weapon. He wasn't guilty, but there was no way he could prove it. He got off on a technicality and suddenly he changed.

He was going to leave Grand Rapids and all the intolerance he faced there."

"He sounds like a rebel."

Lomasi was amazed at how intuitive Rachel could be. "Yes, that is an accurate description of Ahote. He doesn't fit in Grand Rapids. He will be better off in the Twin Cities."

"Were you involved with him romantically?"

"Oh, no," Lomasi retorted. "We are good friends. He is a sweet guy. We grew up together in Wabana Township. I do miss having a friend like that now."

"Maybe we can be good friends now. I have all kinds of ideas for music," Rachel said. "I compose tunes all the time, but I'm no writer. Let's write some songs together. We can play them on open stages at the local coffee shops." Rachel moved closer to Lomasi and put her arm around her.

"I'd like that," Lomasi said. "I love the creative process. Writing a song, a poem, or just some prose gives me a feeling of satisfaction, of being complete."

"I know what you mean," Rachel said. "I have some things to do to get ready for school tomorrow. Why don't we get together next week? We'll write a song and begin our songwriting careers together." Rachel kissed Lomasi on the forehead.

"Songwriting career?" Lomasi asked skeptically. Her emotions were screaming. Here was Rachel, having a perfectly reasonable conversation with her, and at the same time, was she seducing her? Did she want her to stop?

Rachel sensed Lomasi's apprehension and backed off. "Yeah, I've got plans," Rachel explained. "I'd like to write my own songs. I want to find someone with writing skills that will work with me. The fact that you have a great voice is a bonus."

"It might be fun." Lomasi relented. "I'm willing to give it a try."

"Now that you know where I live and you have my cell phone number, I have a feeling we are going to be great friends. Can you find your way back to the dorm?"

"Yes," Lomasi replied. "Thank you for having me over. I'll see you Saturday night."

"Good, I'm looking forward to getting together with you again."

Lomasi walked back to the dorm lost in thought about her new friend Rachel. She felt lighthearted and happy when she was with her.

It was a beautiful sunny day. A leisurely walk home was just what she needed to clear her thoughts.

She liked Rachel. More than that, she was attracted to her. It was almost as if she was meant to meet Rachel. Maybe she would get a chance to use her writing skills to make music that people would like. It was a dream, but why not dream?

Chapter 14

Freedom. Ahote savored the thought. It was a feeling that slowly crept into his conscious mind as he made his way to Minneapolis. It was like being born again, beginning anew. Here was a chance to start over. He was exhilarated. As he rode with Cyrus, he felt like he was an equal, an adult. He luxuriated in the warmth of his newly acquired status until Cyrus dropped him off on a street corner in the business district close to the university. Reality came crashing down on Ahote like a hammer shaping metal on a blacksmith's anvil. He realized that along with freedom came choices. Right now, those choices were problems. Ahote decided he did not want to be the metal being shaped by the hammer. He wanted to be the hammer shaping the metal, his future.

The first problem Ahote had to solve was, where would he stay? He found a Subway restaurant and ordered a sandwich. He picked up a copy of the *Twin Cities Reader* and started paging through it. The first thing that struck him was the variety of entertainment and different activities available to him. He had grown up in an area where you had to create your own entertainment. Now he had his choice of things to do. Suddenly he felt more confident. He was up to the challenge. Life was an adventure.

He finished eating and decided to take a look around. He could see a motel sign east on University Avenue. It looked a little run-down—not a Motel 6 or anything like that—but it was probably what he could afford, at first anyways. He booked a room for the night, paying cash. At least he had a place to sleep and store his stuff while he looked for a place to rent on a more permanent basis.

At first, Ahote sat on his bed and thought to himself, *What am I going to do?* Self-doubt crept into his thoughts again. *Here I am in Minneapolis all alone. I don't know anyone that lives here except Lomasi, and she is new to the area, too. She is a student. She's making new friends now and probably wants to forget about Grand Rapids and her old life. There is nothing she can do to help me. I don't even know if she would be all that happy to see me.* He picked up his guitar and started playing chords at random. It occurred to him that he could write about his experiences. As he strummed and played, he thought to himself, *I must enjoy my life to the fullest.*

The next problem Ahote faced was employment. All he ever heard about since he was a young boy up north was the glory days on the Iron Range and how unemployment now was high, but he had noticed a help-wanted sign prominently displayed in the restaurant he ate in earlier. It appeared to him that in Minneapolis, there were jobs available for the taking. He wondered how much those jobs paid. He would have to make a wise decision about how he made a living. He needed enough money to live and enjoy life, but he also needed the flexibility to play his music and meet other musicians. Of course he couldn't be too picky at first.

Ahote decided the best thing he could do right now was get some exercise. He had to stay in good physical condition. He jogged every day when he was at home. Bluewater Road was the perfect place to exercise. Now he would jog on University Avenue SE. It was an excellent way to explore the area and work out some of his apprehensions about being in a new environment—the city. Grand Rapids had a population of ten thousand people, compared to the Minneapolis/Saint Paul metropolitan area, which had a population of over three million—the difference was staggering to Ahote. He put on his jogging clothes, did his warm-up exercises, and went out the door. He started jogging east on the sidewalk. He thought he would jog to Saint Paul, anyway. He could get an idea of what the two towns looked like. The first thing that struck him was that University Avenue had a lot of storefronts and a lot of traffic. The houses and the buildings looked old, some in disrepair. His self-doubts started to leave him as he jogged along. Jogging always made him feel that he was in control of his environment, his destiny. As he looked around at the people and the buildings, he saw the opportunity for a new start. He was excited.

As he jogged along the sidewalk, Ahote was struck by the indifference. People did not meet his eye—they just looked the other way and went about their business. To Ahote it was almost an epiphany of freedom. The traffic, the people, even the squirrels didn't care about him at all—they barely took notice. He really was free!

At home in Grand Rapids, older people had a parental attitude towards Ahote. They felt they could actively supervise his upbringing. There seemed to be a preordained outcome for him. He was ostracized because he was not like everyone else. He didn't want to be like everyone else. He wanted to create music. He wanted to create art. In Grand Rapids, there seemed to be a few people in charge of the art scene. You had to be on their "good side"; otherwise, you were not going to be successful. Ahote could sense that in the Twin Cities, you had to be able to draw attention to yourself to be noticed. You would be rewarded if you were good at what you did!

Ahote was caught up in these thoughts as all of a sudden he heard, "Hey, handsome, where are you going in such a hurry?"

Ahote stopped and looked at the gorgeous young woman in shorts and a tight top speaking to him. He stopped. "I'm just out for a jog."

"Well, you should stop and get to know Leona," she said.

"I'm Ahote. I just moved here."

"We should get to know each other better if you know what I mean," Leona said suggestively.

"I'm sorry; I did not know what you meant at first." Ahote was embarrassed. "I just moved to Minneapolis. I was just getting to know the neighborhood—looking around. I wasn't looking for....ah; well, you know what I mean."

"That's okay, sweetheart," Leona replied. "I just wanted to make you feel good. Where are you from?"

"I'm from Grand Rapids. I'm a musician. I moved here to get more experience in my field."

"I'm from northern Minnesota, too," Leona said. "You'll like the Twin Cities. There's a lot more to do."

"You look like you're Native American, like me."

"I am," Leona said. "But I'm going for that exotic look for business."

"You're not only exotic, you're really hot."

"You're sweet. Here," Leona said as she handed him a piece of paper with her phone number on it. "Call me if you change your mind or if you just need some friendly advice."

Great, Ahote thought as he kept on jogging. *The first person I meet in Minneapolis is a prostitute. She's Native American. I wonder if there is a connection—prostitution and the reservation.* He started paying attention to where he was going again. He noticed he was jogging up a hill. When he reached the top, he saw a green and white sign saying *Saint Paul.* He kept jogging until he was tired, then returned to his motel room.

Ahote was exhilarated. He got his exercise and was ready to tackle the world. He fired up his laptop and went to the *Star Tribune*'s website to look at the classified ads. He needed a job and a place to stay. To his surprise, there were plenty of jobs advertised on the newspaper's website. Sure, the jobs he was qualified for were not the most desirable jobs, but Ahote did not have a job right now. Everyone had to start someplace and he was not too proud to start at the bottom.

Next Ahote started looking for a place to live. He wanted to have his own apartment. He did not want roommates. He found that in this area there were a lot of places for rent because of its proximity to the university. He selected a few that he could afford and got on the phone. He would not be accused of inaction.

Ahote looked at several apartments and settled on a basement apartment in the Prospect Park neighborhood. It was an ideal location between Minneapolis and Saint Paul. It was close to the public transit system and had easy access to the freeway system. He had been driving one of Duane's cars. He would have to buy one of his own. The apartment was small—one bedroom with a combination living, dining, and kitchen area. It was just the right size for a single guy.

Ahote paid the first and last months' rent and signed a one-year lease. Now he had an ideal place to live, but solving the problem of where to live increased his problems also. He had bills now. He needed a job. Ahote spent the next two weeks applying for jobs. When he first arrived in the Twin Cities, he saw help-wanted signs at the windows of local businesses and all kinds of help-wanted ads in the paper. He soon found out that it was not as easy as it looked. He needed to have enough money to pay his rent and have some left over to live. After applying for fifty jobs, he swallowed his pride and took a job as a waiter in a restaurant in downtown Minneapolis.

Ahote was not excited about his new job at first. He had to work nights and was getting paid minimum wage. He soon found out that he could take advantage of his handsome features and sparkling personality. When he coupled those attributes with excellent service to his customers, he found he got great tips. He was settling into a routine. He worked five nights a week at his waiter job and he could practice his guitar and write songs during the day.

Ahote was starting to feel comfortable in his new home. He was able to purchase furniture and get satellite television with his new income. He was starting to get to know people in the area. He jogged every day after work to stay in shape. However, his music career was not progressing. He wanted to go out to clubs and see other musicians play, but he found the same nights that he could watch other musicians were the most profitable nights as a waiter. Friday and Saturday nights were his bread-and-butter nights—the nights he made most of his income.

One night when he waited on a bunch of Minnesota Vikings players, he made excellent tips and decided to treat himself. He and some of his coworkers went out to an all-night pizza place for something to eat. Afterwards Ahote decided to take a taxicab home. It was about 4:00 AM and he had to wait for a cab. When it finally showed up, he got in.

"Take me to 923 Franklin Avenue Southeast, please," Ahote said politely to the driver.

"Is that over in Prospect Park?" the driver asked. He was an older man with one of those old-fashioned taxi-driver's hats. Ahote guessed he was probably in his later forties, maybe fifty.

"Yup, right across the Franklin Bridge."

"Any special route you would like to take?" the driver asked politely.

"You're the expert; take me the best way," Ahote said. He had learned from his job as a waiter to be respectful of other people in the service industry. Besides, this was one of the few cabs available this time of night. There was little wisdom in making the driver mad.

"Sounds good," the driver replied as he turned on the meter and started driving.

"Busy night?" Ahote asked.

"I don't know," the driver answered. "I just started work—you're my first fare."

"You start early," Ahote observed.

"Yeah, I own the cab, so I get up early and work late."

"How many hours do you work?"

"It varies day to day," the driver said. "I used to have a night driver, so I would work until early afternoon, then turn the cab over to him. He moved to California last month so I am looking for a new driver."

"How does it work?" Ahote asked. He noticed a sign on the back of the seat of the cab saying *Night driver wanted.*

"It works pretty well when I can find someone reliable to work with," the driver said.

104

"No, I mean what kind of a deal is it for your night driver?"

"Oh, I lease the cab to the night driver. Right now I charge thirty-five dollars per night. The driver pays for his own gas and keeps any money he makes over that."

"How much money can you make?"

"It depends on the person."

"What do you mean?" Ahote asked.

"Well, you can decide the days you want to work. I need a commitment of five nights a week or one hundred seventy-five dollars per week. The night driver can have the cab from 3:00 PM to 3:00 AM. A driver can work as many hours as he likes during that time frame. The more hours you work, the more money you will make."

"It sounds interesting," Ahote said. "I might like to try it. Could I make a living at it or is it pretty much a minimum-wage job?"

"If you work reasonably hard five days a week, you can make four hundred to six hundred dollars a week. Maybe more if you work the full twelve-hour shift. You can work more than five days a week if you want. I charge thirty-five dollars per night—five nights minimum."

"I'm a musician," Ahote explained. "Right now I am working as a waiter. The tips are good, but I end up working the hours that I should be out playing my music. I need a job with a flexible schedule. How would that work with cab driving?"

"Cab driving is about as flexible as you get. There is no one watching over you saying you have to work twelve-hour shifts. If you want to work five hours a night, that is fine as long as you pay the lease for the night and the gas."

"Could I work a few hours, take a couple hours off, then work the rest of the shift?"

"Sure," the cab owner said. "The problem most drivers have is being disciplined to work. You have to spend the time to learn the job—how to make money. Then you have to work hard enough to pay the lease and gas and make some money."

"It sounds like a great deal. I would like to give it a try. How would I start?"

"Well, you could drive around with me one day this week and see how you like it. I will pay you twenty-five dollars to ride along. Then if you would like to try it, you have to get a cab-driver's license from the City of Minneapolis. You can use the twenty-five dollars to pay for the license. Do you have a driver's license?"

"Yeah, I've been driving since I was sixteen."

"How is your driving record?"

"It is good," Ahote lied. He did not want to mention that he was arrested for possession of drugs and a gun earlier this year.

"My name is Bob Lundeen. I will leave you this job application. Fill it out when you have the time. Here is my business card with my cell phone number on it. Call me when you complete the application. I will stop by and pick it up. We'll take it from there."

"Sounds good, Bob. My name is Ahote. I will fill out the application this morning and call you back."

"Great. I'll be working until 3:00 PM today, maybe longer. You owe me $4.95."

"Here's a ten-dollar bill; keep the change."

Ahote was excited. After he left Bob, he went inside his apartment and started filling out the job application to be a cab driver. He liked waiting tables as much as anyone likes any job, but the freedom driving a cab would offer him would dovetail nicely with his career as a musician. He called Bob and left a message that he had completed the application and that he was ready to start work.

Bob called Ahote back later that day. "I got your message; you'd like to give cab driving a try."

"Yeah, it sounds like a good opportunity for me."

"I'll stop by and pick up your application later today. If you like, you could ride with me tomorrow and see what it is like."

"Tomorrow would be great," Ahote replied. "What time?"

"I start at 3:00 AM every day. That is probably a little early for you. Let's plan for about 8:00 AM. You can ride with me until noon."

The next day, Bob called Ahote and picked him up. He explained that he drove early in the morning to pick up regular customers and then he went downtown and sat outside the hotels to wait for customers for the airport.

"You do that routine every day?" Ahote asked.

"There are a lot of different ways you can work," Bob explained. "You can choose what you want to do at any given time. There are certain times I like to use the automated dispatch system to get orders. Then there are times I like to sit outside of hotels, and sometimes I like to pick up customers at the airport."

"How do you decide what you are going to do?"

"Most of the time it just happens," Bob said. "I just do what I have to do to make the most money I can at any given time. You will learn from experience. At first it will be all new to you, but with time you will find how you like to work and you will start making more money. If you decide to work the night shift, 3:00 PM to 3:00 AM, you will work differently than I do.

After riding along with Bob for four hours Ahote made up his mind. "I'd like to give it a try," he said. "It seems like it will be a lot more fun than waiting tables—I will have more opportunities to make money."

"Sounds good, Ahote," Bob said. "The first thing you have to do is get a cab-driver's license."

"Is it very difficult to get one?"

"Just go down to the courthouse in Minneapolis and tell them you want a cab-driver's license. You pay a fee and they will issue you one. Call me when you get it. I'll go out with you the first night for a couple hours for training purposes."

"Thanks," Ahote said as he got out of the cab at his apartment.

Chapter 15

Ahote was pleasantly surprised at how easy it was to adapt to life in the Twin Cites. He thought it might be a difficult transition. He found he enjoyed the anonymity. In Grand Rapids, someone new was scrutinized by everyone—he or she was a topic for discussion. In the Twin Cities, there was no scrutiny—no one cared. *That's how I like it,* he mused. He amazed himself with his progress. It seemed like he had found an apartment and a job as a waiter downtown in no time. Now he was going to be a cab driver, all in the span of a few weeks.

Ahote walked to University Avenue and waited for the bus to take him to the courthouse. One of the first things Ahote did when he started working downtown was purchase a bus card. He could travel on the bus as much as he liked for the cost of the bus card, one monthly fee. It was a practical form of transportation and it was a good way to get to know other people in the area.

Ahote felt confident and just a little cocky. When the bus finally stopped to pick him up, he hopped on with swagger, like he'd lived here all his life—it felt natural. When he got downtown, he strutted into the Minneapolis courthouse. He walked up to the information desk and said, "I'm here to get a cab driver's license." The person at the desk directed him to the second-floor office. It was a simple matter to get the license. He just paid a fee, was fingerprinted, and they issued a license to him.

The first thing he did when he left the courthouse was pick up his phone.

"Hi, Bob, this is Ahote. I got my license."

"That's great!" Bob replied. He was excited to finally find someone to lease his cab at night. Now he would not have to work so many hours. "When would you like to start training?"

"How about tomorrow?" Ahote asked.

"Tomorrow would be great. I can pick you up around 3:00 PM."

"Sounds good," Ahote said. "I'll see you then."

Lomasi was fascinated by her new environment. Everything was new and interesting, but she was getting tired of explaining her background. It was always the same. Every time she met someone new, they would say, "Lomasi—what an interesting name. What nationality is that?" She had to go through a long, drawn-out explanation of her background, which would inevitably lead her thoughts, if not the conversation, to the fact that her parents had deserted her. *I am a Native American and I am proud of it,* Lomasi thought, *but do I have to proclaim it to the world with a Native American name? Lomasi is not exactly a sexy name. I have a new life at the university; I am making new friends and learning new things. I need a new name.*

A new name! That is exactly what was needed to go with her new identity. But what name? *I want to be exciting,* Lomasi thought. *I want to be sexy and attractive. Still, I want to be a writer. It has to be an intellectual name also.* She started to look at names in magazines and novels that she had to read for classes. The name had to be original. She did not want a common name. Finally, it came to her: Lola. It was intriguing. It was a sexy, maybe even suggestive, name. Perhaps it wasn't a name that connoted intellectuality, but her work, writing, would display her abilities. Who would want to read a book written by Lomasi? She liked it but she wanted to ask someone else. She picked up her cell phone.

"Rachel, I want your opinion on something." Lomasi asked, "Do you have a minute?"

"Sure, I'm just studying," Rachel replied. "Anything has to be more interesting than that. What is it?"

"I'm thinking of changing my first name to Lola. What do you think?"

"I like it. To be honest, since I met you, I have thought that Lomasi was an unusual name. Everyone I introduce you to comments on it. It makes you seem different from the rest of us."

"That is the issue exactly," Lomasi replied. She was impressed by how intuitive her new friend was. "Everywhere I go I have to explain my name, that I am Native American….besides, Lomasi is not exactly sexy."

"It's a unique name," Rachel said. "You are a unique person. Besides, if you are going to change your name, now is a good time to do it. Since you just started school, everyone you meet will know you as Lola. It will not be a change you will have to explain to everyone."

"My thoughts exactly," Lomasi replied. It was astonishing how connected she was with her new friend. "We're on the same wavelength."

"Ditto," Rachel replied. "Remind me—I will start introducing you as Lola at the party Saturday night. You are still coming, aren't you?"

"I wouldn't miss it," Lomasi replied. "I like school, but it can get kind of boring studying all the time. A party will be a welcome change and a chance to let loose a little."

"I can tell we are going to be great friends. See you Saturday," Rachel said as she hung up the phone.

Lola, Lomasi kept saying to herself. She was pleased. *My new name is Lola.*

It was a beautiful day in Minneapolis. Ahote luxuriated in the warmth of the sun as he sat on the front stoop of his new home and waited. When he had time to think about it, he was in awe of how the city seemed to extend forever. Like starting a new job, it was exciting.

His thoughts were interrupted when Bob pulled up to the curb. He felt a twinge of excitement as he got in the cab and Bob began to show him the ropes of driving a cab. They drove downtown and parked the cab on a cabstand in front of the Pillsbury Building. He explained to Ahote, "When you start at 3:00 PM every day, the demand for cabs will be just starting for the rush hour. If you park on a cabstand downtown, there will be a lot of traffic to the airport. When you park on a cabstand, you wait in line until you're the first cab, then you take whatever fare walks up to your cab."

At first Ahote was skeptical. "I have always liked to do something, make something happen. I don't know about sitting around waiting."

"This time of day, you do not have to wait long," Bob replied. Just as Bob said that, people walked up to the first cab and got in. In a few minutes, their cab was the first in line.

"Airport," a businessman dressed in a suit said as he got in the back seat of the cab.

"Sounds good," Bob said. "Would you like to take the freeway?"

"Yes, the quickest way. I am cutting it close time wise."

"We'll get you there on time," Bob promised.

"It takes two of you to drive a cab?" The man had a New Jersey accent.

"I'm Bob; I own the cab. This is Ahote, my new driver. It's his first day. I am giving him some pointers."

The businessman seemed satisfied and started making calls on his cell phone. Bob showed Ahote the best way to get to the airport and where to drop his customers off.

"When you get to the airport this time of day, it is a safe bet to wait for a fare returning to the city. A lot of people are coming into town now to do business tomorrow or they are returning home from a business trip," Bob explained. He showed Ahote where to get into line at the airport. "The line is long, but it moves fairly fast this time of day." In about half an hour, they were the first cab in line and had another fare downtown again. They dropped her off at a hotel downtown.

"You have a good start," Bob said. "So far we have collected thirty-six dollars and your lease for the day is thirty-five dollars. That means everything you make the rest of the night, you can keep. Just remember, you have to fill the cab with gas when you finish."

"This seems easy enough," Ahote said. "What about coffee breaks and lunch?"

"You can take a break whenever you want," Bob explained. "I always try to time my breaks with the least busy times. For example, the hours from 3:00 PM to 7:00 PM are the busiest on your shift. I would try to work hard those hours and make as much money as I can. Then I would take a break for lunch."

"That makes sense," Ahote replied. "What if I just want to knock off after those hours?"

"That is fine," Bob answered. "Just have the cab back in front of my house before 3:00 AM with the gas tank full. Leave the lease money under the seat and the door locked. We'll get along fine."

"I play the guitar, Bob," Ahote explained. "If I wanted to work the first part of my shift, then take time off to play somewhere and come back to work, that is all right?"

"Sure," Bob replied with a smile. "The best possible scenario for me is if you don't drive it at all and pay the lease." He laughed. "Realistically, I want you to make a good living doing this so you will continue to lease my cab."

"This is great," Ahote said. "It is exactly the kind of job I am looking for."

"Good," Bob said. "Remember, too, that the bars close at 1:00 AM, so it will get busy again around that time, especially on Friday and Saturday nights."

"Where are we going now?" Ahote asked.

"I am going to show you where I fill the cab with gas around my house and where I live so you know where to drop off the cab. Then I am going to turn the cab over to you along with the thirty six dollars we collected. You can drive the cab for the rest of the evening. Just remember to return the cab to me at 3:00 AM and fill it with gas."

"What would you do the rest of the evening, if you wanted to make money?" Ahote asked.

"I would go back downtown. That is where all the money is," Bob replied. "But pay attention to other cab drivers. There are drivers out there making good money; watch what they do. A lot of drivers like to take radio order; that can be good business, too. Also, there are lots of regular customers out there. Some will like you. Give them your cell phone number and they will call you when they need a ride."

"Sounds good, Bob," Ahote said. "I'm going to get out there and make some money."

"Good—you have a great attitude, Ahote," Bob said. "Go make some money and have the cab back by three o'clock."

Ahote drove cab the rest of the night. It was a little frustrating at first. He did not know the city well. He learned that all he had to do was explain this to his customers. Most of the people who got into the cab knew where they were going and didn't mind showing him the best way to get there. By the time the end of his shift came around, he was tired. He filled the cab up with gas and went to Bob's house to leave the cab.

"How did it go?" Bob asked. He was waiting for Ahote to get done.

"It was hard work, but I finished the shift okay. I made almost a hundred dollars, so it was worth it," Ahote replied.

"Good—I'll give you a ride home," Bob said. "Are you game to try it again tomorrow night on your own?"

"Absolutely," Ahote replied. "I like it a lot better than waiting tables."

"Great! I'll pick you up at 3:00 PM; you can drop me off at home. Then if you have any questions, give me a call."

112

Bob dropped Ahote off at his place. Ahote went straight to bed. He fell asleep as his head hit the pillow. He felt secure knowing he had a job that better suited his lifestyle.

Chapter 16

Saturday night—party night at the university. It was a night of firsts for Lomasi. It was the end of her first week of classes. It was her first party of many as she began her new life. Excitement reverberated throughout the whole day. She became concerned that anticipation would spoil the party for her, that her expectations could surmount reality. *Tonight is the first night I will be known as Lola,* she thought. She loved her new life as a student. She looked in the mirror. *I am Lola. I am sexy. I am inquisitive. I am beautiful, charming, and witty.* She said to her self, *For the first time, I feel genuinely feminine.* The friends she made this evening would be the first friends she made with her new identity.

Lola found it hard to concentrate all day. Saturday was the perfect day to get things done. She should spend her time doing the necessary reading to start on the paper due next week. She should start her novel. A novel would be the ideal senior project—she should get started on it early. She should wash her clothes and clean her dorm room. Yet, she did everything but what she should do. She spent most of her time in front of the mirror, trying on different clothes. She wanted to create a good impression for the new friends she would make. She wanted to appear cosmopolitan. She picked up her cell phone and dialed.

"Hi, Rachel, it's Lola."

"Lola?" Rachel replied. "Lola, of course, how are you?"

"I'm fine. I just called about the party tonight. I am at a loss for what I should wear."

"It's casual. Just come as you are."

"Do I need to bring anything?" Lola asked.

"We are going to have a keg of beer," Rachel said. "If you want any other beverage, you will have to bring it."

"Would you like me to bring a snack along?" Lola asked.

"No, just put on a pair of old jeans and a comfortable sweatshirt; bring yourself. We'll start around 7:00 PM."

"See you then," Lola said. She wasn't going to wear a sweatshirt. *I want to look attractive, yet I don't want to be the center of attention,* she thought.

At eight o'clock, Lola was approaching her destination. Rachel's house overlooking the river was lit up, displaying all its grandeur. Lola was a little intimidated by what she might find. After all, this was the West Bank of the university—it was *l'avant garde.* She thought about the trailer that she lived in on Bluewater Road and compared it to the mansion in front of her that one of the pioneers of Minneapolis built from the fortune he made in wheat. *This is an adventure,* she said to herself. *I am Lola and I am up to it.*

Lola walked through the door confidently and looked around. There were a lot of people at the party already. There was a fire in the fireplace that not only warmed the room but created an atmosphere of welcome. She was wearing faded blue jeans and a blue sweater— clothes that showed off her figure but were not ostentatious. She headed for the kitchen. If she did not find Rachel there, she knew she would find the keg. *There's always someone around the keg who is talkative,* she thought to herself. She spotted a familiar face.

"Diane, do you remember me? It's Lola."

"Oh, hi, Lola, thanks for coming," Diane said as she tried to remember where she had met this attractive black-haired girl before.

"Is Rachel around?" Lola asked.

"She is here somewhere," Diane replied. Now she remembered. "Aren't you Lomasi?"

"I changed my name to Lola. I'll explain later, but please call me Lola," she said imploringly.

"Lola, how charming." Diane nodded understandingly. "Let me introduce you to some one of my roommates. This is Harmony."

"Hi, Harmony," Lola said. "I love your house."

"It's not mine," Harmony corrected her. "I just rent a room, but I love it, too. Where do you live?"

"I live on the East Bank," Lola answered. She did not want Harmony to know she lived in the dorm.

"Did you just start school?" Harmony asked.

"Yes, I'm a freshman," Lola answered. "I met Rachel during the lunch break at orientation. She talked me into skipping the rest of the orientation. We spent the afternoon walking by the river and became friends. She invited me to the party."

"Well, you're always welcome here," Harmony said. "We were thinking of turning the house into a sorority, just to show the sorority girls on the East Bank that they have nothing on us. We decided it would be too snobbish. Still, we're a close-knit bunch of girls and you're welcome to join us."

"Thanks," Lola said. "I've met so many new friends recently; it has been a great experience." Lola felt a little self-conscious, so she looked around and said, "I'm going to look for Rachel to let her know I'm here."

"Last time I saw her, she was going upstairs," Harmony said. "She has been giving everyone a tour of the house."

Lola was relieved. She didn't have to make any explanations of her name. Lola was accepted without question. She went upstairs to find Rachel.

"Where did she come from?" Harmony asked Diane. "She has unusually dark skin."

"She's a friend of Rachel's," Diane said. "She is from northern Minnesota somewhere. I think she's Native American."

"That's what I thought," Harmony said. "She acts like she's from the reservation."

"Not everyone can be as sophisticated as you." Diane's sarcasm escaped Harmony.

"Well, at least you don't have to worry about keeping me away from the fire water," Harmony retorted. "I'll keep an eye on the squaw for you."

They turned their attention to the new arrivals coming through the door.

"Hi, Rachel, thanks for inviting me to your party. It looks like it is getting off to a great start," Lola said as she finished ascending the stairs.

"Lomasi...I'm sorry, Lola." Rachel blushed. "I'm glad to see you could make it."

"I wouldn't have missed it for the world," Lola replied. "I just finished my first week of school and already I am tired of studying."

"Lola, this is Stanley," Rachel said. "He's an architecture student. I was just showing him around the house."

"Nice to meet you, Lola," Stanley said as he shook her hand. "Rachel has been telling me about her home off campus, but I just thought she was exaggerating about how nice it was."

"Yeah, there is even a widow's walk," Rachel told them. "I have to put on some more music. Stanley, why don't you take Lola to the kitchen and get her something to drink?"

Rachel winked at Lola as she walked away. Lola gave Rachel a knowing smile. They both thought Stanley was a hunk.

"Well, shall we?" Stanley asked.

Lola smiled and said, "Why not?" as she and her new friend descended the stairs back into the party.

Lola was impressed by the party. Her only social experience had been high school parties until now. Grand Rapids had a population of ten thousand. The Minneapolis campus alone boasted sixty thousand students. Lola thought this was the most sophisticated party she had ever attended. People were discussing everything from literature to current events. Everyone seemed to be up on the latest trends on campus. As a matter of fact, that is how she would describe the scene if she were writing about it—trendy. She had a desire to be a part of it. She was excited because everyone treated her as if she belonged.

As the night wore on, Lola was getting tired and looked for her friend.

"I'm exhausted," Lola explained to Rachel. "I'm thinking about going home."

"Lola, it's too early to go home. We are just getting started."

"But almost everyone has left or is leaving," Lola explained. She thought that Rachel was a little tipsy.

"I know," Rachel admitted. She did not want the night to end. "All of the girls are going out for pizza afterwards. You've never been to Mama Rosas Restaurant? You should come with us."

"I don't know—I've got to start my novel in the morning," Lola replied.

"Nonsense," Rachel said assertively. "You need something to eat after drinking beer. Besides that, how will you get home—walk? We'll get some pizza, then I'll give you a ride home."

"Okay," Lola acquiesced.

"Diane, you ride with Lola and me," Rachel said. "Harmony and Carol, you ride with Colleen. We'll meet at Mama Rosas."

They all got in their cars and drove a short distance to the landmark Italian restaurant. It was 2:30 AM. The bar crowd was just finishing their meal. They found a table for six in the corner and ordered two large pizzas.

"Well, I'd say that the party was a success," Rachel said.

"There's going to be a lot to clean up tomorrow," Colleen pointed out.

"Yes, but we wanted to set the tone for the school year. I think we did that," Carol said.

"Yeah, my first two years of school, I lived in a dumpy place. I was ashamed to entertain my friends there," Rachel said. "I never felt a part of the university experience. I felt like an outsider. Now we have a great place to live not too far from school."

"Yeah, life will be a lot more interesting for us now," Harmony said. "Especially Lola—Stanley followed her around the party like a puppy."

"He was just being friendly. He's shy," Lola replied. She had never thought of herself as being attractive. She noticed at the party that she was getting a lot of attention from the male students who attended. She did not want to admit it, but she was secretly pleased.

"You had him wrapped around your little finger," Diane said.

"I didn't know you were so interested in architecture, Lola," Harmony said sarcastically.

"Yeah, you seemed really interested in how things were built, especially Stanley," Diane said. She seemed a little under the influence still.

"Here comes our pizzas," Lola said. She seemed happy for the distraction. She did not care for Diane's crass comments. So what if a boy was attracted to her? It was her business.

"Taxi," someone yelled at the front door. All the girls looked. Here was this gorgeous-looking taxi driver. He was tall, dark, and muscular. He had dark eyes and long, shiny black hair.

"It looks like my taxi is here," Rachel said in a low voice to the group. "I better get going."

They all giggled.

"You drove," Diane said with a smirk. "You can't just leave us here."

"Why not?" Rachel asked. "You can ride with Colleen, or walk, for all I care."

While her friends ogled the cab driver, Lola tried to sink further into the corner. She did not want her friends to know that the cab driver was her childhood friend Ahote and she did not want Ahote to see her here.

"I think he looks like a wretch," Harmony said. "He's probably just waiting to get some drunk, young, unsuspecting girl in the cab so he can take advantage of her. He's obviously a low life."

"I just wish it was me," Rachel said.

"Harmony, you are always so straight-laced," Colleen said. "Don't you ever let your hair down and have some fun?"

"I'm not some tramp that lets anyone pick me up," Harmony said. "I have standards!"

"Oh, Harmony," Diane said. "You just don't want anyone to have any fun. Face it—you think sex is for procreation and even then a girl should feel guilty while she's doing it."

Harmony was turning crimson. It was hard to tell if she was mad or just embarrassed.

"There he goes," Rachel said as Ahote walked out with the person who ordered the cab. "While we sat around talking, we missed our chance. Now let's eat our pizza. We need our strength in case he comes back."

Everyone started to focus on the business at hand—veggie pizza. They finished eating, then got in their cars to return home. Rachel and Lola rode together; ostensibly, Rachel had to drop Lola off at the dorm.

"It's getting late. Why don't you stay over at my place tonight?" Rachel asked. "We could all have breakfast in the morning. I'll take you home after we eat."

It wasn't a very persuasive argument, yet Lola was tempted. She wondered what it was about Rachel that made it difficult to say no. "Thanks for asking," Lola said. "I'd like to but I have a lot to do tomorrow and need to get up early. I really like your house; maybe some other time."

"It's already early," Rachel said. "It'd be the perfect ending to a perfect evening. Are you sure you won't change your mind?"

Why am I so attracted to her? Lola wondered. She wanted to say yes. "No, I need to go home. Thanks anyways," Lola said. "I can just walk home if you are tired."

"I'll give you a ride," Rachel said. "It's not safe for a girl to be walking around alone this time of night. I feel responsible for my friends."

Rachel dropped Lola off at her dorm. Lola went inside and went straight to bed. She was tired but could not sleep. She stared at the drawing of her mother on the wall. Her mother always seemed to have a knowing smile. Did she understand what her daughter was experiencing?

Lola pondered the evening. The party was great—she got to meet a lot of new people and enjoyed more stimulating conversation than she had previously experienced. She was disturbed by how she reacted to seeing Ahote though. Where did he come from? She had no idea he was driving cab in Minneapolis. Why was she ashamed of her old friend? Finally, she thought about Rachel. She was pleased with her new friend. It was nice of Rachel to invite her to her party and include her in her circle of friends. She had taken Lola under her wing in many ways. Lola wondered what she meant by "the perfect ending to a perfect evening." She decided not to read too much into what her friend had said. There was not any sense in looking for meanings that may not be there.

Chapter 17

Spring 1982

It was the end of spring quarter. The relief was visible on the faces around campus. Mike and Cyrus finished their final exams and were getting ready for the long trek up north.

"I am so tired of studying! I am so glad it is summer break," Mike said. "If I had to write one more paper, take one more final, I'd go mad."

"I hear you," Cyrus replied. "I don't know how people are able to go to school in the summer. I'm burnt out after three quarters of school."

"Let's pack our things and get out of here," Mike said. "We deserve a break."

"Yeah, I have been looking forward to Bluewater Lake," Cyrus said.

"I've been looking forward to seeing Sandy again."

"Is that all you can think about?" Cyrus asked. "Here I'm dreaming about the peace and solitude of northern Minnesota and all you can think about is getting laid."

"Of course," Mike replied. "I have Sandy to think about. She'll be happy to see me. She missed me."

"She's married, Mike. You're amazing. Life for you is one continuous party."

"Cyrus, you're so naïve. You'll see when we get up there. And what's wrong with partying? A man has to enjoy himself. I work hard!"

"Well, let's get ready; the northland is waiting for us. School will be here when we get back," Cyrus said.

"Yeah, it is time to replenish our money supply and do some real work instead of all of this academic crap."

"I don't know how you do it," Cyrus said.

"What do you mean, Cyrus?"

"You don't seem to take school seriously. You're a party animal. Still, you have a B average."

"Live in the moment," Mike said. "Do what you are doing right now to the best of your ability. Enjoy life to the fullest."

"Is that another one of Mike King's homilies?" Cyrus quipped.

Mike just shrugged it off. They started packing. Mike was the financial manager. He was a financial phenom. The money he received from his nightclubs, he plowed back into the business and built up a reserve to purchase more clubs in the future. He took the profits they made from managing the resort, created a budget, and ran their household in Miami. He paid Cyrus a wage that allowed him to support himself while going to school and shared some of the profits at the end of the summer. Mike purchased an older Lincoln Town Car to drive back to Minnesota in comfort and still have room for their belongings. Even though Mike was becoming a wealthy man at an early age, he was unassuming and down-to-earth.

They left mid morning. It took about thirty-three hours to drive from Miami to the resort. Mike figured if they took turns driving and drove straight through the night, they would arrive at their destination the next day in the afternoon. Cyrus was not for the marathon drive, but Mike insisted and he acquiesced.

Bluewater Lake was like glass. The springtime sun warmed everyone and everything. The northwoods were just coming to life with a green hue that delighted their eyes. The only sound was the song of birds celebrating the triumph of spring. They had one week to get the resort ready. They unpacked their belongings and got the lodge ready for their stay.

"This should be old hat to you by now," Mike said.

"Yeah, I remember what to do," Cyrus said. "But, I think the first thing I am going to do is go for a swim."

"Do you know how cold that water is?"

"Aw, come on," Cyrus replied. "What are you, a wimp?"

"I guess the shower would be cold anyways," Mike said as he put his swimming trunks on.

The water was cold, and the swim was short but invigorating. Afterwards they decided to put one of the docks in the water for their own use. Then they launched a fishing boat so they could catch their supper. A couple weeks after ice-out was the perfect time for fishing and they soon had their limit of crappies. They cleaned the fish and Mike coated the fish with cracker crumbs according to his secret recipe.

"Nothing like fish, straight from the lake to the frying pan," Cyrus said as they sat down for their dinner.

122

"You're right," Mike replied. "You know, what we need around here is a woman's touch. I wonder if Sandy would be willing to come back to work here. We can afford to hire some help and it would give us more time to enjoy the summer break."

"It wouldn't hurt to ask her," Cyrus replied. "Why don't we just run an ad in the Grand Rapids newspaper and see what happens?"

"I'd rather just hire Sandy," Mike said. "She has worked here before and knows what to do. She lives right down the road. I wonder if that loser husband of hers would let her work here."

Cyrus gave a sly look to Mike and said, "Is there any other reason you would like her to work here?"

"No," Mike said emphatically. Then, knowing he didn't fool anyone, he added, "Well, maybe—there is something about a woman you can't have. When she worked here the last time, I thought she was just playing hard to get. Then I found out she had a boyfriend—her husband, now. I was crushed. I was younger then, but I find I still think about her. I wonder how she is doing."

"Well, go for it," Cyrus said. "If you don't, you will always wonder why you did not even try."

Mike grabbed the phone book. He picked up the phone and called Sandy.

"Hi, is Sandy there?"

"Who is this?" Sandy asked.

"Mike King from Bluewater Resort."

"Hi, Mike, this is Sandy. Why are you calling?"

"We're just opening the resort. We're looking for someone to help out. Are you available?"

"I don't know—what did you have in mind?"

"It would be the same job as before. You will get the cabins ready for new guests. Keep an eye on the office," Mike said.

"I'll think about it," Sandy replied.

Sandy put down the phone and turned her attention back to the television. She was bored. As she thought about Mike King, an impish grin revealed her thoughts. He always had a lech for her and she had led him on those summers she worked for the resort. She was in a relationship now. Still, the naughty side of her couldn't help but think about Mike's offer. What did it mean? She had heard that another guy, Cyrus, ran the resort with Mike last summer. She wondered if both of them would fall in love with her if she took the job. That could be interesting. She had been laid off from her job in town. It would be convenient for her to work close to home and it was only for the summer. It might even be fun.

On the other hand, she was committed to Dan. Was it right for her to work at the resort, knowing that Mike had hired her because he was still attracted to her? She couldn't stop thinking about the resort and the mischief she could cause. It was a lot of fun to work there and many of the guests were the same people every year. They knew her; it would be fun to see them again. She would talk it over with Dan. They could use the money.

"It looks like we have hired help," Mike said.

"When does she start?" Cyrus asked.

"She said she would think about it," Mike replied.

"That doesn't exactly inspire confidence, Mike. We could use someone to watch the office. Thinking about it doesn't necessarily mean she will help."

"I know, but you have to give her time," Mike said. "She is not working now and she could probably use the money. Besides, you have to admit, the working conditions here are not bad."

"I wish I had your confidence," Cyrus said. He had only met Sandy once last year, but he knew he would be happy to work with her.

"She'll see it our way," Mike said. "We are going to have a great summer!"

"Dan, I have a job offer," Sandy said. "Bluewater Resort called. They would like me to work there for the summer."

"I don't know." Dan thought about it for a minute. "I don't like the idea of you working with that Mike King."

"I know—I wonder about that, too, but we need the money and it is convenient to work close to home."

"Still, I don't like it," Dan said. "Maybe we should move away from here—there are better jobs in a large metropolitan area."

"I like it here," Sandy said. "My mother is right next door. When we decide to have children, she can be our babysitter."

"Sara works full-time," Dan pointed out. "She won't be able to provide day care; besides, we can't afford to have a family right now."

"Well, I like the idea of working at the resort, at least until something better comes along. It will give me something to do and we need the money."

"I want to think about it," Dan said. "We'll talk about it again tomorrow. Let's take advantage of this beautiful weather and go for a walk, then I have to go to work." Dan knew when he had lost an argument. Maybe if he put off the decision, Sandy would forget about it.

"All right, I'll get ready."

Dan and Sandy walked the trails behind their home, then Dan left for work.

Mike and Cyrus spent most of their time the first week preparing for the first guests that would arrive the next Saturday. They opened all of the cabins and cleaned them. They put fresh linen on the beds. Once the cabins were ready, they started preparing the outside amenities. The big job was the docks. There were four of them. No matter how they tried to avoid it, one of them had to put on waders and get in the cold water to adjust the dock level correctly. Once that was done, they set to work on the grounds.

"We're all set for the first guests," Mike said.

"Yeah, we finished a day early," Cyrus replied. "What should we do?"

"We should play," Mike said. "Come on—there is something I did not show you last summer."

"Where are we going?" Cyrus asked.

"We're going for a jog."

They got their jogging clothes on and started up Bluewater Road. They took the path that led to the Joyce estate. They came to a path going off to the west.

"Look at this rock," Cyrus said. He pointed to a rock just before the path that was partially covered by the underbrush. "It looks like a marker."

"Maybe it is," Mike said cryptically as they turned left down the path.

Cyrus was beginning to wonder where they were going when suddenly they emerged from the forest into a clearing. Cyrus found himself looking at a majestic waterfall with a large pool in front of it. Opposite the waterfall, there was a stream that exited the pool and flowed into the woods.

"Wow, when did you find out about this?" Cyrus asked.

"I used to explore the area when I was a kid," Mike replied.

"Is the pool very deep? It looks like a great place for a swim."

"It's not deep and the water is clear. It's probably a little cold this time of the year. Follow me," Mike said as he moved toward a little-used path that was hardly distinguishable from the vegetation that surrounded it. "Wait till you see what's next."

They followed the path to the falls. Cyrus could not keep his eyes off the pool. The water had a bluish tint that captured his imagination. He pondered what had taken place around here over the centuries. When they got to the waterfall, Mike started to go behind it. Cyrus was concerned.

"Where are you taking me?"

"Come on, Cyrus. Quit being so timid—you are going to like this."

Mike went behind the waterfall and disappeared. Cyrus did not know what to think. He mustered up his courage and ducked under the waterfall. He saw an opening in the rock wall. Mike stuck his head back outside and said, "Follow me, you coward."

Cyrus could hardly believe his eyes. "It's a cave," Cyrus said as he stepped inside.

"Yeah, it is an old Indian cave," Mike explained. He shined the flashlight he had brought along. Cyrus could see little portions of the cave the flashlight beam illuminated.

"Look at this artwork," Mike said to Cyrus as he pointed the flashlight at the wall. Time passed quickly as he gave Cyrus a tour of the cave.

"I don't know how long we have been in here. We should get back to the resort," Cyrus said. "It could be dark outside already."

Mike turned his flashlight to the totem pole. "Look at that mug," he said as he pointed to the carving of Chief Wabana.

"What's that?" Cyrus asked.

"It's a totem pole."

"No, I mean, what's that noise? It sounds like voices."

Mike stuck his head outside the cave. "Take a look," he whispered to Cyrus. "Careful, so they don't see us."

Cyrus and Mike peeked outside the cave. They were concealed by the waterfall. At the other end of the pool, they could see a group of people dressed in traditional Native American garb approach the pool at the opposite end of the waterfall. They started a fire in the pit and gathered around it. One of the Indians started playing the tom-tom drums while the rest began to chant and dance around the fire.

126

"I didn't realize anyone else came here," Mike told Cyrus. "Quiet—we'll see where this leads."

"It looks like these people came from a different century. I don't want to see where this leads," Cyrus pleaded. "Let's get out of here before they find us."

"We can't leave without them seeing us," Mike reasoned. "We're trapped. We have to wait it out." Mike took out his camera from his pack and started taking pictures.

"You brought a camera?" Cyrus asked.

"Yeah, I wanted to take pictures of the artwork in the cave, but this is better."

The leader took a woman by the hand and started dancing with her around the fire. The rest of the group sat in a circle around the fire and continued to chant. They were passing a bottle of liquor, smoking marijuana, and egging the dancers on. Soon it was just the woman dancing. She was moving suggestively to the beat of the drums.

Mike kept taking pictures and the scene unfolded. "Now that's what I call a squaw," he said.

"I can't believe we are watching this," Cyrus said squeamishly. "I just hope we get out of this alive."

"Relax, they're getting so high that they'll never notice us," Mike assured Cyrus. "Just give them a little more time to get really drunk, then we'll duck behind that rock and sneak out through the woods. In the meantime, I want to see what happens."

Cyrus was seriously frightened, but Mike continued on. He took pictures as fast as he could. The woman started to disrobe while she danced. When she was naked, she picked up the pace of the dancing. Then she took a younger woman by the hand and brought her into the circle. The younger woman seemed reluctant, but the crowd kept singing and chanting. She had no alternative but to start dancing, too. After a while, she looked like she was enjoying herself as she disrobed to the music also. The drums kept beating faster and the dancing, drinking, and smoking became more intense. The men got up and started dancing with the women. Then the whole scene degenerated into an orgy with the young girl the center of attention.

"All right, let's make a break for it," Mike said. "Follow me." He crouched; using the foliage as cover, he moved quickly to a large boulder, followed by Cyrus. While they hid behind the boulder, Mike said, "On the count of three, we run into the woods. They won't notice us." He counted to three and they ran into the woods. They didn't stop running until they reached the main hiking trail.

"Am I ever glad to get out of there," Cyrus said.

"Yeah, I don't like the feeling of being trapped," Mike said. "On the other hand, it was entertaining. We should have joined the fun."

"Your new camera certainly got a workout. Are you going to be able to find someone that is willing to develop those pictures?"

"I can develop them myself," Mike said. "I can rig a darkroom in the lodge. I have all the equipment necessary to develop negatives and print pictures."

"You're amazing. Did you ever think this was going to happen?"

"There have always been rumors of strange things going on around here. About Chief Wabana and wild parties, but I never believed them until now."

"Why were you going to take pictures in the cave?"

"I was planning on taking pictures of the artwork. I thought I might be able to sell some of the pictures to a magazine. The publicity would be good for business at the resort."

"Well, you've got some porno pictures now," Cyrus said. "What are you going to do with them?"

"First, we'll see how they turn out," Mike said thoughtfully. "Then we'll see what happens. Did that woman dancing look familiar to you?"

"No, it was like nothing I have ever seen before. Why? Do you know who she is?"

"I have my suspicions."

Mike and Cyrus started jogging back to the resort. When they got back to the lodge, Mike started working on the darkroom right away. He was anxious to see how the pictures turned out. The lodge had a large basement. Mike covered the window with cardboard and set up his equipment on a table in the corner. He brought a special light bulb along so he could see what he was doing without damaging the light-sensitive film. He developed the negatives and printed a few of the pictures. The quality was excellent.

"Cyrus," Mike said as he walked into the office. "Look at these—they really turned out good."

"Wow, you would think from looking at the pictures that you were standing right next to them. You're a good photographer," Cyrus said as he ogled the pictures. He didn't want to put them down.

"Thanks. Sandy really is quite a babe."

"That will be an afternoon I'll remember for the rest of my life," Cyrus said. "Maybe you should change your major to photography."

"You get back to getting ready for the guests while I finish printing the rest of the pictures."

"Yeah, I almost forgot our guests will be arriving tomorrow," Cyrus said with a sense of urgency.

The next day as the guests were arriving, the phone rang. "I'll get it," Cyrus said as he answered the phone. "Bluewater Resort," Cyrus said. "How can I help you?"

"Hi, is this Mike?" A female voice asked.

"Just a minute, please. I will get him for you."

"Mike, it's for you."

"This is Mike."

"Hi, Mike, this is Sandy."

"Sandy, thanks for calling. I was just thinking about you," Mike said with a sly smile.

"I was thinking about your offer to work at the resort this summer," Sandy said. "I would be able to work four days a week."

"That would be great," Mike said. "We need someone to work in the office and give us some help with the chores. You're already familiar with the job."

"Good. It's for the summer, then?"

"We close the resort after Labor Day weekend."

"When do you want me to start?" Sandy asked.

"The guests have already started arriving. Would tomorrow be too soon?" Mike asked. "We could use help as soon as possible."

"Tomorrow will work. I'll see you about nine o'clock."

"I'll look forward to it," Mike said as he hung up the phone.

"Who was that?" Cyrus asked.

"That was our hired help, Sandy," Mike replied. He looked like the cat that caught the canary.

Chapter 18

"FIVE DOLLARS!" Rachel screamed. Lola and Rachel hadn't anticipated paying a cover charge to get into Bennington's, one of the hottest new bars in downtown Minneapolis. They grudgingly paid the five dollars each and went inside. They were early enough to get a table. As their eyes adjusted to the light, they could see the plush surroundings in the bar. It was tastefully decorated; black leather covered the chairs and booths. The floor was plush with thick black and scarlet carpet. There was a large bar and ample room to dance. The band was setting up their equipment when the waiter came to take their order.

"Two drafts," Rachel told the waiter. "This is my treat; you've been stuck inside the library too long. We are going to have some fun tonight."

"You didn't have to do that." Lola saw the finality in Rachel's eyes and said, "Thank you."

"Don't worry about it," Rachel said. "I remember those student days. Now that I have graduated and have a respectable job as a barmaid, I can afford to treat."

Rachel's sarcasm was not lost on Lola. The time Rachel spent mastering her instrument and studying for her bachelor's degree did not guarantee employment as a musician.

While they were talking, the waiter brought their beer. A steady trickle of patrons entered the bar. The beer was as cold as the day had been hot; it was the perfect night for listening to music. Lola and Rachel were having a great time talking about everything under the sun. The band started playing and people started dancing.

"Care to dance?" a handsome young man said to Rachel.

"No, my friend and I are just here for a quick drink," Rachel replied tactfully as the young man walked away dejected.

"Men are always falling all over you," Lola said to Rachel. "In school I was jealous of you. The good-looking guy would always come up to you while I always sat and tried to make conversation with his shy friend."

"You make me feel guilty," Rachel said. "I was jealous of you because you were so smart. If I could write like you, my musical career would skyrocket."

"Rachel, I am complimented by your high opinion of my writing," Lola said carefully. "But my lyrics are lousy."

"You just don't realize how talented you are," Rachel replied.

"Lomasi, what are you doing here?" a man asked as he approached their table.

"Cyrus." Lola forced a smile as she stood up. Cyrus was the last person she would like to see again. "I could say the same thing about you. Did my mother pay you to follow me around?"

"No, nothing as glamorous as spy work," Cyrus replied. "I'm attending a conference at the university. They recommended this establishment at my hotel. I am surprised to see someone I know."

"Cyrus, this is my friend Rachel," Lola said.

"Nice to meet you, Rachel," Cyrus said. "I'm Cyrus Longfell, a friend of Lola's family."

Cyrus couldn't believe his luck. He had been dying to see Lomasi outside the office. When they were working together in the summer, Lola's grandmother, Sara, was always around. Even though Cyrus supervised Sara's work as a nurse practitioner, she was pretty much a chaperone when it came to Lomasi around the office. Besides, Lomasi looked grown-up now, out with her girlfriend at a bar in Minneapolis.

He remembered the incident in the supply closet—she was like putty in his hands. He longed to be alone with her again. It was surreal, like the movies, where even though the bar was full of people, Cyrus could just see Lomasi and himself.

Rachel exchanged a look of recognition with Lola. Rachel remembered the story Lola had told her regarding the incident with her former employer. The look she received back from Lola told her that this was the guy.

"Come on, Cyrus," Lola said. "Be honest—you were my boss when I worked at the clinic."

"True, I own the clinic. I like to think the people that work for me think of me as a friend, not the boss," Cyrus replied. "Speaking of being friends, as long as we're here, why don't we dance?"

"Maybe in a little while—I don't like this song." Lola did not want to say no; she wanted Cyrus to hang around. She could tell Rachel had something in mind.

"Do you mind if I leave my drink here while I go to the restroom?" Cyrus asked as he put his drink down and walked away.

"Is he the guy from the supply closet?" Rachel asked.

"Yes," Lola replied. She was still repulsed thinking about it. "He is also my grandma's boss, so I have to be careful that what I do does not affect her."

"Well, he gives me the creeps," Rachel said. "I can tell he likes you."

"Yeah, I'll try to ignore him," Lola replied. "He's old enough to be my father."

"We should teach him a lesson," Rachel said.

"What did you have in mind?" Lola said. She looked at her friend with a mischievous smile.

"You know how men are," Rachel said. "Give them a few drinks and they think with their pecker."

"So," Lola said, "tell me something I didn't know."

"He obviously would like to be with you," Rachel said. "Let's lead him on. Make an excuse; leave him here with me. I'll take care of the rest."

"Okay, but be careful," Lola said. "Here he comes."

"I meant to ask you," Cyrus asked as he sat down with them, "how is school going?"

"It seems like a lot of work just for a four-year degree," Lola replied. "It's taking forever."

"The time will go by fast enough," Cyrus replied knowingly. "You will look back on college in time and be glad that you did it."

"Thanks, Cyrus, I know you are right," Lola said. "That reminds me, I have a paper due tomorrow. I have to go home and work on it. Why don't you two get to know each other better?" Lola winked at Rachel as she got up to leave.

"It was nice to see you, Lomasi," Cyrus said as he looked at her lustfully.

"She is really working hard to do well in school," Rachel observed. "I'm glad she had the chance to get out a little and enjoy herself."

"Yes," Cyrus observed. "This is the time in her career she needs to sacrifice some of her free time. In the future, she will be happy she did. How did you two get to know each other?"

"We were undergraduates together at the university," Rachel explained. "I was a music major."

"That's an interesting area of endeavor," Cyrus said.

"Yes, I play the guitar. Lola would write words to my music. She has a lovely voice."

"She is a talented person," Cyrus said. "Enough about her—what about you? What do you do?"

"I'm a musician," Rachel explained, "which means I am a full-time waitress who plays whenever I get the chance."

"Sounds like a tough way to make a living," Cyrus said.

"It is challenging," Rachel replied. "But once you get established, you can make a lot of money in the music industry. It's also my passion—I love doing it."

"Enough about work," Cyrus said. "We came here to play. Let's dance."

"Sounds great," Rachel said as she got up, took Cyrus by the hand, and led him to the dance floor.

Cyrus was pleasantly surprised at what a great dancer Rachel was. She moved naturally to the music. She was wearing tight-fitting blue jeans and a knit top that highlighted her large breasts. She moved rhythmically with artful yet primitive moves that gave her a sultry appearance on the dance floor—something that was not lost on the other males in the bar. The band started playing a slow dance and Cyrus asked Rachel if she would like to sit down. She gave Cyrus an impish look and put her arms on him in slow-dance position. It was a romantic song and Rachel pressed her breasts against Cyrus' chest while they danced. At the end of the dance, Rachel put her arms around Cyrus and ground her hips into his body. Then they sat down again.

The band took a break. Cyrus was mesmerized by this woman he had just met. He had forgotten about Lola completely. Rachel smiled at Cyrus as she rubbed her leg against his under the table.

'You're quite the dancer," Rachel said to Cyrus. She moved her chair so she was sitting next to him at the table.

"You just bring out the best in me," Cyrus replied. "I don't get a chance to dance much in Grand Rapids. It's a quiet town."

"How long will you be staying in Minneapolis?" Rachel asked.

"My conference was over today," Cyrus said. "I did not want to fight rush-hour traffic to get back to Grand Rapids tonight. I'm going to leave tomorrow morning. Now that I met you, I'm glad I was in no hurry to leave."

Rachel put her hand on Cyrus' leg under the table. "You're sexy," Rachel said. "Too bad you're leaving so soon. We'll have to make good use of our time," she said as she gently stroked him between the legs. Cyrus almost lost control right then and there.

"I have to go to the ladies' room." Rachel smiled coyly as she got up and started towards the restrooms. Cyrus could not take his eyes off her lovely behind as she got lost in the crowd. All that was left of her was a devilish giggle that hung in the air as she walked past the restrooms and snuck out the back door.

Chapter 19

Summer 1982
It's show time! Suggestive music blared from the loudspeakers. Sandy stepped onto the stage timidly. She could feel the warmth of the spotlight as it illuminated her. The brightness interfered with her vision; everything else in the theater was enveloped in darkness. There were applause and catcalls emanating from the audience. She felt embarrassed and at the same time thrilled; a bolt of excitement traveled through her body. She was living her fantasy of performing an exotic dance in front of a live audience.

"We love your resort," a voice interrupted her daydream. It brought her back to reality. She was at the front desk of the resort.

"We are going to take some wonderful memories of Bluewater Lake home with us," Bob Westerman said to Sandy. "We hate to check out. It seems like we just got here, but it is time to go home already."

"Thank you," Sandy said. She was flushed. Instead of performing a graceful dance, she was stumbling over her words. She hoped Bob didn't notice. "I can't take credit for running the resort, but we do work hard to make sure everyone enjoys their stay."

"Don't you live here?"

"No, I live down Bluewater Road a little ways. I have been helping out at the resort since I was a kid. It's a nice place to work in the summer."

"You've have done a very nice job—our children are going to miss you."

"I will miss them, too. They are adorable," Sandy replied.

"What do you do in the winter?" Bob asked.

"Good question," Sandy replied. She flashed back to her fantasy of being an exotic dancer. "I'll cross that bridge when I come to it."

"Well, you have made our stay here very enjoyable. Can you put us on the mailing list for the resort?"

"Sure. I have get it from the office—I'll be right back."

Mike King walked into the lodge as Sandy went into the office. "Hi, Bob, can I help you?"

"I'm waiting for Sandy. She is going to put us on your mailing list. We really enjoyed our stay at your resort. We plan to come back next year."

"We book our cabins pretty quickly. If you reserve your cabin now, we can ensure you will stay in the same cabin next year. Would you like to do that?"

"You know, that might not be a bad idea. My wife was going to finish packing and meet me here. I'll ask her, but I think this week next year will be perfect."

"I was planning on having a cup of coffee while I wait for my Ann. Care to join me?"

"It's such a beautiful morning. I'll buy," Mike said. "Why don't we sit at the table on the deck. It would be a shame to waste the sunshine by sitting inside."

Mike and Bob grabbed a cup of coffee and went out the front door.

"You're a lucky guy to work here for the summer," Bob said as they sat down. "How'd you get a job like this?"

"My dad owns the resort. I've worked here every summer since I was eleven years old. I took over managing it last year when the guy that managed it previously retired."

"I was wondering where you went, Bob," Sandy said as she handed him a clipboard. "Just put your name, address, and phone number there and we'll include you when we do our mailings."

"Thank you," Bob said as Sandy walked back inside the lodge.

"Yeah, thank you," Mike said suggestively as he leered at Sandy in her cutoff jeans and tank top. "She's one of the perks of working here."

"She is pretty hot—it's those enticing long legs," Bob mused. "But isn't she married?"

"It doesn't hurt to window shop." Mike and Bob shared a chuckle.

Bob's wife, Ann, came in with their two children and the male banter stopped. *Back to reality,* Bob thought. "Ann, should we sign up to come here again next year? Mike suggested we reserve the cabin now; that way, we can guarantee we stay in the same cabin next year."

"I don't know, Bob—should we just wait?"

"Come on, Mom, we have to come back," the children cried in unison. They had fallen in love with the resort and the Irish Setter, Fletcher. The dog was their constant companion for the entire week. "We want to have the same cabin and the same dog again."

"Okay, let's book it now," Ann said. "We had such a nice time and Sandy was so helpful with the kids. You're really lucky to have her working here, Mike."

"Yeah, we are going to miss Sandy and Fletcher," the kids rang out. "Can we take Fletcher with us?"

Ann laughed. "Then it is settled. We will come here next year to see Sandy and the dog. The car is packed and we have a long drive ahead of us. Let's get going."

"You get the kids in the car; I'll reserve the cabin," Bob said.

Bob and Mike went back into the lodge.

"Sandy, would you help reserve cabin number five for Bob and Ann? They are going to vacation here again next year," Mike said as he walked behind the front desk and into his office.

Mike began taking care of the routine office work while Sandy helped Bob. He prepared a file for Bob and Ann. All the time he was doing this, he could not help thinking about the scene he had witnessed at the waterfall. He still had the pictures locked in his desk. That had to be Sandy in those pictures. He looked out the office door. Sandy was standing there with her back turned to him. He relished the sight of those tight-fitting blue-jean shorts. He had dreamed about those lovely long legs. He made up his mind. He took two of the more sexually explicit pictures of the woman that looked like Sandy and the medicine man from his desk and put them under the file he had made for Bob and Ann on top of his desk. *She can't miss seeing these,* he thought.

"I made a file for Bob and Ann and put it on my desk," Mike said as he walked out of the office toward the door of the lodge. "When you are done helping Bob, put the paperwork in the file. Then put them on our guest calendar, please."

"Sounds good," Sandy said. She rolled her eyes as she looked at Bob and Ann. Sometimes Mike could be overbearing. She finished with Bob and Ann's paperwork and put it on the desk, grabbed a cup of coffee, and sat down on the deck to take a break.

After Sandy finished her break, she went into the office, and picked up the paperwork and the file. Looking down, she saw the pictures that Mike placed under the file. At first she just thought it was a childish prank, leaving porno pictures for her to see. When she recognized herself in the pictures, she almost fainted. She sat down at the desk and tried to gather her thoughts. At first she was inclined to bolt out of here. She could just leave now and never come back. But what would happen to the pictures? Were there more pictures? Had anyone seen the pictures besides Mike? It was embarrassing, but the only logical thing to do was confront Mike when he returned. She went back to the front desk in the lobby and continued her work as if nothing had happened. She didn't have to wait too long.

"You did a nice job with Bob and Ann, Sandy," Mike said as he casually walked through the lobby and into his office. "It's working out really well for us having you work here for the summer."

"Quit beating around the bush, Mike," Sandy said angrily as she followed him into the office. "I saw those pictures you left on your desk underneath the file. Where did you get them?"

"I took them just after we got here this year. We were exploring the cave under the waterfall and we heard some noise outside. Fortunately, I had my camera with me."

"Fortunate for whom?" Sandy asked. Then she happened to think. "What do you mean 'we'?"

"Me and Cyrus. We shot a whole roll of film. It was quite entertaining."

"You mean you and Cyrus watched what happened there?" Sandy said. Now she understood why Cyrus kept leering at her. She thought it was just a boyish crush.

"We captured the event in color. Bob seemed awfully pleased with you. Is there a reason for that?"

At first Sandy just wanted to get out of there. She moved closer to the door. Where would she go? She could quit her job and go home, but she liked working here. Could she continue to work for someone who was in a position to blackmail her? She needed to get away to think these things through.

"What do you want me to do with these pictures?" Mike casually asked her as she went out the door.

"What are you going to do with the pictures?" Sandy said. She was surprised she was smiling. She thought it was odd that instead of feeling resentful toward Mike, she was actually attracted to him. She felt warmth spread throughout her whole body. "That is the question."

"Come back in here and close the door. We don't want guests to overhear us."

Sandy complied.

"I thought I could mail them to the *Herald Review* newspaper. I could envision the headline *Ancient Native American ritual on Joyce estate.*" Mike smiled. "Next time, you could have an even bigger audience."

"You wouldn't dare!" Sandy protested. Secretly, she wondered how Mike seemed to look into her soul. She was becoming excited by his brashness and the idea of an audience.

"Why wouldn't I?"

"Drag your name and the resort through all that?" Sandy retorted. "Even you are smarter than that."

"The newspaper takes anonymous leads to stories," Mike suggested. "Come back here let's talk some more."

Sandy walked back and stood in front of the desk. She watched as Mike slid his chair back and pulled down his zipper.

"We could work something out," Mike said suggestively.

"Mike, you're disgusting. To suggest such a thing is perverted." She wondered if Mike could see her nipples becoming erect through her tank top.

"Would you rather I mail these pictures to the paper?"

"Maybe we can work something out," Sandy said as she slowly slid her tank top over her head and tossed it on the floor.

"Come here," Mike said as he pointed to his open zipper. Sandy slowly walked around the desk. Mike grabbed her by the hands and pulled her to her knees.

Chapter 20

As Sara drove Lola back to Minneapolis, she began to appreciate the time she had to herself now that her granddaughter was away at the university. She missed Lomasi. It was nice to have her home for the weekend, but the constant barrage of questions—the same questions, over and over again—was as monotonous as a broken record. Sara gave the same answers over and over again. Sara realized that her granddaughter was upset. She needed information. Did they need to have this discussion again on the way to Minneapolis?

"Why didn't the sheriff conduct a thorough investigation?" Lola asked.

"There were no leads. There still aren't," Sara replied. "You can't expect the sheriff's office to spin their wheels investigating your parents' disappearance. They had other cases, too."

"So they just pushed my parents' disappearance aside?"

"Most missing persons turn up eventually. I suppose that is what the sheriff thought at the time. As time went on and there was no further evidence, they did put it on a back burner, where it remains today."

"Well, I'm going to put it on the front burner again. I am going to solve this mystery."

"Lola, please forget about it," Sara said as they pulled up to the dorm. "You're here at college to develop your career skills, not investigate something that is just as well left alone."

"Why do you always say that? It is not better to leave it alone. There's more," Lola said accusingly to Sara. "You're not telling me everything!"

"There are some things I didn't tell you for your own good. You were too young to understand."

"Too young?" Lola echoed.

"Sandy had her problems. When she was a teenager, she became involved with a crowd from the reservation that got her addicted to drugs."

"My mother was a drug addict?" Lola considered this new information.

"Yes, there were wild parties; alcohol was involved, too. There were drunken brawls and arrests."

"My mother was arrested?" Lola thought of the portrait of her mother; this was incredible.

"Finally, Sandy was admitted to a treatment center. She took the cure. That is where she became involved with an old classmate from school, Dan."

"So they met in a treatment center and got married."

"Not exactly," Sara said. "Dan and Sandy were never married. They just lived together."

"This is so hard to believe," Lola said. "I never dreamed my mother was like that. Why didn't you tell me this before?"

"You were too young. It could affect your development. I was waiting for the right time, but it never seemed appropriate until now."

"You hid things from me purposely!" Lola was livid. "I'm an illegitimate child!"

"Settle down," Sara pleaded. "Now you know everything I know. Arguing with me will not help you." Sara was wondering how much she should tell Lola. She decided this was enough for one day.

"I know, Grandma," Lola said. She calmed down. "I am grateful for everything you've done for me. I do not wish to cause problems for you or anyone else. But this is important to me. This is about who I am. I will solve it and I will solve it in my own way. I am starting my book. As I research my writing, I will uncover information that was overlooked or never came to light. It will become part of my education."

"I understand how you feel, Lola. I just want the best for you. What if you don't like what you find?"

"That is the chance I will have to take," Lola said. She grabbed her backpack and got out of the car. "I love you, Grandma. Thank you for the ride. I'll call you later in the week."

"I love you, too—be careful. Don't let this become an obsession and forget about school," Sara said. She pulled away from the curb and began the long drive home.

Lola felt like she had the tiger by the tail. She could not let go of the tail or her anger. Her desire to solve the mystery was overwhelming. The disappearance was like a radioactive isotope slowly decaying while emitting harmful radiation, exposing her life to the disastrous side effects. Resolution was the only cure to her malady. Where to start was the question.

Lola determined the only thing she could do was to start at the beginning again, to call the sheriff's office. She had spoken to Pat Medura on her first attempt to get information. He was the sheriff during the time her parents disappeared. He sympathized with Lola but could not help her. In reality, he was a manager. He was not an investigator. She felt he was trying to get rid of her. Lola resolved to speak to the person who actually investigated the incident. She was able to get the name of the deputy, Brent Foster. He had retired a few years ago but still lived in the Grand Rapids area. She decided to give him a call.

"Hi, Brent, this is Lola Whitecloud."

"Hi, what can I do for you?"

"You don't know me, but you investigated my parents' disappearance fifteen years ago."

"Sure, I remember—Sandy and Dan."

"They were never found."

"Yes, I know. It was frustrating for me. It was one of cases that bothered me, off and on, all of my career in the department."

"Why do you say that?"

"Well, usually cases like this resolve themselves. There is usually a reasonable explanation. In this case, both husband and wife disappeared, leaving a child behind. We never heard from either of them again. It is highly unusual."

"So you have no idea what happened to them?"

"Nothing we could prove."

"Prove? What do you mean by that?" Lola asked.

"It is just a hunch. Your mom was working for the resort on Bluewater Lake before she and Dan disappeared. I always suspected there was something going on between her and the owner of the resort."

"Like what?"

"I don't know; I could never put my finger on it. I had a gut feeling that Mike King and Cyrus Longfell were somehow involved."

"You mean Cyrus from the Longfell clinic?"

"Yeah, he was going to school with Mike in Miami back then. They would run the resort for the summer, then go back to school in the fall."

"Did you know my parents?"

"Sure, Sandy was a troublemaker when she was young. She got involved with the wrong crowd. I arrested her a couple times. Then she went through treatment, settled down with Dan. He was good for her. Yes, I remember them well."

"Why did you abandon the investigation?"

"I didn't really abandon it. Like I said earlier, the disappearance always puzzled me. It's just that the trail went cold. When we didn't turn up any clues to what happened, we got other calls to investigate. Your parents were put on the back burner. It was something I thought about once in a while but never had time to pursue. I always had the feeling that this incident was just the tip of the iceberg. If we could get the investigation started, we would uncover a lot of illegal activity involving Mike King."

"Did you know my parents when they were in school? What were they like?"

"Sandy was a great student, always at the top of the class. She was popular with the guys."

"What do you mean, 'popular'?"

"She was very attractive. Even though she was younger, most of the guys would have liked to date her. Everyone always wondered what she saw in Dan."

"Why do you say that about Dan?"

"He was just the opposite of Sandy. He wasn't really popular. He was one of the guys that had truancy problems, bad grades—a loser."

"He got a job at the paper mill and worked there for a few years before he disappeared," Lola retorted.

"I know—high school is not necessarily an indication of how successful people will be, but that is the impression everyone had of Dan."

"Is that why the investigation was put on the back burner?"

"No, we just ran into a brick wall. Sandy worked at the resort for several summers. I always thought there was something going on there. All my career as a deputy, I felt that there was something suspicious about Mike King. He made a lot of money over the years. No one knows how much money or how he made it."

That last statement made Lola curious. "Do you think that Mike and Cyrus had something to do with my parents' disappearance?"

"It could be. Your parents disappeared right after they closed the resort for the season. Mike always ran everything. I always thought

Cyrus was a follower. It turned out, Cyrus is pretty smart. He went away to medical school and came back here to work. He has a successful clinic. He's kind of a big shot around here now."

"That doesn't answer my question."

"I know I am being vague, but my suspicion is vague. It regards the whole area up Bluewater Road. We've had numerous calls over the years. There was everything from burglaries of seasonal properties to complaints from hikers walking to the Joyce estate. I could never put my finger on it. I just had a hunch."

"Do you think my parents were involved in it?"

"No, there was nothing to indicate your parents were involved in anything illegal. I just think there was more going on in that area than meets the eye and obviously there was more to your parents' disappearance than we were able to discover."

"So you suspect Mike and Cyrus?"

"You are full of questions," Brent said. "Yes, I suspect those two. However, it is just a hunch. There is something about them that I cannot put my finger on. I have a feeling they could clear up some of the mysteries of what has happened in that area. Whether that would help us solve your parents' disappearance, I don't know."

"Well, that is sufficiently vague."

"I know, but it is the best I can do. You've aroused my curiosity again, but I'm no longer a deputy. I'm retired, so I have no official capacity in this case anymore."

"Well, thank you for helping me," Lola said.

"I don't know if you could call that help."

"I know more than I did before I called you and I am grateful. Would you mind if I called you again?" Lola asked.

"No," Brent replied. "Feel free to call any time. I will be as helpful as I can."

Lola hung up. She sat down and started to summarize the conversation. Her thoughts were scrambled. One thing she knew for sure: she would get to know more about Mike King and Cyrus Longfell.

Chapter 21

1982

A spectacular summer morning, the sun peeking through the window warmed the room. The birds were singing, their joy contagious. The sunbeams reflected off the water onto the ceiling, creating a wave-like light show. Still, Cyrus did not feel like getting out of bed. It was the ideal morning to be lazy and take things as they came.

Cyrus enjoyed helping Mike run the resort. It was a perfect way to spend the summer unwinding from the stress of the school year. The problem was that summer slipped by too quickly. It was August already. He was enjoying himself so much, he did not want the summer to end.

Why, then, did Cyrus have this uneasy feeling about what he was doing? He couldn't put his finger on it, but it was there, gnawing at him. He wasn't looking forward to going back to school—he liked it here. But that wasn't it. There was something about this whole setup—the resort, working there for the summer—that seemed too good to be true. It was Mike. Intuitively, he could feel it. There was something going on that Mike was not telling him about.

It was time to snap out of it. What could be wrong? *Exercise,* he thought. *There is nothing like a good run in the morning to start the day.* He would shake off the morning's cobwebs with a vigorous workout. Cyrus did his warm-up exercises and started jogging north on Bluewater Road. One of the things he loved about the area was that he had his choice of routes to run. He decided to take the path that led to the cave on the Joyce estate. The history of that cave and the surrounding area fascinated him. It was a three-mile jog. It was a splendid way start to the day.

When he reached the pool in front of the waterfall, he decided to take a swim. He dove in and swam under the surface. The water was cool and refreshing. Cyrus opened his eyes. The water clarity was excellent—he could see a fish swimming in the distance, darting in and out of his vision. It was a dream that came true for someone majoring in natural sciences. The world that surrounded him was his laboratory. His lungs were about to burst, forcing him to surface. As he stood, his head was barely above the water; he gulped in the air. He noticed his feet were sinking in the sand that covered the bottom of the pool. He pondered what might be buried in the sand. What had fallen in the pond over the last century? What secrets did the sand hold?

He was distracted by voices in the distance. He could not make out what was being said, but he could tell it was an argument. He had no reason to fear for his safety, but somehow, he felt vulnerable, naked, in the pool. He quietly swam back to shore, put his clothes on, and started jogging back to the resort. As he got closer to the main hiking path, he heard the voices again. One voice sounded familiar. It was Mike King. The other voice was female. He couldn't tell for sure, but he thought it was Sandy's voice. The woman said something about pictures. Then he heard an engine start—perhaps an all-terrain vehicle. The argument stopped as he heard the vehicle drive off. *Oh, well— another mystery,* Cyrus mused as he jogged back to the resort. He took a quick shower and got ready for work.

Cyrus was in the office, anticipating what demands the guests would put on his time, when Sandy walked into the room. She had been shy lately and had not paid much attention to Cyrus. He was curious what had changed her attitude toward him.

"Good morning, Sandy," Cyrus said cheerfully.

"Oh, hi, Cyrus," was Sandy's reply. She seemed listless, uninterested.

"It's a beautiful morning," Cyrus said, trying to put a positive spin on things. "I was just thinking, a couple more weeks and we'll be closing the place down for another year."

"I'll be unemployed by the end of the month," Sandy said. "I'll have more time to work on my art."

"That doesn't sound that bad. I could use some time to pursue the things that interest me," Cyrus said, thinking out loud. "School gets to be a grind."

"Oh, Cyrus, cut the crap," Sandy said. "You know what's going on. Why pretend you don't?" Sandy blurted out. She started crying, then ran to the door. Cyrus tried to catch her but she was already gone. *It's just as well,* he thought. He was never good at consoling crying females.

"What's going on with her?" Mike said as he entered the office. "She went running by me like I didn't exist."

"I don't know," Cyrus said. "She just started crying and ran out of here like something was wrong."

"I wonder if she is going to come back to work today."

"What is going on, Mike?" Cyrus said. "She didn't just start crying for no reason. She was obviously upset."

"I don't know, Cyrus. It could be anything."

"Mike, did you show her the pictures we took of her by the waterfall?"

"Yes, I did," Mike replied sheepishly.

"What did she do?" Cyrus eyed Mike suspiciously.

"Come see for yourself. I put a surveillance camera in the office so I could see what was going on in here. I filmed what happened when I confronted Sandy with the pictures."

They went into the office. Mike played back the film clip. Cyrus looked on in amazement.

"Mike, how could you do that? She's a married woman. She works here with us. Have you no respect for the relationship we have with her?"

"Cyrus, you wouldn't understand. I've had the hots for her ever since I was a kid. She's a tease. She's been teasing me for years. I finally got the upper hand."

"You should be ashamed."

"I'm not ashamed—she's an adult. What do you think she was doing with those guys dressed up like Indians by the waterfall when we took the pictures?"

"That was none of our business and who knows why she did that?"

"You're just jealous, Cyrus. She'll be back. She knows I still have the pictures—I haven't shown her the film clip yet. You want to try her out when she comes back? I can arrange it."

"You're sick," Cyrus said. "If I were Sandy, I would sneak in here when you are not around and steal the pictures."

"Even if she found the pictures, I have backup."

"I feel sorry for her," Cyrus said. He shook his head in disgust as he walked out to do his chores.

The next day, Sandy was back, just as Mike predicted. She was great with the customers, as always, but with Cyrus, she was moody. One minute, they would have a serious conversation about the resort; the next, she was lost in thought and hard to approach. Cyrus was perplexed.

Cyrus had outdoor chores to perform, which took him most of the day. When he returned to the lodge, he noticed Sandy and Mike in the office. The music was loud enough that they did not notice Cyrus arrive. When he peered inside the door of the office, he saw Sandy snorting a line of white powder into her nose through a dollar bill.

"Thanks, Mike—I needed that," Sandy said.

"Just another perk of working with me," Mike smiled as he spoke. He was proud of himself.

Sandy sat back in her chair. Cyrus could tell she was zoned out. He was really disgusted with Mike and how he treated women. *Mike is a sociopath,* Cyrus thought. *He doesn't care about anyone but himself. Yet Mike treats me almost like a family member.* It was confusing.

Sandy perked up, looked at Mike, and said, "What am I going to do when you leave?"

"Don't worry about that—it's still a couple weeks away. Come over here and sit on my lap, babes I need you close to me."

Sandy got up, sat on Mike's lap, and rubbed against him seductively. "Is that what you wanted?" she asked.

"You should divorce that loser Dan and come with me."

"Divorce?" Sandy asked. "He's not my husband—we just live together. I met him in drug rehab. I'm getting tired of him anyways. He's like a puppy."

"Don't worry about a thing; I'll take care of you."

"You? What can you do? You work for your daddy."

"Don't be naïve, Sandy—a girl that looks like you could make a lot of money. Instead of living in a trailer, you could be living in a condo on the beach in Miami, driving a nice car, and spending your time bathing that beautiful body in the sun."

"What do I have to do, marry you?"

"No, I own a couple nightclubs in Miami. You can be one of my entertainers."

"Entertainer?" Sandy asked.

"Okay, you could be a dancer, a stripper."

"A stripper." Sandy smiled at the thought.

"Yeah, you are wasting your talents here. Stick with me—we'll get rich."

"I've never danced in front of an audience before," Sandy objected weakly.

"Well, you can audition right now," Mike said. "Close the door."

Cyrus watched the office door close and moved quietly to the front door of the lodge. He could only imagine what happened next.

Cyrus was troubled and went for a long walk in the woods. He wondered what he was getting himself into. He was dependent on Mike for income and a place to stay during school. He wondered how many other people were dependent on Mike. Mike was like a plague, corrupting everyone he encountered.

Chapter 22

Everything was new to Ahote, he was excited. He could feel the pulse of a city much larger than he was accustomed to living in coursing through his veins. He felt alive but at the same time he was intimidated. It was the kind of challenge he liked. Even though he had been driving the cab for a couple of weeks, Ahote found that he did not know the Minneapolis streets as well as he should. Cab drivers had to wait on cabstands for orders when they were not busy. The cab dispatcher auctioned the orders over the radio to the closest cab to the order. Ahote still had to think about where in the city those cabstands were located. He was learning the locations a little bit at a time. For example, he did know where the general hospital was, so he decided to find it, park on the cabstand there, and wait.

His first fare of the evening wanted to go to the lower north side of Minneapolis. Ahote did not have a prejudiced bone in his body. On the other hand, he was not used to being around African Americans. It was his first experience in the projects—low-income housing in north Minneapolis. He picked up an elderly woman and drove as she directed through downtown. When he arrived at the row house, she wanted Ahote to help her into her home. He made the mistake of leaving his cab door open while he helped her inside. When he returned to his cab, he saw a young boy running away from the cab. It took him a while to realize that the young boy had the radio that Ahote planned to listen to later in his shift. Ahote drove the neighborhood trying to find the kid, but by that time, the thief had vanished. Ahote learned a hard lesson about the Twin Cities. He was glad it was only a radio and not his guitar, which he kept in the trunk of the cab.

Ahote was afraid to take another fare in that part of town, so he deadheaded—drove with his cab empty—back downtown to the general hospital. He reasoned that anyone coming from the hospital had to be relatively harmless. He kept taking fares like that for the next few hours. He would pick a person up at the hospital, take them to their destination, and return to the hospital for another fare.

Finally, about 7:00 PM, a man in a suit carrying luggage got into his cab and said, "Airport."

Ahote had to think, *How do I get to the airport from here?* Finally, he said, "I'm new to cab driving. I don't know the best way to get to the airport from here."

"Don't worry about it—I go there all the time," the man said. "I will show you. Just go straight until Fourth Avenue South and turn left. That street will take you to the freeway. After that, just follow the signs."

"Thank you," Ahote said gratefully. He was a little embarrassed that he did not know where the airport was. He was happy because he knew it would be a good fare and that he could wait his turn at the airport. If he was lucky, his next fare would go back downtown.

Ahote kept working at his new job, determined to be good at it. When bar closing time—1:00 AM in Minneapolis—came around, he decided to call it quits. He filled the cab with gas, drove to Bob's house, and left thirty-five dollars on the front seat of the cab for his lease. He called a cab to take him home. He counted his money when he got home. He made sixty dollars. Not bad for a rookie. He was exhausted. He grabbed some supper and went to sleep.

It was a slow night driving cab. Ahote was sitting on a cabstand not far from home, thinking that he should knock off early. He had made enough money to pay his lease and gas for the cab tonight with a few bucks left over to go out. One of the things he liked about his new job was that the cab was available for personal use during his shift.

One of the bars that Ahote had picked up a lot of cab fares from was the Cabooze bar. It was located a few miles from his home. They always had good bands there and it always seemed crowded. He was still eighteen, but his height and his muscular appearance made him look much older than that. As a cab driver, Ahote made it his business to talk to bouncers and bartenders. Now that he was known to them, no one questioned his age.

Ahote had a premonition that he would be a great entertainer. He took his guitar playing seriously and practiced assiduously. Even though he was intimidated by the quality of the musicians who performed in the Twin Cities, he also felt that he could be like them—even better. If he paid the price for success with practice and took every opportunity to play in public, he would succeed. He was on a mission; American

Indians were not a relic from the past. It was a stereotype created by post-World War II television. His ancestors were a proud race of proud, talented, and thoughtful people.

Ahote thought about Lomasi. He wondered if she was happy studying to become an author. She could write songs and sing with him. Her words and his music—they could go far. Well, it did not work out that way. Her grandmother was very controlling. She would not let Lomasi's natural talents flow. He thought about the nights sitting around the campfire. Now she was getting to be quite a looker, too. She would be a real asset on the stage. He wondered if he was just missing home or if it was her that he missed.

"Well," Ahote said to himself out loud, "if I want to be a great guitarist, it is time to get started." He picked up his guitar and headed to the Triangle bar. It was an open stage tonight. He would get fifteen minutes to play his best stuff. The crowd would be the judge. He had played for parties and friends in Grand Rapids, but never for complete strangers. He was shy when it came to playing in public, so it took self-persuasion to get him through the front door of the Triangle bar. Once he was inside with his guitar case in hand, there was no turning back. He was the last to come in, so he would be the last to play. He wondered if that was good or bad.

"Just sit over there," the bartender/MC said as he described the open-stage process to the customers. Ahote sat on the edge of his chair. The first performer was a young woman who was playing old Joan Baez songs. She had a good voice but could not play the guitar like Joan. Ahote was starting to feel more confident. The woman playing Baez got some good applause. He wondered if it the crowd was just being nice of if they enjoyed the performance. Next there was a poet, then a comedian.

"Our next performer is Ahote," the bartender said. "You might recognize him as our cab driver. He comes in here all the time to give people a safe ride home. Did you know he was talented? Let's listen."

"Thank you," Ahote said as he got up on the stage. "I started playing guitar when I was fourteen. Last year, a friend of mine and I started writing music. I would like to play a tune we wrote about an American Indian Chief named Wabana. It also describes our home in Wabana Township." Ahote started the tune in A minor. As the chords wafted softly through the bar, the acoustic sound captured the crowd. Now everyone was staring at him. At first, his voice broke as he sang, *"Wabana, Wabana you call to me."* Then he played his heart out. The crowd must have felt the emotion with which he played, for they applauded loudly after the song.

"Thank you," Ahote said, accepting the applause. The crowd seemed to like him more than the other performers. He wondered if that was really true or did it just seem that way because he was on the stage in front of everyone. He sang three more songs and his time was up. The bartender asked everyone to give the performers a big hand of applause as Ahote sat down. He was drained but happy over all that he had performed live in Minneapolis. He had done his best.

Ahote packed up his guitar and sat down to have a beer. After overcoming his fear of performing in his new hometown, he needed a reward. A local band started to play and he was enjoying the music when a sultry brunette approached him.

"Hi, my name is Reena," the woman said. "I enjoyed your performance. Mind if I join you?"

"That would be great," Ahote said.

"I like to come here on open-stage nights," Reena said. "The local bands here play the same stuff you hear on the radio. It's refreshing when you hear something original."

"I like to write songs," Ahote said. "I started out learning popular music but found that I like to create. Music is a way for me to express my thoughts and feelings."

"Where do you get your ideas for songs?" Reena asked.

"I'm an American Indian—you probably guessed. My father was one of the last medicine men. He taught me many of the old ceremonial songs. I've adapted some of those songs and adopted them as my own."

"Does that give you your inspiration?" Reena wanted to know. "I'm an artist of sorts myself. It's something I always wonder about."

"That first song I sang, 'Ode to Wabana,' I wrote about Chief Wabana and the land he used to own," Ahote explained. "He was the last functional American Indian chief of our tribe. Since then, the tribe has been Americanized and mostly fallen apart. It's sad."

"I know what you mean," Reena said. "I am from Czechoslovakia. There were a lot of old traditions there that were very charming that are largely forgotten now. Everywhere you look, people have their faces in the their cell phones now."

"Yeah, I know," Ahote replied. "Everyone would like to be doing something else and be someplace else. I'm like that, too."

"What do you do for work?" Reena asked as she looked closer at Ahote. She liked his shiny dark eyes and genuine smile. He was younger than her but that was what she liked. She could see his naturally muscular build and slender waist. She wondered what he looked like from behind.

"I drive a cab at night," Ahote answered. "I usually work this time of night, but I took time off to play at the open stage."

"Where are you from?" Reena asked, her interest piqued.

"I grew up in Grand Rapids, Minnesota," Ahote explained. "I moved to the Twin Cities to have a bigger market for my music career. I figured there would be a lot more opportunity in a larger town. So far, I haven't been disappointed. How about you? What brought you here from Czechoslovakia?"

"I just live here in the summer when I am between jobs," Reena explained. "I live in Los Angeles in the winter. I like to get away from work. Besides, it is more temperate here in the summer."

"What do you do?" Ahote asked.

"I'm a model," Reena said. "I'd like to break into movies, but it is competitive."

"Looks to me like you've got what it takes," Ahote blurted out.

"Thanks." Reena seemed genuinely pleased. "I have to go to the ladies' room; don't let them take my beer while I'm gone."

Ahote could hardly believe his luck. *What a woman,* he thought as he watched her walk in the direction of the restrooms. Her long, straight, black hair almost reached her waist, accentuating that lovely rear. Her form-fitting jeans and that skimpy top made her look like a supermodel. He noticed that her appearance was not lost on others in the bar. She was the kind of woman men dreamed about.

When Reena returned from the ladies' room, she sat back down again. They made small talk. They danced to some rock and roll music, then went back to their table. She was sensual and flirtatious. Ahote was enjoying himself and lost track of time.

"I should be going," Reena said.

Ahote had a disappointed look on his face that Reena picked up on right away.

"Why don't we go out to my car and smoke a joint before I go?" Reena suggested.

Ahote had only smoked a little marijuana in his life, but he did not want to appear to Reena like a hick from northern Minnesota. "Sure, why not?" he replied.

Everyone noticed they were leaving and he could feel the jealousy from the guys sitting at the bar watching him leave with the best looking woman in the place. They walked down Riverside Avenue. Ahote put his arm around her. He was hoping the night would not end. When Reena took her car keys out of her purse and activated the remote to unlock her car, the lights went on in a new red corvette. She opened the door and motioned for Ahote to get in.

"Nice ride!" Ahote said.

Reena smiled coyly and said, "I am." She turned on the radio and took a joint out from under her visor. They took a few hits off it and Ahote pulled Reena toward him and kissed her a long, lingering kiss. Reena responded to his kiss with her tongue and rubbed her hand up and down his chest. Ahote cupped his hand over her breast and gently massaged. He was having trouble controlling himself.

"Why don't we go to my place?" Ahote asked.

"Whoa, down boy!" Reena kidded Ahote. Then seriously she said, "I can't, Ahote—I have to get up early tomorrow. I'm going back to Los Angeles for a few days. Besides, I never sleep with a man the first day I meet him."

"But you are so hot!" Ahote exclaimed. "I have to see you again. I can take you to the airport tomorrow from my place." Reena was tempted. "I have to go home and pack. Here's my phone number. Call me next week. I'd like to see you again."

Reena picked up the phone when she got home. "Hi, Mike, I met him."

"How did it go?" Mike asked.

"He's just a kid. It was easy. He thinks I can't resist him."

"Let's proceed with the rest of the plan, then."

"I've got some guys lined up that can help us. He'll never know it was you behind it."

"Good—he'll get what he deserves, the stinking Indian."

Lola started her novel. It wasn't as easy as she expected. In school, writing had always come easily to her. She found that writing a novel was different. If she was going to use the book to solve the mystery of her parents' disappearance, she had to research. She had to investigate. She knew she could count on the deputy, Brent Foster, for any information he could provide, perhaps even help. In Brent's opinion, was there was something going on at the resort that involved Mike King and Cyrus Longfell. She decided her first step would be to just go talk to Mike. He still lived on Bluewater Lake for the warm months of the year. It was the logical first step.

"Hi, Rachel, it's Lola," she said when her friend answered the phone.

"Hey, what's up, Lola?"

"I was thinking about going home next weekend. Want to come along?"

"How were you going to get there?"

"I'm going to let you drive."

"That's really big of you. Why would I like to go to Grand Rapids?"

"I thought we could do some songwriting. No distractions; we could concentrate, use the northland for inspiration."

"Why else did you want to go there?" Rachel knew when she was being manipulated.

"All right, I admit it—I have an ulterior motive. I want to find out what happened to my parents. I spoke to the deputy who did the investigation. He gave me some ideas. I thought we could check out one of them. It would be fun. There is a beautiful area called the Joyce estate we could explore. I'd also like to try to speak with Mike King, a guy my mother used to work for at the resort just before she disappeared."

"Do you think that it is wise to start investigating on your own? Will you be safe?"

"It's the only way the mystery will be solved. No one else cares. Besides, I've decided to write a novel about their disappearance. I am going to use it for my senior thesis. That way, I can kill two birds with one stone."

"Actually, it sounds like fun. I could use some time out of the city to relax. We could stay at my lake home."

"Great, I'll call my grandmother and let her know we are coming. She might be hurt if I don't stay with her."

"Tell her we are going to be doing some brainstorming and need to be alone."

"Well, maybe I can spend one night with her anyways. She's paying for my school."

"We can discuss that on the drive," Rachel replied. "We'll leave after you're done with classes on Friday. We'll be there by dinner time."

That part was easy. Now comes the hard part, Lola thought as she dialed the phone.

"Hello," the voice on the other end of the line answered.

"Is this Mike King?"

"Yes, it is."

"Hi, Mike, this is Lomasi Whitecloud."

"Who?" Mike asked.

"I am Sandy Whitecloud's daughter. She worked for you several years ago."

"Oh, yes—I remember her," Mike said.

"I'm writing a book about her disappearance. I will be in the area this weekend. Would it be possible to stop by and speak with you? I'd like to get some background information."

"I don't know what I could tell you that you don't already know."

"I'd appreciate it if I could stop by and talk," Lola said. "I have no memories of my mother and father. They disappeared when I was too young to remember, so anything you could tell me would be helpful. Would 2:00 PM Saturday work for you?"

"Sure, since you put it that way, how could I refuse? Do you know where I live?" Mike had no choice but to see her. It would sound suspicious if he declined her request.

"Yes, I grew up on Bluewater Road."

"Fine, I'll see you Saturday, then," Mike said as he hung up the phone. His mind raced as he thought about what might happen. Why was she digging around after all this time? A book—why would she be writing a book?

As Lola hung up, she was thinking ahead also. *That was easy enough.* The tough part would be talking to him. What could she ask without making him suspicious?

"Cyrus, this is Mike." Panic had driven Mike to call Cyrus. Since Cyrus had established a successful practice, sometimes Mike felt that he did not like to speak with him. It was almost like Cyrus wanted to distance himself from Mike now that he was a respectable doctor. It was Mike who had helped him with a job at the resort when Cyrus was in college. He had given Cyrus a place to stay rent free. It was ironic. Even though they were different in many ways, one could not mistake the similarities in their attitudes. Both were confirmed bachelors.

"Hi, Mike. It's been a while since we spoke. How are you doing?"

"I'm fine. I'm calling because someone named Lomasi Whitecloud just called me. Do you know her?"

"Yes, she's worked here at the clinic in the summer. Her grandmother, Sara, is a nurse practitioner here. What does Lomasi want?"

"She wants to know about her mother, Sandy. She said she is writing a book about her disappearance. Why would she be writing a book, for Christ sakes?"

"Lomasi is a student at the University of Minnesota. She wants to be a writer."

"Why would she call me about Sandy? What does she know?"

"She's a nice kid. When she worked for me in the clinic, she was polite and always worked hard. Of course, her grandmother was her supervisor. I suppose she always wondered what happened to her parents. You can't blame her for that."

"How did she connect us with her parents?" Mike asked.

"What do you mean 'us'? I told you back then that nothing good would come of this."

"Cyrus, quit being so high and mighty. You were involved with this, too."

"It was your idea. I was just young and impressionable."

"We were both young. The question is, does she know what happened?"

"How could she?" Cyrus said. "She was just out of infancy when it happened. I am sure she is just on a fishing expedition."

"Well, I would feel better if I knew more about what is happening. Can you see if her grandmother sent her in our direction?"

"I will mention it to Sara tomorrow at work."

"Thanks, Cyrus—I knew I could count on you."

"All right, I'll let you know what I find out."

Chapter 23

Ahote basked in the glory of his night of fame, the open stage. He kept replaying it over and over again in his mind. Now it was back to reality, driving a cab. He was becoming known, not as a performer but as a cab driver. The bartenders recognized him when he came into the bar and directed the people who called a cab to him. Tonight, when he pulled up to the bar, two men got into the back seat. *That was easy,* he thought.

"It's the rock star," one of the men said. "I saw you play at the Triangle the other night."

"Thank you," Ahote said, pleased that someone recognized him. "I enjoyed playing there."

"Yeah, you were pretty good," the man said. "Some of the people that play open stages, you wonder where they got the idea anyone would be interested in hearing them sing. But you're the genuine article, the real deal."

"Thanks," Ahote said. "Where you guys going?"

"Stand Up Frank's," the man said.

"We're on the way," Ahote said. He turned on the meter and started driving. Stand Up Frank's got its name serving strong drinks. It was in a rough area of town known for bars, hard drinking, and fights. It was straight down Washington Avenue to their destination. He dropped his passengers at the bar and parked on the cabstand at the intersection of Broadway Street and Washington Avenue.

The intersection of Broadway and Washington was typical, four corners. There were bars on three of the corners. Ahote knew he would not have to wait around long for another fare. He was reading the paper when a man got into his cab. It was not unusual for people to just get into his cab while he was sitting on the cabstand.

"Take me to Plymouth and Irving," the man said. Ahote turned on the meter and started driving. He was going to an area of north Minneapolis that was the "bad" part of town. The houses were decaying. It was a high-crime area. Ahote did not mind driving there, but he was reluctant to pick up fares in the area because they never went very far and sometimes he had trouble getting paid.

"Nice night," Ahote said to the man in the back seat. The man did not reply. Ahote did not mind. He did not always feel like talking, but there was something about this guy in the back seat that was strange.

"Wait here—I'll be right back," the man said as he tossed a twenty-dollar bill over the seat to Ahote to hold the cab. It wasn't that busy that night, so Ahote did not mind waiting, but he never felt that comfortable in this part of town. Everyone had an agenda. Someone was always trying to take advantage of the other. *The meter is running—what do I care?* Ahote thought.

The man got back into the cab after a few minutes. "Take me to James and Highway 55," he said.

Ahote drove to the intersection. He turned to collect the fare. The last thing he remembered was a sharp pain in the back of his head—then darkness.

It felt like a dream—a bad dream. Ahote woke up slowly. Was he hung over? It came back to him slowly. His head pounded and his mouth was dry. He was in his cab. He felt the back of his head—there was blood, dried blood, covering the back of his head. Then he remembered the last fare he took. He searched his pockets for his money; they were empty. His wallet was on the front seat of the cab. It was empty. He had to wake up, regain his alertness.

He heard the cab dispatcher over the radio. He realized that he had to call the police. He keyed the microphone of the radio. He said his cab number. "Eighty-seven."

"Eighty-seven," the dispatcher repeated. "We have been trying to reach you. Your shift is over and the owner of the cab is wondering where you are."

"I was robbed. Someone hit me over the head. I am at Highway 55 and James Avenue North."

"Are you hurt?" the dispatcher asked.

"Only my pride," Ahote replied. "I do have a large lump on the back of my head."

"Stay put—we will have a squad car there in a few minutes," the dispatcher said. "Do we need an ambulance?"

"No, I will be okay," Ahote replied as he slumped over in the cab, once again unconscious.

160

When Ahote woke up again, he was in the hospital. *Is this all a bad dream,* he wondered. *How did I get here?* Then he realized Bill, the owner of the cab he drove, was in the room with him.

"How are you, Ahote?" Bill said.

"I'm okay, I guess," Ahote replied. "Where am I?"

"You're in Hennepin County Medical Center's emergency room," Bill explained. "By the time the squad car reached your location, you were unconscious on the front seat of the cab. We were all pretty worried."

"I didn't mean to cause everyone so much trouble," Ahote said as he slipped back into oblivion.

Lola and Rachel started for Grand Rapids early Friday.

"I'm glad we left early," Rachel said. "It's a long drive and I hate to get caught up in the weekend rush to go up north."

"I'm looking forward to getting home. I made an appointment to meet with Mike King on Saturday. I'd like to ask him some questions about my mother. She worked for him the summer she disappeared."

"Do you suspect that he was involved?"

"I don't know what to think. The deputy seems to think he's a shady character. It could be he knows something. Someone knows something about the disappearance. I just have to find them."

"Well, I'm just excited about going to my lake home again. I don't get there often enough. It's a great place to relax. Besides, I am looking forward to a weekend alone with you."

"I've been looking forward to it, too," Lola admitted. She felt comfortable with Rachel. She had never been attracted to another female. Rachel seemed to be pulling Lola to her like a magnet. It was difficult to resist. It was pleasant yet disturbing.

"I thought it was your father's lake home."

"It is, sort of." Rachel wondered how much to disclose to Lola about herself. *A little at a time,* she thought. "He put it in my name for tax purposes. I'll inherit it anyways."

"Kind of like your house?" Lola asked. *There is so much about Rachel I do not know,* she thought to herself.

"Yes, like my house," Rachel said irritably.

"Rachel, would you come with me to see Mike King?" Lola quickly changed the subject.

"Of course—I couldn't let you go there alone. Besides, I'm driving."

"Good, we can stop at my grandmother's for lunch, then go visit Mike. Then I have a special surprise for you."

"I love surprises—I just hate waiting for them. What is it?"

"It's a cave behind a waterfall. We could write a song about it. It's not too far from my grandmother's place."

"Great, we'll make a day of it. Now where should we eat tonight?"

"I know just the place. It's called Brewed Awakenings. It is a coffee shop in Grand Rapids. They have great food and there is a nice atmosphere."

"It sounds great—I'm getting hungry already," Rachel said.

The next day, Rachel learned a lot about her friend from college. When they arrived at Sara's for lunch, she saw a trailer home. Even though Sara worked as a nurse practitioner and earned a six-figure income, she lived modestly. The property looked nice. Sara maintained it well; there were flower gardens and shrubs, yet the property exuded an aura of austerity.

Sara came outside to meet them. She was dressed in blue jeans and an old flannel shirt that was not tucked in at the waist. She had a warm smile and there was a twinkle in her eyes. She seemed genuinely pleased to see Rachel. It was obvious that she was happy to see her granddaughter.

"Grandma, this is my friend Rachel," Lola said.

"Nice to meet you, Rachel," Sara said.

"Thank you for inviting me."

"It is nice to see you, Lomasi," Sara said with joy. "Duane will be happy to see you, too."

"Grandma, I've changed my name to Lola."

"I know—it is just hard for me to get used to it. Is that going to be your pen name or is it going to be your legal name also?"

"I'm not an author yet, but Lola will be my legal name soon. I have not decided on a last name yet."

"Young people—always something new. Well, it is probably for the best." Sara did not like the idea of her granddaughter changing her name, but she knew better than to express her displeasure. "Why don't you two come inside? I have lunch ready."

Rachel was fascinated by the interior of the trailer. She could feel Sara's personality in it. Black-and-white pictures of people from previous generations, parents, aunts, and uncles adorned the wall. Native American heritage was on display, including a headdress of feathers that looked like it belonged on a chief. The furniture was antique. They sat down to a round oak table in the dining room that appeared to have been in the family for generations.

"That's a fascinating headdress on the wall," Rachel said both from interest and to make conversation.

"Yes, that belonged to our ancestor, Chief Wabana."

"Your ancestor?" Rachel asked.

"Yes, both my grandfather and my father were chiefs. Probably their fathers, too—it is a shame there is no written history to trace. My brother, Duane, would have been a medicine man, a shaman, had he remained with the tribe. Of course, those days are gone now."

"Duane lives next door," Lola explained.

"He is going to stop by to say hi. It has been a while since he's seen you," Sara said to Lola. "He's not really my brother," she said to Rachel. "We're just close friends. We grew up together."

"It's funny, next door has a different meaning up here. In the cities, next door means less than fifty feet away. Here there must be a quarter mile between you," Rachel said.

"We both have twenty-acre parcels," Sara explained. "So the distance between own probably seems like a quarter mile but it is a little less than that. We value our privacy."

Rachel sat in silence as Sara and Lola caught up on the local gossip. When they finished, Sara said, "Why don't you take Rachel for a walk to the Joyce estate? It's a beautiful walk this time of year."

"Is that the place you were telling me about with the cave?" Rachel asked Lola.

While Sara wasn't looking, Lola made a signal for Rachel to button her lips.

"What cave?" Sara asked.

"Oh, we've been talking about taking a trip to the Wisconsin Dells," Lola lied. "Rachel, we should get going—it is getting late."

"You have an appointment or something?" Sara asked sarcastically. She was disappointed that they would not spend more time with her.

"Yes, we have to meet a guy named Mike at 2:00 PM," Rachel explained.

Lola could not believe Rachel could be so naïve to say that in front of her grandmother. On the other hand, she did not warn her that Sara would not be keen on them talking with Mike King.

"You didn't tell me you were going to meet with Mike," Sara said with parental authority. "Why do you need to talk with him? Is this about Sandy and Dan?"

"Grandma, I am just writing a book. It's going to be my senior thesis."

"You're a freshman. You have three more years before you become a senior and you have to worry about a thesis now?"

"It takes a long time to write a book when you work on it part-time, Grandma. I have to start working on it now. Besides, I want to discover more about my parents. What better way is there to do it?"

"You'll get yourself into trouble messing around with Mike. I can save you the trouble. Sandy used to work for Mike at the resort—period. That was her involvement with Mike. Your parents disappeared because of Dan. He was involved with crime—guns and drugs."

Lola was getting mad. "Like Ahote was involved with guns and drugs?" she retorted. "Everyone knows he was set up. Someone planted a gun and painkillers in his car to get rid of him."

"Now, Lola, let's not start that again," Sara chided her granddaughter.

"Guns and drugs are just an excuse to not investigate further," Lola said angrily.

Rachel was looking out of the living-room window. She was sorry she had brought the appointment with Mike up in the conversation. She wanted to change the subject. Just then, Duane walked into view. Rachel wasn't expecting such an attractive man.

Duane knocked on the door and walked in with such confidence and poise that Rachel was dumbstruck. Fortunately, he spoke to Lola, so Rachel did not have to say anything.

"Lomasi, it is nice to see you again."

"Duane, I'm glad you came. I miss you. This is my friend, Rachel Hargrove."

When Duane shook her hand, Rachel felt a chill up her spine. His deep blue eyes seemed to look right through her. He smiled salaciously. "Nice to meet you," he said.

"Likewise," Rachel managed to mumble.

Duane turned his attention to Sara and Lola. Rachel walked to the picture window to regain her composure. She was admiring the view while Duane and Lola talked for a few minutes. Then Duane took his leave.

Duane was in and out of Rachel's life in minutes, but his image remained indelibly imprinted in her mind.

"Who is that guy sitting up the road on a four-wheeler staring at the trailer?" Rachel asked, pointing across the road.

That brought Lola and Sara to the window.

"That's just some guy who hangs around here watching things. Don't pay any attention to him. He is not playing with a full deck," Sara said.

"He gives me the creeps," Lola said.

"How long has he been doing that?" Rachel asked.

"We started noticing him last year. Who knows how long he's been hanging around?" Sara said.

"Can't you call the police?" Rachel asked, glad to change the subject from Mike King.

"There is no law against what he is doing, it is just unusual," Sara said.

"Well, you would think he would have better things to do with his time," Lola remarked. "We have to be going. I'll call you tomorrow, Grandma."

"You two be careful around that Mike King. He is a shady character. No one knows for sure where he got his money. He has a powerful influence around here."

"We won't do anything foolish. I love you, Grandma," Lola said as they left.

There was silence as they pulled out of the driveway. Finally, Rachel said, "Sorry, I didn't mean to let the cat out of the bag."

"That's okay," Lola said. "I didn't warn you that the subject was taboo. You have to understand that people around here think that Mike King has a lot of money and that he is powerful. There is resentment among the locals of people from out of town, especially big cities. It's complicated to explain, but my grandmother probably thinks that Mike is more powerful than he really is."

"We'll soon find out what he is really like. It never hurts to be cautious," Rachel said.

They found the right address sign and pulled into the driveway. The home made a statement. It was not very large or ostentatious. It was tasteful. Both home and garage were made from hand-scribed white-pine logs. Rachel guessed each log was twelve inches in diameter. The lawn was manicured and studded with sixty-foot red pines. The elevation to the lake was perfect. Everything about the property was perfect and said *Welcome.* Even the lake welcomed them, shimmering with the afternoon sun.

Rachel took one look at the property and said, "Who cares what your grandmother thinks? I'm in love with him. Is he married?"

"Let's not get carried away," Lola said. "There are a lot of log homes around here. Remember, we came for information."

They knocked on the door and Mike answered. "Hi, you must be Lomasi," he said as he looked questioningly at Rachel.

"Hi, Mike. Yes, I am Lomasi and this is my friend Rachel."

"Welcome to my home. Come in."

Rachel could not believe her eyes. The home was absolutely charming. It had oak wood floors, a vaulted ceiling with log beams supporting the structure above. The fieldstone fireplace reached the ceiling and had a bearskin rug in front of it. The house exuded an aura of warmth that exemplified up-north ambiance.

Mike was six-foot-three. He had a large frame and looked like he was in terrific shape. There did not seem to be an ounce of fat on him. His hair was gray and he had piercing blue eyes. He was strikingly handsome.

"I prepared some coffee, or perhaps you would prefer tea."

"I'd like tea," Lola replied.

"Me, too," Rachel chimed.

"It's such a lovely day—why don't we sit outside on the deck? Have a seat while I heat the water."

While Mike was in the kitchen, Lola and Rachel had a chance to take in the view. Mike had a pontoon boat and a speed boat on either side of the dock, and there was a sailboat moored in the shallows. He had three hundred feet of lakeshore and thirteen acres, the neighboring homes were not visible. The shoreline across the lake was undeveloped, it seemed like they had the whole lake to themselves. They were so captivated by the view that they hardly noticed when Mike returned with the beverages.

"Here's your tea," Mike said. "How do you like the view?"

"It's perfect," Rachel said.

"Thank you. I love to show people my property. Now how can I help you?"

"I started writing a novel for my senior project at the University of Minnesota," Lola explained. "I chose as a subject the disappearance of my parents. We came to visit you because Sandy, my mother, worked for you before she disappeared. I was hoping you could point me in the right direction for my research."

"You look like your mother," Mike replied. "It was unfortunate that Sandy and Dan disappeared. No one has ever seen either of them again."

"Is there anything you remember? Anything at all you can tell me would be helpful. I never got to know my parents because they disappeared when I was very young, so writing this book and researching are a way of seeking resolution."

"It must be difficult for you, Lomasi," Mike said. "You have my sympathy. I told the police everything I know when they investigated. I have nothing more to say except we miss her. She did a wonderful job around the resort with the guests. She was a part of the resort, and she provided excellent service; she contributed to the atmosphere of enjoyment that brings our guests back again year after year."

"Was there anything with any of the guests at your resort that would relate to their disappearance?"

"No, the people that stay at our resort come here on vacation. They are here for a week or two and then go home. All they are interested in is enjoyment. Sandy just helped them with checking in and out and getting ice, things like that."

"Would you mind if I spoke with some of the guests who were here that summer?"

"Yes, I would," Mike said. "I sympathize with your situation, but I have to think of the business at the resort. Questioning guests of the resort who had nothing to do with your parents' disappearance could give them the impression of impropriety. That would hurt my business."

"Is there anything else you can tell me about my mother or father?" Lola asked. She was disappointed.

"No," Mike replied with a sad expression. "I would just like to say that I hope you get resolution. I liked Sandy and I was sad when she disappeared."

"Thank you for your time, Mike," Lola said.

"Thank you for coming over. It was nice to meet both of you." His smile lingered on Rachel.

Chapter 24

Ahote recovered quickly from the physical damage he received from the robbery. He was released from Hennepin County Medical Center and returned to driving the cab. He became wary of taking fares in some parts of the city. He considered quitting cab driving because of the danger, but he did not know what else he could do. Cab driving allowed him the luxury of taking time off when he wanted to—no one cared. He made better money than when he was a waiter and the working conditions were better. He was able to pursue his music career. Who was he kidding? He hadn't played anywhere since the open stage at the Triangle bar.

What am I afraid of? he asked himself. He decided to go to a concert at the Target Center. Perhaps he could get some inspiration. He parked his cab and bought his ticket. The show was great. Ahote was a natural when it came to music. When he listened to live music, he could feel its essence mingle with his soul. He knew he belonged in the music business. It was what gave his life meaning. The problem he had to solve was how could he make the transition from cab driver to performer? That answer was waiting for him as he approached his cab.

"Are you the cab driver?" a man asked Ahote.

"Yeah, I was just going home," Ahote replied, trying to avoid the man.

"Could you take me to my hotel before you do?" the man asked.

"Which hotel are you staying at?" Ahote asked. After the robbery, he was skeptical of people who walked up to his cab.

"The Hyatt Regency," the man replied.

"Hop in," Ahote said.

"Thanks, I was afraid I was going to have to walk," the man said. "I'm not so sure it is safe to walk downtown at this time of night."

"There are worse places," Ahote said.

"How did you like the concert?" the man asked.

"It was okay," Ahote replied. "I've seen them before. I'm a musician myself. I like to see how other musicians perform."

168

"Where do you play?" the man asked.

"Nowhere right now," Ahote explained. "I'm just starting my music career in Minneapolis. I am from Grand Rapids, Minnesota. I moved here so I could make more money and eventually break into the music business."

"I'm in the music business," his passenger said. "I manage the band you were just listening to. I get everything set up for them so all they have to do is show up and play."

"Wow! That sounds like a great way to make a living," Ahote said. "How did you get that job?"

"I used to think I wanted to be a musician, but I didn't have the talent or drive," the man explained. "I started out helping carry the equipment and setting it up—the grunt work. Eventually, I worked my way up. I'm the boss now."

"Do you need any help?" Ahote asked. "I'd love to do that kind of work. I was robbed the other night. That is why I was careful when you asked me if I could take you to your hotel. That's how robberies happen. People approach you on the street and ask for a ride. The next thing you know, you are unconscious on the front seat and your money is gone."

"I wish I could help you," the man said. "My name is Avery. Here is one of my cards. Give me your name and phone number. Next time someone leaves, I'll give you a call. People burn out on this job because there is a lot of traveling involved."

"I'd love the traveling," Ahote replied. "I'd like to see how this business actually works."

"All right—I'll call you in the future." Avery paid his fare and disappeared inside the hotel.

"Well, that was a waste of time," Rachel said as they drove away from Mike's house.

"I don't know—there was something he was not telling us. I think he was more involved with my mother than he let on," Lola said.

"What do you mean?"

"I think he was attracted to my mother. I don't know—it is just an intuitive feeling I got from being with him. If he was not involved in their disappearance, then he knows something about it."

"I'll volunteer to go over to his place again, alone, to do further research," Rachel said with a salacious smile.

"Cut it out, Rachel. This is serious."

"Okay, Miss Superdetective, where to next?"

"We go for a walk," Lola said. "There is something I want to show you."

"The nature trail with the cave?" asked Rachel.

"You have a good memory."

They drove back along Bluewater Road until they reached the parking area for the hiking path to the Joyce estate. Rachel parked. They started walking down the trail to the Joyce estate. When they reached the path that led to the waterfall and the cave, Lola said, "Wait till you see this."

"Wow," Rachel said as the waterfall came into site. "What a beautiful spot. This is like a picture from a postcard."

"Yeah, I know. We used to come here and swim when we were kids. There is never anyone here. Even though this is a public place, I've always had it to myself."

"Let's go skinny dipping," Rachel said.

"We can go swimming later. Let me show you the cave."

Rachel followed Lola gingerly as they took the path that led under the waterfall. Rachel was surprised when Lola's trim figure disappeared through the crack in the rock. She followed Lola cautiously.

"How did you find this?" Rachel asked. "You can hardly tell that this is an entrance to a cave."

"We discovered it when we were children. We were scared to explore it at first. We thought it was haunted," Lola said as she shined her flashlight on the walls. "You can see the primitive artwork on the walls. Someone lived here, used it for shelter—probably in the winter. It was an artist or artists."

Rachel was wowed by the appearance of the cave. She checked out the artwork all along the walls. The totem pole at the center of the cave captured her attention. Lola and Rachel moved closer to examine it. The pole was ten feet tall with a bald eagle on the top. There was a firepit in front of it with a large spike extending up in the air about four feet. It was exactly in the center of the firepit.

"What is that?" Rachel asked, pointing at the spike.

"It's a stalagmite," Lola explained. "It's limestone that was built up by water dripping from the cave's roof over the centuries."

"It looks like it was used to impale things. It looks like there were sacrifices here—maybe recently."

"Relax. There is nothing to be afraid of now. We've had fires in here before. I doubt there have been sacrifices here for centuries."

"Don't tell me that totem pole is centuries old. It would have rotted away long ago, and what is the deal with that eagle looking like it is ready to attack on top?"

"Totem poles were constructed to ward off evil spirits, not for evil purposes. Before this area was logged, the eagle was abundant. It was revered as the supreme hunter, a god. The population of eagles has made a comeback in recent years."

"Still, the cave looks like a temple or a ceremonial gathering place for some strange cult."

"There is nothing like that going on around here. This is Wabana Township. It is one of the quietest areas in Minnesota."

"Look, there is a drawing of a deer," Rachel said.

"It's probably an elk. Before the white pines were logged, this area was populated by elk. Once the land was logged, the elk disappeared and were replaced by deer."

"This place gives me the creeps—let's get out of here."

"Wait, let me show you the rest," Lola said. "You see this little stream?"

"Yes, it doesn't look like much."

"Well, this stream probably carved out the entire cave at one time. Now it is just a trickle. It starts at the back of the cave, then flows through the entrance underneath the waterfall. What is not apparent is that there is another cave. Come on, I'll show you."

Rachel followed Lola reluctantly as she led her to the back of the cave.

"Here is where the stream enters the cave. You can see, there is a narrow passage—just wide enough to squeeze through."

"I'm not so sure about this," Rachel said apprehensively.

"Don't be afraid," Lola said as she lead the way though the opening. They slid through a narrow entrance that was six feet long. It extended through solid rock. When they emerged at the other end, they were in another cave. This one looked twice as large as the first.

"Wait until you see this," Lola said as she walked toward the back of the cave. "There is a tunnel here that leads to another chamber. Follow me."

Rachel followed reluctantly. The walls of the cave slowly narrowed for a hundred yards, then opened into another chamber. There was light in the chamber from the roof of the cave, which was almost translucent. The floor of the chamber was sand and there was a large pond that took up half of the chamber. The water had an aqua-blue glow that gave the chamber an eerie atmosphere.

"How did you find this?" Rachel asked.

"I was playing when I was a kid and found it. I don't think anyone knows about it. It's a great place for a swim," Lola said as she started taking off her clothes. She was wearing a swimsuit underneath her clothes. Rachel just sat and watched Lola, mesmerized by the chamber and the luminescent water. Lola dived into the pool and swam around a bit.

"Is the water deep?" Rachel asked sheepishly.

"It gets to be about ten feet in the middle. There is a sand bottom. Come on in."

"It looks cold," Rachel replied. Lola had never seen Rachel so unsure of herself.

"Watch this," Lola said as she submerged and started swimming underwater. She disappeared. Rachel was starting to get worried. It had been a minute at least and Lola still had not surfaced. Rachel's adrenaline started flowing. She started stripping off her clothes to rescue her friend. Just as Rachel was about to jump into the water, Lola surfaced.

"Lola, you scared me to death. I thought you drowned."

"No, I'll show you what I did. Now that you have your swimming suit on, come on in the water."

Rachel entered the water gingerly. She was a good swimmer but had never swum in a pool in a cave before and was a little uncomfortable.

"Follow me," Lola said. "There is another way out of this cave. It is an easy underwater swim."

Rachel followed Lola. The water was clear and now that she was submerged, she could see the light source. It was from a tunnel. Lola was swimming through the tunnel. Rachel's sense of adventure kicked in, and she rigorously swam underwater after Lola. They emerged outside the cave in a lake.

"This is fantastic," Rachel said as she pulled herself to the sandy shore. "Lola, I had no idea anything like this existed."

"You can imagine how I felt as a kid discovering this."

"Does anyone else know about this?"

"I'm sure quite a few people know about the first chamber. The other chambers were my secret until now."

172

"All of the paintings on the wall seem prehistoric, but the totem pole has to be recent. It looked like it was in good condition. It couldn't be as old as the paintings."

"That is true," Lola said. "There was an old legend that the spirit of Chief Wabana occupied the cave. That is why a lot of kids knew about the first cave but did not explore further. They believed the rumor that the evil spirit of the chief haunted the cave."

"Speaking of evil spirits, I think Mike King fits the bill."

"I agree," Lola said. "I think he is hiding something and I would like to know what it is."

"Does he still own the resort?"

"Yes, but he no longer manages it. His father died and he inherited a chain of nursing homes and who knows what. He is independently wealthy."

"So how do we find out the truth?"

"He must have some records of some sort. I doubt he will share them with us. I have a hunch he was involved with my mother. How he was involved remains the question."

"Well, why don't we just wait until he leaves and break into his house?" Rachel said sarcastically.

"Rachel, that is not a bad idea," Lola said.

"Oh, come on, Lola. I was just kidding. We don't want to go to jail."

"Who said anything about going to jail? We just wait until he goes someplace and find a door that is open to his house."

"How do you know how long he will be gone?"

"That's where you come in. You need you to keep him busy so I can search his home."

"What do you mean 'keep him busy'?"

"Call him, invite him to lunch. You saw how he looked at you. He'll jump at the chance to have lunch with you."

"I don't want to be involved with this. What if you are caught?"

"Don't worry about me."

"I am worried about both of us. We could both go to jail."

"I will tell the judge that I operated alone. That you had nothing to do with it."

"Lola, I am worried about you, too. I don't want something to happen to you. What if Mike has surveillance cameras? What if he has an alarm system?"

"Rachel, this is Grand Rapids, Minnesota. People around here don't lock their doors."

"If Mike has something to hide, which it looks like he does, he will have a security system. Sitting behind bars is not the way you want to begin your writing career."

"I'll be careful. All I want to do is copy the hard drive on his computer and search his desk while I'm waiting."

"All you want to do is break and enter!"

"Okay, what do you suggest?"

"You have a point. We're not going to be able to just ask him to confess being involved in your parents' disappearance."

"Let's get our stuff from the cave, grab a pizza at Papa Murphy's, and go back to the cabin. We'll start a fire and make a plan."

Ahote kept working at his job as a cab driver while he practiced playing his guitar and writing music. He was becoming acclimated to living in a larger metropolitan area and was starting to make friends. The robbery he experienced made him gun-shy. He drove the cab mostly in the area surrounding the University of Minnesota. It seemed safer. There was plenty of business from the hospital and the local bars to keep him busy.

Ahote was a thoughtful person. He was polite to his customers. He was respectful of older people who needed special attention caused by the infirmities of age. In many ways, he felt that he was performing a service more valuable to society than the money he received in compensation for his work. On the other hand, he felt that many people, some customers included, did not feel he performed a valuable service at all and looked down on him as an individual who was not skilled and was uneducated. It did not fit with his self image as a composer, musician, and poet. He was going through an identity crisis.

When his cell phone rang one day and he heard Avery say, "Hey, man, what's happening?" he did not know how to reply. He thought it was a telemarketer hustling him for a buck. He almost hung up. Instead he replied, "Not much—why are you calling?"

"You probably do not remember me. My name is Avery," the caller replied. "You gave me a ride to my hotel one night after a gig the band I manage played at the Target Center."

"Oh, yeah, Avery," Ahote said. "Thank you for calling."

"No problem," Avery said. "One of our roadies just quit so he could get married—he had to. I remembered talking with you about working for us. Are you still interested?"

"Very interested," Ahote replied.

"We will be playing in Milwaukee next week," Avery said. "You could start there. We pay six hundred dollars a week plus expenses."

"What are the expenses?" Ahote asked.

"Basically, we pay for your meals and a place to stay," Avery replied. "You will carry the band equipment, set it up, and take it down after the gig."

"It sounds good," Ahote replied. "I'd like to give it a try."

"We'd like a commitment from you to stay with us for the rest of the tour," Avery said. "It will last another twelve weeks."

"Sounds great," Ahote said.

"Good," Avery said. "Meet me in Milwaukee Monday. I will give you my cell phone number. You start Tuesday."

Ahote was psyched; he would get experience with a touring band. He could watch the inner workings of the group. He could gain experience that he would use the rest of his career.

He told Bob he would be leaving the cab business next week. Bob said he would miss Ahote and said if he ever wanted to drive a cab in Minneapolis again, he would help him find a job.

Ahote went home and started packing. He gave notice to his landlord. Suddenly, it dawned on him that he would be leaving this place that was his home for the last few months. He was finally getting settled in and now he would be starting on a new adventure.

Ahote picked up his guitar and started to play. It was times like this that he felt inspired, creative. He favored the key of A minor in his music. It had a certain melancholy that suited his mood. He thought of his forefathers and how they conquered lands. How his ancestors provided for their families. Now he was going to conquer in the music business. He started playing "Ode to Wabana." He thought about the great American Indian chief and the trials and changes that the chief guided his people through. He sang:

Wabana, Wabana you call to me
Wabana, Wabana you set me free
It's here I feel my spirit soar
This wild beauty that I adore.

Ahote thought of his home in Wabana Township. The words had special meaning for him. His spirit was soaring. Some day he would return home, victorious. The young man who had left Grand Rapids with his tail between his legs would return a conquering warrior—the most successful musician/poet in the country.

Ahote played with more intensity—it was almost intoxicating. He had a good voice, but he missed those days he played outside his trailer on Bluerwater Road with Lomasi. He felt that she was his musical compliment. She wrote words to his music that flowed. Her words were interesting, even provocative. He put his guitar down and lay on the sofa. He was thinking about how it would be to tour with a band. He would learn the ropes of his business from the bottom up. He slowly drifted off into a deep sleep.

Chapter 25

"Cyrus, this is Mike."

"Hi, Mike, what's up?"

"I just had a visit from Lomasi and her friend Rachel."

"So, why are you telling me about it?"

"I just wanted to let you know. They are probably going to be contacting you next. Lomasi was asking questions about her mother working for us at the resort."

"I have nothing to hide regarding that."

"Quit acting so high and mighty. You were involved with her just as much as I was."

"No, it was your idea. You were the one who had to have her. I was just there. You were the one who got her addicted to drugs again. You were the one who talked her into working for you in Miami."

"You said it. You were there. This concerns you as much as it concerns me."

"Okay, what do you want?"

"We need to be on the same page in our playbook. Your story has to match up with mine. We need to stand together on this."

"I am going to tell the truth."

"What do you mean 'the truth,' you little pipsqueak?"

"Relax, Mike. I am going to tell them I know nothing about Lomasi's parents' disappearance. I just happened to work with her mother at your resort years ago."

"That's exactly what we both should say. Our story is exactly the same and rings of the truth. I know I have not seen the last of those two. Any chance you can get Sara to call Lomasi off?"

"You make it sound like she's a dog. She's just a college student inquiring after her parents. If I approach Sara, I will just arouse suspicions. It will make it worse."

"Just mention to her that Lomasi and Rachel stopped by my place asking questions. That will be enough. Sara will take it from there. She'll tell them to quit bothering us."

"Okay, I'll do that Monday at work."

"Thanks. Are you still coming over to my house tomorrow?"

"Yes, I'll see you then," Cyrus said as he hung up.

"This pizza is good," Rachel said as she sat with Lola in front of the fireplace with a glass of wine.

"It was a good day. We got the mandatory visit to my grandmother out of the way. We visited Mike King and you saw the cave."

"It was an adventurous day."

"All that remains is for you to call Mike and ask him to lunch tomorrow."

"I'm sure he'll fall for that. 'Hi, Mike, why don't we have lunch tomorrow so Lola can search your house? By the way, do you use surveillance devices?'"

"You saw how egotistical he was. He will probably think you fell in love with him."

"I fell in love with his house. It was gorgeous. He wasn't bad either, really. It's just that he is old enough to be my grandfather."

"Since when did that stop you?"

"Okay, I get your point. But somehow this does not fit with my image of modern women. We are using feminine wiles to take advantage of Mike. It seems rather underhanded."

"You think Mike would not do the same thing to you? What do you think he did to my mother?"

"I got the impression he has a lot of integrity."

"He's a clever person. It's just lunch. Go ahead and call him now."

Secretly, Rachel liked the idea. She picked up her cell phone and dialed Mike's number.

"Hello, this is Mike King."

"Hi, Mike, this is Rachel. We met this afternoon at your house."

"Hi, Rachel, what can I do for you?"

"Nothing, really—I enjoyed meeting. I am wondering, would you would think I am too forward if I asked you to lunch tomorrow?"

There was a moment of silence on the phone. "Sure, we could have lunch. What is this all about?"

"Nothing, really—I would like to get to know you better."

"It sounds like fun. Have you ever eaten at Forest Lake restaurant?"

"Yes, that sounds good. Shall we meet at noon?"

"Noon is fine—I'll see you then," Mike said as he hung up the phone.

"See, it wasn't that hard," Lola said.

"Actually, it was kind of fun. I think it will be an interesting lunch."

"Who knows where it might lead?"

"Probably to a jail cell for you. Are you crazy?"

"I am going to wear one of those stocking caps that cover your face with holes for the eyes and mouth. Every bit of my skin will be covered, so even if there is a surveillance camera, he won't know it was me."

"He'll know it was me and you—he just will not be able to prove it. But what if your grandmother is right? What if you are right? What if he did have something to do with your mother's disappearance? Do you think civility alone will stop him from doing something about it? We are stepping out on a thin limb."

"He will not even know it happened," Lola said. They finished the pizza.

Rachel sat next to Lola on the bearskin rug. She put her arm around Lola. "I'm scared of what might happen to you. I care about you."

"Come on, quit acting like a mother figure." Lola could feel the effects of the wine. She was coming to realize that she cared about Rachel in more that just a friendly way.

"It's not that. I just met you a few weeks ago, but I feel like I've known you a long time. I'm worried." Rachel kissed Lola. This time, Lola did not resist. She relaxed and enjoyed it. She liked being with Rachel, even though she got the impression there were a lot of things Rachel was not telling her—not the truth anyway.

Rachel stood and took Lola's hand. "It's time to go to bed." They walked hand in hand into the bedroom.

The next day, Lola dropped Rachel off at the restaurant early and went to her grandmother's house. She parked the car and took a roundabout path through the woods to Mike King's house. She concealed herself in a spot that had a clear view of Mike's door. She took out her field glasses and watched as Mike was preparing to leave for lunch. He was carrying boxes out to his car. Lola wanted to see what he had in the boxes. Did her visit with Rachel precipitate a reaction, paranoia in

Mike? Mike looked at his watch, closed the trunk, locked the front door, and drove away.

Lola waited five minutes—it seemed like hours. There was not activity in the house. She looked for a camera as she approached the house. She couldn't see any cameras, but there could be one in the trees surrounding the house. Every inch of her was covered anyways—the only way someone could recognize her was her size, and that would not be positive identification. It didn't look like Mike had turned on an alarm before he left. She tried the front door—locked. She worked her way around to the back of the home. It had a walk-out basement; she tried the basement door. It was locked also. She climbed the stairs to the deck. She was going to try the sliding patio doors when she heard an outboard motor. She laid flat on the deck behind the table and chairs. She was concealed from view from the lake because the house was on a slight incline to the lake. She raised her head to see a family driving by on a pontoon. She could hear them saying what a beautiful home it was. Lola lay still for another few minutes while the pontoon leisurely passed from view. She got up and tried the sliding doors. They were locked. She went around the house looking for an open window. She might have to physically break into the house. She was about to go into the woods to look for a stick she could use to break a window when she decided to take a better look at the woodpile underneath the deck. Sure enough, there was a chute with a trap door to put wood into the basement. It was open.

Lola waited a minute to gather her courage. Was she really going to break into this house? In the end, her curiosity about her parents won over and she plunged through the trap door into the darkness. She landed on a pile of logs and rolled to the floor. If there was anyone in the house, all her attempts at stealth were for naught. She had made enough noise to wake the dead. She took out her flashlight and surveyed her surroundings. She climbed over the firewood to the door. She breathed a sigh of relief. It was open. She was in the basement. She looked around. Like the upstairs, the basement was immaculate. She felt like looking around, but she had a mission to accomplish.

Lola made her way upstairs, taking care not to leave any sign of her entry. She went straight for the computer on the desk. The house had an open floor plan. The great room took up most of the space on the main floor. Lola turned on the computer; while she was waiting for it to boot up, she started searching the desk drawers. She systematically made her way though the desk until she found the drawer on the bottom left was locked. She turned her attention back to the computer. It was asking her to log in with a password. She started trying common passwords. She tried *Mike, King, password*...etc. She was afraid she would lock up the computer. The only response she got from it was to check if the caps lock was on. She was about to give up when she typed her mother's name, *Sandy.* It worked! The computer finished booting. Lola put a USB drive in the slot and started to copy the contents of the computer's hard drive to it.

Lola turned her attention back to the locked desk drawer. It didn't look like a very complicated lock—maybe she could pick it. She took out her Swiss army knife and slid it between the drawer and the desk frame. She could feel the knife hit the bolt portion of the lock. She applied pressure and felt it give. She slid open the drawer. She stopped and listened. She thought she heard something. She remained perfectly still. Nothing. She started going through the locked drawer. She heard it again. She slid the drawer closed and started toward the stairs. She heard the front door open. She bolted down the stairs and hid in the firewood room.

Mike pulled into Forest Lake restaurant's parking lot. It dawned on him that he had made an appointment to meet Cyrus at his house. He forgot about it completely. Cyrus would have left by now. He tried Cyrus on his cell phone. There was no answer. *He must be close to my place by now,* mused Mike. It was amazing what a lunch appointment with an attractive young female could do—he had forgotten his commitments. *Oh, well.* Cyrus watched Mike's house when he was on vacation. He had a key to the front door. Cyrus could go inside and call him from there.

Mike looked around as he walked in the door of the restaurant.

"Can I help you?" The waitress smiled from behind the cash register.

Mike spotted Rachel. "No, thanks, I'm meeting someone here."

"Hi, Rachel," Mike said as he approached the table overlooking Forest Lake, which the restaurant was named after.

"Hi, Mike, thanks for meeting me," Rachel said. She was a little unsure of herself. What was she going to talk with him about?

"It's a pleasure to have lunch with you. Thanks for inviting me."

Rachel blushed, even though it was true—she did invite him. "I'm glad we're doing this."

"Hi, Mike, the usual?" the waitressed asked.

"I'd like some coffee and a chance to look at the menu. What would you like?" he asked Rachel.

"I'll take some tea and a menu also."

"Where's Lola?" Mike asked.

"She's at my place working on her book."

"I thought you were from Minneapolis. You have a home in Grand Rapids?"

"My father has a home on Pokegama Lake."

Mike was suspicious. He had already checked the county records online. The house was in Rachel's name. She seemed young to have a second home on a lake. He decided to confirm what he already knew. "Lola is writing a book about her parents' disappearance?"

"Yeah, it is something that has bothered her all of her life. This is a way to get some closure. It's going to be her senior thesis for school. She is majoring in writing."

"I hope that goes well for her. I remember my college days—they were great."

"That's what everyone tells me, but it seemed like nothing but hard work to me."

"Life is hard work. That's why we should take time to smell the roses. Having lunch with you, for example."

Rachel was starting to like Mike. *He is handsome,* she thought. *What could be more charming than to lunch with him?* She was relaxing and starting to enjoy herself.

"Here comes the waitress again. Let's order," Mike said.

Cyrus pulled into Mike's driveway. Something did not seem quite right. The garage door was closed and it looked like no one was home. He remembered distinctly telling Mike that he would be over around 12:30 PM. Mike was disturbed about the two young women who came over to his house yesterday.

Cyrus thought about calling Mike but he did not have cell phone reception in the area. Then he thought maybe something had happened to Mike, a heart attack or health issue. Realistically, Mike had probably forgotten. He decided to go in Mike's house and check on him. Besides, he could always use Mike's landline to call Mike on his cell phone. Cyrus found his key and inserted it in the lock. He turned

182

the key, heard the bolt slide, and opened the door. He thought he heard a commotion in the great room, so he moved stealthily into the house. He called out Mike's name. He could see Mike's computer was on, but that was not necessarily unusual. He thought he heard something in the basement. He decided to call Mike on the landline on the desk.

"Mike, Cyrus. I thought we were going to meet at your house."

"I'm sorry, Cyrus. I tried to call you on your cell phone, but you must have been out of the coverage area."

"So what happened?"

"I had a lunch date and I forgot you were coming to my place. I'm at Forest Lake."

"Well, she better be good looking or I'm going to be pissed."

"She is. You're at my place?" Mike asked. He recognized his home phone number on his cell phone display.

"Yeah, I was worried about you. I was concerned you had a heart attack or something."

"I'll be home in about an hour if you care to wait."

"No, I have some things to do today. Did you leave your computer on?"

"I didn't—well, maybe I did. I don't remember. I was preoccupied with something before I left."

"I thought I heard something when I came in. I'll have a look around before I leave to make sure all the doors are locked."

Lola was standing in the dark in the firewood room. She tried not to breathe too loud. It was difficult; it felt like her heart was in her throat. She would not be able to climb out the chute without making enough noise to alert whoever was in the house. She thought she recognized the voice. It belonged to her grandmother's boss, Cyrus, the lecherous Cyrus. She was scared to death. What if he caught her? Breaking and entering was a serious crime. It carried jail time. What would happen to her writing career?

Then she realized she was not alone in the darkness. She could hear the squeaks of an animal. She could barely hear it moving though the woodpile. Was it a mouse? She hoped it wasn't a rat, or even worse, something bigger. It made her skin crawl, but she could not move. She would be discovered. As she stood there in the darkness, she felt the animal sniffing at her toes. She wanted to cry out, but she didn't dare. She kicked it. Whatever it was flew back into the woodpile. The logs shifted. The noise was nerve-racking. Lola was sure it could be heard across the lake. Whoever was upstairs must have heard the logs shift. She had her hunting knife with her. She took it out. She held it above her head and was ready to strike.

Cyrus heard the noise downstairs. Something was wrong. His first inclination was to call the police. It could be nothing. He decided to go downstairs to investigate. He tried to be as quiet as he could as he went down the stairs. He looked around the basement. Everything was in order. The walk-out door was locked. He looked at the woodshed.

Lola could feel fear gripping her spinal cord. This was it. Could she actually stab Cyrus? He deserved it after what he did to her. She could hear him put his hand on the doorknob and twist. The door slowly creaked open. Lola got ready to strike. Suddenly, a huge rat ran out the small opening of the door. Lola could hear Cyrus scream in fear, then laugh. "You scared me to death, you little devil," Cyrus said to the rat. He sighed in relief. *Mystery solved,* he said to himself as he went up the stairs and out the front door.

Lola could hear the front door close but waited another five minutes, listening carefully for any movements in the house. Finally, she left the woodshed and stealthily moved up the stairs. She slowly looked around the house and then went back to the computer. The screensaver password was *Sandy* also. The copy program had finished. The contents of Mike's hard drive were on her USB drive. She decided to go through the contents of the desk drawer that was locked. There was nothing of interest in the drawer except a USB drive that Mike probably used as a backup. She inserted it into the USB port of the computer. When she tried to view the files, she was prompted to enter a password. This time using *Sandy* as a password did not work.

Lola decided she had enough excitement for one day. She shut down the computer and replaced everything on the desk the same as when she found it. Then she went downstairs. She crawled out the wood chute and snuck through the woods to her grandmother's house.

"I'm back at my grandma's. Do you want me to pick you up?"

"No, Mike gave me a ride home."

"How did lunch go?"

"I'll tell you when you get here."

Lola contemplated her afternoon adventure as she waited for Rachel to arrive. She could not help but think about Mike's computer. Why was the password *Sandy?* Was it just a coincidence? That seemed unlikely. Was she close to a breakthough regarding her parents' disappearance?

"How did it go?" Rachel asked when Lola answered the door.

"I'll tell you later. I copied the contents of Mike's hard drive. Let's get going—I want to see what is on it."

Rachel sat next to Lola and watched as she fired up her laptop.

"Guess what the password was to login to Mike's computer?" Lola said.

"I don't know—*alluring?*" Rachel was a little tipsy from the drinks at lunch.

"Well, I can tell how your lunch went. The password was my mother's name, *Sandy.*"

She plugged in the USB drive and viewed the contents of the copy of Mike's hard drive. She opened the *my documents* folder and saw that there was actually a folder called *Sandy.* She tried to open the folder but found that the contents were encrypted.

Chapter 26

Everything is always an emergency with Mike King, Cyrus thought as he parked in Mike's driveway. He got out of his car and knocked on the door.

"What's so urgent?" Cyrus asked when Mike answered his door.

Mike led him over to his computer and said, "Watch this."

Cyrus watched the screen as Mike fast forwarded through the part where Cyrus was looking through the house. He slowed it to normal speed when the stranger dressed in black appeared.

"Who do you think this is?" Mike asked.

"I can only guess, but based on what you've told me, Lomasi?"

"That's my guess too. Watch what she does," Mike said as they watched her unplug the USB drive from his laptop and search the drawer."

"How did she get in?"

"She must have come in the wood chute. That is the only thing I can think of. I have motion detectors monitoring the doors and windows. She eluded those. The video camera didn't start recording until you came in the door."

"I thought I heard someone in the house when I came in yesterday."

"You did hear someone. Why didn't you investigate?"

"I did. I looked around the house. I thought I heard a noise in the room you use to store firewood, but when I opened the door, a rat ran out."

"It turns out there were two rats in there. One was human."

"Then it wasn't just a rat I heard, it was Lomasi."

"Lunch with Rachel was just a distraction," Mike said.

"I'm glad I didn't discover her. What would we have done if we caught her?"

"Blackmailed her, just like her mother."

"That's your answer for everything, Mike. What could she find on your computer or in your drawer?"

"Nothing is missing from the drawer."

"What do you think she was searching for?"

"She copied something from my hard drive. I'll tell you what she wants. She wants to cause trouble over her mother."

"What do you think she knows?"

"I don't know. She had to log in to my computer. The means she must have guessed the password."

"So?"

"The password is *Sandy*. I have a *Sandy* folder on my hard drive with the pictures we took of her that day at the waterfall."

"She's seen the pictures?"

"The file is encrypted."

"Why do you have pictures of Sandy on your computer?"

"You know how I feel about her."

"How long until some computer geek opens the file for her? After she sees the pictures, what do you think will happen?"

Mike gave Cyrus a serious look. *In for a penny, in for a pound,* he thought. "Cyrus, we are in this together. You have to help me."

Cyrus just sighed in resignation.

Lola could not get the *Sandy* folder that was on Mike King's hard drive off her mind. Rachel had a friend from college that was a computer guru. If anyone could open the file, it was Gary. He had it for a day now. She wondered if he had time to work on it.

She called her friend. "Rachel, this is Lola. I was curious if you had heard from Gary yet about the contents of that folder."

"I did—I was going to call you later on today to let you know. You're lucky Mike uses old technology. Gary was able to crack it easily. It seems our friend is a pornographer."

"There was pornography in that folder?"

"Yes, I asked Gary to email it to me. He wouldn't do it. I can see his point. He did not want to email porn and have someone intercept the email. He said he copied the decrypted file to your USB drive. He is going to drop it off at my place later today. It looks like you took a big risk for nothing."

"What do you mean?"

"Gary said it was just some weird stuff. It looked like something from an ancient sex ritual. Our friend Mike may be a little weird, but there is nothing illegal about that."

"I don't know—I have a hunch about him."

"Actually, I like him. I might go out with him if he ever calls me again."

"Be careful, Rachel. What if he knows that the purpose of that lunch was only a diversion to break into his house?"

"I don't think he has any idea about that. He was smitten with me."

"I think both him and Cyrus are smarter than you think."

"I'll call you when Gary drops of the USB drive. I'll wait till you come over. We can look at the pictures together."

"Okay. I'll wait to hear from you."

Lola came right away when Rachel called her. They settled into the privacy of Rachel's apartment upstairs. Rachel fired up her laptop and they started looking at the pictures.

"I can't believe it."

"What can't you believe?" Rachel asked.

"I think that's my mother. It looks exactly like her pictures."

"I can see a resemblance between you and her."

"What are they doing?" Lola said incredulously.

"You don't know what they are doing?" Rachel smirked.

"No, I mean…it seems to be a Native American ritual of some type. Do you recognize the setting?"

"It's by the waterfall. The place you brought me to explore the cave."

"That's right, and they seem to be conducting some kind of ancient rite. But look—the pictures must have been taken from the area of the waterfall looking back over the pond."

"Are the pictures recent?" Rachel asked. "Does this mean you mother is still alive?"

"The date on the properties of the pictures is seven years ago. I can't tell for sure, but I think that these pictures were probably scanned."

"Why do you say that?"

"Because…look…you can see they are tilted slightly. Who knows when they were taken? My parents have been missing for eighteen years."

188

"I can't tell for sure, but it does not look like she is being forced to do anything."

"What are we going to do, Rachel?"

"What can we do? We can go to the police, but what do we tell them when they ask where we got the pictures? It would mean a ticket to jail for us. Breaking and entering, stealing private property—how long do you think they would lock us up, a few years?"

"We can't just let this be swept under the table."

"If we found this evidence, there has to be more."

"I can't believe the sheriff didn't find this evidence years ago. Obviously Mike King is involved with my mother in other ways than just employing her at the resort."

"What about your father? Is he in these pictures, too?"

"I can't tell. The men are painted and dressed for ceremony. If he is, I don't recognize him."

"We have to go back up north dig into what happened some more. I could call Mike and let him know I'll be at my father's lake home again this weekend. I think he'll jump at the chance to see me again."

"We'd be taking a big chance. Are you sure you want to do that?"

"I liked him. I enjoyed having lunch with him."

"How much do you think he knows? We show up at his house and ask him about my mother. He has to be suspicious of us. I don't think you should do it."

"I know this isn't a television show where the good guy always wins, but there is a certain amount of intrigue involved in this."

"Maybe we should think of it as a television show or, better yet, a novel. We're the heroines. What should we do?"

"We should trick Mike and Cyrus into confessing, but how?"

"We have to make them overconfident."

"They already are overconfident. What do they have to be afraid of? Mike is even arrogant enough to keep those pictures on his hard drive."

"But why? Why would he keep those pictures on his hard drive all these years?"

"Unless my mother is still alive and Mike is using these pictures to blackmail her. Could she still be alive?" Lola asked hopefully.

"That would be a lot to hope for. If your mother was still alive, wouldn't she have contacted you? How could she leave her only daughter and never want to see her again?"

"The answer is, she wouldn't. There has to be something that we are missing."

Rachel's phone rang. "Hello…No, I did not…No, we were there but came home Sunday…I can't go there now….No, don't report it to the police. It was probably just an animal."

"That was my security service," Rachel explained. "They were wondering if we were at the cabin. The alarm went off last night."

"It sounds suspicious to me."

"It could be. In the past, we have had animals set off the alarm."

"Did you mean it about us going up north again next weekend?"

"Of course—this is the most exciting thing I have done for a long time. We have to plan a strategy. Do I call Mike?"

"Let's wait. I want to think about it."

"That cave is fascinating. I'd like to visit it again."

"Let's think about it and I'll contact you Thursday. We'll plan our weekend."

Ahote met Avery in Milwaukee and toured with the band. He learned the ins and outs of the business from the ground-floor perspective. He also learned how to set up a stage and take it down quickly. He learned that the music business was just that—a business. He finished the tour with the band in Miami. After twelve weeks on the road, he was tired and glad to be done.

Ahote had to make a choice. He could head back to Minneapolis or stay in Miami. A lot of the people he worked with on the tour, including the band, were from Miami, so he decided to stay there. Avery assured him there would be a job for him on the next tour. He thought about what he could do for a job and decided that he would get a cab license and drive a cab until the band started touring again.

After learning to drive a cab in Minneapolis, it was an easy transition to drive a cab in Miami. He would get to know the layout of the city one fare at a time.

Ahote learned in Minneapolis that there were ways to make money in his cab other than fares. He was asked for drugs and prostitutes when he picked up passengers at hotels. He already had drug connections from the friends he made touring. Ahote was becoming quite the entrepreneur.

After a couple of months, Ahote became known in the area. He had an engaging personality, which drew people to him. He liked Miami because the population was diverse. In Grand Rapids, he was treated like an outsider, a Native American, even though he had lived there all his life. It was better when he lived in Minneapolis, but there was still that stigma of being a minority. In Miami, minorities were the majority. He felt comfortable there and accepted.

Ahote worked hard on his music career. He learned that he had to pay the price to be successful. That meant learning to master his instrument and his singing and songwriting skills. He often thought about the band he worked for on tour. Although the band was made up of talented musicians, they were just people like everyone else. He knew that his goal was attainable.

Ahote also enjoyed the seedy side of life in Miami. He learned to work the cabstands close to the strip clubs. He liked to meet the dancers. He learned to treat them as entertainers, which they were. He became friends with them. He partied with them and slept with some of them. They found him charming.

One day, he got an order for the Barracuda Club. He parked outside the door and walked in. "Hi, Tony, who called a cab?"

"Ahote, how ya doin?"

"All right, man. Don't talk to the boss man too often; business good?"

"Yeah, everything is good. I've been looking to talk with you. We got something new in I think you'll like."

Just then, a sultry blond walked up and asked, "Are you my cabbie?"

"Ahote, this is Cassandra. She called the cab," Tony explained. "Stop by later on and we'll talk some more."

"I will," Ahote said as he walked out of the club with his fare. He opened the door for her.

"You're a gentleman," Cassandra said to Ahote as he got into the front seat. "Handsome, too!"

"I usually get nervous around good-looking women, but you bring out the best in me."

"Thanks. Take me to the Belmont. I've gotta work a double shift tonight. What's your name?"

Ahote introduced himself. He explained that he was relatively new to town. He was experiencing great rapport with Cassandra. He explained he was from northern Minnesota originally.

"I am, too," Cassandra replied. "I grew up in Grand Rapids."

"Me, too," Ahote replied. "Maybe we know some of the same people. I grew up on Bluewater Road, north of town."

Suddenly the conversation stopped and there was silence until they reached the Belmont Club. Cassandra threw a twenty-dollar bill over the front seat and said, "Keep the change," as she got out of the cab.

Ahote thought he must have said something to offend her, but at least she had given him a decent tip.

Ahote went back to the Barracuda Club later that night. "Is Tony around?" he asked the bartender.

"He's in his office. He didn't call a cab."

"I know, he wanted to talk to me about something. Tell him I'm here, would you?"

Tony came out of his office. "Ahote, glad you came back. Let's talk in my office."

They went back to the office. Tony said to Ahote, "We got a shipment of some super fine stuff. Would you like to get in on it?"

"Yeah, probably—I would need to try it."

"We can do that in a minute. Let me ask you this first: how would you like to get into something really profitable?"

"I'm always interested in more money," Ahote replied cautiously. He wondered what Tony had up his sleeve.

"Here." Tony pulled out a plastic bag with a small amount of white powder.

"Cocaine?" Ahote asked.

"Heroin—it's making a comeback."

"A comeback?" Ahote asked.

"Yeah, it's clean, not cut at all, and the price is reasonable. We had one of our guys quit. We need someone to sell it. You've been doin' okay with weed. We thought you might like to give it a try."

"I don't know. I'll have to think about it."

"Take this sample. Give it a try. See if you like it."

Ahote took it. He wasn't sure he would try it. On the other hand, he did not want his source of marijuana to dry up. He wanted to keep Tony happy. They went out in the alley to try the new weed.

"Cassandra could be your first customer," Tony offered Ahote.

"I didn't get on too well with her when I took her to the Belmont."

"She's moody. She's been with us since the beginning. She's at an age where she might not have too many more years as a dancer."

"What will she do?" Ahote asked.

"Who cares? There are plenty of young girls out there. She'll probably work on the streets."

Ahote agreed to buy a kilo of the weed. He left Tony and went back to driving his cab. He was disturbed by the revelations during his meeting with Tony. He thought about the heroin he had. Maybe he would give it a try—just snort it. There was a lot of money in the drug-dealing business. He could sell enough to produce his own music CD. Once his music career took off, he could quit driving a cab and dealing drugs. He went back to work.

Chapter 27

"It's been four days and nothing has happened. You've erased the folder off your hard drive and destroyed all the evidence. Are you satisfied?" Cyrus asked Mike.

"I'm suspicious. What makes you think they haven't seen those pictures of Sandy we took at the waterfall?"

"You worry too much. What if they have? Do you think they will be able to tell that Sandy was in the pictures? We didn't do anything."

"Lomasi isn't stupid," Mike replied. "She'll look at those pictures, recognize Sandy, and wonder what the connection is between them and the disappearance of her parents. All I need is a couple of young girls sniffing around in my business."

"Are you sure she copied the folder from your hard drive?"

"You saw her remove the USB drive. She must have copied it. She probably copied my whole hard drive."

"What else is on your hard drive?"

"Nothing and everything; I keep all my financial records on my hard drive. There is a lot of private information on it."

"We didn't do anything," Cyrus speculated. "There was no crime on our part."

"Yeah, but we didn't exactly cooperate with the sheriff—we withheld information from the investigation. Besides, if I have those two sniffing around my business, there is no telling how much trouble they can cause."

"What are we going to do?"

"I already searched the house on Pokegama Lake. Nothing turned up. It had an alarm system, but it was not very sophisticated."

"So now we wait. What else can we do?"

"I did not get to where I am by waiting. I am going to call Rachel and set up another date. I had a great lunch with her. She's very charming. Too bad she is in cahoots with Lomasi."

"All we know so far is there are a couple girls having fun. Wouldn't you be curious about what happened to your parents if you were in her situation?"

"Yes, I would be curious. I would also be cautious. I wouldn't break into someone's house."

Mike scares me, Cyrus thought. *He is not telling me everything.*

Mike King was a chapter of his life that Cyrus had buried deep in the recesses of his mind, only to be dragged up again. In some ways, Mike's role in his life was a blessing—he had helped Cyrus when Cyrus needed help. In some ways, Mike was a bad dream that would not go away. He looked at his friend and wondered how he became so involved in his schemes and what it was going to cost him. The price tag could be large.

"So what are we going to do?" he asked Mike.

"So what are we going to do?" Rachel asked Lola.

"We have to go on the offensive."

"I thought breaking into Mike King's house was pretty aggressive," Rachel said. "Don't you think that he may have an inkling that happened?"

"If Mike had a surveillance camera in his house, he probably has a recording of me."

"It makes me nervous. Who knows what Mike King is capable of doing?"

"We are going to find out," Lola said thoughtfully. "You are going to invite him to lunch again."

"Why don't you invite him to lunch? It was your mother."

"You're the one he was interested in. Nothing is going to happen at lunch. Besides, you liked him, didn't you?" Lola found it hard to hide her jealousy.

"I don't know why I do these things for you," Rachel said as she picked up the phone. She listened to the ringing, wondering, *Is there any wisdom in doing this?*

"Hi, Mike, this is Rachel Hargrove."

"Rachel, thanks for calling." Mike could hardly believe his luck.

"I wanted to tell you I enjoyed having lunch with you last weekend."

"I enjoyed it, too, Rachel. I'd like to do it again."

"I would, too, Mike—that's the reason I called. I am going to be in Grand Rapids next weekend. Perhaps we could get together then?"

"I'll pick you up Saturday at noon?"

"That sounds good, Mike; I'll look forward to seeing you then," Rachel said as she hung up the phone.

"Well, that was easy," Rachel said to Lola.

"That was great, Rachel," Lola said

"He's falling into our trap."

"I'm not so sure," Lola speculated.

"What do you mean? That's exactly what we wanted him to do."

"Are you sure they aren't planning for me to go back there?" Lola asked.

"How else are we going to find out what happened to your parents?"

"I think they have set the trap for us and we have to be careful not to walk into it."

"You could be right. We have to think about how we can turn this to our advantage," Rachel said thoughtfully.

"We have to make them think we are a couple of dumb girls. That they are in control so that they become overconfident."

"That is already the case. Mike isn't impressed with my intellectual abilities."

Lola giggled. "You're right, but I didn't mean it that way."

"We have to think about what they expect us to do."

"They probably think that I will try to break into Mike's house again. Someone will be waiting for me at Mike's place or will be waiting to follow me while you are having lunch with Mike."

"We should give them what they expect. Then surprise them."

"Are you crazy? Do you think I want to go to jail for breaking and entering?"

"What should we do, then?"

"We have to flush them out, find out what they are hiding. There is a lot we do not know, but what we know for sure is that Mike has some pictures of my mother engaging in some erotic acts."

"But how does that help us?"

"We have to make them think that we know what happened to my mother."

"Do you think Mike was part of what happened at the waterfall?"

196

"No, it is just a hunch, but I think Mike was blackmailing my mother and Cyrus was somehow involved. It's just speculation, but maybe she fought back and they killed her."

"That explains what happened to your mother, but what about your father?"

"Maybe they killed him, too. He must have known something about what was going on."

"I'm glad someone knew something about what is going on, because I'm lost."

"Don't feel bad—I'm lost, too. But, out of all of this confusion, maybe we can get Mike and Cyrus to make a mistake."

"So what's the plan?"

"We both go up to your lake place this weekend. After Mike picks you up, I'll go to my grandmother's house. I'll bet you that Cyrus will follow me there."

"Okay, so we get them to tip their hand. What does that accomplish?"

"We'll make more plans on the way up north. In the meantime, let's think about our options and see what kind of strategy we can develop. Besides, a weekend getaway for the two of us could be romantic."

"I'm looking forward to it," Rachel admitted.

"They played right into our hands," Mike said when Cyrus answered the phone.

"What are you talking about, Mike?"

"Rachel just called me—she will be in Grand Rapids this weekend and we are going to have lunch at the Sawmill."

"That means Lomasi will be visiting your home again."

"Exactly. They must think we're stupid."

"Do you want me to wait at your house while you have lunch?"

"No, I have a better idea. I'll tell you about it later."

Rachel picked up Lola after their morning classes at the university and they started the four-hour drive up north. It was shaping up to be a beautiful weekend. They were going to spend a great weekend on the lake, but they had to decide on their strategy to make Mike King disclose his role in the disappearance of Sandy and Dan.

"Now I'm worried about what will happen at lunch. What if he tries to kidnap me or something?"

"He won't do that—too much risk in a public place. I think they will focus on me. They will know that lunch is just a ploy and will want to find out what I do."

"You're right. Now that I think about it, what will you do? I thought about what you said about going back to Mike's house. That would be walking right into their hands. What we have to do is make them think we know something we do not know. But what is that?"

"It doesn't have to be anything. The only thing we have right now is some pictures by the waterfall. We know that Mike must have taken the pictures. I would guess from the background of the pictures that he must have been at the waterfall or close to it. So I am going to my grandmother's house in the morning. I can sit in the front yard, read a book, and wait for Mike to drive by. Then I'll wait another ten minutes and drive up Bluewater Road. Instead of going to Mike's house, I will drive right by it and go to the path that leads to the waterfall."

"I get it—you can see if anyone is following you."

"Yes, I will find a location with a good vantage point of the parking lot and wait to see if anyone takes the bait."

"If someone shows up—Cyrus, for example—you can take pictures."

"I never thought of that; I will take pictures. But pictures of Cyrus will not prove anything. If he shows up in the parking lot, it will be time to lead him on a merry chase."

Mike and Cyrus were sitting on the deck at Mike's house. It was a beautiful afternoon, but Mike and Cyrus were not there to enjoy the sunshine.

"So it's agreed—you will follow Lomasi to find out what she is up to," Mike said.

"Yes, we'll catch her red-handed breaking into your house. She will have a one-way ticket to the county jail."

"We can't send her to jail, Cyrus. What if she has copies of the pictures? We will have a lot of explaining to do."

"Why did we ever get involved in this in the first place? It just keeps getting more complicated all the time. We should just disclose what we know and leave it at that."

"Cyrus, don't get cold feet on me now. You're in this just as deep as I am."

"Okay, okay—we'll set up a webcam and record the break-in on your computer. I'll be there to catch her red-handed."

"We'll show those two girls they can't mess with us. As long as we stick together, we'll be all right. Once we catch her red-handed, we can blackmail them into leaving us alone."

"What if Lomasi doesn't go to your house? What if they have something else in mind?"

"We'll have to just play it by ear, then."

"I think I should just follow Lomasi. If she goes to your place, the webcam is in place. If not, at least we'll know what she is up to."

"Do as you like, Cyrus, just don't screw it up. She'll end up at my place anyway."

Lola and Rachel arrived at Rachel's lake home late Friday afternoon. After a quick swim, they went for a cruise on the lake. They pulled their boat up to the dock at Zorbaz and went into the restaurant for dinner.

"Are you ready for tomorrow afternoon?"

"As ready as I'll ever be," Lola replied. She looked at her friend and wondered what they would find out. "It will be a new chapter in my book."

"I hope we are around to see if it is a bestseller."

"It's exciting—I feel like a detective in a movie, only the danger is real."

"Do you know where Mike is going to take you to lunch?"

"No, he just said he would pick me up at my place."

Lola raised her glass to Rachel's and said, "To success."

They turned their attention to enjoying their meal.

While Rachel and Lola were in the restaurant, an intruder dressed in black approached Rachel's car. He found it was locked. He lay on his back next to it and placed something behind the rear bumper. He wondered if he could disable the alarm system on the house. He moved stealthily around the house to the walk-out basement door that faced the lake. As he got close, a motion detector turned on the light above the door. He ducked down as low as he could and slunk into the nearby woods at the side of the house. There he waited patiently.

It was dark when Rachel and Lola returned to their cabin. They left the light on the dock shining brightly so they could find their way back.

They went inside and started a fire in the fireplace. Lola took her laptop out to work on her novel. Little did they know, they were being watched.

The intruder was still there. He was cloaked in darkness and the nearby woods. He crept close to the window to get a better look at his prey. He was in control now. He would know where they were at all times now. He would find out their intentions.

The next day, Lola drove to her grandmother's house. She had a chance to visit with Sara and catch up on the local gossip. Then Lola sat in a lawn chair in the front yard and read a book. She was casually watching Bluewater Road to ensure that Mike King drove by before she started her journey up the road. She sat there patiently waiting. Mike had to leave by 11:30 AM to get there by noon. It was a quarter to the hour and he still hadn't driven by.

It dawned on Lola that perhaps Mike had gone downtown earlier. Besides, what did she have to worry about? She was not going to go to his house. It would have been nice to have Mike see her sitting there when he drove by, but really, what difference did it make?

Lola told Sara she was going for a walk to the Joyce estate, got in Rachel's car, and drove to the parking lot. She was sure she would be followed. She walked down the hiking path to a tree she used to climb when she was younger and climbed it. She had a clear view of the parking lot.

She only had to wait a couple minutes for a familiar car to pull into the parking lot. Cyrus surveyed the area and then got out of his car. He tried to open Rachel's car door; when he found it locked, he started walking down the hiking trail. Lola remained perfectly still and let Cyrus walk by her. She almost giggled when she saw how cautious he was being. She thought, *If he goes to the waterfall, then I know he was involved with my mother.*

Lola carefully followed Cyrus from a safe distance. He took the path to the waterfall. When he got within sight of the pond, he left the path going into the woods, taking a position that gave him a good vantage point of the area.

Mike sat in front of his computer and watched Rachel's car leave her house and drive toward Bluewater Road. The real-time GPS tracking system transmitter he installed on Rachel's car last night was working perfectly. He saw the car park at what must be Sara's house. He waited until the car started moving north on Bluewater Road and picked up the phone. "Hi, Rachel, this is Mike."

"Oh, hi, Mike. What's up."

"I hate to do this to you, but I am feeling terrible. Do you mind if I cancel lunch?"

Rachel, trying to sound disappointed, replied, "I was really looking forward to lunch with you, but if you're not well, I guess we'll have to do it another time."

"Thanks for understanding." Mike said goodbye and hung up. *It is all working out the way I want it to,* he thought. *It's too late for Rachel to call Lomasi on her cell phone. There is no cell phone reception. Lomasi will be on the way to my place in no time and Cyrus will be following her. The trap is sprung.*

"Is Lola there?" Rachel asked when Sara answered the phone.

"No, she just left to go for a walk."

"This is Rachel. Do you know where she went?"

"She went to hike on the trail that leads to the Joyce estate. She has your car. She said you were going on a date."

"It got canceled. She doesn't answer her cell phone."

"You have to get used to northern Minnesota, Rachel. There is no cell phone reception where we live."

"Thank you, Sara. Tell her I called."

"Is there something wrong? You sound concerned."

"No, my date canceled. I was just wondering if she wanted to do something for lunch."

"She said she would be going back to your place after her walk."

"Thanks, Sara. It was nice talking to you," Rachel said. She tried not to sound concerned about Lola, but she could not help wondering what Mike was up to. *Is he really sick? Does he know we had something planned? He is smarter than we gave him credit.* Rachel was intrigued, yet in a way, she wished she would never have been involved in this. She felt helpless. She thought, *I have to do something, but what can I do?*

Mike, still sitting at his computer, felt like the cat that caught the canary. Using his GPS tracking system, he could see that Lomasi was walking into his trap. All he had to do was wait for her to pull into his driveway. To his surprise, she drove past his house and kept heading north on Bluewater Road. He asked himself; *Where is she going? Is this some kind of trap? I wonder if Cyrus is following her.*

All he could do was wait. The car stopped at a curve in Bluewater Road. He asked himself, *Is that the parking lot for the path to the Joyce estate? The car did not move. Is she going for a walk or to the cave behind the waterfall?*

There was only one way to find out what Lomasi was doing. Mike shut down his computer, grabbed his Glock nine-millimeter, and activated the alarm for his house. He hopped on his ATV and sped down Bluewater Road. He deliberately drove past the parking lot; he noticed both Rachel's car and Cyrus' car in the lot. He was relieved to know that Cyrus had a handle on things. *At least I hope he does*, he thought. He concealed his ATV in the woods close to the parking lot and set off on foot.

Lola was torn between two alternatives: *Do I confront Cyrus and ask him why he is following me? He could deny it. What then? Or should I continue on as if I did not know he was following me?* The latter seemed to be the best alternative.

Lola utilized all the skills she had developed as a child growing up in the northwoods to quietly circle around Cyrus and emerge from the vegetation at the pond. She tried to pick the spot where the pictures of her mother in that pagan ritual were taken. At first she was nervous—after all, Cyrus was her grandmother's boss—but after a while, she started to enjoy herself. There was something exciting about knowing someone was watching you. It was like being on a stage.

She pretended to find something. She started digging in the sandy earth that surrounded the pond. She had her back turned to Cyrus, trying to draw him in. She stood up, pretending to examine a stick she had picked up in her hands for a couple of minutes. Then she slipped the stick into her backpack and walked toward the waterfall. It was a hot, steamy evening, so she decided to take a swim. She would give Cyrus something to look at. She slowly took off her clothes until she was nude and dove in the water. The pool was not very deep, but it dropped off quickly by the waterfall and had a sandy bottom. Lola had swum in this pool so many times as a child that she knew every inch of it. She would swim underwater, putting her hands on the sand occasionally so she could follow the bottom to the other side of the pool and surface again. She kept repeating this procedure, enjoying the cool, clear water and the erotic feeling she experienced knowing Cyrus was watching her. Suddenly, her hand scraped across something metallic on the bottom. Pain shot through her hand. She surfaced and was relieved to see her hand was not cut. She would probably just have a bruise.

Lola dove to the bottom of the pool again and retraced the route she took to the metal. At first she was unable to find what her hand had struck; even though the water was crystal clear, it was hard to see the detail at the bottom of the pool. Eventually she found it. She surfaced to catch her breath and dove back down to the bottom. The object seemed to be a metal ring. She pulled on it. There was resistance at first, and then the object gave way. She found she was pulling a chain out of the sand. She had to surface again for air. When she resubmerged, she pulled a rusty chain out of the sand. She dragged the chain out of the pool and sat down on shore. She was exhausted. She examined the chain. It looked like it was about two feet long and at the end there was a broken link. She wondered how the chain broke. What was it holding?

Cyrus was so engrossed in the scene in front of him that he didn't notice Mike King approaching him from behind.

Cyrus jumped when he heard Mike say, "The same old Cyrus. I can see you are working hard."

Cyrus looked at him. He could not disguise his surprise. "Sometimes a guy can enjoy himself and get the job done at the same time. What are you doing here? I thought you were having dinner with Rachel."

"I called her and canceled. I told her I was sick. I wanted to see if Lomasi would break into my house again. When I saw she came here, I was curious what she was up to. Now I can see she was entertaining you."

"Yeah, I noticed last summer when she worked at the clinic that she was not the same little girl Sara used to bring to the office."

"From my perspective, this was just a waste of time. Girlie shows are a dime a dozen."

"I wouldn't jump to conclusions, Mike. I just saw Lomasi find something at the bottom of the pool. She dragged it up on shore. I don't know what it is. She was poking around in the area where we took the pictures years ago. It looked like she found something there, too."

"Let me see those binoculars."

Suddenly, Lola remembered she was being watched. Cyrus must have seen her pull the chain from the pond. Did he suspect anything? Did she dare go back by the path? No, it might not be safe. She quickly dressed, grabbed her stuff, and retreated into the cave.

"Where is she going?" Mike asked Cyrus.

"I don't know," Cyrus replied. "Why would she go into the cave?"

"One of us should follow her."

"You're the one with the flashlight."

"It would be stupid to follow her in there," Mike said. "If she discovered we are following her, we would lose the element of surprise and she would be aware we were following her in the future."

"Then we wait. We can search the cave once she leaves."

Cyrus and Mike patiently waited for Lola to leave the cave and go home.

Lola entered the second chamber of the cave and found her way to the pool. She dove in and made her escape to Kremer Lake. She waited for a few minutes, then cautiously started making her way back to the parking lot. She noticed an ATV in the woods on the way. When she reached the parking lot, Cyrus' car was still there. Was there someone else with Cyrus? She couldn't be sure. The best thing to do was to get out of there safely. She put her stuff in the trunk and drove away.

On her way back to Grand Rapids, Lola called Rachel. "Hi, this is Lola. Can you talk?"

"Yes. Did you get my voicemail?"

"I haven't checked it yet. Are you through with lunch?"

"Mike called and canceled lunch. I left you a message."

"There's no reception by my grandma's house. Cyrus was following me. I waited in the woods by the parking lot for the Joyce estate. I took some pictures with my phone, then followed him. He hid himself in the woods where he could watch the cave, so he guessed where I would be going."

"What did you do?"

"I gave him what he expected. I snuck around in the woods and started searching the area where my mother was when those pictures were taken. I pretended to find something. Then I went to the pool under the waterfall. It was hot. I wanted to give Cyrus something to think about, so I went skinny dipping. While I was in the pool, my hand hit a hard object on the bottom. I pulled out a chain that was broken. It was mostly buried in the sand. I realized I did not want Cyrus to find out what I found, so I went into the cave and escaped him by swimming underwater to Kremer Lake. When I left the parking lot, Cyrus' car was there along with an ATV. I'll bet the ATV belongs to Mike."

"You did the right thing. You would not want to be out there alone at the mercy of Cyrus and especially Mike," Rachel said.

"I wonder if that chain had anything to do with the disappearance of my mother?"

"It could just be a coincidence that the chain is close to the place where the pictures were taken of your mother."

"I know that it is a long shot, but I would like to explore the bottom of that pool further. You never know what we might find."

"Maybe we could get some kind of underwater metal detector."

"We'll have to check to see what is available."

"What happened to her?" Mike asked Cyrus. They had been waiting outside the cave for two hours.

"Maybe we should go in after her," Cyrus suggested.

"She's probably waiting for us to come in there."

"Well, one of us should go in there and one of us should wait out here. That way, if she is going to try to slip by us, one of us will see her."

"What are we going to do if we catch her?" Cyrus asked thoughtfully.

"Good point—let's get out of here. We're better off not confronting her."

They weaved their way back to the parking lot to avoid running into anyone who would witness their presence. They were surprised when they reached the parking lot.

"Where's Lomasi's car?"

"She's already gone."

"We waited there for almost two hours. She had plenty of time to get away. There must be another way out of that cave."

"If there is, we never found it. We've been around this area for a long time."

"I can find her; let's go back to my place," Mike said.

"What, are you clairvoyant?"

"No, but I have the technology to do it. I installed GPS tracking software on my computer and put a small device on Rachel's car that allows me to keep track of the car's location."

Cyrus followed Mike back to his house.

"She's back at Rachel's place. It takes at least a half an hour to drive there, so she was way ahead of us," Mike said.

"Well, there is no way we will find out what she found now."

"All we can do is wait."

"I'm going home to get some rest. I spent a lot of time doing this for nothing. Let me know if you find out anything more," Cyrus said as he left.

Mike resolved that he was not going to be beat up by a couple of college girls. He would scare them off.

Chapter 28

The week dragged by for Rachel. She was infatuated with Lola and was looking forward to getting together with her again as soon as possible. She decided to call her.

"Lola, why don't you come over to my house tonight?" Rachel said over the phone. "I am going to make some lasagna."

"That sounds great, Rachel, but I am getting together with a friend of mine from Grand Rapids tonight," Lola replied.

"Is it a male-type person?"

"Yes, but it is not what you think. He was my neighbor on Bluewater Road when I grew up. We are kind of related."

"How can you be kind of related?"

"It's a long story. He was adopted by Duane, Sara's neighbor."

"Well, as long as it is something platonic, why don't you bring him along? We could open a bottle of wine. Then if you two would like to go out later by yourselves, I'll just stay home."

"That may not be such a bad idea. I have been wondering how I would entertain him."

"Why don't we plan on seven o'clock?"

"That sounds great, Rachel. Thanks for calling."

Ahote felt awkward picking up Lola at the dormitory. The university was an environment so foreign to his world. He missed the comfort zone of his cab.

"Hi, Ahote," Lola said. "It's nice to see you again."

"It's nice to see you. Thanks for getting together with me."

"Cab driving must be treating you well," Lola observed. "You're driving a new Camaro."

"A lot has happened since I saw you last, including a new name for you," Ahote said, changing the subject.

"Yes, I changed my name to Lola. I got tired of explaining to everyone that I was Native American and answering all their questions, so I adopted a more conventional name."

"I like it. Where should we go to eat?"

"A friend of mine from school invited us over for a lasagna dinner."

"Sounds good to me, just tell me how to get there."

"Drive across the Franklin Bridge and take a left on River Road. Rachel lives in a house on the river."

"Sounds like big bucks."

"She lives there and rents it out to four other girls. I might move in next year if there is an opening."

They pulled into the driveway at Rachel's house and went to the door. Rachel was waiting for them and opened the door before they could knock. "Welcome," she said.

"Hi, Rachel, this is my friend Ahote."

"Nice to meet you, Ahote. Thanks for coming."

"Thanks for inviting me," Ahote said. "I like your place."

"It's such a nice evening, let's sit out on the porch and have a glass of wine. The lasagna is done—I took it out of the oven—we just have to let it cool a little bit. I have some great white merlot."

"I'll take a glass," Lola said.

"Nothing for me," Ahote said. "I'm driving."

"How about some pop, Ahote?"

"Just a glass of water is fine."

Rachel returned with the water and the wine.

"You have a nice place here, Rachel," Ahote said. "It is nice to have a view of the river."

"Yes, it reminds me of lazy summer days. And it gives me inspiration for my music."

"Lomasi tells me you were a music major."

"Ahote, I changed my name to Lola!"

"Sorry, I just found out about the name change tonight," Ahote said to Rachel. "It is hard for me to get used to it."

"I think the name Lola suits her," Rachel said thoughtfully.

"I'm a musician, too," Ahote said.

"What instrument do you play?" Rachel asked.

"I play guitar and sing."

"In college, my instrument was piano, but I play guitar for fun," Rachel explained.

"We should play sometime," Ahote suggested.

"I'd like that," Rachel said. "Right now the lasagna is ready. Let's go eat."

They all sat down to dinner.

"You're a cab driver/musician?" Rachel asked.

"When I first moved here from Grand Rapids, I worked as a waiter. Then I found out about cab driving. It allows me a have a flexible schedule."

"Can you make much money driving a cab in Minneapolis?" Rachel asked. She saw Ahote and Lola pull up in a new car.

"I moved to Miami. I drive a cab there. The money is all right. The hours are long."

"What are you doing in Minneapolis?" Rachel asked.

"I'm on my way to Grand Rapids to visit my adopted father, Duane."

"We're going to Grand Rapids this weekend," Lola said. "Rachel has a house on Pokegama Lake."

Ahote was impressed. A house on the River Road and one on Pokegama Lake—Rachel must be doing all right. "Can I use your bathroom?" Ahote asked.

"Sure, just go to the end of the hall. You can't miss it."

When Ahote was in the bathroom, Rachel said, "You didn't tell me he was a hunk!"

"I don't think of him that way. He is just the guy next door I grew up with."

"He's gorgeous."

"Yeah, well, wait till you get to know him." Lola was visibly jealous.

"That's what I plan on doing. What are you going to do tonight?"

"I really don't know. Ahote called me out of the blue. I haven't seen him since I left Grand Rapids. I was surprised to hear from him. Could we sing and play guitar with him? It would help me out."

Ahote returned. "Thank you for the dinner," he said. "We should probably get going, Lola."

"Rachel has a guitar and a piano upstairs in her apartment. She suggested we play and sing."

"Great idea—I have my guitar in the trunk of my car," Ahote said. "I'll go get it."

Ahote came back in with his guitar. They all went upstairs to Rachel's apartment.

"This is really nice," Ahote said. "You have plenty of room and a view of the river."

"I like it. It can be trying having roommates at times. Someday I'd like to have it to myself." Rachel thought of living with Lola.

"You could do it with the royalties from your music."

Rachel laughed. "I think that is a long way off."

They tuned their guitars and Ahote started strumming in A minor. He was surprised when Rachel took the lead. She improvised with an A minor pentatonic scale lick, then moved into the harmonic minor scale. It was beautiful. Ahote was impressed. He could not take his eyes off her. Here was this charming woman, playing guitar at a much more advanced stage than him.

"That really sounds good, Rachel," Ahote said. "I'd like to play this song I wrote with Lola called 'Ode to Wabana.'"

"You're a songwriter?" Rachel asked.

"That is one of the things I would like to do," Ahote replied. "I like to sing and play the songs I write."

"Well, go ahead and play your song. I'll follow along."

Ahote started playing rhythm guitar for the song, Lola joined in singing, and Rachel played fill-ins and took the lead in the bridge of the song. Ahote was impressed. He had never played with someone who was a trained musician. It was a new experience that he liked. Rachel knew exactly what to do and when to do it.

"Wow, Rachel—that was great!"

"I am surprised how well we play together. Lola has a lovely voice."

"Yeah. What other songs do you know?"

They played together for an hour. Rachel noticed that even though Ahote had rough, muscular features, he had a warm personality and was particularly sensitive to the nuances of the music they played.

"We should do this again," Rachel said.

"I would enjoy that," Ahote said. He was thinking how attractive Rachel was and how well she played the guitar. "How about this weekend?"

"Maybe we'll do that. As I mentioned, we're going to Grand Rapids this weekend," Lola explained. "We have some detective work to do."

"Detective work? What happens in sleepy old Grand Rapids that requires detective work?"

"Lola is trying to solve the disappearance of her mom," Rachel explained. "It has become an obsession with her."

"That happened so long ago, I wasn't old enough to remember it," Ahote remarked. It was no surprise to him, though—it had always been an obsession with Lola. "How can you possibly expect to find out what happened now."

"You'd be surprised," Lola said. "We found some interesting pictures. They were on Mike King's computer."

"Mike King? How did you access his computer?"

"We have our ways of getting information," Lola said. "Anyways, we found there was some kind of a celebration going on at the waterfall on the Joyce estate that my mother was involved with. We are going back up there this weekend to do some more investigating."

"I'll be at Duane's house. I haven't visited him in a while. Let me know if I can be helpful," Ahote suggested, hoping he would see Rachel again.

"You can help us search by the pond if you like," Lola said. "I found a chain at the bottom of the pond. I'd like to find what it was attached to."

"Have you discussed any of this with Sara?" Ahote asked.

"No, I have asked Sara about my parents many times, but she sweeps the subject under the carpet. It is almost like she does not want me to know something. I think Mike King and Cyrus Longfell are somehow involved in this, and when it comes to them, she clams up," Lola said.

"I have had similar thoughts," Ahote said. "Duane has never been forthcoming when I ask about my parents."

"Yes, I thought about showing these pictures to Sara, but I think she would just act shocked. Perhaps she does not know anything about them. Anyways, she worked her way up from janitorial duties at the hospital to being a nurse practitioner. She thinks doctors are gods. In her own way, she worships Cyrus. I think she fears Mike King. I need something more substantial to confront her. Besides, she raised me as if I were her daughter. I should be grateful."

"I am curious, too. It doesn't hurt to search the pond. We could have a campfire at your place Saturday night. Roast hot dogs and marshmallows.

"It sounds like a plan," Rachel said. She had been silently amazed at the revelations that occurred in front of her. "I really enjoyed playing guitar with you," she said to Ahote. "I hope we can get together some more and write some songs. We can use Lola's help with the lyrics."

"It sounds like a musical adventure," Lola said.

"Lola, I'll pick you after classes Friday," Rachel said.

"I'll meet you two up north," Ahote said.

They said goodnight. Ahote drove Lola home. "How long have you known Rachel?"

"I met her my first day at school. She was at the orientation. We've become good friends over that time."

There was silence for a moment as Ahote was lost in thought about the evening. He had never met anyone like Rachel before. His pursuing a musical career always made him the bad boy, so to speak, in the neighborhood. Now he had met someone who had a degree in music. She seemed interested in him and his music. It gave him a lot to think about.

"Thanks for giving me a ride home. I enjoyed myself this evening," Lola said.

"I enjoyed myself, too. I'll look forward to seeing you this weekend," Ahote said as Lola got out of his car.

Mike was simmering. He was mad at Rachel and Lomasi. He had watched their progress on the tracking system installed on his computer as they drove back to Minneapolis the following day. He knew they had slipped through his hands without him accomplishing what he wished to accomplish. He wanted to scare them into submission. He did it with Sandy and he would do it with her daughter. Her friend was just a bonus. He needed to stop them from investigating Sandy's disappearance, but how?

He had a good start. They could not make a move without him knowing about it. With his global tracking system, they could not come close to Grand Rapids, particularly Wabana Township, without him knowing about it. He had to assume they had the pictures he and Cyrus took so many years ago. It was no proof of anything. Still, it would cast the shadow of suspicion on him regarding the disappearance of Sandy.

Then there was Cyrus. Mike had been manipulating him ever since they were kids. Cyrus was smart, but in the end, he was timid. Yet when they started all this at the resort years ago, Cyrus had wanted no part of Mike's relationship with Sandy and, in truth, his part in it was small. Was it still enough to extort his help? Looking at it realistically, Cyrus was his weakest link. Would he remain silent? There was only one way to find out.

"Cyrus," Mike said into the phone, "this is Mike."

"Hi, Mike, what's up?"

"I was just thinking about those two girls. What do you think we should do about them?"

"What do you mean *we?*"

"You're in this just as deep as I am."

"I told you years ago we should just forget about those pictures, get rid of them. But no, you had to keep them. It's your own fault we're in this mess."

"Get off your high horse. There is nothing we can do about the past. What happened has happened. We have to focus on the future, our future."

"You're right. We have no choice."

"That's the Cyrus I remember. Now let's make a plan."

"I don't see how we can plan anything. We don't know what they are going to do."

"We know Lomasi is going to write a book about her parents' disappearance. She intends to do research."

"The sheriff didn't find anything—what makes you think it will be any different for Lomasi?"

"For one thing, she's smarter than the sheriff. Also, she is focused and can take her time. She doesn't have every crime in Itasca County to investigate."

That is true, Cyrus thought. "Now that I think about it, the sheriff wasn't out sniffing around the waterfall or the cave."

"They have the potential to do damage—real damage. It is just a matter of time."

"We could be jumping to the wrong conclusion, Mike. Are we just being paranoid? Let's just wait and see what happens."

"I think you are wrong. We have to be proactive. Bad things happen to those who sit around and wait."

"What can we do, question them?" Cyrus said sarcastically.

"Cut the crap, Cyrus. Think about it—Lomasi's grandmother works for you. Wait for the appropriate time and ask her how Lomasi is doing in school. Get Sara talking about her. See what you can find out."

"That makes sense."

"Of course it makes sense. In the meantime, I can keep track of where Rachel drives her car. Call me after you talk to Sara."

"Okay."

"One more thing—who is Rachel Hargrove?" Mike asked.

"I don't know. I only met her once." Cyrus was embarrassed when he thought about his encounter with Rachel.

"She's involved with Lomasi, we know that. Could she be instigating all this? I'll call Tony and have him look into her."

The next Friday, Cyrus spent most of the day in his office. It was a day to catch up on paperwork. He wondered how he would approach Sara. He felt guilty about what was happening, but letting Mike down would be letting himself down. He had to learn as much as he could. As the day wore on, he tried to the think of a nonchalant way to discuss Lola with Sara.

He heard a knock on his office door. "Come in," he said.

"Hi, Cyrus." It was Sara. "Sorry to disturb you, but would you mind if I left an hour early today. Lola is coming up to visit this weekend. I need to get ready."

"I don't see any reason why not," Cyrus replied. *Sometimes things just work out,* he thought. "How is Lola doing now?"

"She is doing well. She likes college; so far, her grades have been excellent. It's just that she wants to be a writer. I'd like to see her go into something stable like the medical profession."

"I remember those days. When you're young and in college, the choices can be daunting. You have to be patient. Is Lola interested in being a journalist?"

"No, I would consider that sensible at least. It's a career. She is interested in writing novels. She already started writing one. It's for her senior project."

"Actually, that sounds interesting," Cyrus said, trying not to sound too interested. "What is she writing about?"

"She is writing about the disappearance of her parents."

"That's a tough subject. I thought that was pretty much an unsolved mystery. It's a shame."

"It is," Sara replied. "I think that is part of the problem. Sandy is something that is missing in her life that she somehow has to resolve. She is working on solving the mystery."

"Has she made any progress?"

"No. She's young; she thinks she can solve the problems of the world. I try to explain to her that she needs to be practical. If Sandy's disappearance couldn't be solved by the sheriff, what chance does she have of solving it? Anyways, she is coming up here this weekend with her friend from college to do some more investigating."

"That's interesting. What more is there to investigate?"

"I don't know. I'm glad she is coming to visit. I guess the best thing I can do is let this thing play out for itself."

"I think a lot of you, Sara. We have worked together for too many years to count. If you would like to discuss this further or if I can do anything at all, please feel free to ask."

"Thank you, Cyrus. I'm glad we had this conversation. I feel better."

"Don't mention it," Cyrus said as Sara left his office and went back to work.

"I hope you don't have plans for the weekend," Cyrus said to Mike when he answered the phone.

"I don't have any plans as it turns out. What's up?"

"I spoke with Sara earlier today. She wanted to leave work early so she could get ready for Lola's visit."

"Lola?"

"I forgot to tell you. Lomasi changed her name to Lola when she went to college."

"I'd like to get those two out of my hair, whatever their names are."

"Let's not do anything drastic. Sara told me that they are going to be over to her house Saturday. She knows that Lola is looking into her parents' disappearance."

"How much does Sara know?"

"She didn't seem to know anything new. She wishes that Lola would forget about it and focus on her career."

"That makes three of us. I'll monitor the tracking system. We have to keep an eye on them. I'll be able to reach you by cell phone?"

"Yes, we'll keep in touch," Cyrus said as he hung up.

Chapter 29

Rachel kept playing her last visit to Grand Rapids over and over again in her mind. It was like a puzzle—the pieces were there, she just had to put them in their proper places. She thought about her involvement with Mike King. He was handsome, rich, and very smooth. She was curious about his involvement with Lola's parents. Rachel admired Sara, someone who pulled herself up by her bootstraps. She could identify with that. Sara had an aura about her radiating integrity and stability. Duane, on the other hand, exuded animal magnetism. She could feel the attraction spreading through her when she thought of him. Was he purposely trying to seduce her? *He probably doesn't even realize he has that effect on me,* she thought. She decided the best way to find out was to call him. What was there to lose?

"Hi, Duane, this is Rachel, Lola's friend."

"Hi, Rachel, it's nice of you to call."

"I really enjoyed meeting you," Rachel replied. "Lola thinks highly of you."

"She's a little darling. I think of her as my grandniece."

"You mean she isn't related to you?" Rachel already knew Sara and Duane were not related, but she was interested in hearing what kind of a relationship Lola had with Duane.

"We're not related in the familial sense, no."

"So you are not related at all to Lola?"

"Sara and I are very close, but I am not her brother," Duane explained. "I watched Lomasi grow up, spent a lot of time with her. We have a strong bond, but we are not family."

"Interesting. The reason I called you is, Lola is frustrated. She feels that everyone knows more about her parents' disappearance than her, but they are not telling her because she will be hurt or something."

"I understand." Duane's mind was racing. He was hoping to see Rachel again. "Perhaps there is more. I never thought of it that way. We always just wanted to protect Lomasi when she was young and impressionable."

216

"Is there more you can tell me?"

"Maybe I can be helpful—I don't know. I feel uncomfortable discussing this on the phone," Duane replied, hoping she would take the bait.

"I understand completely. Would it help if we talked in person?" *Why did I say that?* Rachel thought.

"I would like to help Lomasi, of course. I just don't think I should discuss her mother with her directly. Sara would not approve."

"I have a house on Pokegama Lake; I like to visit the area. I could drive up there tomorrow."

"Great. Why don't you stop by my place? We could have a leisurely talk. Later in the evening, I am having some friends over. You could stay for the party if you like."

"That sounds like fun."

"All right, why don't you stop by around 4:00 PM?"

"Okay, I'll see you then." Rachel hung up the phone. She smiled to herself. *I think he likes me.*

The next day, Rachel could not concentrate. She was riding an emotional roller coaster with peaks and valleys—riding a beast that mirrored her own inner passions. It was disconcerting, yet she was enjoying the ride. She packed a few things for an overnight stay and left for Grand Rapids. She drove to her house on Pokegama Lake. She freshened up a bit, then drove to Duane's house.

"Hi, Duane," she said when he answered the door. "Thanks for having me over."

"I have been looking forward to seeing you again," Duane said as he looked her up and down.

He's leering at me, she thought. She felt a tingle in her spine. She was hoping Duane did not notice that she was flushed or that she was at a loss for words.

"Sit down," Duane said as he motioned her towards the sofa. "Would you like something to drink? I just made some lemonade."

"Lemonade sounds great," Rachel stammered. She felt like a young girl on her first date.

Duane went into the kitchen and brought lemonade for Rachel and a beer for himself. He sat and said thoughtfully, "Why do you care about what happened to Sandy?"

Rachel was unnerved by his frankness. "I care because she is Lola's mother. I care about Lola," Rachel said. She felt Duane's piercing stare. He had asked a valid question.

"I'm sorry if I am too direct. Even though I am not really related to Lola, I care for her, too. I was involved in her upbringing, taught her Native American customs. Don't you think as a white girl you are intruding on Native American family matters?"

"No," Rachel replied. She tried to hide her anger. "This is not about racism—everyone has a mother. Lola is my friend."

"Are you sure it is just about friendship?" Duane asked.

"Yes, I feel sorry for Lola. She never got to know what happened to her mother and father. If you know anything that would be helpful, please tell us." Rachel was feeling an incredible attraction to Duane. She felt like he was looking straight through her. She felt a little lightheaded. She wondered why she was defending her actions. Somehow she cared what Duane thought of her.

Duane got out of his chair and sat next to her on the sofa. She could feel his demeanor had changed. "I'm sorry. I feel very close to Lola. I guess I resent the fact that she likes you so much."

"Thank you for being so understanding. I was feeling intimidated." *He's playing me like a fiddle,* she thought. To her surprise, she liked it. "What can you tell me about Lola's mother?"

"I am reluctant to discuss this with you, but Lola is an adult now and she has the right to know," Duane said as he moved a little closer to Rachel. Silence hung in the air.

"Tell me—I'd really like to know." Rachel leaned into Duane.

"Sandy was a wild child. She was talented, intelligent, and charming, but she had a feral quality about her."

"Do you think she is still alive?" Rachel asked.

Without waiting for a reply, Rachel put her arms around Duane's neck and kissed him. She surprised herself and him. Duane, of course, responded to her unexpected move by kissing her back. Rachel slowly lay back on the sofa, drawing Duane with her until they were prone. She was hot with passion. She began to grind herself against Duane. He cupped her breasts and started gently massaging. She slid her hand inside his trousers, his hardness filling her hand. She gasped, then began unbuckling his pants and fumbling with his zipper. He stood and quickly slid his trousers down, his manhood erect. Rachel slid her pants off and then he was on top of her. She moaned with pleasure as he penetrated her—she was lost in pleasure.

218

When Rachel woke up, she was alone on Duane's sofa. She wondered how long she had been there. She was covered with a sheet; underneath, she was completely naked. Her body ached everywhere. She smiled as she thought about Duane.

Rachel looked around the living room. There were beer cans and fast food wrappers strewn across the floor. The ashtrays were full and the smell of marijuana still hung in the air. She wondered what had gone on. She had missed the party—or had she?

Rachel looked at the time on her cell phone. She had stayed there overnight. What had she done? She grabbed her purse and rummaged through it. Nothing was missing. She looked out the window and saw her car where she had left it. She was groggy. It felt like the morning after. As she came to her senses, it felt like she had been making love all night. What had Duane done to her? Why did she come here in the first place? It wasn't the wisest decision. She heard snoring. She went to the bedroom and peeked in. Duane was sleeping; there was a woman in bed with him. She didn't remember what happened—all she knew was that she wanted to get out of there. Rachel went back to the living room, found her clothes, and dressed quickly. She grabbed her things and went out the door. She got in her car and looked around. There was nothing amiss. She started the car and left.

By the time Rachel reached her home on Pokegama Lake, she was awake. She went inside, took off her clothes, and got in the shower. The warm water had a soothing effect. She got out of the shower, dried herself, and went straight to bed. Her head hit the pillow and she was asleep.

Chapter 30

The pitter-patter of raindrops accentuated the gloom of the day as Lola scampered from her dormitory to join Rachel for the journey to Grand Rapids. It was an inauspicious start to their weekend up north. Both of them hoped the stormy weather was not a harbinger of things to come. Friday afternoon was always an upbeat time for Lola and Rachel. It was hard not to be in a good mood with the entire weekend in front of you. The weather worsened as they drove, tempering their spirits. When they arrived in Grand Rapids, the storm became severe. They stopped at Rachel's house to drop off their luggage, then began the trek to Sara's house. When they reached Bluewater Road, they had to dodge fallen trees and branches. Tornadoes were rare in this part of the country, but northern Minnesota was no stranger to severe winds. Rachel couldn't avoid getting a tree limb stuck under the car as she drove. The car dragged the limb along over the gravel road, making an annoying noise as they went. Rachel stopped and tried to pull the tree limb free, but it would not budge. Lola pitched in to no avail.

"We'll ask Ahote for help," Lola said.

"I hate to drive all that way like this."

"It's only a little ways."

When they pulled into the driveway, Ahote waved from the window.

"Thanks for helping us clean up after the storm," Ahote joked as he came outside to greet them.

"It's not funny," Rachel replied. "This tree limb could damage my car. Can you help get it out from under there?"

"Sure." Ahote reached under the car to dislodge the branch. He could not pull it loose. "It must be really stuck. I'll have to crawl under the car."

Rachel brought a blanket from the trunk so Ahote could lie on it. He slid underneath the back of the car. After he pulled the branch loose, he started to slide out from under the car when he noticed something that looked out of place attached to the underside of the car behind the rear bumper. He was wondering what kind of new invention they had thought of now and was surprised when the grabbed it and was able to pull it off with relative ease.

"Look what I found," Ahote said.

"What is it?" Rachel asked. She and Lola were both looking at what Ahote had in his hand. It was a small black object that looked like half a sphere that fit easily in Ahote's hand.

"I don't think it is part of your car," Ahote said. "It came off too easy."

"What does it say on that label?" Lola asked.

"I can't tell without my glasses," Ahote said and handed the device to Rachel.

"Global tracking transmitter," Rachel read. "What is that?"

"Have you been dealing drugs?" Ahote said to Rachel and laughed. A guilty look came over Rachel's face. He had an impish charm to him when he was amused. "I saw a news story on TV about these. The police use those to keep track of suspects. They can track your location on their computers."

"What in the world is going on here?" Rachel said. "Why would the police be keeping track of me?"

"Come on, Rachel, come clean," Ahote said with a sly smile.

"I have noticed a couple squad cars following me in Minneapolis, but I thought it was because of my lead foot," Rachel joked.

"Are these available commercially, too?" Lola asked.

"I think you can buy them on the Internet," Ahote said.

"You don't suppose someone other than the police may have planted that device on your car?" Lola asked.

"I think I know who you have in mind," Rachel said.

"Well, let me in on the secret," Ahote said.

"Mike King," Lola said.

"Why would Mike want to keep track of Rachel?" Ahote asked.

"There are a few things you do not know about," Lola said to Ahote. "We interviewed Mike a couple weeks ago. I told him I was writing a book about my parents' disappearance." Lola looked at Rachel, wondering if they should tell Ahote everything that had happened.

"Can you keep a secret?" Rachel asked Ahote.

"If it regards Mike King, yes, I can keep a secret. I hate the bastard."

"Most of the people in the neighborhood hate him," Lola explained to Rachel.

Lola explained how she had crawled into Mike's house through the wood chute and hacked into his computer. "We think Mike may know that we broke into his house," Lola said.

"What do you mean, *we?*" Rachel said.

"You kept him busy while I did it," Lola said. "We think he had surveillance cameras. I was wearing a stocking cap over my face so no one could recognize me, but if he had me on film, Mike could probably guess who it was. He probably knows we copied his hard drive," Lola explained to Ahote.

"What did you find on his hard drive?" Ahote asked.

"We found the normal stuff anyone would save on their computer, plus an encrypted folder called *pictures,*" Lola replied.

"Were you able to decrypt the folder?" Ahote asked.

"A friend of Rachel's opened it for us. It had pictures of my mother in it."

"Pictures?" Ahote asked.

"Pictures of my mother in compromising situations," Lola said reluctantly.

Ahote knew he had hit upon a nerve and wisely changed the subject. "What should we do with the transmitter?"

"Destroy it," Rachel said.

"That will alert Mike that you found it," Ahote said.

"Wait a minute—it may come in handy sometime in the future," Lola said. "Let's put it back where it was. We won't let on that we found it."

"Yeah, who cares if Mike King knows where we are? I'm glad he is worried about what we are doing," Rachel said as she gave the device back to Ahote. He crawled under the car and put the transmitter back where he found it.

Mike was watching his computer off and on all day. He knew Rachel had arrived in Grand Rapids the day before; when he saw her car stop at Sara's, he knew Lola was with Rachel.

Rachel's car did not leave her home on Pokegama Lake all morning. Finally in the afternoon, Rachel was on the move. He followed the car's progress as it traveled to Bluewater Road and stopped close to Sara's house, then continued on to the parking lot for the hiking trail.

"Cyrus, this is Mike. The girls are on the move again. They parked their car at the parking lot for the hiking trail."

"What do you want me to do?" Cyrus asked.

"Come out here and help me with them. Let's see if we can put an end to this."

"Okay, I'll meet you on the way to the cave."

After picking up Ahote, Rachel and Lola parked in the lot for the hiking trail.

"Should we post a lookout for Mike?" Ahote asked. "I think we have to assume he will follow us here."

"That is a good idea," Lola said. "Ahote, would you watch for Mike?"

"Wasn't it Cyrus who followed you last time?" Rachel asked.

"You are right. It could be either one of them, perhaps both," Lola replied.

"What if they are following us? Does it make a difference?" Rachel asked.

"What do you mean?" Ahote asked.

"We came here to search the area and the bottom of the pond for clues to what happened to Lola's parents. Are we going to do anything different because they are watching us?"

"Last time when Cyrus was watching me, I pretended to find something at the site of the ritual with my mother. I wanted to make them show their hand. Then I really found something at the bottom of the pond. Just knowing we are searching has to be affecting them. They must be wondering what I found," Lola said.

"They are not going to tell us what they know. We somehow have to trick them into disclosing their involvement in the disappearance," Rachel observed.

"Either way, we have to know if they are watching. If they are, we can put on a show for them," Ahote said.

"Yes," Lola agreed. "Ahote, will you let us know right away if they are following us?"

"All right," Ahote replied as he disappeared into the woods to watch for Mike or Cyrus."

"I suggest we just go ahead with what we came here to do. Let's search the pond and see what we can find," Lola said.

"I agree," Rachel said as they veered off the hiking trail toward the waterfall.

Lola inspected the shoreline of the pond looking for the spot closest to where she had found the chain. She made a show of stripping down to her bathing suit and entered the pool. This time, she brought a diving mask and snorkel. She would swim along the surface first, to see if she could find anything obvious, before she searched the bottom in earnest.

While Lola was in the pool, Rachel used the metal detector they brought with them to search the shore. She watched her friend move along the surface of the pool. She wondered if Lola was looking for something that was not there. Were they on a wild goose chase? Would she ever be able to find out what happened to her parents? Just because Mike King had some photographs on his hard drive didn't mean that he was involved in Sandy's disappearance.

The beeper on the metal detector startled her back to reality. Rachel had found something. She dug into the sand to no avail. She kept digging until she was about two feet down—nothing. Rachel had brought a sifter with her and started to sift through the sand she had dug out of the hole. After she had sifted through roughly half the pile, she found a metal object encrusted with sand. As she cleaned it up, she realized it was a spent ammunition cartridge, probably from a pistol. She continued to sift through the sand in the pile. She found another cartridge.

Rachel tried to get Lola's attention, but Lola was busy surveying the bottom of the pond. Finally Lola looked toward shore. Rachel held up one of the spent shells and pointed to it. Lola swam to shore.

"Look what I found," Rachel said.

"Is that what I think it is?"

"If you think it's a shell from a gun, probably a pistol."

"You found it here?"

"Yes, I haven't finished going over the whole area. We know someone was shooting here at one time. The shell was encrusted with sand. It is hard to say how long it has been here."

"I didn't find anything in the water. I think I will have do dig in the sand at the bottom of the pond, an impossible task. We need a metal detector that will operate underwater."

"I'll bet we can rent something like that. We'll look on the Internet when we get back to my place."

Ahote waited patiently, watching the parking lot of the hiking trail for any sign of Mike or Cyrus. After an hour, he decided to give up. He followed the hiking trail and took the path to the waterfall. He was wondering how Lola and Rachel were doing when he saw someone in a spot overlooking the pond watching his friends. This had to be Mike King. His first thought was to confront Mike. He didn't like him very much anyways. *What if he's armed?* Ahote wondered. *We're out here in the middle of the northwoods with a maniac.*

Ahote pondered his options. He was watching Mike King take pictures of his friends. He could see that Lola and Rachel were involved in some kind of activity on the shore. It looked like they had found something. He decided he would take pictures of Mike.

He took out his phone and started to take pictures when he felt a hand on his shoulder. He turned to see Cyrus.

"What are you doing here?"

Ahote was startled—he jumped and turned his body away from Cyrus. Cyrus lost his grip. Ahote seized the opportunity and fled into the woods. Cyrus ran after him. Ahote tore through the underbrush as fast as he could. Cyrus was no match for him but kept up the chase.

Mike heard the commotion behind him. He could see someone hightailing it through the woods with Cyrus in close pursuit. Then he saw Cyrus trip on something and go down. He rushed over to Cyrus, who was brushing himself off with his hands.

"What happened?" Mike asked.

"I caught Ahote taking pictures of you with his phone. I grabbed him but the little devil was too fast for me and got away."

"We better get out of here fast. It won't take long for Ahote to warn the girls. I don't want them to catch us here watching them."

"Why? We're not doing anything wrong," Cyrus said.

"I just don't want to confront them here. Let's go back to my place. It will give us a chance to talk about how we should proceed."

Ahote came running out of the woods to warn Lola and Rachel. They knew something was wrong right away when they how quickly he was approaching.

Ahote could barely speak—he was out of breath. "Mike and Cyrus are out there," he said as he gasped for air. "Cyrus caught me taking pictures of Mike. I barely got away."

Lola and Rachel grabbed their equipment. The three of them retreated into the woods. After they had gone a ways, they stopped and listened.

"I don't think they are following us," Lola said.

"I thought Cyrus was going to kill me," Ahote said. "Fortunately, he can't keep up with me in the woods."

"They probably don't want us to see them," Rachel said. "Let's head back to the parking lot."

"What if they are waiting for us?" Lola said nervously. This was not what they had planned.

"We have to go there sometime—we might as well do it now," Ahote argued.

They circled around the waterfall area and approached the parking lot from a roundabout direction. They stopped short of the parking lot in a spot where they could observe yet remain concealed. The only car in the parking lot was Rachel's. There was no activity. They approached the car cautiously, got into the car quickly, and drove away.

"What a relief," Rachel said as she drove Bluewater Road.

"Yeah," Ahote said. "I thought those two would cause us problems. It was the perfect opportunity to get rid of all of us."

"What do we do now?" Rachel asked.

"I promised Sara we would come over for supper. It's getting late. Let's go to her place. We'll roast hot dogs over the fire. We can talk about what we should do later."

"Drop me off at Duane's first," Ahote said. "I want to clean up."

Rachel pulled into Duane's driveway.

"We'll see you in a little while," Lola said to Ahote.

"I'll be over with Duane in about an hour."

Rachel and Lola drove to Sara's house.

Chapter 31

"We got away just in time," Mike said to Cyrus. They were sitting on Mike's deck overlooking the lake relaxing with a beer.

"What do you think they found?" Cyrus asked.

"A couple of old fools," Mike replied sarcastically.

"I won't argue with that, but you said Rachel found something buried in the sand."

"I would like to know what that was, too. I should have known when I saw them on my tracking system stop near Sara's house that they were in cahoots with Ahote."

"Yeah, where did he come from? I gave him a ride to Minneapolis well over a year ago. I thought we had seen the last of him then."

"We have to do something about them. Mislead them or scare them. I'd like to just be rid of them."

Ahote and Duane walked over to Sara's house. Lola and Rachel were sitting next to the fire.

"It's about time you showed up," Lola said to Ahote and Duane.

"I suppose all the food is gone already," Duane retorted.

"You don't think we wanted you to eat it?" Lola said.

They all laughed. Duane gave Lola a hug. "It's nice to see you again. You look good."

"I'm glad to see you, too. Duane, you remember my friend from college, Rachel."

"It's nice to see you again, Rachel," Duane said with a coy smile.

"Thank you, Duane, it is nice to be here." Rachel was pleased to find out that no one else knew about her visit to Duane's house.

Sara came out of her trailer with the hot dogs. "It's about time you two got here," she said to Ahote and Duane. "We were going to start without you."

"Lola and Rachel already have," Duane replied. "Would anyone like a beer?" Duane asked as he opened the twelve-pack he was carrying.

"I'll take one," Sara said. "I'll go get the baked beans and salad while you start roasting the hot dogs."

"Are you two staying with Sara?" Duane asked.

"No, we are staying at Rachel's lake home," Lola replied.

"We're just up here for the weekend," Rachel added

"We were hiking by the waterfall today," Lola said.

"That area used to be a ceremonial site for our tribe," Duane said.

"Do you know a lot about the waterfall, Duane?" Rachel asked.

"Sara and I are members of the last generation that was raised by the tribal community. The tribe used to occupy that area. Our ancestors are buried near there. The township and the lake are named after the last chief, Wabana."

"So the song Ahote and Lola wrote, 'Ode to Wabana,' has historical significance?" Rachel asked.

"Yes, it does. To our tribe it is sacred ground."

"How long did they occupy the area?" Lola asked.

"It is hard to say. The history of our people was passed down in story form. I know some of the stories, but they do not convey specific dates. That is why I was glad that Ahote and Lola wrote the song about Wabana. Young people today do not want to learn the ways of their ancestors. They want to live in the present. We are immersed in an electronic society. Our culture can't compete and is disappearing. Ode to Wabana speaks of our glorious past. I hope they write more songs like that."

"So you know about the cave and the paintings on the wall?" Rachel asked.

Duane shot a concerned look to Sara. "Of course, the paintings represent a history of our people and their lifestyles. We have tried to keep the cave a secret, so it does not become overrun by tourists. We like our quiet lifestyle up here. We don't want that to change."

"What kind of ceremonies went on around the waterfall?" Lola asked Duane.

"I do not know all of them," Duane replied. "I was young boy when the last remnants of the tribe relocated to the reservation. The ceremonies were usually celebrations or supplications to the gods."

"Supplications?" Rachel asked.

"Yes," Duane replied. "Ceremonies to bring the rain, ensure good hunting, fertility—things like that."

"Enough of the past," Sara said. "I have my granddaughter and her friend visiting me. Let's have a good time in the present."

"I agree, Grandmother," Lola said. "It is nice to be here with you again."

Mike was still brooding about what had happened earlier. Those kids were smarter than he thought. Were they aware he was monitoring the location of Rachel's car? It had not moved. He drove by Sara's trailer. There was a gathering there tonight. Was it a family gathering or were they plotting a strategy against him? That was his question. Cyrus had gone home. Unlike Mike, Cyrus recognized there was nothing more to be done today. They would have to wait until the girls tipped their hand.

Mike could not accept sitting around doing nothing. He wanted to make things happen. He parked his car. He was going to creep up on the party to see what was happening. Then he realized there was more to lose than to gain by invading their privacy. Maybe they had web cameras out there. Reluctantly, he went home.

Sara and Duane retired from the gathering around the fire early, leaving Lola, Rachel, and Ahote to themselves.

"It was an interesting day," Rachel said. "We were followed by Mike and Cyrus. We found cartridges from a pistol in the sand by the pool. I wonder what it all means?"

"It is hard to say," Lola replied. "We can't assign any importance to the cartridges, although it makes for a good show. Mike and Cyrus are concerned about what we are doing or they wouldn't be watching us."

"How can we ferret out why they are watching us so closely?" Rachel wondered.

"Mike has hated me ever since I was a kid," Ahote said. "Whatever he and Cyrus are up to, I want to catch them. Revenge would be sweet."

"I think the key to what happened to my parents can be found by the waterfall and cave. There is something there. I just do not know what it is."

"We are close to something—I can feel it. We just have to keep digging until we find it," Rachel replied.

"I am going to research where we can rent an underwater metal detector," Lola said. "There is more at the bottom of the pond to be found."

"It seems the more we dig, the more dangerous it becomes," Rachel observed.

"I thought Duane was interesting tonight," Ahote said. "Normally he jumps at every opportunity to talk about our ancestry. He loves to tell stories. Tonight, it seemed he was reluctant to speak."

"Do you think it was because I was here?" Rachel asked sheepishly.

"It could be," Ahote said.

"I got the feeling he knows more than he is telling us," Lola said. "I have never been able to get as close to Duane as you."

"I know what you mean," Ahote said. "Duane is as kind as a person can be. He wouldn't hurt a flea. I think he is just protective of the lore that surrounds our ancestry. He yearns for the old days."

Chapter 32

"I'm perplexed by the whole situation," Lola said to Rachel. "It is such a challenge to find out what happened." Lola was beginning to cherish the time she spent with Rachel at her lake home.

"Yes, I definitely think we got more than we bargained for," Rachel replied. They were sitting in front of the fireplace enjoying a bottle of wine. "The one bright spot in the whole affair is I met you."

"Yes, I never thought I would be attracted to another woman, but here we are." Lola moved closer to Rachel. She thought back about her sexual encounters in the past. All of them were rushed—she didn't even know if she had enjoyed them. It seemed to her that men thought of her as a piece of meat. Rachel, on the other hand, took her time nurturing their relationship. She felt comfortable. Their lovemaking was…well, fantastic.

"How is your book coming?" Rachel asked.

"I have an outline of what I want to write. Only it's a jumbled outline."

"It's very confusing," Rachel said thoughtfully. "It seems to be a jigsaw puzzle where some of the pieces are identical."

"That's an interesting analogy. I feel the same way. Sometimes I think that Mike King is the cause of my parents' disappearance. I know he is hiding something from us. Other times, I think he plays a minor role in the the whole thing. The truth is probably someplace in between those two scenarios.

"Mike is a clever guy. I think he is involved in illegal activities other than the situation with your parents. We are just looking at the tip of the iceberg."

"I know what you mean, but he seems very polite and refined."

"I planned to flirt with Mike when I had lunch with him. I thought I could get him to chase me. When we were sitting at the table, I felt like a child. It was like he was in control and danger lurked in the background. It was exciting, really."

"Were you attracted to him?"

"Yes and no," Rachel explained. "It was definitely sexual excitement. It was not love. I felt like I was playing with fire."

"Maybe that's what we are doing. We could be getting in over our heads."

"You are right. I don't feel I am getting in over my head, though. I know exactly what I am doing. There are some things about my background that I have been meaning to tell you, Lola," Rachel confessed.

"I was hoping we might have a talk like this. I am getting more involved with you than I thought I would. When we are not together, I think about you; there are some things that do not seem to add up."

"We are just getting to know each other. That makes sense. What were you wondering about?"

"This house on Pokegama Lake, for example; you say it is your parents house, but everything in it seems to be yours."

"It is mine—I bought it myself. I've had it for a few years."

"How can an unemployed musician afford a property like this? Did your father lend you the money?"

"I didn't borrow any money—I paid cash."

"Did you inherit money?"

"No, Lola, I made my own money. I used to deal drugs."

"You were a drug dealer?" Lola repeated in shock. "You seem so sweet and innocent."

"I think we should talk about this if we are going to continue seeing each other."

"It won't make any difference, Rachel, I love you. I realize that now."

"I love you, too." Rachel felt a flood of relief travel all through her. "But I have to be honest with you. I had a hard time when I was young. I know what a lot of people say. 'What is so hard about having rich parents and growing up in Edina?' My parents are very strict and very religious. They had to control my life. I rebelled. I ran away from home several times."

"What is so unusual about that? You were lucky to have parents."

"I know, but it is hard to see when you are that age. The last time I ran away, I left for good. My parents will not even talk to me anymore."

"Why?"

"They are not proud of the fact that I became a prostitute. I was sixteen. I needed a way to support myself. I was walking down the street wondering where I was going to get my next meal and some guy pulled up next to me and motioned for me to get into his car. I did. I figured, *What is the harm in a little oral sex?* I earned forty dollars. After I did that a few times, a pimp noticed me. He pretty much forced me to work for him or not work at all. He got me addicted to drugs."

"Rachel, how could you do that?" Lola said sympathetically.

"I know what you think. But you have never been in a situation like that. It happens quickly and it is easier than you think to succumb to temptation. I was clever, though. When I saw how much profit you could make dealing drugs, I decided to use the money I earned on the street as seed money for my drug business. It took a while to earn enough money because my pimp was always all over me for money. Anyways, I saved the money and started making money buying and selling drugs. The rest is an American success story."

"An American success story?" Lola questioned. "How can you call drug dealing a success story?"

"Well, at first it was just me dealing drugs on the street. I saved my money and bought drugs in larger quantities. Soon I had people working for me. I did not have to work on the street. The risks were not as great. I bought the house on River Road. It was a wreck. I got a great deal on it. Every year it seemed I became more successful. After ten years, I was rich. I bought this house in Pokegama Lake. I had more cash than I knew what to do with. I realized that if I invested my money, I would never have to work again. I quit dealing drugs."

"Is that why you quit? You had enough money?"

"There were other reasons. I was a physical wreck. If I continued that lifestyle, I knew it would be an early grave for me. I checked myself in to Saint Mary's rehabilitation program and kicked the habit. While I was there I started playing the piano again. I had taken lessons when I was younger, but I never took it seriously. It turned out I have musical talent. Some of the counselors at rehab took interest in me and helped me get my GED and get into college."

"Is that all you have to tell me?"

"No, since I met you that day at the university, my life has taken on new meaning. I realized that a lot of my problems were caused by me not recognizing that I was a lesbian. I was ashamed of my urges. Now that I have met you, I feel like a new person. I am in love and I don't care who knows about it."

"Rachel, I am glad you told me all this. You removed the cloud of uncertainty over our relationship. I feel the same way about you."

Rachel embraced Lola. They made love in front of the fireplace.

"Let's go to town and have breakfast," Rachel suggested. It was early morning. They looked out on Pokegama Lake, it was like glass. A mist blanketed the lake, painted copper-orange by the morning sun.

"I'd rather just sit here and watch the sunrise. I'll make some coffee. We can eat later," Lola said.

"That sounds great. I'm enjoying being alone with you."

"I'm glad we had that conversation last night. I am comfortable in our relationship now that it is based on honesty."

"I was afraid to tell you the truth. Sometimes you seem so idealistic. I thought I might drive you away from me. I would hate to lose you, Lola," Rachel explained as they embraced.

"I love you the way you are now—nothing else matters. I'm still very troubled about my mother and father, though."

"I have some ideas about that," Rachel said. "I think you are on the right track with Mike King."

"What do you think his role was in my mother's disappearance?"

"That I don't know, but what I do know is that Mike King has *drug dealer* written all over him."

"You think so?"

"Yes. It's the perfect setup. He imports drugs and distributes them, then uses his nightclub business to launder the money. He probably has large bank accounts in the Cayman Islands."

"You have a vivid imagination." Lola was skeptical. "Do you really think he is a criminal?"

"Yes, a very intelligent criminal. He is the kind of criminal that does not get caught."

"If you are right, how does this help me solve the mystery surrounding my parents?"

"You will never get Mike to confess willingly. You may never solve the mystery. What we can do is use Mike's greed to make sure he gets caught."

"How do we do that?"

"We do a drug deal with him and turn him in to the police."

"How are we going to get Mike to do a drug deal with us?"

"Not with us, with me. I'm sure Mike has checked us both out by now. He probably knows that I dealt drugs in the past."

"I don't see how that helps us. He is probably leery of us."

"I'm sure he is, but he probably would like to get back at us, too. I will see if I can set up a drug deal with Mike, a big drug deal. We'll see if he will fall into our trap."

"What if he does? Aren't we just as guilty as him? After all, we are the buyers in the drug deal. We should just go to the police."

"Mike has the local police in his back pocket. Anything we say to them will get back to Mike. I know his type. He will double-cross us. Mike will pretend to make a deal with us. He will sell us the drugs, but ultimately he will plan to walk away from the deal with the drugs and the money. He will try to leave us empty-handed. Perhaps even in jail."

"Let's talk about this some more later. I am confused. We can discuss this further over breakfast."

"Okay, but there is one more thing I have to tell you about. I hope you won't be mad at me."

"There's more?"

"Yes. How much do you know about Duane?"

"I've known Duane all my life. He's a well-intentioned person. He has been like an uncle to me. But sometimes I feel that I don't know him. There is a darker side to Duane."

"I visited Duane earlier this week. I found out about that darker side."

"Rachel, you are full of surprises." Lola was hurt. "What do you mean *visited?*"

"I called him and asked him if he knew more than he was letting on about your parents' disappearance. He invited me to his house to talk with him."

"So what did you do?" Lola asked.

"I drove up Tuesday and met with Duane at his place."

"What happened? What did you learn?"

"I think Duane drugged me."

"What do you mean?"

"He served me some lemonade. The next thing I knew, it was early Wednesday morning. When I woke up, I was sleeping on his couch. I was sore all over—I mean, all over."

"Do you think Duane took advantage of you?"

"My memory slowly came back to me. At least I think they were memories. It seemed like a dream. Maybe it was. Anyways, it reminded me of the pictures of Sandy. It was like I was a sex object in a Native American ritual around a campfire."

"Were you raped?"

"I really don't know what happened. It is just a vague memory, but I felt like I was fucked in every hole. I hate to sound crude, but I am still sore."

"What are you going to do? Are you going to press charges against Duane?"

"No, I have no proof."

"I can't believe that Duane would do such a thing."

"I was wondering if something like that happened to your mother."

"The paintings on the wall in the cave," Lola said.

"Yes, that's what a couple of those paintings are depicting."

"Mike King captured that on film. I'll bet he was using those pictures to blackmail my mother."

"Do you think it is possible that Duane had something to do with your parents' disappearance?"

"I think both Sara and Duane know more than they admit."

I don't know how to say this to you, but your adopted uncle reminds me of my pimp. I think he is involved in all of this.

Chapter 33

"I would like to know what is going on here, Cyrus," Mike said.

"I don't know, Mike—life used to be so simple," Cyrus mused.

"Yeah, I know what you mean. Now we have those two girls bird-dogging us. They don't know what they are getting themselves into. Why are they bringing up something that happened years ago?"

"They're idealistic and young. Lola wants to solve the mystery of her parents."

"I wonder what Lola found in the pool at the waterfall," Mike speculated.

"It looked like a bone to me. Who knows what went on there over the centuries? Those paintings in the cave suggest it was an area where the inhabitants performed their religious ceremonies."

"It looked more like orgies to me." Mike was always brash and to the point.

"It looks exactly like the pictures you took of Sandy years ago."

"I hope Lola didn't see those pictures."

"There is no telling what they know. Or even what they imagine happened."

"Well, I think getting rid of them at the first opportunity is the best idea."

"What do you think will happen if we get rid of them? If two young women are missing, they will not just forget about it if they don't have any leads. We could even see the FBI involved," Cyrus pleaded.

"We have to have a plan."

Mike's cell phone rang. "Hi, this is Mike."

"Hi, Mike, this is Rachel."

"Rachel, I was just thinking about you."

"You were? We must be on the same wavelength. I had the urge to call you," Rachel improvised.

"I agree," Mike said, not sure what he was agreeing with.

"I would like to get together with you again. Let's have lunch next weekend."

"We could do that. Should we try the Sawmill Inn?"

"Yes, I like that restaurant. Does noon Saturday work for you?"

"I'll put it on my calendar. See you then," Mike said as he hung up.

"They have something planned for next Saturday," Mike said to Cyrus.

"They are trying to trap us some way or another."

"I think you are right. We have to have a strategy in place."

"I think you should go to lunch with Rachel. See what she wants."

"I know what I want. I'd like to take her to one of the rooms at the motel. The next day, the maid will find her body in the room."

"You would never get away with that."

"I know, but it's a great idea. Here's what we will do."

Mike planed to have lunch with Rachel and find out what she and Lola were up to. Cyrus would stay at Mike's house and monitor Rachel's car.

Mike parked in the lot at the Sawmill Inn early. He had a good view of the front door, so he could see Lola drop Rachel off. Cyrus would be able to tell where Lola was going. To Mike's surprise, Rachel was alone when she pulled into the parking lot, got out of her car, and went into the restaurant. Mike went over to her car—it was empty. He went into the lobby of the Sawmill Inn and met Rachel."

"You're early," Mike said to Rachel.

"I try to be punctual. Thanks for meeting me."

"My pleasure—it is nice to see you again."

"Let's get a table before they are all taken."

Mike and Rachel were seated at a table toward the back of the restaurant that was semiprivate. Mike ordered a bottle of white merlot. They exchanged small talk. Finally, Mike leveled with Rachel.

"Rachel, I don't trust you. Last time we had lunch, someone broke into my house. I have her on videotape. She was wearing a ski mask and dark clothes to hide her identity. Did you have anything to do with that?"

"It was concidence," Rachel replied with a straight face.

"I don't believe in coincidence, especially when the coincidence involves you."

238

"Okay, so what do you want to know?"

"Where is your friend Lola? Is she breaking into my house again as we speak?"

"I left her at my house. She is working on her novel."

"The novel about her parents' disappearance?"

"Yes, she wants to know what happened to them. She wants to have a normal life. She needs closure regarding her parents."

"What does that have to do with me?" Mike asked.

"You knew her. She worked for you before she disappeared. Lola thinks you have information that you are withholding. She wants to know what it is that you are hiding and why."

"I have nothing to hide regarding Sandy. She was just someone who worked for me."

"You have more information than that," Rachel said.

"Yeah, I do have more information than that. It's about you."

"You leave me out of this!"

"Come on, Rachel. Who do you think you are fooling? I've seen you and Lola together. You're a couple of lesbians. You're not here because you are attracted to me."

"So what? You're no angel yourself. You act like an upstanding citizen around here, but you own a string of strip clubs throughout the United Sates. You have *drug dealer* written all over you."

"It takes one to know one," Mike replied calmly, knowing he had hit his mark.

"What do you mean by that?"

"I looked into your past, Rachel. You ran away from home when you were sixteen years old. You became a prostitute. You became involved in drug dealing and made it big. Rumors are that you retired, but I know better. You are just too smart to get caught. You have a house in Minneapolis that is paid for, a house on Pokegama that's paid for, and bank accounts who knows where."

"Can I take your order, please?" the waitress asked as she approached their table. Both Mike and Rachel were surprised. They were so engrossed in intense conversation, they had forgotten they were in a restaurant. They ordered and resumed their conversation when the waitress left.

"Level with me, Rachel. What do you want?"

"I want money, Mike."

"You've got plenty of money—you don't need any of mine."

"I don't want any of yours. What I want from you is heroin."

Silence. Mike had to take a minute to digest the statement Rachel had just made. He thought this change in direction might be something he could turn to his advantage. "Wait a minute—where did you get the idea you could get heroin from me?"

"Cut the crap, Mike. I have a million dollars burning a hole in my pocket and I have a customer in Australia who will pay my price for pure heroin."

Mike looked at her skeptically. "What are you going to do with the money?"

"It's for me and Lola—we are going to disappear to some deserted island."

Mike looked around the restaurant cautiously. It didn't look like anyone was listening, but that was the time to be careful. "Let's not talk here. We'll continue this discussion further at my place."

They finished their lunch. Rachel followed Mike back to his place.

"We can talk in private here."

"You don't think I'm that stupid, do you, Mike?"

"What do you mean?"

"You told me over lunch you have a video camera here. Let's take your pontoon out on the lake—we can talk there."

The azure water of Bluewater Lake shimmered in the sunlight. Ripple waves created by the summer breeze reflected the image of the pontoon in a surreal display of tranquility. Boats of anglers studded the lake. Others were enjoying a leisurely cruise. A young woman was maneuvering her kayak along the shoreline photographing the wildlife. All oblivious to the drug deal that was be negotiated near them.

"I want to do a couple more big deals and get out of this business. I can take a million dollars' worth of heroin, smuggle it into Australia, and double my money. I want you to supply the heroin."

"Okay, let's say for the sake of argument that I could supply you with heroin. How am I going to get paid?"

"You will get paid in hundred-dollar bills, ten thousand of them."

This sounded appealing to Mike. So far, Rachel had all the right answers. "Where are we going to make the exchange?"

"We can do the deal at the waterfall on the Joyce estate. There's plenty of open space."

"All right, I'll think about it."

They finished their cruise. Rachel drove back to her home on Pokegama Lake.

Lola was anxiously waiting for Rachel at the door.

"How did it go?" Lola asked.

"Different than I thought," Rachel replied.

"Did you get any information from Mike?"

"Nothing that was helpful."

"What took you so long?"

"We had lunch, then we started talking about a drug deal. We went back to his house and took the pontoon out so we could continue the conversation in private."

"Did you make a deal?"

"No, but we might have a deal—he is thinking about it. Lola, he knows that we are lovers. He knows I was a prostitute and a drug dealer. He confronted me with the fact that I own my house in Minneapolis and the house on Pokegama Lake. I was surprised that he knew so much."

"So we are at another dead end?"

"No, he is thinking about the drug deal. It may be that his greed or his desire to get back at us will overcome his suspicions."

"You asked him about my parents?"

"Yes—he avoided the question, but I think he knows something."

"Mike is pretty influential around here. Do you think he will call the sheriff? Then it will be us that end up being arrested."

"I doubt it. He could end up casting suspicion on himself. It could jeopardize his business interests. He is greedy. My guess is that he will make about a half million dollars on the deal. He will not want to miss out on that much money."

"I can't wait to see him in custody."

"Be patient, Lola—you will get your chance."

"Cyrus, can you come to my place? We have something to discuss," Mike said cryptically.

"I'm busy, Mike. Can't we talk about it on the phone?"

"No, we have to do it in person. You always have time for your old school chum."

Reluctantly Cyrus replied, "All right, I'll come over after work today."

Later that day, Cyrus arrived at Mike's house.

"Well, what is so important this time?" Cyrus demanded.

"It turns out that Rachel is ambitious. She wants to do a drug deal with me."

"It's a trap," Cyrus said. "You know they are just trying to trip you up."

"You could be right. If it is a trap, we will find out about it from my contacts in the sheriff's office."

"Why take the chance?"

"There's a half million reasons for me to take the risk.

"You can count me out. I won't risk my license to practice medicine to help you."

"You've already risked it. Where did I get the codeine to plant in Ahote's car? Where did you live for three years during college? What kind of activities were you involved in?"

"Quit reminding me."

"All right, let's make a plan. I don't want to walk away from the deal without the money and I do not want to go to jail."

"When is the deal going to take place?"

"I left Rachel wondering. I told her I would think about it. The first thing I'm going to do is call Miami and see if we have that much heroin available."

"I've got to get home. Call me when you're ready," Cyrus said as he walked out the door.

Chapter 34

The silence was overpowering, magnifying the anxiety Lola was already experiencing. She was replaying the same scenario over and over. The scene was Lola visiting Rachel in prison. She could not sleep the whole night. She looked at Rachel resting peacefully and wondered how she could be so calm in the face of the events planned for the next day. She tapped Rachel on the shoulder.

"Wake up—it's nine o'clock in the morning. I'm scared. I didn't sleep all night," Lola said to Rachel. "I don't want to be involved in something illegal."

"You don't have to become involved." Rachel was groggy.

"How are we going to do this?"

"You worry too much. Go back to sleep."

"I can't sleep. I'm concerned about what might happen ," Lola said.

"I am going to do the exchange of money for drugs," Rachel explained. "You are going to stay in Minneapolis. You have nothing to be concerned about."

"I want to be in Grand Rapids, close to you, in case something happens."

"You have to stay as far away as possible. You are my insurance policy."

"I don't understand what you mean."

"The nice thing about Mike is that he is predictable. His plan is to keep both the money and the heroin. "

"You're right. He is despicable."

"He probably plans to get rid of both of us at the same time."

"I never thought of that."

"Yes, everything will be neat and tidy."

"I get it. As long as I am not there, Mike doesn't dare harm you because I will be around to point the finger at him."

"Exactly. What we have to figure out is how I am going to get out of there with the heroin."

"I thought we were going to have the sheriff arrest Mike."

"We can't go to the sheriff. Mike has someone in the sheriff's office that will tip him off. We have to be careful."

"So you are going to go through with the drug deal?"

"Yes, once we are sure that Mike will sell us heroin, we can get the FBI involved."

"So what are you going to do with a million dollars' worth of heroin?"

"I'm going to sell it."

Lola could not hide her disappointment. "Rachel, you have been leading me on. This isn't really about getting back at Mike. You're going to make money on this deal."

"That's the beauty of it, Lola. We are going to take the profits from this drug deal and give them to Sara. She is going to be able to open her home for Native American women who are being abused."

"What if you are caught? What am I supposed to do then—visit you in jail?"

"I won't get caught. Now let's plan this out."

Rachel's phone rang. "Hello."

"Hi, Rachel, this is Mike."

"Hi, Mike. I've been looking forward to speaking with you."

"Good, I think we can go ahead with what we have planned."

"I'm glad to hear that. When can we meet?"

"Would tomorrow at two o'clock in the afternoon work for you?"

"Yes, that will be fine."

"All right, I will see you then," Mike said has he disconnected.

"Everything is falling into place. We are on for tomorrow," Rachel said to Lola.

"I don't like it," Lola said. "Why take the risk?"

"Trust me—I know what I am doing."

"It's all set up," Mike said to Cyrus. They were sitting on Mike's deck overlooking Bluewater Lake enjoying a cold beer on a sweltering summer afternoon.

"I don't see why you need to take the chance."

"This is our opportunity to get rid of Lola and Rachel at the same time! If we can accomplish that, we end up with a million dollars' worth of heroin and a million dollars cash."

"Why are you bringing the heroin if you plan to get rid of Lola and Rachel?"

"I have to plan for the downside. Those two are clever. The very least I expect to do is walk away from the deal with a half million dollars' profit."

"Don't let your greed get the best of you."

"Think of it this way." Mike took a sip of beer. "If we make a half million, we can hire a hit man to take care of them."

"What do you mean *we?*"

"Your fate is tied up in this just as much as mine is. Getting rid of Lola and Rachel would put an end to the connection between us."

"You are going to retire?"

"Yes, I have had enough of this. I want to sit back and enjoy my life. We'll sell our nightclubs and head for the Cayman Islands. You will get your share and we will dissolve this partnership."

"That is the best idea I have heard in a long time," Cyrus said. "I've been very uncomfortable being a silent partner. If we sell out, I can focus on practicing medicine without looking over my shoulder all the time."

"You won't have to practice medicine—you will be independently wealthy."

"How much money will we get from the sale?"

"Cyrus, we have forty-one nightclubs. Unless we find someone who would like to buy all of them at once, it will take a few years to sell them, so don't be in a hurry to spend the money. Your share will be several million."

"Wow, I have never really thought of myself as being rich."

"Let's forget about that for now and focus on the matter on hand."

Mike and Cyrus continued to work on the upcoming drug sale.

"Wish me luck," Rachel said. She kissed Lola goodbye and got in her car.

"Be careful," Lola pleaded. "Call me as soon as you get done." She was visibly worried about her lover.

"Don't worry—it will be all right."

Rachel got on the freeway and drove toward her home on Pokegama Lake. She turned on the radio and tried to get her mind off the upcoming confrontation with Mike. The drive to Grand Rapids went quickly. She called Lola to let her know she had arrived safely.

She went to town and ate at El Potro, her favorite Mexican restaurant in town, went back to her house, and started a fire in the fireplace. She poured herself a glass of wine. She started reading her favorite book, *Vanity Fair*. She fell asleep. In her own way, she identified with Becky Sharp.

Cyrus arrived at Mike's house at noon. Lunch was on the table. Cyrus was surprised to see his old friend sitting at the table.

"Hi, Jake. It's been years since I've seen you."

"Nice to see you, Cyrus. It has been a while."

"You're not looking any worse for wear. What brings you to northern Minnesota?"

"I brought some merchandise for Mike."

"Will you be staying long?"

"No, I'll be leaving after lunch. You've been keeping this place a secret. This is my first visit to the northland. It's beautiful country."

"It truly is a nice place to live. It probably is a little cold for you Floridians in the winter."

"I'll have to visit again. Sit down. Let's eat. Mike has been holding lunch for you."

They ate lunch and Jake left. Unbeknownst to Cyrus, he was headed to Minneapolis, not Florida. He had to complete the second part of his assignment.

Mike and Cyrus were at the waterfall. Mike had the heroin with him. They were waiting for Rachel and Lola. Rachel drove an ATV into the clearing. There was a suitcase in the back basket of the ATV. She stopped ten feet in front of Mike and Cyrus.

"You made it," Mike said.

"Of course. It is going to be a profitable day for both of us."

"Where is Lola?" Cyrus asked.

"She stayed in Minneapolis. She didn't want to be involved in this."

"So it's just you?" Mike asked.

"Let's get down to business," Rachel said, ignoring his question. She grabbed the suitcase and put it between her and the two men. "One million dollars in one-hundred-dollar bills."

Mike placed a brown grocery bag full of drugs next to the suitcase for Rachel to inspect. "Uncut heroin, Mexico's finest," Mike said as he carried the suitcase back to where Cyrus waited for him. He started to inspect the money.

Rachel grabbed the sack of drugs and retreated to the ATV. She inspected the bag, then stuck her finger in the heroin and had a taste. "Good," is all she said.

Satisfied that he had a million dollars, Mike and Cyrus got on their ATVs and drove off.

A shot rang out. Rachel ducked behind her ATV. She could not spot the shooter, so she zigzagged her way to the entrance of the cave, dodging bullets on the way.

Mike circled back to the waterfall cautiously. After hearing multiple shots, he knew his plan had gone awry. Rachel could very well have her own shooter. When he arrived at the scene, he saw his man with the rifle stealthily approaching the waterfall.

"Where is she?" Mike asked.

She's trapped in the cave."

Cyrus said to Mike, "I thought you were going to keep the heroin and the money."

"Rachel is no dummy," Mike replied. "She left Lola in Minneapolis as an insurance policy. I sent Jake there to take care of that loose end. Otherwise, we would have a visit from law enforcement if just Rachel disappeared."

"Well, we're a half million dollars richer. Not bad for an afternoon's work."

"Yeah, well, first we have to smoke out Rachel." Mike had brought some tear-gas canisters along. He had anticipated something like this happening.

They approached the entrance to the cave carefully, ever vigilant for a trap set by Rachel. Once they reached the entrance, Mike yelled inside, "You're trapped. Come out or I'll fill that cave with tear gas."

Silence hung in the air.

Mike took a tear-gas canister, pulled the pin, and threw it into the cave. "There. She'll come running out of there shortly."

They waited; still, no Rachel. "Maybe she passed out from the tear gas," Cyrus suggested.

Mike started to enter the cave but the fumes were still too powerful. "Let's get out of here. We made a half million dollars today. Let's settle for that.

"Yeah, I guess we should be happy," Mike said as they started their walk back to the parking lot.

"It's done," Rachel said when Lola answered the phone. "I'm on my way home."

"Thank God. I have been worried sick."

"Mike and Cyrus looked disappointed when I told them you stayed in Minneapolis. I was there early scouting. I saw someone in the woods with a rifle. If we were both there, we would probably be in a shallow grave. Mike and Cyrus would have left with the drugs and the money."

"I'm amazed at how clever you are, Rachel," Lola said. "But I'm worried about you driving back to Minneapolis with the drugs in your car."

"I parked my ATV close to the entrance to the cave at an awkward angle for the shooter. He shot anyways, so I ducked into the cave and escaped out the back. I delivered the drugs to the buyers already. The deal is done."

"Well, hurry home, then—I'm looking forward to seeing you."

"Be careful, Lola—if they shot at me, it probably means someone is in Minneapolis to take care of you."

"I'll stay at your place until you get here."

Chapter 35

Mike's mood was dismal. He tried to work, but he could only stare at his computer. He felt listless. He had been melancholy all week. He had made a half-million dollars on a drug deal that took very little effort on his part. He used to get a high, almost like using drugs, when he finished a deal. Instead of feeling euphoric, he was depressed. *It is time to retire*, he thought. He had run his drug operation laundering the profits through his chain of nightclubs without getting caught. He was always one step ahead of law enforcement. He had never been indicted or even questioned about illegal activities. Now two young women threatened to uncover the whole operation. Ironically, they seemed to be one step ahead of him.

Mike resolved to take a walk and think things through. He climbed on his ATV and drove Bluewater Road, parking in the lot for the hiking trail. It was a sunny summer day, a perfect day to seek the shade of the forest. The gentle breeze whispered through the leaves and kept the mosquitoes at bay. As he approached the waterfall, Mike felt compelled to investigate the cave. He grabbed the flashlight he stored on the ATV and meandered down the path to the waterfall. *This is where it all started*, he thought to himself. *If I had not taken those pictures of Sandy back then, I wouldn't be in this mess*. Mike entered the cave. Even though he had a powerful flashlight, the dank and dark environment sent a chill up his spine. He looked at the totem pole. The eagle that crowned the totem reminded him of the symbol for a Roman legion. It occurred to him that this one looked like a screaming eagle, the symbol for the U.S. Army's 101st Airborne Division. Wasn't Duane a screaming eagle? He turned his attention to the paintings on the wall. There was something of significance he was missing but he couldn't quite put his finger on what. He wondered what had taken place in this cave over the centuries.

Mike moved toward the wall for a closer examination of the paintings. The second to the last painting depicted an orgy not unlike the one he photographed. As a matter of fact, the woman at the center of the ceremony had a striking resemblance to Sandy. It was unlike him to miss so many details. Mike turned his attention to the stream of water that ran though the cave and out the entrance to join the waterfall. He followed the stream to the back of the cave. He inspected the opening the water traveled through. *I wonder if this leads somewhere. What do I have to lose?*

He entered the crevice sideways. He found it got bigger as he went. Instead of being at a dead end, he found himself in another cave. *This must have been carved out centuries ago*, he thought. Mike followed the stream. He could feel the cave narrowing the further he went until it opened into large cavern. There was a pool of water glowing an aqua color in the dark, giving the chamber an eerie ambiance. The pool must have a light source—why else could it glow in the dark? His curiosity got the best of him. He stripped down to his underwear and carefully waded into the pool. He swam underwater to the bottom of the pool. He could see a tunnel that was the source of light for the pool. He surfaced and took some time to catch his breath. Then he submerged and entered the tunnel. He swam about ten feet underwater and then emerged from the tunnel into open water. He swam four feet further and broke the surface of what looked like a lake. He got out of the water and explored the area. He recognized the landscape. *This is Kremer Lake,* he thought.

A light bulb went on in his head—this was the proverbial light at the end of the tunnel. This was how Rachel escaped while he and Cyrus thought they had her trapped. They had waited outside the waterfall for her to come out of the cave, while she left by the back entrance. She wouldn't get away with that again.

Mike swam underwater into the cave. He dressed, then navigated his way back through the cave and out the entrance under the waterfall. He walked quickly back to the ATV, then he went home. He was going to call Cyrus when his phone rang.

"Hello," Mike said.

"Hi, Mike, this is Rachel."

"Hi, Rachel. Thanks for calling." Mike felt like blurting out that he had found the secret exit to the cave, but he wanted to save that information. He would catch her and Lola using that escape route. He would enjoy the look on their faces when they realized he had outwitted them.

"It's nice to talk to you, Mike. My customers really like the merchandise."

"That's good to hear."

"Yes, the good news is, they are going to become repeat customers."

"That is good news, Rachel. Perhaps we should talk about this face to face rather than on the phone."

"You're right. I will be in Grand Rapids this weekend."

"Should we meet at the Sawmill Inn again for lunch?"

"Sure, Saturday noon at the Sawmill Inn. I'll put that in my schedule," Rachel said.

"Good. I'll look forward to seeing you then," Mike said as he disconnected.

Mike called Cyrus. "We've got them," he said when Cyrus answered the phone.

"Is this Mike?"

"Of course it's Mike. Don't you look at your caller ID display before you answer the phone?"

"We don't have them, Mike. I don't want anything further to do with drug dealing."

"This is it. It is our chance to get rid of those girls for good and make some bonus money, too. Then we get out of the business."

"I've been thinking about our conversation last week about selling our nightclubs. It sounds like a good idea to me. We've been lucky so far. Our luck won't last forever. I think it is time to retire."

"You're right," Mike replied. "I have to tell you this—I found out how Rachel got away from us that day at the waterfall. There is a back way out of the cave. There is an entrance to a second cave at the back of the first cave. The little stream of water flows through it. You squeeze through that entrance into the second cave. If you follow the little stream, there is a third chamber with a pool in it. You swim underwater from that pool to Kremer Lake. That's how Rachel got away from us."

"I don't want anything to do with this," Cyrus said. "You go ahead. I'll be out of town when it happens."

"Come on, Cyrus," Mike said. "Wouldn't you love to see the look on those girls' faces when we're waiting for them to surface in Kremer Lake?"

"No, you do it yourself. We do not need the money, Mike. Why take the risk?"

"Have it your way, Cyrus. I'll put the nightclubs on the market when I get done with this last deal. We have those girls right where we want them. They are going to lay out big bucks for heroin. This time I am going to walk away with everything and we are going to be rid of those girls for good!"

"Lola, this is Rachel. I have good news."

"Oh, hi, Rachel. What's up?"

"I just talked with Mike. We are going to get together at the Sawmill Inn Saturday for lunch."

"I told you not to get involved with Mike. He is bad news."

"I thought you wanted him to get what he deserves."

"What do you mean?"

"I am going to talk him into doing another drug deal. Only this time, the FBI is going to be waiting for him."

"So what does this have to do with my situation? I want to find my mother and father. I want to know what Mike had to do with it. If we can prove he had something to do with their disappearance, or most likely their death, then I want him to be punished."

"I think that Duane and Mike are in cahoots on that score. Maybe even Cyrus. You will never get any information from any of them."

"What should I do?"

"Sara knows more than she lets on. She is the weakest link."

"You think my grandmother is involved in all this?"

"No, that is not what I think at all. I think she knows more than she lets on. If we keep investigating and uncovering more information, eventually she will relent."

"So that is why you want me to come up north with you?"

"You're such a sweetheart. I want you to come up north with me because I love you. I want to be with you."

"I love you, too, Rachel."

"Together we can solve the mystery of what happened to your mother and father. You can complete your novel for your senior thesis."

"Okay, I'll come up there with you."

"Good. I'll pick you after your classes Friday."

Chapter 36

Rachel expressed frustration as she picked up Lola at the dormitory after classes Friday.

"I get tired of picking you up all the time at the dorm. Why don't you just move in with me?" Rachel asked Lola as they started the three-and-a-half-hour drive to Rachel's lake home. She had never been drawn to another person like this before.

"My grandmother paid for the dorm room. It would be ungrateful to leave it now."

"I understand, but think how convenient it would be to live with me on River Road."

"Convenient—we would never get anything done." Lola smiled at the thought.

"I think it would be just the opposite—we would get more done because we could spend the nights together rather than liaisons during the day. It would eliminate all the time driving back and forth."

"What would my grandmother think?"

"She is going to find out eventually."

"I know, but she is paying for my school. I don't want to have a conflict with her."

"I can pay for your school. You won't have a thing to worry about."

"Sara raised me as if I were her own child. How can I be disrespectful to her?"

"How do you know she will think you are being disrespectful?"

"I've heard her and Duane discussing homosexuality before."

"You make it sound like it's a stigma. Same-sex love has been practiced in all the great civilizations of the world."

"I know, but this is my grandmother and Grand Rapids, Minnesota. We have to give her time."

"Well, we can at least bring the subject up. Tell her you are going to vote for same-sex marriage when they put it on the ballot."

"Let me do it in my own way, Rachel. I'll consider moving in with you, but let's just take it a little at a time right now. There are too many things going on in my life for me to make major changes."

"I'm just frustrated because I love you and I want to be with you. I've never felt this way before."

"I feel the same way, Rachel. I just have to take it slow. We have a weekend together—let's just enjoy it."

"All right. I'm looking forward to lunch with Sara tomorrow. I like her."

"Yes, she is a spunky old gal."

Lola and Rachel arrived at their destination. It was dinner time when they finally finished unpacking.

"Did you leave anything behind in your dorm room?" Rachel asked sarcastically.

"Let's pick up a pizza and eat here tonight," Lola said, ignoring her.

"I'm tired of eating in," Rachel replied. "Pizza sounds good, but let's go out somewhere we can have a meal and relax. I can do without the cleaning up after we eat."

"Okay, there is a pizza place in Grand Rapids called Sammy's. They have good pizza and it's right on Pokegama Avenue, not too far away."

"Sounds great," Rachel said as the left the house. They got back in the car and made the short drive to downtown Grand Rapids.

They parked outside the restaurant, went inside, and took a table by a window.

"It's a nice place," Rachel said. "I think any place would be nice right now. I'm starved!"

"I am, too. Let's get a veggie pizza."

"Lola, you're so bland. Why don't we order pepperoni and Italian sausage?"

"Let's order half and half—pepperoni always upsets my stomach. I won't be able to sleep."

"Okay." Rachel ordered for them. They both ordered beer. They were enjoying each other's company. After the long drive, it was nice to relax. Two women approached their table.

"Lomasi, it is nice to see you," they said.

"Hi, Denise, Martha," Lola said. "It's nice to see you again, too. This is my friend Rachel from the university."

"Hi, Rachel. Nice to meet you"

"It's always fun to meet Lola's friends," Rachel said.

"Lola? Who's Lola?" Martha asked.

"I started going by the name Lola recently."

"Lola—I like it. It has a mystique about it," Martha said.

"Lomasi isn't sophisticated enough for you anymore?" Denise asked. Denise had always been jealous of Lola. Denise's application to the University of Minnesota was turned down. She was attending the community college in Grand Rapids.

"No, it's pretty obvious I'm Native American without having a Chippewa name. It's just that every time I meet someone new, they ask what nationality my name is and I have to explain my heritage. I have been meeting a lot of new people lately at school. Whereas Lola is a name easily accepted without question. Besides, I have to admit, I think it does sound more sophisticated. What is wrong with that?"

"Well, I like it. It's you," Martha said. "We have to get going. We're going to the early movie."

"It's nice to see you again, Martha. you, too, Denise," Lola said.

"Yes, it was nice to meet you," Rachel said as Denise and Martha walked away.

"They're a couple of lesbos," Denise said after they walked out the door. "They live together in Minneapolis."

"How do you know that?" Martha asked.

"The Longfell clinic," Denise said. "I stopped there for a physical. The receptionist, Ashley, told me that when I was waiting. You remember Ashley from school. She was a year ahead of us. She heard Doctor Longfell and Lomasi's grandmother discussing it one day."

"Well, I don't care. I've always liked Lola. I like her new name. What she does in her personal life is her own business," Martha said.

"I believe marriage should be between a man and a woman. Most of the people in Grand Rapids feel the same."

"Well, they're not married, are they?"

"How do you know? They could be."

"We'll never agree on some things, Denise. Let's just go to the movie," Martha said as they got into the car.

The next morning, Rachel got up early and went jogging. When she got back to the house, Lola was up having coffee at the kitchen table.

"Well, it's about time, sleepyhead. I thought you were going to sleep all morning," Rachel said.

"It was so nice just to lie in bed and know I didn't have anything to do all day except what I want to do. I'll never schedule classes early in the morning again," Lola remarked.

"Well, I'm exhilarated when I wake up here. It is so nice to run early in the morning in the fresh air. I saw three deer on the side of the road. I was within twenty feet of them before they ran."

"I used to have a pet deer when I lived with my grandma," Lola said. "I used to put corn out in the backyard every day for her. She became so tame, she would eat out of my hand."

"I'd love to see that deer. Do you think it will be there tomorrow at lunch?"

"My grandmother doesn't believe in feeding the deer corn. It's not good for them. They are used to eating from the trees and grass, wild vegetation. She thinks eating corn will upset their natural diet and cause health problems."

"It sounds logical. I hope we can see your pet deer."

"We can go there early Sunday if you like. I can take you for a walk out in the woods behind our place. We have a lot of trails there. We can have lunch with Grandma and I can have my talk with her. Then we'll go home to Minneapolis."

"We'll see how I feel tomorrow morning. Right now, I have to get ready for my lunch with Mike."

Rachel put on a tight-fitting pair of jeans and a sweater to show off her figure. She drove to the Sawmill Inn. Mike was waiting for her in the lobby. He stood up as she came in.

"Hi, Rachel. It's nice to see you."

"I've been looking forward to lunch."

"I have, too. Let's get a table before it gets crowded."

They walked into the restaurant area of the hotel and asked the hostess for a seat by the window.

"You look great," Mike said to Rachel.

"Thanks. It's nice to be up north. I always feel rested after a good night's sleep here."

"I know what you mean. I've been living here so long, I am used to it."

"That house of yours on Bluewater Lake is lovely. Log homes are very fashionable."

"Thanks. It's made from hand-scribed red-pine logs that were harvested locally. I designed it myself."

"Well, it's very charming."

"So are you," Mike replied smoothly. "Why don't you come over after lunch? We can take a ride on my pontoon."

"Let's do that," Rachel said.

They both were very careful regarding their conversation. They couldn't make a drug deal in the restaurant—too many people around. They made small talk. Rachel was surprised how much she enjoyed Mike's company. They finished lunch and went back to his house. Mike disabled the alarm and let Rachel in the front door.

"Would you like something to drink?"

"I'll just have some water, thanks."

Mike grabbed a couple bottles of water from the refrigerator. He gave Rachel her bottle, then put his arm around her and gave her a kiss. Rachel did not resist. Finally, Mike pulled away.

"Let's go out on the pontoon," Rachel said. She wanted to get out of the house. She was alarmed by how aroused she was from a simple kiss.

"Sure, right this way," Mike said as he took her downstairs. "It's nice to have a walk-out basement. I keep my stuff for the lake close to the basement door. It's convenient."

"You really designed it nicely," Rachel said as they walked down to the dock.

The pontoon was stored on a lift that kept it out of the water. A green-canvas canopy served as a roof over the pontoon, protecting it from sun and rain. Mike lowered the pontoon into the water, then pulled it from under the canopy, fastening it to the dock so Rachel could get in. He put the key in the ignition and started the motor. He untied the pontoon from the dock and began a leisurely trip around the lake.

"It's a perfect day for a cruise in the pontoon. It happens every time you come here, Rachel."

"It's the perfect day to make money, Mike. Let's talk about it."

"I like the sound of that, Rachel. What do you have in mind?"

"The same as before—I want a million dollars' worth of heroin. How are you going to spend your profits, Mike?" Rachel enjoyed this type of banter.

"You got rid of the last batch fast."

"I have unlimited demand. It's an ever-expanding market and we've got a corner on it."

"Unfortunately, I don't have an unlimited supply. I'm looking for more now."

"Aw, come on, Mike—what do you want, more money?"

"That will probably be the case. I have my people looking for more right now." He wanted to impress Rachel. He acted casually even though the quantities were large.

Mike and Rachel took a full tour around Bluewater Lake. When they got back to Mike's house, Rachel helped him dock the pontoon and made her excuses to leave, resisting the temptation to go inside his house.

"Call me next week. I'll have more information for you then."

"All right, Mike. Thank you. I had a really nice time," Rachel said sincerely, then drove away. She had charmed him and she knew it.

Mike watched her drive away. *I'm twice her age,* he thought. *But maybe, just maybe, it could work.*

"What took you so long?" Lola said to Rachel as she walked in the door.

"We couldn't talk in the restaurant. I had to go back to his place."

"You had to go back to his place?" Lola asked with more than a hint of jealousy and skepticism.

"Yes, we just took a pontoon ride. We didn't even go inside." Rachel told a little white lie. She didn't dare mention the kiss, though it was on her mind. "We talked on the lake, where there was not chance of being overheard. We didn't settle anything. I'll call him next week and we'll arrange the exchange."

A silence hung in the air. Rachel could tell Lola didn't like the situation.

"I've got a great Idea. Let's call Sara and see if she wants to go out to dinner tonight instead of lunch tomorrow. I'll buy. Then we can spend tomorrow morning together here and get going home a little earlier to avoid the traffic."

Lola cheered up a little. "That's a good idea. I'll call Grandmother."

"Where should we take her? I'm tired of the Sawmill Inn."

"Her favorite restaurant is Forest Lake."

"Go ahead and call her." Rachel was happy to get Lola's mind off Mike and drugs.

Lola called Sara. They agreed to meet at Forest Lake restaurant.

"Grandma said she would be there at six o'clock."

"Great. We better get ready."

They drove to Forest Lake restaurant on the east side of Grand Rapids. The complex was situated across the street from a lake of the same name, Forest Lake. It was considered fine dining by locals. Great food and excellent service earned the restaurant its reputation. They arrived early enough to get a seat by the window. They were just getting ready to order something to drink when Sara arrived.

"Hi, Grandma," Lola said as she got up from her seat and gave her grandmother a hug.

"Every time I see you, I am amazed at how grown up you are. Hi, Rachel," Sara said.

"It's nice to see you, Sara," Rachel replied. "I'm glad we could get together this evening."

"So am I," Sara said. "I didn't have any plans for this evening and it is quiet around the house with Lomasi—sorry, I mean Lola—gone."

"I miss you, too, Grandma."

"Well, we're all together now. Let's order something to drink."

They called the waitress over. Sara just wanted water. Rachel ordered a pitcher of beer for her and Lola.

"Lola, you're too young to drink beer," Sara said after the waitress left.

"Don't tell anyone," Lola whispered to her grandmother. "No one seems to notice when I am with Rachel."

There was a moment of awkwardness—both Lola and Sara had something to say to each other, but they didn't know exactly how to bring the subjects up.

Finally, Lola blurted out, "Grandma, I have always felt that there was something that you have not been telling me about my mother. I've been thinking about the paintings in the cave under the waterfall. I think mother painted some of them. There, I said it!" Lola looked at Rachel and smiled.

"I do know something about that," Sara said. "And I have some things to talk with you two about also. But this is probably not a good place to talk about it. Why don't we go to my house after dinner? We can talk there."

Everyone agreed to postpone the conversation until after dinner. The waitress returned with their drinks. They ordered food and caught up on everything that had happened since they saw each other last. When they finished dining, they drove to Sara's house for coffee and conversation.

Rachel and Lola settled into comfortable chairs in Sara's living room.

"Rachel, would you like a glass of wine?" Sara asked. "I don't serve alcoholic beverages to people underage," she said to Lola. "Would you like some pop or something?"

Lola looked at Rachel as if to say, *Some things never change.* She replied, "Just some water, Grandma."

Sara went into the kitchen and prepared the refreshments.

"Are you ready?" Rachel asked Lola.

"As ready as I'll ever be," Lola said.

Sara came back with the drinks. She sat on the sofa and said to Lola, "You go first."

"Grandma, I think the last two paintings in the cave behind the waterfall were painted by my mother. She was an artist. I think this was information that she was leaving behind for me."

"Well, it may be that she wanted to leave information behind for you, but Sandy was not the artist who painted those paintings," Sara said matter of factly.

"I think she did. One of the people depicted in the painting looks like her," Lola asserted. "How do you know she didn't paint them?"

"Because I painted them," Sara replied.

"You painted them?" Lola was flabbergasted. She didn't know what to say next.

"Yes, didn't you know that I paint? Where do you think Sandy got her talent? She got it the same place you got your good looks—from me."

"All the time Ahote and I played in that cave, we thought it was our secret."

"I was quite an item in my time. You just weren't around to see it," Sara said.

"I found some pictures of Mother at one of those parties depicted in the paintings—it looked like she was having fun." Lola handed Sara a couple of the pictures she got from Mike's hard drive.

"Where did you get these?" Sara asked as she looked at the pictures. She was clearly disturbed that Lola had these pictures in her possession.

"Does it matter?" Lola posed the question. "I am wondering how my mother became involved in something like this."

"The same way I became involved in it. That is why I was always so careful with you. I did not want the same thing to happen to you that has happened to so many Native American women over the years. Of course, times are different now. You went to school in Grand Rapids. Now you are going to college."

"I don't understand, Grandma."

"Sitting around the fire at night was the only entertainment we had in the old days. The only laws were those enforced by the chief or the medicine man. There were practices that involved women captured from other tribes that would not be considered moral by today's standards. But since there were no laws, the men could do anything to these women."

"We know there were atrocities performed on women by all races in primitive societies," Rachel rationalized. "Why should Native Americans be any different?"

"Once alcohol was introduced to the tribes, these practices sometimes extended to our own young women. Then drugs became available. There were elements in our social circles that took advantage of the effects of alcohol and drugs and abused our young women."

"Is that what happened to Mom?" Lola asked.

"That is what happened to a lot of our young women. They developed addictions, they participated in activities that would be illegal in the white man's world, but because these things happened on the reservations or in private among 'Indians,' everyone looked the other way. There was prejudice. We were considered savages. The Native American was not considered a human being. Native American women were even lower. There was exploitation of females. There was rape, incest, and riotous living. These attitudes are starting to change."

"What do you mean 'starting to change'?" Lola asked. "This is the 21st century. Things have changed."

"Not for everyone," Sara continued. "The reservations are way behind the times. Registered sex offenders can hide on the reservations and there is little or nothing law enforcement can do about it. The tribal police look the other way."

"What does this have to do with my mother and father?" Lola was afraid to ask.

"You mother was a wild young woman. I was surprised you had these pictures, but not by their content."

"Wild young woman?" Lola asked.

"Yes, Sandy was talented. She could draw, she could paint, she could write. She excelled in just about everything she did. But she was not disciplined. She was just the opposite—uninhibited. She wanted to try everything. I didn't want to tell you this because you held such a high opinion of her and I wanted things to turn out differently for you."

"Tell me everything, Grandma," Lola said as she looked at Rachel. "I deserve to be told."

"I can leave you two alone if you feel it would be better to talk in private," Rachel offered.

"No, there are things I would like to say to both of you," Sara said to Rachel. "Perhaps we should talk about it now."

Lola looked at Rachel inquisitively. "What do you want to know, Grandma?" she said to Sara.

"I heard from a reliable source that you two are more than just friends. Is that true?"

There was an awkward silence. Then Lola asked, "Where did you hear that?"

"Quit avoiding the question; answer me."

"It's true," Lola said. "Rachel and I are lovers."

"I'm glad we got that out in the open. By now it's probably all over Grand Rapids. I could probably read it in the gossip column if we had one."

"Are you shocked?" Rachel asked.

"Not anymore," Sara replied calmly. "Actually, I'm neutral about it."

Lola was surprised. "What do you mean by 'neutral'?" she asked.

"Well, at first, I didn't like the idea at all. I didn't want you to turn out like Sandy," Sara explained. "Since I have gotten to know Rachel, and after spending time with you two, I can see that you are in love."

"Does that mean you will not oppose our relationship?" Rachel asked.

"I didn't think I would say this, but actually, I'm more than neutral—I approve," Sara said. "I was opposed, but who am I to tell you how to live? You have your whole lives ahead of you. Do what you want."

"What did you mean when you said you didn't want me to turn out like my mother?" Lola asked.

"Lola, I will be honest with you because you are no longer a child and you do deserve to know. Life was not easy for me when I was a young. There was a lot of prejudice against Native Americans. We were generally thought of as lazy, alcoholics and drug addicts. Native American women were even lower on the totem pole. We were considered squaws. In tribal terms, we were possessions. Men could use us as they liked and no one cared."

"So what is different now?" Lola said sarcastically.

"In many ways, your question is a good one," Sara said. "The answer is that I am different now."

"What do you mean, Grandma?"

"That painting on the wall of the cave is of me. It is just a small part of what I was subjected to when I was young. I was an alcoholic, a drug addict, and considered a whore by the people around me. I was abused sexually and physically. I had a low self-worth and I just thought that was what I deserved."

"What happened to make things different?" Lola asked.

"I got pregnant with Sandy." Sara let that statement hang in the air for a minute. "I realized if I kept on drinking and doing drugs, I would end up in an early grave. I would leave the child I was bearing at the mercy of the world. I checked into a treatment program and took the cure."

"Grandmother, why didn't you tell me this before?" Lola asked. There were tears in her eyes.

"You were young and you looked up to me. I cared about what you thought of me. I still care about what you think of me, but I realize that this is a part of your life, too. You should understand the events that led you to where you are now.

"I spent months in a treatment facility. It seemed like years to me. When I got out, I found a job at the hospital. It was an entry-level job for a person with no skills and no education. I didn't complain. I had health insurance. When Sandy was born, I took the minimal time off and went right back to work. I started taking classes at night. I was surprised that I could do well at those courses. I learned that I was intelligent. I became a licensed practical nurse and eventually a registered nurse. It took time and sacrifice. When the opportunity presented itself to become a nurse practitioner, I stepped forward. You probably remember me driving to Duluth and back three nights a week. I had to leave you alone at nights. You have always been trustworthy and hard-working, so I did not worry about you.

"What does all this have to do with my mother?" Lola asked.

"Sandy was a wild child," Sara said as she shook her head. "She could have graduated close to the top of her class if not at the top of her class. She could have done so many things with her life. Instead, she lived for the moment. She became involved with young men who treated her poorly. She drank and became addicted to drugs, then was passed around at parties. I tried to get her to come to her senses, but she enjoyed it.

"I take partial blame, too. I was away at work and school, so she had the opportunity to do what she wanted to do. I talked to her, she seemed to understand, but the same behavior continued. Finally, she overdosed on drugs. She was taken to the hospital emergency room. I was at work when it happened, so I was there immediately. She barely survived. The court ordered her to undergo treatment. She met Dan in the treatment center. They knew each other from school but never really noticed each other until they were thrown together by their problems. They became lovers.

"When Sandy discovered she was pregnant, she was a changed person. She moved in with Dan, and they bought the trailer next door with some help from me. Dan worked full-time at the paper mill. It was a good-paying job, but it was shift work. Sandy was alone a lot. She tried to make it as an artist, but it isn't easy for a Native American artist to make a living, so she worked at part-time jobs. There was no one around to give her guidance. After you were born, she worked at the resort for a few years. That's where she got to know Mike King. She worked hard at being a good mother to you, but she just had this wild streak. She would go on binges and be gone for several days. Dan didn't know what to do. He just put up with it.

"Eventually, Sandy disappeared. It was the last time I saw Dan also. He came over with you and asked if I had seen Sandy. I told him no. He asked if I could watch you for a while. I said yes. He went home, got drunk, and disappeared. I didn't know what happened to Sandy. I assume Dan disappeared looking for Sandy."

"Why didn't you tell the sheriff the truth?" Lola asked. Sara could hear the resentment in her voice.

"The sheriff, everyone just assumed that Sandy and Dan disappeared together. They both had a reputation for being wild. I had to think of you. I didn't want Sandy to be arrested if she decided to come back. I did what was best for you. I let the authorities assume what they wanted to assume. It didn't matter to them—they just thought Sandy and Dan were irresponsible savages who never fit into society. Perhaps they were not all that wrong."

"Why didn't you tell me the truth a long time ago?" Lola was mad with Sandy now.

"I didn't tell you the truth because I love you. I was afraid of what might happen to you. When you were young, I didn't know if you would turn out like Sandy. Both Sandy and I had drug and alcohol problems. I thought you might have inherited the same traits. Neither Sandy nor Dan came back; it just was easier to go along with the established story."

"I'm just so glad that you turned out the way you did," Sara said to Lola. "You're a talented young woman and you are doing the right thing. You're going to school to develop your talents. When I heard you were having an affair with Rachel, I thought the worst. Now that I have spent some more time with you, I am happy for you both."

Rachel chimed in here. "I am glad you approve, Sara. Lola and I love each other. This has been a lot for Lola and me to comprehend in one evening. I think we should go home and get a good night's sleep."

"I think you are right, Rachel," Sara said. Then she turned to Lola and hugged her. "I hope you don't feel betrayed. I did what I thought was best for you, Lola. I love you."

"I love you, too, Grandma," Lola replied. She returned Sara's hug.

Finally, they let each other go. Lola and Rachel said goodbye to Sara and drove back to Rachel's house.

The next day, Lola and Rachel drove home in silence. When they got back to Minneapolis, Rachel said, "Lola, would you like to come over to my place for a little while?"

"No, I just want to be alone with my thoughts for a while. This is a hard to accept."

Rachel dropped Lola off at the dorm. Lola went to her room and locked the door. She stared at the picture of her mother. She was heartbroken. She burst into tears. *You're not trying to tell me anything—you're laughing at me. How could I be so stupid? You're just stoned!* Lola turned off the lights and cried herself to sleep.

Chapter 37

It became a daily habit. In truth, an early morning jog along the river was a great way to start the day, the week. Cool, crisp morning air produced a wisp of mist, decorating the Mississippi as it journeyed silently toward the Gulf of Mexico. Exercise was one of Rachel's favorite activities. Not a soul stirred on the road along the river, which would soon be bustling with rush-hour traffic. Rachel relished the solitude of the morning. It was her opportunity to focus her thoughts not only on the activities of the day, but also on her future with Lola. Rachel was pleased that Sara had accepted her love relationship with Lola so graciously.

The atmosphere in the car during the long drive home from Grand Rapids yesterday was pregnant with anxiety. Rachel wisely left Lola to her thoughts. Even though it was a weekend of revelations, Rachel could not help but think the answers Lola obtained to her questions only begged more questions. *Where is Sandy now? Where is Dan? Did Dan find Sandy?* These had to be the big questions for Lola. She resolved to call Lola after her jog.

Rachel turned her thoughts to the impending drug deal. *Was Mike going to get her heroin? How much would it really cost? Had she set the hook hard enough?* It was obvious Mike was fascinated with her. Guile and duplicity would serve to reel him in. The rising sun tinted the mist on the river orange as light reflected off the water. Rachel took solace in the fact that everything seemed to be going as planned. She had faith that would continue.

Rachel was lost in thought and was surprised when she looked up and saw she was approaching her house. It was amazing how quickly forty-five minutes of exercise flew by. She quickly showered and dressed, preparing for the new day. Her phone rang.

"Hi, Rachel. I'm sorry I wasn't any fun yesterday. I was really shocked by what my grandmother told me."

"That's okay. I knew you would feel that way. I was pleased that Sara said she approved of our relationship."

"Yeah, that surprised me. It almost seemed too easy. I cried my self to sleep last night. This morning I feel better."

"I knew you would. I was out jogging earlier—I just finished up. I was just going to call you, so I'm glad you called me."

"My grandmother is cagey. She told me a lot, but she never said what happened to my mother and father."

"Do you think she knows?"

"I think she knows more than she is letting on. I have to be persistent with her. I was shocked when she told me she was the artist who created the paintings in the cave. Then when she revealed the truth about my mother, I was stunned. I wasn't thinking straight enough to ask her more."

"I think it merits another trip to Grand Rapids next weekend."

"You just want to be alone with me at your cabin," Lola accused mockingly.

"What's wrong with that?"

"Nothing—it sounds like fun."

"Let's plan on going up there next weekend, then. You can drag whatever information you can out of Sara. I think we should make a more thorough search of the cave. I am still intrigued by the objects you found in the pond."

"That sounds like a plan. I better get ready for classes."

Lola dialed Sara's number. She was surprised at how long the phone rang.

"Speak," Duane answered the phone. He was always abrupt when he answered.

"Hi, Duane, I was calling Grandma."

"Is this Lomasi?"

"Yes, is Grandma around?"

"She just went outside to get something from her car...here she is now."

"Hello."

"Hi, Grandma," Lola greeted Sara.

"Hi, Lola, I'm glad you called. How are you feeling?"

"All right. At first I was shaken by our conversation, but I am coming to accept it."

"No one is perfect, Lola. Some things you have to accept in life."

"It's just a little harder to accept the truth about Mom. Rachel and I are coming up again this weekend. Are you going to be around?"

"Yes. Why don't you come over for lunch? We can talk some more."

"That sounds great, Grandma."

"Stop by Saturday around noon. I have to go now—Duane is waiting for me."

"See you next weekend," Lola said as she disconnected.

Later that week, Rachel called Mike. "Hi, Mike, this is Rachel."

"Hey, Rachel, it's nice to hear from you."

"Lola and I were thinking of making a trip to Grand Rapids this weekend. I was wondering if you would have anything for me?"

"Nothing yet—I'll keep you posted."

"Okay," Rachel said dejectedly.

Mike thought Rachel sounded disappointed. He wondered if she was a user who could afford her habit. Perhaps he could employ that knowledge to exploit her. She would make a great dancer.

"Why don't you come over to my place for dinner while you're here? I'm a gourmet cook."

"I'll have to think about it."

"I'll call you Friday. I'll have more information for you then."

"Okay, bye." Rachel hung up. She smiled to herself. She knew she had Mike right where she wanted him.

Mike and Cyrus got together at Mike's house to talk business.

"Just like old times," Mike said to Cyrus.

"Too much like old times. I'd like to leave old times behind me."

"Awe come on, Cyrus," Mike replied with a smile. "You can never have too much money."

"So you're going to do the drug deal with Rachel?"

"Yes, I'm just waiting for Tony to find more heroin. Then I want to get Rachel to pay me enough to make it worth my while."

"Mike, you're greedy."

"It has served me well in the past."

"It will be the death of you, Mike."

"What do you want me to do? Do you want me to waste those two girls when they come up here next weekend?"

"If you knew what was good for you, you would. And leave me out of it, when you do."

"I'll think about it."

Mike returned Tony's call. "Are we all set?"

"We could be. I found what we were looking for. I made the connection today. It's expensive."

"How expensive?" Mike asked.

"Twice what we thought it would cost."

"How long will it take to get it?"

"I'll be there with it by the weekend," Tony replied.

"I'll count on you being here by Saturday morning, early."

Mike wondered how much Tony was skimming off the transaction. He would have to deal with that later. He needed his help this weekend.

The school week flew by for Lola. Ever since Sara had given her tacit approval of Lola and Rachel living together, Lola had been staying at Rachel's house every night. Friday morning when they got up, Rachel said to Lola, "I'll pick you up at your dorm after classes. Call me when you're finished packing. We'll drive up north from there."

"I have to wash some clothes first," Lola explained.

"We'll take the clothes with us. You can wash them at my cabin."

"Why do we keep calling it a cabin? It's a house, a year-round home."

"I know, but there's a certain romance to calling it a cabin."

"I wish I would have lived in a home like it when I was growing up."

"I'll pick you up at noon. We'll eat lunch along the way."

"Hello," Rachel said as she answered her cell phone. She recognized Mike's number on the display. It was hard to hide her excitement—her plan was working.

"Hi, Rachel, this is Mike."

"Mike, I'm glad you called. Do you have good news for me?"

"Good and bad—the good news is, I found what you are looking for and I can get it for the weekend."

"That is good news."

"The bad news is, it will cost three times what it cost last time."

270

"Ouch! How can you do that to me, Mike?"

"I'm just passing my costs on to you, Rachel."

She paused for a moment—silence.

"I guess I have no choice." Rachel feigned reluctance.

"Good. We'll meet Sunday at the same place?"

"Yes, Sunday, same time, same place."

"See you then," Mike said as he hung up.

Rachel was elated. Mike was walking right into her trap. What did she care what it cost? The FBI would be waiting for Mike on Sunday.

Rachel parked by Lola's dormitory and helped her carry luggage and laundry to the car.

"Is that all you're bringing along?" Rachel asked Lola sarcastically. They had to make two trips and filled Rachel's trunk. They stopped at the Sportsmen Café in Milaca for lunch on the way. They arrived at their destination mid-afternoon.

"I had the feeling all the way up here that we were being followed," Lola confessed to Rachel after they finished unpacking.

"By who?" Rachel asked.

"Mike."

"Why would Mike follow us? He has the tracking system installed in my car. He knows where I am all the time."

"Doesn't that give you the creeps?"

"If I didn't want him to know where I am, I could just remove the device and leave it in my garage."

"Maybe that is what we should do when we to go my grandma's house."

"If it makes you feel more comfortable, we will."

"It does," Lola explained. "If Mike knows we are snooping around the cave, he might decide it is better to be rid of both of us at the same time. We could end up at the bottom of the pond."

"I doubt that. He wouldn't get rid of me before he got his cash. He probably will try to get rid of us afterwards," Rachel said thoughtfully.

"Doesn't that worry you?"

"Not at all," Rachel said nonchalantly. She acted like she was just swatting an annoying mosquito from her arm. It was one of the things that attracted Lola to Rachel. She never let anything bother her, distract her from her goal.

Mike had grown to love northern Minnesota over the years. It was a perfect summer morning. The rising sun warmed the cool, crisp air. Joyous birdsong wafted through the air. Mike enjoyed his first cup of coffee on his deck. *Time to get to work*, he thought. He entered his attached garage and engaged the garage door opener. He had stocked his ATV with explosives the night before. He checked to make sure that he had everything he needed, then pulled out of his garage; using his remote, he watched the garage door slowly close.

Mike drove his ATV up Bluewater Road to the hiking-trail parking lot. He kept driving his ATV up the hiking trail. This was a non-motorized trail, but who cared? Especially this time of the morning, he had the hiking trail to himself. Mike made his way to the waterfall and the cave. He made sure no one was following him.

Mike took C-4 plastic explosives out of his backpack and placed them at the entrance of the cave. He selected the location carefully. There was enough explosive to seal the entrance of the cave. It was out of sight. He would be able to detonate it remotely.

Mike's next task was the rear entrance to the cave. This required Composition H6, an Australian-produced explosive compound he could use to seal the underwater tunnel that led to Kremer Lake. He drove his ATV to Kremer Lake and placed the explosives strategically to seal the escape route. He was done. Mike drove his ATV back to his house. He changed clothes, got in his car, and drove downtown to Springer Realty & Auction Service. He listed his home on Bluewater Lake for sale.

Mike looked at his surroundings like he was looking at them for the last time. He had an exit strategy. He had sold his resort. The sale was kept quiet so as not to disturb the flow of repeat customers. He was in the process of selling his string of nightclubs. He didn't need the money anyways. He already had enough money in banks on the Cayman Islands to last his lifetime.

This was his last deal and he would go out in style. He would keep the three million dollars cash, the drugs, and he would eliminate Lola and Rachel. The cave would be their grave. No one would suspect him. Another perfectly executed plan. It was high time he left. *When they find Rachel and Lola, I will be safely tucked away in the Caribbean, never to be heard from again,* he thought.

Chapter 38

Lola was groggy. Defeat had raised its ugly head like a beast and deflated her will to fight. She could not understand how everything could go so wrong. How did Mike get the upper hand so easily? Obviously they had underestimated him. Did she tip her hand? How did Mike find out about the rear entrance to the cave?

"All right, Lola, or Lomasi, or whatever your name is—you have caused me untold problems since you started poking your nose into my business. It's payback time," Mike said.

They were in the cave behind the waterfall—Mike, one of his henchman, and Lola. Torches used to light the cave flickered, exaggerating the shadows of objects until they appeared to dance on the walls. Coupled with a fire in the pit in front of the totem pole, the shadows haunted Lola. It was a harbinger of things to come.

"You thought you and Rachel would get away with using that back exit from the cave again, didn't you?" Mike said accusingly. He grabbed Lola under the chin and squeezed. "Answer me!"

"Yes." Lola was barely able to talk. Her grandmother lay on the floor of the cave with a bullet hole in her forehead. The back side of her head was blown off by the exiting bullet. The acrid smell of spent gunpowder hung in the air.

Lola looked into Mike's eyes. They were vacant and cold. There was no emotion visible yet she could feel the hate. It was a side of Mike she had not seen before. Tony, the henchman, was enjoying himself. *He's sadistic,* Lola thought to herself.

"What are you going to do to me?"

"You are going to end up like your friends," Mike explained. "Only with you, I am going to take my time."

Lola looked at Rachel. Her eyes were open. Her throat was slit. Rachel had tried to step in and help Lola after Mike grabbed her. It happened so quickly, Lola almost missed it. Rachel had dived at Mike. Tony slit her throat in midair. She was bleeding out before she hit the ground.

Now it was just Lola left. She wished she was dead, too. It was humiliating. Mike had forced her to strip in front of him and Tony. While Tony held the gun on her, Mike stretched her arms behind her on either side of the totem pole and tied her wrists together. Then he wrapped a piece of rope around her legs and the totem pole several times, eliminating any possibility of self-defense.

"I will give you a preview of what is going to happen to you. The fire pit is full of hot coals. I am going to treat you the way the Apaches used to treat the women they captured. First I am going to take one of those hot coals and start to slowly burn off your nose. In between those sessions, I am going to make tiny cuts all over your body—a torture the Chinese invented—Death by a Thousand Cuts. Before you slowly die from the cumulative effect, I am going to skewer you on the stalagmite—a sacrifice to your ancestor, Chief Wabana. Then you can join your friends, slowly sinking though the layers of sand at the bottom of the pool in front of the waterfall. By the time you are missed, you will be buried so deeply in the sand that you will never be found."

Mike reached down with a pair of tongs and picked up a red-hot coal. He put it in front of Lola and slowly moved it toward her nose. Lola began to feel the heat radiate on her face. She tried to move away, but she was tied to the totem pole. When she turned her head, Tony came over and held her in place. The coal touched her nose. Lola felt a searing pain and let out deathly scream.

"Ahhhhhhhhhhhh......"

Rachel shook Lola. "Wake up." Lola had the sheets wrapped around her tightly. There was down from the pillow strewn across the bed. Lola was visibly sweating. "I'll have to make sure you are awake next time I go jogging," Rachel said to Lola.

"Rachel, you're alive!"

"Of course I'm alive, silly. You were having a bad dream."

Lola looked around the room and slowly came to her senses. "You would not believe the nightmare I was having."

"Looking at the condition of this bed, I can imagine. Was he cute?"

"Stop kidding around. Mike was going to burn my nose off."

"Well, I'm glad you woke up—I kind of like your nose. Why don't you get dressed and clean up a little bit and we'll get some breakfast?"

"It's not funny, Rachel. I'm worried about what will happen. Mike is dangerous. You should keep away from him."

"Stop your worrying. We're not going close to him, Lola. The only thing Mike is going to see closely is the inside of jail."

"I hope you're right."

"Of course I'm right. Now get ready. We'll go to Country Kitchen for breakfast, then take a cruise on the lake before we go to Sara's house."

Lola and Rachel left for Sara's house. Their plan was to lunch with Sara, then move on to the waterfall to search for answers. Having left the tracking device behind, they did not anticipate any interference from Mike.

"Hi, Grandma," Lola said as Sara opened the door. "We're hungry."

"The soup is just about ready," Sara said. "Sit at the table— we'll have some coffee while we wait."

"Good. I hope you don't mind me asking some more questions, Grandma. Last weekend was quite an experience for me."

"I'm glad we took the opportunity to talk. I have wanted to explain to you what happened for quite a while, but I never thought the time was right," Sara explained. "After our discussion last week, I felt like a weight had been lifted from my shoulders."

"I guess there is never a good time," Lola said thoughtfully. "You just have to make time for some things. I forgot to ask you last week—do you have any idea what happened to my mother and Dan?"

"No. I always suspected Mike King had something to do with Sandy, but I was never able to find out what."

"Do you think that Dan ever found her?"

"I don't know. I haven't heard or seen either of them since they disappeared. Dan was heartbroken. I'm not sure Sandy felt the same way about him."

"Mike put a tracking device on Rachel's car," Lola told Sara. "Ahote found it when he was here last. He helped remove a branch that got stuck under Rachel's car. When he crawled under the car, he found it."

"How do you know Mike put it there?" Sara asked.

"We were going to the waterfall and cave. Rachel and I went ahead and started searching. Ahote concealed himself in the woods and watched the parking lot. Both Mike and Cyrus turned up. How else would they know we were there?"

"Did they cause you any problems?"

"Who knows what they had planned? Ahote warned us and we snuck out of there," Lola said.

"You're not going to give up looking for your mother, are you?" Sara asked.

"We're going to go to the waterfall after lunch. I found a bone there last time we searched the area."

"I guess I understand how you feel. I would like to find out what happened to Sandy, too. We both need closure."

"I'm glad you understand," Lola said.

"Do you still have the tracking device on your car?" Sara asked Rachel.

"It's in my garage right now," Rachel explained. "We try to use it to our advantage. We would like Mike to know we are in Grand Rapids, but we don't want him to know where we are going to be this afternoon."

"Be careful," Sara advised them as she put the soup on the table.

There were no cars in the parking lot for the hiking trail when Lola and Rachel arrived. They parked and went directly to the waterfall.

Rachel rented an underwater metal detector. Lola was wearing a swimsuit under her clothes so she did not have to change in front of anyone who might be watching them.

Equipped with a snorkel and the metal detector, Lola mad a systematic search of the bottom of the pond. She found that whenever she got a positive reading on the detector, she could not reach whatever was triggering the alarm. She would move a little sand with her hand and an equal amount of sand would immediately take its place. When she stood on the bottom of the pond, she slowly sank into the sand despite her swim fins. If she wanted find solid bottom, the pond would have to be drained. *A perfect spot to dispose of my mother's and father's bodies*, she thought.

Lola gave up searching the bottom of the pond. She found Rachel in a clearing next to the pond sunning herself on a blanket in her bikini.

"Find anything interesting?" Lola asked sarcastically.

"I don't think there is anything interesting to find," Rachel replied. "I think we are on a wild goose chase."

"So why did you come along?"

"Because I like it here and I wanted to be with you."

"So, maybe we should search the cave. We aren't going to find anything in this pond. It doesn't have a bottom. At least not one I can reach."

"You mean it is quicksand?"

"Something like that—whatever falls in there will sink through the sand until it reaches bedrock. I would call it a perfect burial place."

"Will it be any different in the cave?"

A shot rang out. A bullet ricocheted off rocks directly behind Rachel. Lola and Rachel started running toward the entrance to the cave. The bullets kept coming. Rachel and Lola zigzagged back and forth until they reached the entrance of the cave. They hid behind the boulder guarding the entrance, then waited for the firing to stop before they crawled into the cave.

"That was close," Rachel said.

"We're not out of it yet. Whoever is out there shooting can come in the cave easily enough. It's dark in here, too. I can't see a thing."

"I came prepared," Rachel said as she pulled a flashlight and a Beretta 3032 Tomcat handgun out of her bag.

"Do you know how to use that?" Lola asked.

"Of course. I have a permit to carry it. Come on—let's get out of here before that shooter gets lucky."

They hurried their way to the back of the cave.

Lola and Rachel were directly in front of the entrance to the second chamber when suddenly they were hoisted in the air. They found themselves trapped like fish in a net that had been hauled out of the water on a winch. It dawned on them that they were herded into a trap and the trap was sprung. Rachel had her Beretta out, ready to shoot, but she could not see anything. The shooter, on the other hand, could see Lola and Rachel perfectly using a night-vision scope.

There was a popping sound. Rachel felt a sharp pain in her neck. She pulled out a dart as she passed out, dropping her Beretta noiselessly on the sand floor of the cave. Before the handgun hit the ground, Lola had a dart in her neck. Lola and Rachel were slumped together in the net, oblivious to their dilemma.

Lola and Rachel woke up tied together, sitting on the floor of the cave. They were still groggy from being drugged. There was a fire in the pit, and there was someone dressed in ceremonial Native American garb sitting by the fire smoking from a glass pipe.

"Are you awake?" Lola whispered to Rachel.

"Yes," Rachel whispered back.

"Hey, shut up, you two," their captor yelled.

The voice was familiar to Lola—she just couldn't place it in her drugged state.

"Duane!" Lola cried out, realizing who was holding them. "What do you think you are doing?"

"What do you think you are doing, little one?"

"I'm looking for my mother."

"Well, you won't find her here."

"How do you know that?" Lola asserted.

Duane was feeling the immediate effects of the methamphetamine—he was in the mood for verbal sparring.

"Ooooooh, little one, you aren't in a position to demand anything." Duane took another hit off the pipe.

"He's a madman," Rachel whispered to Lola.

"You're right, you bitch!" Duane said. "I'm mad at you, you upper-class slut. You weren't so high and mighty when you were here last."

"What have you done with my mother?"

"I haven't done anything with her. The last I heard, she was enjoying herself in Miami."

"She's dead. You killed her. Admit it," Lola said in anguish. The thought of her mother alive and not contacting her was too much for her to believe.

"You're wrong about that," Duane said with a malevolent smile. "She left you with Sara so she could enjoy her life."

"She would never leave me behind. You killed her," Lola said.

"No, I didn't kill her, but I am going to kill you two. You couldn't leave well enough alone. You had to keep digging into the sacred ground of our ancestors. For that, you will be sacrificed to the great Chief Wabana!"

Duane started dancing around the firepit in a drug-induced trance, his chanting in a language that was unintelligible to anyone else. His dancing was becoming more frenzied. Lola wished she could see Rachel's expression. She wished she could speak to her friend. She thought this might be the end. Rachel just sat there saying nothing. Then the dancing stopped.

"What are you going to do with us?" Lola blurted.

"You will see, little one. I will offer your friend to Chief Wabana first. I will impale her on his phallus," Duane said, pointing at the stalagmite in the middle of the firepit.

He cut Rachel loose from Lola. He grabbed her roughly and slapped her face. When she did not respond, he dragged her to the firepit and started ripping off her blouse. Rachel startled Duane when she suddenly came alive. She had loosened the ropes that held her hands while Duane was dancing. She delivered a powerful right hook to Duane's chin and followed up with at left uppercut into his belly.

Lola was amazed at what was happening. She could not believe her friend was so resilient. Rachel had delivered blows to Duane that would stagger a normal person, but Duane, in his drug-induced state, was barely affected. He slipped behind Rachel, put his left arm around her neck, and pulled her tightly toward him in a stranglehold. His right hand pulled his hunting knife from the sheath on his belt. He held the blade to her cheek.

"Now, my dear, you are going to dance for us like the last time you were here or your young friend is going to die," Duane said as he pushed Rachel toward the firepit. "Now dance for us, you slut."

Rachel looked at Duane. She could tell he was crazed. He had moved behind Lola and put his knife close to her throat. She had no choice. She started to dance around the firepit.

"Now take off that blouse," Duane ordered as he watched Rachel dance.

A deafening gunshot rang out. The impact of the bullet knocked Duane onto the floor. The shot was errant, only grazing Duane's shoulder, but he could feel no pain. He got up and looked at Sara as she came into view.

"It's all over, Duane," Sara said. "You're done abusing young women."

She held an ancient Colt 45 on Duane. It was a wonder she could hit anything with that weapon. She moved to untie Lola.

"Sara, how can you do this to your lover?" Duane said as he slowly moved toward her.

Sara fired a shot at his feet to stop him, but it had the opposite effect. Duane sprang forward like he was on a diving board at a swimming pool. He wrested the Colt 45 from Sara while he was in midair and knocked her to the ground with his impact. He rolled and came up on his feet. He fired a shot in the air.

"Don't get any ideas now—any of you," he threatened. "I know how to use this old Colt. Rachel, you just continue what you were doing. Sara, you get over and dance with Rachel. It's just like old times."

Lola could not believe this was happening. This was a nightmare. It was a different version of the nightmare she had last night coming true. They were all going to die. They would end up at the bottom of the pond.

Duane stood there, stoned out of his mind, looking at the women in front of him, completely in his element. The flames from the fire lit his face through the shadows. He had a demonic look. It suddenly dawned on Lola that this was the same face that was pictured on the totem pole.

Someone appeared from the darkness behind Duane. He dived at Duane's back, wrapping his arms around Duane's midsection. Duane fired the Colt as he fell. The bullet went harmlessly to the roof of the cave. The stranger lost his grip on Duane as they fell to the ground. The stranger got up and hit Duane with a solid right hand to the jaw. Duane let loose a kick that hit its mark between the stranger's legs.

Lola could not loosen her bonds as she watched all this unfold in front of her. It dawned on her that the stranger was the weirdo that watched everything from his ATV. The person she thought was some kind of a pervert was rescuing them, or trying to anyways.

The stranger struggled with Duane. They wrestled each other on the floor. They both got up. Duane swept his leg in an arc, hitting the stranger in the knee. He fell to the ground. Duane had his back to the fire. Rachel crawled behind Duane on her hands and knees between him and the firepit. The stranger saw his opportunity and sprang at Duane. He knocked Duane backward. Duane tripped over Rachel. Duane twisted his body so he could break his fall with his hands. He let out a scream that would haunt the cave for the millennium as he impaled himself on the stalagmite. His legs and arms were flailing in the air. The stalagmite stuck out of his back at least twelve inches. The scream turned to a gurgle and blood gushed from Duane's mouth. His eyes were popping out of his head as he died a slow death.

Sara, ever alert to danger, picked up her Colt 45 and pointed it at the stranger. His long hair and beard were disheveled. He watched Duane die as he caught his breath.

"Put your hands up in the air," Sara said to the stranger. She would have no more violence.

"Grandma," Lola said. "He saved our lives."

"The stranger raised his hands in the air. When his breath came back to him, he said, "Sara, don't you recognize me? I'm Dan."

Chapter 39

Ahote was pleased with himself. He was the cat that got the cream, and like cream, everything he attempted rose to the top. In truth, he had a feline-like grace that seemed to quietly attract success. Of course, Miami's population was much more diverse than he had experienced elsewhere. A Native American could easily fit in. It was the second time he chose to live in a large metropolitan area starting from scratch. It was easier this time; he had learned from his previous experiences. A casual observer might have concluded that everything came with ease. In truth, it was not easy, but Ahote was a hard worker—he focused on his goals. He drove a cab at night. He practiced guitar and wrote songs during the day. Then there was his drug business. It was booming. Ahote always had money in his pocket—he had no worries financially. He dressed in a way that wasn't lavish, yet his clothes conveyed a style, personal charm.

He met a woman when he first settled in Miami who he couldn't get out of his mind. She was a stripper. She was gorgeous. Her name was Cassandra and she was obviously older than him. Probably twenty years older than him. Perhaps that was one of the things that attracted him to her. In reality, he was attracted to her because she behaved as if he did not exist.

Ahote waited on the cabstands outside the clubs where she danced. She didn't call a cab at the end of the night like the rest of the girls. She walked out to the cabstand at the end of her shift and selected the cab she would ride in. It was never Ahote's cab. He wondered what he had done to make her mad at him.

Ahote decided it was impossible to understand women. He would just forget her. Besides, he had to get ready to perform. He was going to sing his songs and play his guitar at a dinner club tonight for an hour. He didn't make very much money doing it, but he got a chance to display his talents.

Ahote wished that Lomasi could have come to Miami to visit. It was so different from Grand Rapids. He didn't experience the same prejudices here that were common in a town where every one knew everyone. There were some pretty progressive nightclubs in Miami. The Vagabond, the White Room, and the Nocturnal, to name a few, all had events that catered to the eighteen-year-old-plus crowd that could not legally drink but enjoyed good entertainment and dancing. Plus, Miami was warm. No snow and ice here in the winter.

Tony had been to Mike's house in Minnesota before, but he had never stayed overnight. He wondered what Mike had going on this time that merited his help. He said he wanted Tony to help him with the drug deal. He wondered what help Mike needed. After all, if he found someone stupid enough to pay that much money for drugs, wouldn't he want the goose to keep laying golden eggs? Why did he have to have the drugs, the money, and the girls? Mike was greedy. *On the other hand,* Tony thought, *I'm working for Mike, not the other way around.* Tony decided to content himself with skimming money off Mike's transactions.

There was a knock on the door. "Tony, are you ready?"

"Yeah, just waiting for you," Tony replied. He opened the door and started down the hall with Mike. They went out to the garage and got on the John Deer Gator that Mike kept for doing tasks in the yard. It was perfect for the job. There was room enough to comfortably transport two people and room in the bed of the vehicle to carry their equipment.

"We'll drive this to the spot I showed you. I want you to wait there. At a little after 10:00 AM, you should see two women surface from the underwater tunnel I showed you earlier. All you have to do is hold them here until I get back here."

Mike left Tony in place. He took the bicycle out of the Gator and rode it back to his house to prepare for the morning's activities.

Mike didn't feel threatened by Lola or Rachel. Nevertheless, he felt more comfortable when he slid his Glock 21 under his belt. He grabbed a flashlight in case he needed to pursue the young women into the cave. It never hurt to be prepared for the worst.

At 9:30 AM, Mike drove to the parking lot for the hiking trail. He got out of his car and walked to the waterfall. He sensed cautious eyes following his every move. It was difficult not to smirk. He was prepared—his trap was set. He'd anticipated Lola's and Rachel's plans. This time, he would walk away with the drugs, the money, and he would be rid of those pesky young women forever.

Mike sat confidently by the boulder that sheltered the entrance of the cave from sight. Even if those young women got past him and into the cave, they would never leave the cave alive.

"Freeze! FBI. Put your hands in the air!" Mike couldn't believe his ears. He looked at the clearing surrounding the waterfall and saw FBI agents emerge from their places of concealment in the woods, moving to converge on him. He ducked behind the boulder, quickly fleeing inside the cave. He turned on his flashlight. The first thing he saw was Duane's body impaled on the stalagmite in front of the totem pole. It was a bad omen—he had been set up.

"You're trapped. Come out with your hands up!" Mike heard an amplified voice behind him. Fortunately, he had a surprise for them. They obviously did not know there was another exit. Mike ran to the back of the cave, turned sideways, and slipped through the narrow entrance to the second chamber. He detonated the explosive he had planted by the entrance of the cave. There was a flash of light, then a huge explosion. The entrance to the cave was sealed. By the time the reverberations reached him, he was in the second chamber of the cave. He ran to the back of the cave. He dove into the pool and swam underwater, then surfaced in Kremer Lake.

"Hold it right there," Tony said, pointing his gun. He did not recognize Mike wet.

"It's me, you idiot," Mike said. "Come on, let's get out of here."

Mike hopped behind the wheel of the Gator, started the engine, and drove away, barely giving Tony a chance to get into the front seat. He drove like a madman, taking the back way to the road. He detonated the second charge he had placed in the underwater tunnel. It wasn't necessary, but there was no sense in leaving behind evidence that might be traced to him. Mike took a left onto Bluewater Road.

"Hey, you're going the wrong way!" Tony panicked.

"I'm going the right way," Mike explained. He was visibly upset. "Those girls set us up. The FBI is back there to arrest us—we need to get out of here fast."

Mike kept driving down Bluewater Road until he came to the public access to Wabana Lake. He pulled onto Wild Rose Lane, a private road that lead to some remote cabins on the north end of the lake. When they reached the last cabin on the road, Mike pointed the Gator directly at the woods and kept going. Tony thought Mike had gone crazy, but after they traveled two hundred yards, they pulled into a clearing. Mike navigated the Gator to a large brown pole barn one hundred feet from the lake. He jumped off the Gator and ran to the side of the building facing the lake. He unlocked the large garage door and engaged the electric opener. He motioned for Tony to pull the Gator into the barn.

Inside the building was a Cessna Skyhawk SP aircraft equipped with pontoons.

Tony parked the Gator and walked up to Mike. "Where did that come from?" He was amazed.

"You need to be prepared for every eventuality," Mike replied with pride. "This will take us out of here before anyone even knows we are gone."

"How do we get it on the lake?" Tony asked.

"It's on a track system. We just roll it to the lake, start the engine, and fly away."

"But where are we going from here?"

"You let me worry about that, Tony. Now untie the ropes that are holding the plane in place. I'll go through the preflight checklist and we will be on our way in no time."

Tony untied the ropes while Mike prepared for flight. Together they pushed the plane to the water's edge. Mike got in while Tony pushed it the rest of the way into the water. Then Tony pulled the plane to the dock and held it in place while Mike started the engine. Tony hopped into the passenger side of the plane and they navigated to open water. They were on the north end of Wabana Lake. Conditions were perfect. The lake was relatively calm and there were no boats to be seen. Mike gave the engine gas. The takeoff was smooth. Mike kept the plane low, below the radar.

"That was pretty slick, Mike. You thought of everything."

"You have to be prepared in our business. By the time they figure out what happened, we'll have landed on a lake by Virginia, Minnesota. I have a pickup truck parked there. We can drive to Miami. The FBI will be watching the airports, but we won't go close to those. When we get to Miami, you begin the exit strategy we put into place. Leave the businesses running just as we planned. It's time for you and I to disappear, Tony. The rest of the employees are on their own. The Feds will seize the businesses eventually. It will take time to go through the judicial system.

"I'm going to miss working with you, Mike."

"I'm going to miss it, too," Mike said philosophically. "But there comes a time for everyone to retire. How many people do you know who are rich enough to retire when they are fifty?"

"You're right. We're lucky to be able to get out while we can."

"We're not out of this yet. Keep your eyes peeled—I'm going to land on that lake right there."

Mike brought his plane in for a safe landing. They pulled up to the dock on the lot Mike owned. He had another large pole building there.

"What are we going to do with the plane?" Tony asked.

"There is another track system here. We'll pull the plane into the pole building and lock it up. Then we'll drive to Duluth and stay the evening there. They might not find this property. If not, we'll liquidate it along with the plane later. Here—take this rope and secure the plane to the dock while I get the track system going."

Tony took the rope from Mike and moved to the end of the dock. When Tony bent down to tie the rope to the dock, Mike hit him in the back of the head with a pipe he had concealed in the plane. He took out a hunting knife and slit Tony's throat.

Mike used the track system to pull the plane into the pole barn.

Mike put the john boat resting on the side of the lake into the water. He tied Tony up in a canvas tarp. He attached cement blocks to the ends of the rope. He took the body to the middle of the lake and threw it overboard.

"That's what you get for skimming money off the top from Mike King," Mike said as he watched the body slowly sink to the bottom of the lake.

Mike drove an old Ford F150 pickup truck to Duluth. He checked into a Holiday Inn under an alias, had dinner, and retired to his room to rest after a hard day's work.

Ahote had just gotten into his cab. He was starting work. He liked owning his own cab. He was his own boss. He could work when he wanted. In truth, he had just completed the biggest drug deal of his career. A couple more deals like that and he could retire. His phone rang. He looked at the caller ID on his phone—it was Rachel.

"This is Ahote," he said when he answered the phone. He wanted to impress Rachel. He didn't want to appear too anxious.

"He's on his way to Miami," Rachel said without identifying herself.

"How do you know?"

"I just know. He has an exit strategy. He'll be going to the Caribbean by boat."

"Okay, I'm ready."

"Good, let me know how it goes," Rachel said as she hung up.

Ahote had been waiting to get even with Mike for a long time. Once he realized that it was Mike who planted the gun and drugs in his car, he vowed revenge. It was not as easy as it sounded, however. Mike was a powerful guy.

Then Ahote talked with Rachel. He found out what Duane had done to her. They realized that Mike and Duane were in cahoots. They were taking advantage of young Native American women. Duane would introduce them to alcohol and drugs. Once they were chemically dependent, Duane would entice them with wild partying and orgies.

Eventually Duane would introduce these young women to Mike. Mike needed a never-ending supply of young women to work in his clubs. Their careers as dancers depended on their youth and appearance. Once they were addicted to drugs, the next logical step was prostitution. Mike would use them until they either became too old or died.

That is what had happened to Sandy. Ahote finally pieced the puzzle together. Sandy came to Miami and was dancing in Mike's club. She had changed her name to Cassandra. *Sandy* was mundane, but *Cassandra* was mysterious, inviting, and contained an obvious reference to Greek mythology—the daughter of a king, a dancer. Now Ahote understood why Cassandra had been careful to avoid him. She did not want him to find out that she was Lola's mother. When this was all over, Ahote planned to bring Lola to Miami for a reunion.

Mike wasted no time getting to Miami. He paid cash for gas and food. The pickup truck he was driving looked old and rusted out, but it was in perfect running condition. Wearing a baseball cap, faded-out blue jeans, and an old T-shirt gave him the appearance of a working stiff. He knew he had to get out of the country, but he also knew that moving too fast created mistakes. He was going to work his plan. He would drive to the wharf in Miami, changing into his boating garb on the way. Then he would take out his boat, ostensibly for a pleasure cruise. It would be a pleasure cruise that never ended.

Mike would lose himself in the Caribbean. He would assume a different identity that he had already created. He would alter his appearance. He would lay low long enough for the authorities to give up on him. At the very least, they would put the search for him on the back burner. Then he would be free to travel and enjoy his life. The only other person that knew of his plans was Tony. Tony would only be talking to fish at the bottom of the lake.

Chapter 40

Ahote exerecised the patience of a cat waiting to pounce on an unsuspecting mouse. In this case, the mouse was really a rat, and not an unsuspecting rat by any stretch of the imagination. If Ahote pounced, his prey would be a formidable foe. So Ahote waited with apprehension in his rented boat in a slip where he could observe Mike King's boat. He inspected his arsenal, an old Cold 45 and a hand grenade, both of which he had obtained from druggies who traded their possessions for their addictions. Did they even work? He hoped he would not have to find out. He wondered how long he would have to wait. Would his persistence be rewarded? He had his doubts, but he also had faith in Rachel. She was beguiling and she was smart. *She could be a con artist,* he mused—*perhaps she is.* She was one step ahead of Mike the whole time.

It happened so quickly, he couldn't believe his eyes. A rusty old Ford pickup parked in the lot next to the wharf. Mike King stepped out of the pickup dressed like a man of leisure going for a cruise. He walked the pier, boarded his boat, and went below deck. Moments later, he emerged, started the motor, and prepared to back his vessel out of the slip. Mike looked like he did not have a care in the world. He displayed no sense of urgency.

Ahote, on the other hand, was experiencing anxiety. It was show time. This was exactly how he and Rachel had rehearsed it, but when it came time to execute the plan, things did not seem so straightforward. He would call the Coast Guard and explain that there was a fugitive fleeing the country in his boat. Then he was going to follow Mike until the authorities could catch up with him. Ahote hadn't taken into consideration that Mike was in his element. He grew up boating in the Miami area. Ahote realized he had to overcome his insecurities and bring the plan he and Rachel had worked on so hard to fruition.

Ahote hated Mike. He was well aware of the fact that Mike had either planted the drugs and gun in his car, then set him up to be arrested, or he had someone do it. Mike's continual backstabbing contributed to the bad reputation Ahote got in the Grand Rapids area. Ahote was disgusted by the fact that Mike was getting young women addicted to alcohol and drugs and sending them to his nightclubs to be strippers, then prostitutes. There was nothing Mike would not do for money. How much money did one man need?

Ahote thought about himself and his situation. He felt like a hypocrite. Was he all that different from Mike, only on a smaller scale? After all, wasn't one of the reasons he was living comfortably because he was dealing drugs? He was using his profits to springboard his career as a musician and poet.

Enough soul searching, Ahote thought. He had a score to settle. As Mike pulled out of his slip and headed toward open water, Ahote started the motor on his boat and prepared to follow him. He speed-dialed the number he had carefully programmed into his phone.

"Coast Guard," a voice answered.

"Hi, my name is Ahote and I am following a fugitive in my boat."

"You are following a fugitive?"

"Yes, his name is Mike King. He is wanted by the FBI. He escaped arrest in Grand Rapids, Minnesota. He is now escaping the United States by boat."

"We have never heard of Mike King."

"He's wanted," Ahote repeated, exasperated that his well-thought-out plan was unraveling in front of him. "He just escaped a drug bust involving the FBI in Grand Rapids, Minnesota."

"I am checking our computerized list of individuals wanted by the FBI. I do not see anyone named Mike King."

"It just happened two days ago," Ahote pleaded. "He eluded arrest and is making his getaway from Miami."

"We have a direct feed from the FBI's most wanted list into our systems. If a Mike King was wanted by the FBI, we would be aware of it. Who is this I am speaking to again?" the voice asked suspiciously.

Ahote hung up. No wonder there were so many criminals going unpunished. Law enforcement was incompetent. They arrested the easy ones and the difficult crimes went unsolved. He dialed Rachel's number.

"This is Ahote," he said.

"Where are you?" Rachel asked.

"I'm following Mike. I called the Coast Guard as we planned. They have never heard of Mike King."

"I know," Rachel explained. "When Mike fled the FBI, he went into the cave. He must have found the back way out of the cave. Anyway, he left the heroin in the cave. There was an explosion and the entrance to the cave was sealed. By the time the FBI cleared the entrance and entered the cave, Mike was long gone."

"So what is the problem? Didn't they know that it was Mike they were after?"

"They found Duane's body impaled on the stalagmite in the firepit and the heroin next to him. That solved the crime and saved them the problem of a trial."

Ahote was shocked. The man who raised him was dead? "How did Duane's body end up in the cave?"

"That is another story. In the meantime, you need to follow Mike. The FBI will recognize their mistake in time. Where is he now?"

"I followed him to Key Biscayne. He pulled into a small cove in Bill Baggs Cape Florida State Park. I am waiting for him outside the bay."

"It's less than two hundred miles from Miami to the Bahamas. From Nassau he can fly anywhere in the world. All he needs is a fake passport and money. Something tells me he has both."

"I'll keep an eye in him."

"Be careful," Rachel said in a pleading way. It was the first time Ahote heard concern for him in Rachel's voice. Of course, she was probably only concerned for his safety.

Mike knew he had been set up. He doubted anyone was able to follow his getaway to Miami. He was sure that someone would figure out that was his destination. It was convenient Duane would be found dead in the cave while he fled. It would confuse things for a little while—not long, but maybe long enough.

Mike had a feeling he was being followed as soon as he backed his boat out of the slip. Once he was in open water, he nonchalantly took out his binoculars to determine who was in pursuit. Lo and behold, it was his old friend Ahote. Well, he was going to finally get the chance to get even on that score. Mike pulled into a small cove on the south end of Key Biscayne. He would not be there long. It would only take a couple minutes to mount his Browning 50-caliber machine gun on his boat. Then he would blow Ahote out of the water. All he had to do was get close enough so Ahote's boat was in range. That should be easy enough.

Ahote waited patiently. He was idling his motor, moving slowly, mimicking a fisherman. Mike blasted out of the cove heading straight for Ahote's boat. It was the last thing Ahote expected. There was a time to stand and fight in life, but prudence dictated to Ahote that it was time to retreat. He put his boat in gear and took off full speed for land.

Ahote heard machine-gun fire. He watched as bullets splashed in the water behind him as the lethal rounds landed closer and closer to his boat. Mike was walking his fire toward Ahote's and soon the rounds would at the very least annihilate Ahote's boat. He had only one choice—evasive action. He had to zigzag back and forth until he could put the ocean liner ahead between him and Mike. Ahote had one advantage—Mike could not operate his machine gun and steer the boat at the same time. Once he was protected by the large travel ship, he could call the Coast Guard and get help. Mike would have to back off. Ahote watched the rounds chew up his deck as he fled behind the ocean liner. The deck of his boat was damaged, but he was not wounded. He speed-dialed the number programmed into his phone.

"Coast Guard," the same voice answered.

"This is the guy that called before about the fugitive. He is now chasing me just south of Key Biscayne. He is using a machine gun. Help, before he kills me."

"Listen, son, we have enough problems right now without someone with a hyperactive imagination calling us. Don't call again!" The Coast Guard hung up the phone.

Ahote knew he had only one chance. He had to make it to Key Biscayne. All that stood between him and death was the ocean liner. He had made sure the boat he rented could outrun Mike's boat. If he chose the right direction, he could leave his adversary behind. Should he take the long way and head for the bow or go back the way he came, the stern? What would Mike guess? Ahote chose the stern. He grabbed the hand grenade from his arsenal. If Mike was waiting for him, he only had one chance. He would have to make a perfect throw with the grenade.

Ahote retraced his route. He put the boat at full speed. As he approached the end of the ocean liner, he pulled the pin on the grenade. He would have to throw the grenade regardless of if Mike was there or not. As he pulled around the stern, he saw his adversary idling his boat.

Mike could not decide what to do. There was a surprised look on Mike's face as he saw Ahote bore down on him at full speed.

Ahote tossed the grenade. It was like time stood still. Every second seemed like a minute as the grenade followed an arcing path toward Mike's boat. Mike took his hand from the machine gun and pushed the throttle full forward. His boat hesitated as the engine revved up. The boat began to move slowly as the grenade approached. Mike ducked as the grenade sailed over his head and just missed the back edge of the boat. The grenade exploded just underneath the water's surface. The noise from the explosion was muffled by the water. Water flew through the air in all directions, some of it drenching Mike. The shrapnel from the grenade was slowed so much by the water that, even though the grenade exploded four feet from Mike's boat, none of the shrapnel reached the boat. The shock wave from the grenade propelled the boat forward.

Ahote did not look back after he threw the grenade. He knew he would be able to outrun Mike's boat. He also realized that he would not be able to outrun a Browning machine gun. It was time to get our of there. When he heard the explosion behind him, he turned to see what had happened. He saw that Mike's boat was not damaged. Ahote thought he probably had enough of a head start to reach Key Biscayne. When he looked back again, Mike and his boat were headed toward open water. Mike's next stop would be the Bahamas.

Epilogue

Rachel drove Lola and Ahote to a brand new building on forty acres in the country. They met Sara. The four of them watched the workers put up the sign for the Bluewater Shelter for Battered Women. Sara was proud of her new facility. She was the director. She had applied for and received a grant from the Blandin Foundation to pay her operating expenses. The construction workers were putting the finishing touches on the building that would open the next day.

"Well, you must be very proud, Grandma—your dream has become a reality," Lola said.

"Thanks to you," Sara said to the three of them. "Rachel, we have you to thank for your generous donation. It seems a miracle that one so young can be so generous."

"It is for a wonderful cause," Rachel said. She gave a knowing look to Ahote and they both laughed.

"Well, we are rid of Duane. He will no longer be preying on helpless Native American women," Sara said.

"Mike King is gone, too," Lola said. "Everyone thought he was a respectable businessman when in reality he was a crook just like his father."

"His end was fitting," Ahote said.

"Yeah, they seized all Mike's ill-gained assets," Rachel explained. "But he had millions in the Cayman Islands no one knew about. "

"How do you know about it?" Sara asked.

"Your granddaughter made a copy of Mike King's hard drive listing his off-shore accounts."

"It's too bad about Sandy, I always knew she would end up that way. She was a wild child. She would do and try anything," Sara said.

"At least I know what happened to my mother. I can finish my first novel with peace of mind," Lola said. "I have learned a lot from this."

"What happened to Dan?" Ahote asked. He missed out on that information because he was in Miami.

"Remember that strange guy on the ATV we saw? That was Dan. He thought if he hung around long enough, he would find out what happened to Sandy," Lola explained. "I had a long talk with him. It turns out he wasn't my father after all. He said he loved me and that we would always be friends."

"He wasn't your father after all?" Ahote asked.

"No, he said he didn't know who my father was. Sandy was pregnant when he met her at the drug rehabilitation clinic. He fell in love with Sandy and accepted me as his daughter," Lola explained. "That is another mystery that cannot be solved."

Everyone looked at Sara. She looked at the ground sheepishly.

"Grandma, what do you know?" Lola asked.

"Well, you might as well know everything now," Sara said. "Your real father was Duane."

Lola was shocked. "You knew all this time but you never told me?"

"Yes, I knew that Sandy was not dead. I knew she was somewhere, but she was no one to be a mother to you. I thought it was just as well that you did not know. I was afraid of Duane—you don't know what he was really like. He was truly a predator. You're an adult now, so you might as well know the truth."

Lola was shocked and saddened. Her father was dead. Her mother was dead. She was confused and frightened by the turn of events. But the future was ahead of her. She felt like she had aged a lifetime when in realty she was still in college.

Lola, Rachel, and Ahote flew to Miami. On the way, they discussed what had happened. "This was one of those experiences that will last me a lifetime. Even though the results were tragic, I feel like a whole person again," Lola said.

"You can begin the healing process now," Rachel added.

"I already feel better, except I wonder about you," Lola said to Rachel. "That was very generous of you to give a million dollars to my mother to build the shelter. I don't know if Grandma would have accepted it had she known it was profits from your drug business."

Rachel glanced in the back seat at Ahote. They exchanged knowing looks.

"What's going on between you two?" Lola asked jealously.

"It wasn't my million dollars. I just didn't want to tell Sara where it came from or she might not have accepted it."

"Where did it come from?" Lola asked.

"It was Mike King's money," Rachel explained. "I gave the heroin we bought for a million dollars from Mike to Ahote. He took it down to Miami and sold it back to Mike for two million dollars. In the end Mike's greed got the best of him."

There was silence in the car for the rest of the drive to Minneapolis. They dropped Ahote off at the airport so he could catch a flight back to Miami.

Lola went back to the University of Minnesota and packed the contents of her dorm room. Rachel picked her up and she moved in with Rachel.

Lola unpacked her things and put the charcoal drawing of her mother on the wall. She stared at it. She could feel her mother looking at her with that impish, coquettish smile.